Praise for

THE ORCHARD

"To be transported, wholesale, into a new and unfamiliar world is one of literature's great gifts, and the opening pages of David Hopen's ambitious debut novel, *The Orchard*, promise exactly that. . . . Hopen is a stylish, atmospheric writer whose characters inhabit sensuous tableaus. . . . Part thriller, part religious inquiry, part love story, and part Tarttian homage. . . . Hopen's talent is evident, his knowledge abundant."
—*New York Times Book Review*

"The most brilliant novel I read this year. . . . A wildly engrossing bildungsroman."
—Book Riot

"Fascinating. . . . [A novel] that settles in the mind and heart, requiring rumination long after turning the last page. . . . Remarkable and thought-provoking. . . . An outstanding debut."
—BookBrowse

"Powerful and stirring, like a 2020 Jewish version of *The Catcher in the Rye*. Structured into chapters by month throughout a typical school year and tackling the 'majestic sadness' that is tragedy, this journal-like book written by a Yale Law School student will definitely take root."
—*Good Morning America*

"Both fresh and affecting. . . . Essentially *The Secret History* set among highly observant Jewish Floridians. . . . Heretics, sex, drugs, and even Talmudic rituals that border on bacchanalia abound."
—*Entertainment Weekly*

"Audacious. . . . With *The Orchard* Hopen may have taken the boldest step yet in the ongoing turn of the American Jewish novel. . . . *The Orchard* [is] something distinctively new in fiction." —*Tablet*

"A poignant and utterly devastating experience. . . . Hopen's novel may call to mind works by Chaim Potok, like *The Chosen*. . . . Harrowing and brilliantly rendered. . . . *The Orchard* is intense and deeply moving. . . . Its questions are not easy, nor are the answers it provides. To discover a thought-provoking young writer like David Hopen this early in his career is a rare privilege indeed." —*Anniston Star*

"A big, ambitious coming-of-age story. . . . *The Orchard* delivers thrills and suspense. It's both heady and playful. It's rich with allegory. Like the most enduring coming-of-age stories, it transports the reader into an alluring world of youth that's unfamiliar and exciting but unmistakably nails the feelings and desires that come with trying to make sense of who you're meant to be." —Goop

"David Hopen's riveting debut joins the urgency of a thriller with the devastating consequence of a spiritual crisis for its hero, who is no less imperiled by his religion than by the threat of its loss. In Ari Eden's story, the clash between youth and experience, godlessness and piety, individualism and conformity, will feel both devastatingly familiar and utterly new. *The Orchard* throws open the doors to this world and introduces a major new voice." —Susan Choi, National Book Award–winning author of *Trust Exercise*

"David Hopen's ambitious debut novel combines the religiously observant world of Chaim Potok's books with the academic hothouse of Donna Tartt's *The Secret History* and F. Scott Fitzgerald's observations of the rich and privileged. . . . A singular addition to the world of Jewish fiction as well as a notable variation on the classic campus novel." —*BookPage*

"*The Orchard* makes good on its promise to shine light on the workings of privilege in every culture."   —CrimeReads

"*The Orchard* is a wildly ambitious, propulsive novel touching on big, life-altering topics, but David Hopen manages that weight by never losing his grip on the story, which blends philosophical questions with a unique thriller and a group of teenagers who command your attention. At the heart of the novel there's a yearning, a reckoning with those moments when we transform and when we wonder if we can ever go back. I'd be so wary of comparing any novel to Donna Tartt's *The Secret History*, but *The Orchard* can handle it because it diverges in such interesting ways."   —Kevin Wilson, author of *Nothing to See Here*

"An entirely surprising tale, rich with literary allusions and Talmudic connections, about the powerful allure of belonging. This novel will likely elicit comparisons to the work of Chaim Potok. . . . But Hopen's debut may actually have more in common with campus novels like Donna Tartt's *The Secret History* and Tobias Wolff's *Old School*. . . . Hopen's debut signals a promising new literary talent; in vivid prose, the novel thoughtfully explores cultural particularity while telling a story with universal resonances. A captivating Jewish twist on the classic American campus novel."   —*Kirkus Reviews* (starred review)

"This is a brilliantly conceived and crafted coming-of-age novel of ideas, replete with literary and philosophical references. . . . Unforgettable."
—*Booklist* (starred review)

"Hopen commingles religious philosophy and dangerous behavior in his ambitious debut. . . . A moving climax. This isn't your average campus novel."   —*Publishers Weekly*

"Magnetic. . . . What I was struck by is how seamlessly Hopen weaved very Jewish concepts and debates about Judaism, morality, and God.

. . . The ending was explosive—and one I'll be thinking about for a long time." —Alma

"I guess it would be accurate to call *The Orchard* a coming-of-age story, or a fish-out-of-water story, or a clash-of-cultures story, or a crisis-of-faith story, or a false-prophet story—the truth is, *The Orchard* is all of these and more. It's a story of profound intelligence, a story of tragic grandeur, and a story unlike any other I've ever read."

—Nathan Hill, author of *The Nix*

"A tremendous read, a brilliant excursion into the world of Orthodox Jews, both thrilling and philosophical."

—Gary Shteyngart, author of *Lake Success*

THE ORCHARD

THE ORCHARD

A Novel

David Hopen

ecco

An Imprint of HarperCollins*Publishers*

A hardcover edition of this book was published in 2020 by Ecco, an imprint of HarperCollins Publishers.

FIRST ECCO PAPERBACK EDITION PUBLISHED 2021

Designed by Michelle Crowe

Illustration by Elizabeth Yaffe

Library of Congress Cataloging-in-Publication Data
Names: Hopen, David, 1993– author.
Title: The orchard: a novel / David Hopen.
Description: First edition. | New York, NY: Ecco, an imprint of
   HarperCollins Publishers, [2020]
Identifiers: LCCN 2020013616 (print) | LCCN 2020013617 (ebook) |
   ISBN 9780062974747 (hardcover) | ISBN 9780062974761 (ebook)
Subjects: LCSH: Jewish teenagers—Fiction. | Jews—Fiction. |
   Jewish fiction.
Classification: LCC PS3608.O633 O73 2020 (print) | LCC PS3608.O633
   (ebook) | DDC 813/.6—dc23
LC record available at https://lccn.loc.gov/2020013616.
LC ebook record available at https://lccn.loc.gov/2020013617.

ISBN 978-0-06-297475-4 (pbk.)

21 22 23 24 25   LSC   10 9 8 7 6 5 4 3 2 1

For my mother and my father, on whose love my world stands

Our Rabbis have taught, four entered into The Orchard. They were Ben Azai, Ben Zoma, Aher, and Rabbi Akiba. Ben Azai gazed and died. Of him it is written, "Precious in the eyes of HaShem is the death of his pious ones." Ben Zoma gazed, and went insane. Of him, it is written, "Have you found honey, eat your share lest you become full, and vomit it up." Aher became an apostate. Rabbi Akiba entered, and exited in peace.

—Hagigah 14b

Fade far away, dissolve, and quite forget
What thou among the leaves hast never known,
The weariness, the fever, and the fret
Here, where men sit and hear each other groan;
Where palsy shakes a few, sad, last gray hairs,
Where youth grows pale, and spectre-thin, and dies;
Where but to think is to be full of sorrow
And leaden-eyed despairs,
Where Beauty cannot keep her lustrous eyes,
Or new Love pine at them beyond to-morrow.

—Keats, "Ode to a Nightingale"

THE ORCHARD

PROLOGUE

s tragedy dead?"

This is what I asked Mrs. Hartman at the end of it all, when I was still obsessed with every fatal flaw but my own.

She didn't ask why I needed to know. Instead she asked me to define tragedy for her. I told her this was impossible: tragedy was a subphilosophy, something to be felt, not defined.

She shook her head. "Majestic sadness," she told me. "That's tragedy."

I thought about that night, standing side by side with Evan and Amir in those waning moments before the policemen, the fire trucks, the body count. I thought about the look on Evan's soot-washed face. "I wonder if Noah is seeing this," he had said, his voice soft, sad. After everything that had happened our senior year, it was the way he said this that made me cry. If that was not majestic sadness, I decided, nothing was.

"Well, Mr. Eden?" She blinked at me. "Did it die with the Greeks?"

"No," I said. "I suppose not."

AUGUST

Come, my friends,
'Tis not too late to seek a newer world.

—Tennyson, "Ulysses"

For the first seventeen years of my life I lived in Brooklyn. From nursery through the eleventh grade—blurred, prehistoric years—I attended a small yeshiva called Torah Temimah, the translation of which ("the Torah is perfect") was our credo. School was single-sexed, with a black-and-white dress code, thirty boys per grade and a reputation for functioning as an academic travesty. Yiddish-speaking rabbis refused to teach anything vaguely related to evolution. Former hippies, plucked from the street, incapable of landing a job in the regular school system, ranted incoherently about civics. Freshman-year math was canceled abruptly after Mr. Alvarez, our lone competent teacher, decided he'd seen enough of our wondrous country and returned to Argentina. The Torah was perfect, our education was not.

None of this mattered much to our community. Never was there any pretense that this was anything but a yeshiva first and a school second, dedicated to "the uncompromising development of students into the leaders of modern-day Torah" and then, with whatever time was left in the day, to a secular education. Most graduates spent years floating aimlessly around the country, studying in a Beis Medresh here, a Beis Medresh there, where their fathers had once studied, where a second cousin once removed was a notable donor, wherever really, they were offered a bed. No one had college on his mind. It took me all this time to realize that this amounted to a beautiful life.

My family wasn't too different, at least back then. My father was an accountant for a small, local firm, which I suppose made us something of a minority in a community in which many fathers spent their days learning or teaching Torah. Still, my father fancied himself a learned man—his grandfather, he enjoyed reminding me, had been a fairly prominent rabbi in Williamsburg and descended from a line of middling Talmudic scholars—and spent his free time engrossed in study. His profession was infinitely boring, but he was satisfied with his lot and prone to pious overgeneralizations: "God-fearing specks in a vast universe do not require fancy careers." He was, in short, eminently suited for our community: graying hair, worn smile, the simplest man I've ever known.

My mother—thin, elegant in the way receding youth clings to certain women—was more unusual. Her parents, third-generation Chicagoans, maintained a semi-traditional household: occasional Friday night gatherings, synagogue on the High Holidays, no pork, some lobster. As a freshman at Barnard, she partook in a Hillel-sponsored trip to Israel and, nearly overnight, became infatuated with the spiritual fulfillment, moral discipline and communal structure offered by Orthodox Judaism. She returned reborn, studying with a local rebbetzin, adopting increasingly complex mitzvoth and, by the end of her fall semester, transferring to Stern College. Soon after, a shidduch was arranged with my father.

I was deeply curious about my mother's early life, but she said little on the subject. She insisted, in fact, that she hardly remembered her childhood in Chicago. I used to ask questions—what was it like eating nonkosher, having Saturdays free, attending public school—but instead of substantive answers received instructions, mostly from my father, to keep private my mother's status as a Ba'alat Teshuva, a newly religious Jew. Her real life, she claimed, began with my father. After marrying, she earned her master's at Teachers College, a rarity for the other mothers I knew. She taught fourth grade at Torah Temimah, which meant she witnessed firsthand its academic horrors.

"Aryeh," she announced after it'd become apparent my fifth-grade teacher took personal offense to the concept of required reading, "enrichment is in order."

And so every day after school we'd sit in the Borough Park Library, my mother and I, and read. She gave me books to devour—*Tom Sawyer* and *To Kill a Mockingbird*, *Flowers for Algernon* and *A Wrinkle in Time*. Soon, I was biking over after school and perching myself in the corner, where the librarian, Mrs. Sanders, with her cherubic-white hair and feline eyes, had grown accustomed to leaving me stacks of "mandatory" books. "Nobody reads these," she'd say. *Night*. *Death of a Salesman*. "You're going to make up for everyone else." Dickinson once described her father as a man who read "lonely & rigorous books." This was what I became: a contemplative boy surrounded always by lonely, rigorous books.

Such was the way I received some semblance of an education. I stood out in English classes, if only because an alarming number of my classmates flirted with illiteracy. Their parents were content with whatever the school managed to teach—astonishingly little—and actually preferred their children study Talmud exclusively.

"What're you doing at the library?" my friend Shimon would probe. He had comically long payot wrapped twice around his ears, a kind, thin face typically covered with acne and was always sweating, his shirt a mosaic of ketchup from lunch and dirt from recess, "Is there a shiur there or something?"

"You're asking if they offer Gemara classes at the public library?"

"Yeah."

I shook my head.

"What do they have, then?"

"Books, Shimon."

"Sefarim, you mean?"

"No," I said. "Real books. Want to come?"

He frowned. "I can't."

"Why not?"

"My father says that stuff stains your neshama."

—

THERE'S A POEM I LIKE by Jane Kenyon. It's three stanzas, ten lines, rather somber. The poem's called "In the Nursing Home"; it likens aging to a wild horse running tight circles that grow smaller, smaller, until eventually they cease. As a teenager, I felt this neatly encapsulated the suffocation of my childhood, the trackless wasteland of tightening circles I inhabited. I felt sometimes as if I existed alone, outside the external world, bearing no true relation to anyone or anything, as if the invisible harnesses that tethered humans to their surroundings had, in my case, come undone. I was accustomed to living unmoored, inured to rappelling through a shrinking reality with neither rope nor anchor. This was all I knew: gazing out at the coming night, alone, waiting diligently, like Kenyon's horse, to be retrieved by some force—any force—that could reinsert me into my own life.

—

MY PARENTS BROKE THE NEWS in February, amid dull snow.

"Aryeh," my father started, nervously setting down his utensils on the table, dabbing his napkin at the corner of his mouth. "Imma and I have something to discuss with you."

We had quiet meals. I was an only child; my mother would serve and we three would dutifully attempt small talk before lapsing into silence. Most families we knew were overrun by hordes of children in small houses—Shimon, for instance, had seven siblings—and though mostly I enjoyed being on my own, I wondered on occasion whether living amid commotion could relieve my solitude.

My father cleared his throat. "I lost my job."

Sadness washed over me, seeing his embarrassed look, the way my mother fixated on a spot of dirt on the floor, the snow falling gray and bleak through the windows. At first I said nothing, willing my silence to transmit commiseration, not apathy. "They fired you?" I asked, probably insensitively, when I thought of something to say.

"Not technically." Again he cleared his throat, this time for momentum. "It's folding, the firm, at the end of the summer."

Four men in a cramped, poorly lit back office in Flatbush, I couldn't help but think, did not a firm make. "The whole—operation?"

"These are difficult times, Ari, what with the state of the economy and all." Sure, I nodded, the economy. "Mr. Weintraub says he can't afford to keep us running anymore."

"Dreadful," my mother insisted, playing with the tablecloth, "isn't it, Aryeh?"

"I'm sorry, Abba," I said. And, truly, I was: my father was proud, decent, content to function on little sleep, resolved never to miss minyan, never to use a sick day, never to complain about the fact that a considerable percentage of the little money he scraped together went directly toward paying my tuition. He was not, in my view, someone deserving of humiliation.

"I'm sure you'll find something soon?"

"The thing is, Aryeh," he said, "there's not much else around here."

I played with the rim of my glass of water. "Maybe Mr. Weintraub can help find you something?"

"He's out of a job, too, *nebach*. But I did get an offer through one of Uncle Norman's business contacts."

"Uncle Norman?" My father's oldest brother was a heavy, balding figure known for peddling disastrous investments: a grimy kosher steakhouse that survived two months, a fledgling Laundromat in Queens, a company that sold malfunctioning vacuum cleaners. My father, like most sensible members of his family, made a habit of steering clear of Norman. "You trust anyone associated with Uncle Norman?"

"No Lashon Hara." He paused. "But, not really, no. Mr. Weintraub, however, is an honorable man. And Mr. Weintraub vouches for this person."

"Oh," I said unsurely, glancing at my mother for some explanation of my father's urgency, "wonderful, then." My mother, in turn, smiled patiently.

"Nothing major, but a better pay grade, actually. Baruch Hashem." A pause. "But it's—well, there's a catch."

I raised my brows. "A catch?"

"The job isn't in Brooklyn."

"So it's in New Jersey?"

He shook his head. "South Florida. A city called Zion Hills."

"Florida?"

"Huge Jewish community. More affordable living, Uncle Norman tells me, plus better real estate. And Imma has already been offered an interview with a local elementary school."

"At a school that believes in little luxuries like, I don't know, literacy and staff bathrooms, can you imagine?" My mother made a face of intense satisfaction. "And there's supposed to be a very *elite* yeshiva high school there. It seems to have a really excellent reputation."

I was overcome suddenly by the silence of my house: heavy, toneless. I looked back to my father and then resumed eating. "Okay, then."

Maybe the way I said this, the fact that this monumental decision failed to elicit emotion, was disconcerting, a red flag that something within me was off. I didn't watch many movies, being that this was Borough Park, where we were wary of spiritual disease, but I did know that the cinematic version of this scene would have been marked by dramatic angst. Yet I felt nothing of the sort: no sadness, no heartache over life's sudden changes. Indeed, the thought of being freed from the unremitting monotony of my current existence gave me an exhilarating sense of escape. I was sick of enduring relentless, Chekhovian boredom, sitting alone in libraries, mourning what I'd never know: torturous love, great voyages, *nostos*. Far away from my present reality, I suspected, unfolded some higher life, one sustained not by mere echoes but by the sound of happiness. Each person, Bacon claimed, worships "idols of the cave," those peculiar beliefs that constitute our character and, at least in my case, our ruin. My own idols, I know now, are these: a fundamental disdain for the gray on gray, an intolerance for what Freud recognized as life's ordinary unhappiness.

My parents gave baffled looks. "Okay?"

"It's okay with me, I mean," I said.

"Maybe you'd like to mull it over," my father said.

"The last thing we want, of course, is to uproot you," my mother said.

"We'd understand," my father said. "If I needed to, I could find other work just for the year, until you finish school. Things might be tighter, yes, but we believe in *hashgochoh protis*, don't we? Hashem has a funny way of making things work out."

My mother took my hand. "Your entire life is here, we realize."

I shook my head. "I want to leave." I looked back at my plate and continued eating. Outside, everything was now white and brilliant with ice.

—

I DIDN'T TELL THEM UNTIL June, on our final day of eleventh grade. We were sitting in the jungle gym behind the school. From the swing set, Shimon, Mordechai and Reuven debated the Gemara we were learning: the conditions for violating Shabbat to save a life.

"You can break it to save a one-day-old baby," Shimon said heatedly. "Rav Shimon ben Gamliel says so."

"Yeah, 'cause it's like being a doctor," Mordechai said. "Cut off the leg to save the body. Break one Shabbat to observe many. It's *pashut*. Easy."

Shimon clicked his tongue in annoyance. "Don't just steal the Rambam's words. That's plaguing."

"Plagiarizing," Mordechai corrected.

"Whatever. *Shtus*."

"Nu." Reuven rocked higher into the air, the chains suspending him above us groaning. "Here's another one." He was tall, lanky and had horrible teeth. He claimed his parents objected to braces on religious grounds. ("Do not alter thy body," he'd repeat pedantically. "It's right there in Vayikra!")

Shimon coughed, wiped his hands on his shirt. "Yes?"

"What if there's doubt?" These questions often lent Reuven a gelid look in his eyes.

"Doubt?" Mordechai asked. "What's a case of doubt?"

"Like, you can't be *sure* someone will actually die."

"No one here remembers Gemara Yoma?" Shimon stroked his right payot for comfort, as if to calm himself. "If there's even a question of emergency, of *pikuach nefesh*, but you still have to ask a rabbi? The Gemara says you're like a murderer."

Mordechai nodded along. "Too much piety can cost a life."

"So you're calling me a murderer?" Reuven was now only half-smiling.

"Not only that," Shimon said, "but if I was your rabbi then I'd be a disgrace, too, rules the Gemara."

Reuven picked at his front incisors, tracing the staggering distance between them. "Why?"

"For letting you even think there's a *havah minah* here," Shimon said. "For letting you delay saving a life by asking stupid questions."

"Okay, okay, now I got it," Reuven announced, snapping his fingers. "What if it's a goy? Goyim can't keep Shabbos!"

Mordechai snorted. "So? What's that got to do with anything?"

"So the initial reasoning is out," Reuven said. "You're not saving future mitzvoth."

"Remember Gemara Sanhedrin?" Mordechai rolled his eyes. "If your neighbor's drowning, you're obligated to save him."

"Yeah, but still," Reuven said, "does that include a goy? You know, necessarily speaking?"

Mordechai shook his head. "You don't believe that?"

"Well, no," Reuven conceded.

Shimon went quiet for a moment. "But for the sake of argument . . ."

"Aryeh," Mordechai said, his voice rising, "Aryeh, talk sense into them, will you? Someone drowns—Jew, Gentile, animal, anyone, anything—you save them, yeah?"

I'd been swinging in silence, mind adrift, until quite suddenly I realized the news I'd been avoiding since February could, at long last, be avoided no longer. "I'm leaving."

Shimon gave me a look, annoyed I'd interrupted the counterargument he was preparing. "What?"

"I'm leaving," I repeated. I rooted my feet to the asphalt, taking myself out of motion.

"*Shkoyach*, you made that clear." Shimon, dripping with sweat, wiped the back of his hand across his face. "Library?"

"I'm leaving Brooklyn."

"Leaving Brooklyn?" echoed Reuven.

Shimon frowned. "What does that mean you're leaving Brooklyn?"

"I'm moving," I said. "Away."

"To the city?" Mordechai asked, dark eyes aglow.

"Why *davka* Manhattan?" Shimon was a skilled Torah student, but his habit of reframing everything as a Talmudic question was grating. "Your father wants you to learn in that yeshiva?"

My hands gripped rusting metal. "Which yeshiva?"

"On the Upper West Side. For kids who aren't serious about Torah." After a pause: "You aren't serious about Torah."

I allowed myself, briefly, to exit my present conversation, to visualize the school and the streets and the neighborhood and the city around me, to meld the clamor of traffic and children and animals and Gemara and crying and laughing and singing and praying into one simple unit of sound, a single emission, to grasp it and, in the palm of my hand, crush it into silence. I waited, I counted to five, and then I relaxed my fist, permitting all noise to untangle back into clarity. "I'm moving to Florida."

"Florida?" All three looked flushed with shock. "What's in Florida?"

Shimon tried coming to a halt, nearly falling out of his sw— "There aren't yeshivas in Florida."

"Of course there are," Reuven said defensively. "My cousin lives there."

"They have beaches," Mordechai said quietly. "Beautiful beaches."

"I've never been to the beach," Shimon said. "My father says beaches aren't . . . *shayich*."

"My father got a job there," I said, stony-faced.

"But he already has a job."

I felt, all at once, emotionally bludgeoned. For stability, I envisioned myself as one of Fitzgerald's characters—neurasthenic, desirous, self-enclosed—for whom unhappiness somehow deepens nobility. The thought was less redemptive than anticipated. "And now he has a new one."

"Well," Reuven said, scrunching his face in thought, "when do you leave?"

"August."

"Wow," Shimon said plainly. He sucked his breath melodramatically. We stood awkwardly for a bit, nobody saying much, save for Shimon whispering "wow" every so often.

"Will there be girls in your new school?" Reuven finally asked, delicately, shifting uncomfortably on his feet.

I nodded.

Shimon looked fairly appalled. Reuven gave a conflicted smile, unsure how to react. Mordechai, most experienced among us—rumor had it he was secretly dating the daughter of Rabbi Morgan, our seventh-grade rabbi, though I was skeptical about that whole affair—clapped my back.

"You're lucky, Ari Eden." His eyes narrowed. "Most of us will never get out of here."

—

MY LAST MONTHS IN BROOKLYN dissolved at a terrific pace. There was
 flurry of packing, everything we owned—quite little—stuffed into
 es and trucks. There were solitary walks through my neighbor-
 There were things I left behind: torn basketball sneakers I'd

worn to death, forgotten birthday letters, discolored Parsha cards I'd won in school raffles. At the end of my days in Brooklyn, I stood in my bare bedroom, staring at my mirror, watching seventeen years fade: the furniture gone, the rooms emptied, everything whitewashed. A general sense of melancholy hit me for the first time since my parents announced the move. Leaving didn't make me sad; on the contrary, the exhilarating prospect of trading my dreary, uneventful life for something new was, at long last, within reach. What was saddening was the realization that, in time, we stand in emptied houses to learn we've never made a mark.

—

ON MY FINAL DAY IN Brooklyn, Shimon and I biked to Brooklyn Bridge Park, only a few miles from where we lived. Mostly we rode in silence, stopping occasionally for water or rest. It was late afternoon when we arrived, the sun retreating into the water, the sky a brilliant violet, a trace of summer in the air.

"Well," Shimon said, drenched helplessly, mopping himself with a towel. "This is it." He wrapped the towel over his head. "Can I ask a question?"

"Go for it."

"Are you scared?"

"To leave?" A sailboat moved across the water. The hull seesawed gently with the wind. I felt an inexplicable sense of vicarious seasickness. "No. I want to start over."

"Know how long we've known each other?"

"Since nursery."

He gave up drying himself. "And you'd say I'm your best friend, wouldn't you?"

"Yes," I said slowly, "I guess I would."

"I was thinking."

"Yeah?"

His hands were deep in his payot. "Saying farewell to a se[...] easy."

"Pardon?"

"You finish a sefer and then you say Hadran Alakh. *We will return to you, and you will return to us.*"

"Or you bury it."

"Well, yeah," he said, "if it's destroyed."

"So your point is that you're more attached to a sefer than you are to me?"

"No," he said noncommittally. "My point is that with a sefer, you know what to do. You know you'll see that Torah again."

"But with me—"

He shrugged.

I gazed empty-eyed at the water, made dim and silvery by twilight. "I see."

"Like, it's hard to say goodbye, but it's also not that hard," he pressed. "I don't know. I mean, you're not that sad yourself about it, are you?"

Aryeh Eden, I thought. *Rav Glick's shiur. Torah Temimah. Borough Park. Brooklyn. New York. United States. Olam HaZeh. The Universe.*

"No," I said, feeling a conspicuous lack of shame admitting this.

"Maybe because most things seem sad with you." Shimon's cheeks flushed. I felt overwhelmed with desire to be away, to slink into dusk and never see him again.

"Think you'll come back?" he asked eventually, breaking the silence snaking between us. In the years since, I've thought a lot about what this meant. Brooklyn? Our friendship? Religiosity? It didn't matter. They were all tied up in each other, they all meant the same thing.

"No," I told him. "I don't suppose I will."

We stayed a while longer, watching night plunge upon the bridge, and then retrieved our bikes. We rode the entire way home in deference to a larger silence. When we turned on to our street, we parted ﹖th a wave.

﹖e seen Shimon only once since.

—

THE FIRST THING ABOUT FLORIDA was the heat, which blasted us the moment the automated airport doors slid open, leading us outside into exhaust fumes and fever-searing sunlight. Within minutes of waiting for a cab, my clothing clung to my skin. Like a good Brooklyn boy, I had worn a white button-down, tucked into dark, formless pants, with the white strings of my tzitzit dancing at my knees. I felt like Shimon, sweating, sweating.

It was a quick drive to our neighborhood. We were restless to see the new house, and my mother urged our driver, who offered broken English and mistaken turns, to go faster. For the last several weeks all I'd heard from her was how jaw-dropping Zion Hills was: immaculate homes, filled with doctors and lawyers and bankers— "professionals," my mother called them, relics of a life before my father. Still, I was floored seeing it in person, the multistoried houses, the golf course, the sports cars parked lazily in paved driveways.

My mother drew down the window and pointed. "That's the high school!" Torah Temimah had been tiny and utterly run-down, a two-story building with cracks in the pavement, perpetually overflowing toilets, unpainted walls adorned with mold and five and a half classrooms, half because, weather permitting, freshman year shiurs were held on the porch, overlooking the parking lot. This school, in stark contrast, was titanic. The building looked a good five stories high and was surrounded by basketball hoops, full-length verdant soccer fields, clay tennis courts. "Breathtaking, isn't it?" My mother had her face against the window. Her voice carried with unfamiliar exuberance.

"Not exactly haymish," my father said under his breath, less awestruck. He turned his attention to one of the far-off fields, where shirtless soccer players jostled in pursuit of the ball. "Looks like goyishe prep school."

Eventually, after several trips down the wrong cul-de-sa

driver found Milton Drive. We pulled onto the street and drove slowly, looking for number 599. "There," my mother motioned. And then, seeing our driver's eyes widen: "Not the gigantic one, I'm afraid. The one on the right."

Our neighbor directly across the street, the house at 598, was indeed gigantic: a red-bricked, vaguely Tudor mansion, built on a double lot, with large, stained-glass windows, a balcony overlooking the driveway, a three-car garage and four cars. I didn't know much about cars, but I knew one was an Audi.

"Goodness," my mother said, "that backyard."

I caught only a glimpse of what seemed to be an Olympic-size pool, since my father decided we'd marveled enough at our neighbor ("a house is a house: what do you do with so many rooms?") and urged our driver to pull into our more humble abode.

That our neighbor towered over us did not lessen my excitement. I felt an immediate surge of attachment to our new house: single-storied, cozy, considerably larger than what we'd ever had before. We had weather-beaten pavement in our driveway, slightly brown grass baking in the heat, two palm trees out front and, I was delighted to discover, a small pool out back, the perimeter of which was overrun by tiny, leucistic lizards.

"What do you think, Ari?" my mother asked nervously after we unloaded the car and loitered in our driveway.

"It's great," I said, and I meant it. For the first time for as long as I could remember, I felt overwhelmed with fluid happiness, overjoyed at the distance separating me from my old life.

—

WE WERE SITTING IN OUR living room that evening, after a makeshift dinner of scrambled eggs and several hours unloading boxes, moving furniture, transferring miscellaneous items from one side of the room to the other and back. I was reviewing a page of Talmud with her when our landline rang. My mother answered; I heard her exaggerated laughs. Foreign sounds to me.

"Our neighbors," my mother said, bustling in from the kitchen. "From the house across the street. Cynthia and Eddie Harris—they sound lovely."

My father stared blankly. "What'd they want?"

"They've invited us to a barbecue tomorrow."

My father's finger held our place in the Gemara. *Damages caused by oxen or by mav'eh are caused by a living spirit. Fire has no living spirit.* "And what'd you tell them?"

She looked rosy-cheeked. "That we'd be delighted, of course."

He nodded slightly, returning his attention to the Talmud. Without another word, we resumed learning.

—

THE BARBECUE WAS ON a sun-dazzled afternoon. Even in the oppressive Florida heat we dressed as we always did: my father and I in black and white, my mother tzniut in her long sleeves, though I noticed she donned a new floral dress for the occasion.

Timidly, we rang the doorbell and waited for several minutes, admiring the flagstone steps and double-hinged oak doors, my mother elated at the prospect of a social life, my father looking as if he'd prefer to be anywhere else. Eventually, when no one answered, we made our way around the side of the mansion, following the sound of laughter. We opened an iron gate and let ourselves into the party.

Horror washed over my father's face as he surveyed the backyard. Wives in short, colorful sundresses, Chardonnay in hand. Men in Burberry polos, gripping beers. Teenage boys and girls thrashing together in the pool, a cardinal sin in our former lives. Dazzlingly alien sights: wealth, charm, hysteria. My stomach turned uneasily.

"Hello, there," a hearty voice boomed behind us. A thick man in a crisp white polo clapped my father on the back, startling him. "You must be the Edens!" Ever so slightly, my father stole a look at the top of the man's gelled hair. No yarmulke. The man extended a beefy hand. "Our new neighbors! You guys know how excited we've been to meet you? Wasn't too much love lost with the people who used to own your house. I mean, nice people, I guess, but kept to themselves too much. We needed new friends." He squinted, his eyes sweeping the backyard—incidentally the most impressive backyard I'd ever seen: an enormous pool, a marble bathhouse, a Jacuzzi and bar, a fence bordering a picturesque golf course—and shrugged. "I don't know where Cynthia went off, she must be inside. Come, I'll bring you in to meet her. Eddie Harris, by the way. Real pleasure."

My father gave a thin smile, his hand comically small in Eddie's. "Yaakov Eden."

"Thanks for coming, Yaakov," Eddie said, before offering his hand to my mother.

An awful moment followed, my mother staring blankly, caught between the social necessity of extending her hand and our strict custom of refraining from touching non-family members of the opposite gender. I winced, but Eddie realized his mistake quickly and holstered his handshake. "Shit, my apologies!" he barked. "I didn't realize, excuse my idiocy . . ."

"No, no," my mother soothed, red-cheeked with embarrassment. "Please, not to worry." My father assumed the face one might adopt when passing a kidney stone, but Eddie and my mother both gave awkward smiles. "I'm Leah."

This would have been considerably more painful, perhaps unsalvageable, with someone else. Yet Eddie released a sonic laugh, diffusing any tension. "Don't mind me, I'm just a shmuck. Most people here aren't terribly strict about, er, what do you call it? Shomer negiah, right, that kind of thing. Between us, maybe they ought to be, I'll show you one couple in particular over there, plenty of rumors, though who am I to judge? So, yeah, that whole no-touching thing isn't really on my radar. But Cynthia'll kill me when she hears." After his laughter, Eddie rested his eyes on me. "And your name, sport?" He had quite the handshake.

"Aryeh."

"No kidding. That was my old man's name."

"Oh yeah?"

"A bona fide tzadik." He paused, sending thoughts heavenward. "I think you would've liked him," he mumbled to my father.

My father nodded courteously, unconvinced.

He turned back to me. "And how old are you, bud?"

"Seventeen."

"Seventeen? So you're a junior or senior?"

"Senior."

"Nice. And you'll be at the yeshiva in Sunny Isles, I assume? They're pretty serious folks, let me tell you. I hear they hold mishmar three times a week."

"I'll be at Kol Neshama, actually."

"That other place was much too far of a drive," my mother said. "Plus, we're told Kol Neshama is, well, a superior education."

"Wow, you're going to the old Voice of the Soul Academy? Who would've thought?" He grinned boyishly. "You've really got to meet my son, you're in the same class." He turned animatedly to my parents. "How great is this?"

They returned his grin politely.

"Noah Harris!" he hollered toward the pool. "Where the heck are you, kid?"

From the water emerged a tall boy with green eyes, long blond locks, an exact replica of his father's smile and an almost excessive collection of shoulder and abdominal muscles. It was obvious he was an athlete. "Nice to meet you all," he said, slinging a towel over his shoulders. "I'd shake your hands but I'm sopping."

"Easy on the shaking," Eddie said, winking at my mother. "Noah, Ari here will be in your grade at the Academy."

"No kidding."

"Yaakov, Leah, what do you say we fix you both stiff drinks, yes? These two don't need us breathing down their necks." Eddie slapped my back playfully. "Yaak, you like cigars? No? Well, you do kind of look like a man I could turn into a lover of single malt. I've got the perfect thing for you to try. Noah, grab Ari a beer, will you, or a hot dog if he wants? Don't worry, everything's kosher." With that, his large hands took hold of my father, while carefully avoiding contact with my mother, and steered them away.

Noah watched them leave. His arms appeared to flex involuntarily, despite the fact that they hung at ease at his sides. I wondered what it would be like to have such a problem. "Say your name was Ari?"

"Aryeh," I said. Then, kicking myself: "Ari for short."

"And you moved from—?"

"Brooklyn."

"Dope. I have friends on Long Island. Know anybody there?"

"Some," I said noncommittally, certain we'd have zero mutual friends.

"I went to camp with Benji Wertheimer. Know him?" he asked, hopeful for conversation. "No? Fantastic point guard."

I shook my head.

"What about Efrem Stern? Okay, Naomi Spitz? Shira Haar? She's from Kings Point. Everyone knows her, throws Hamptons parties, she's super pretty?" He laughed. "Don't tell my girlfriend I said that," he said confidentially, pointing back toward the pool.

"No, I, uh—I won't."

"Where'd you go to school?"

"Torah Temimah."

"Torah Temimah?"

"Yeah," I said, feeling small.

"Never heard of it. New school?"

"No. Not really."

"One of those frum places, then. The shtetl. We talking black hats?"

Just how out of place I was dawned on me. To Noah, whose life, I suspected, involved athletic glory, beach houses, summer parties, I was some staid rabbinical student who had wandered comically into the wrong world, or at least the wrong backyard. And I was not unaccustomed to living as a stranger. I was a stranger in my previous existence, but one who understood that the rules governing each detail

of life—how to marry, how to think, how to tie my shoes—were pre-
scribed, always, by an aspirational morality. Standing before Noah,
I was a different breed of stranger, someone attempting to hide
in plain sight without any understanding of the overarching rules.
Camouflaging here, I realized then, would be harder even than in
Brooklyn. "Yes," I said, itching to leave. "Pretty much."

He laughed. "You'll find it a bit different here, I think. We tend to
have a bigger appetite than Torah . . . what'd you say it was?"

"Temimah."

"Right. That. All boys, wasn't it?"

I grimaced at how quickly he sized me up. "Unfortunately," I said,
attempting to salvage some semblance of self-respect.

"I don't know how I'd survive in a school like that. Go stir-crazy,
probably." He rubbed his bicep. "Come, let me introduce you."

Nervously, I followed him to the edge of the marble-tiled pool.
Two girls swam over. "Ladies," Noah said, "meet Ari Eden. Ari, this
is my girlfriend Rebecca Nadler, and this is not my girlfriend, Sophia
Winter."

"Nice to meet you," I said.

"Hello," Rebecca said, swimming toward me to offer her hand.
When Noah shot her a warning look, she retreated, improvising with
a warm wave. She was tall and athletic looking, with brown, curly
hair, big teeth and wide features. My eyes, however, were fixed firmly
on Sophia, treading silently by the edge: dark hair, milk-white skin,
a sharp, slightly angular nose, wiry arms, cerulean eyes.

Noah slapped my back: I'd been staring too long.

"Where'd you move from?" Rebecca was looking at me curiously.

"Brooklyn."

"New York—everything's beautiful there, isn't it?"

My life in New York, I wanted to admit, was anything but beautiful. Instead, I did the socially acceptable thing and nodded.

"I just think it's way too hot down here. I'm desperate to move
north one day, even though I know Noah will never leave his parents. Ain't that right, kid?" She grabbed his wrist, dragging him back

toward the pool. Laughing, Noah allowed himself to topple over into the water. They resurfaced, Rebecca on his back, her arms around his neck. I stood awkwardly as they groped each other. Water lapped the bottom of my pants, drenching my black New Balance sneakers, though I didn't dare move. I attempted an agreeable smile.

"You'll get used to it," Sophia said, drifting closer. "They have a difficult time keeping their hands off each other." As she spoke, I allowed myself to occupy those sky-blue irises, which, more than the blazing Florida sun, reduced me to a nervous sweat. I became conscious suddenly of how often I was blinking, of how my jaw was unhinged. "They've been together since sixth grade."

"That's a long time."

"It is, but I've known her since we were four. Which means," she paused theatrically, "I enjoy the distinct honor of serving as perpetual third wheel."

"It's really an issue—we just can't get rid of her." Noah gathered water into his mouth and squirted in Rebecca's direction. She responded by directing tidal waves at his face. "Maybe we'll pawn her off on you?"

Sophia smiled uneasily, pushing wet strands of hair from her forehead. Still treading in place, she looked away toward the green over the fence. Something dark, for the slightest moment, passed through her eyes.

"You wouldn't mind, would you? I mean, she's a beauty," Rebecca said, lounging now on Noah's shoulders, "isn't she, Ari?"

My cheeks turned an outrageous red. Yes, I wanted to say, yes, she was gorgeous, unquestionably the most gorgeous human being I'd ever seen. Instead, I mumbled incoherently, refocusing my attention to the dirt on my shoes. When I looked up again, I noticed that Sophia's gaze had returned to me. "Won't you be coming in?"

"No," I said stupidly. "I don't have a bathing suit. And actually I've got to go soon . . . still settling into the new house—"

She laughed dismissively. "They don't do much coed swimming in Brooklyn, I suppose." She swept back her hair, glided toward me and, looking up daringly, presented her hand. Blinking, hesitating for a fraction of a moment, I accepted, helped her out of the pool, ignoring how outrageously close I was to her body, how water splashed from her chin and neck and stomach and hips and landed on my clothing, trying desperately not to stare as she walked to her lounge chair and dried herself, focusing my vision instead on the gold bracelet, engraved with faint treble clefs, on her left wrist. Sophia Winter was the first girl I'd ever touched.

On her chair sat a copy of *Pale Fire*. I'd been mailed the same copy as summer reading. "Are you liking it?" I asked, eager to veer the conversation away from my glaring social deficiencies.

"Meeting you?" She grabbed a towel from a chaise lounge and wiped her face. "I'd say it's been perfectly unremarkable, wouldn't you?"

"Nabokov," I said, pointing to the book.

She seemed amused I so much as knew how to pronounce his name. "You've heard of it?"

"I read it last month. So yes."

"That's an odd coincidence."

"Doubtful. It was for school."

"Which school?"

"Kol Neshama."

"Oh. I thought you were a senior."

"I am."

She draped her towel over her shoulders, like a cape, and adjusted her black bathing suit. "The Academy doesn't take transfers for senior year."

"Yeah, that's right, actually," Noah said. "Remember that kid Stevie Glass? He tried switching in for senior year and they didn't let him. And he was supposed to be pretty bright."

I shrugged. I imagined arriving for my first day of school, only to be informed that some error had been made, that I was never, in fact, accepted. "Well, I'm pretty sure they took me."

Sophia continued to dry herself, wrapping the towel around her waist, wringing water from her hair. I knew immediately that I'd memorize every detail of her face. "So how'd you do it?"

"I applied."

"That much I pieced together."

"They liked my essay, I guess." The application process had been fairly unmemorable, largely informational, with the exception of one prompt: *"No man chooses evil because it is evil; he only mistakes it for happiness, the good he seeks." (Mary Wollstonecraft) Discuss in 2–10 pages.* It was the first research project I'd ever had and I rather enjoyed writing it. I mailed in eight pages, titled: "'Immortal Longings': Human Yearning in Literature and in Gemara Berachot Lamed Amud Aleph."

Sophia made no attempt to hide her shock. "So you're telling me you not only somehow secured a place in Kol Neshama but you're also taking AP Lit?"

"I didn't swim much in Brooklyn," I said, "but I did an awful lot of reading."

Her hands went to her hips. She had a way of downturning her mouth that made my insides freeze. "Well, then. What'd *you* think of *Pale Fire*?"

Noah smirked from the pool. "Check out these scholars."

"It was weird," I said. "But I liked it."

"Really? Because it tries too hard. I don't like when books resort to beating you over the head—Kafka excluded. It's a sign of imaginative inadequacy on the part of the author. Not to mention the whole thing is too, I don't know, voyeuristic for my liking." I knew she was, less than subtly, putting me in my place. "Maybe my appreciation would be deepened if I'd get around to reading *Timon of Athens*."

"Timon of who?" Rebecca asked.

"Of whom," Noah added. Rebecca socked him.

"It's where Nabokov got the title," Sophia said. "*The moon's an arrant thief, / And her pale fire she snatches from the sun.*"

"Yeah, I don't know about that," I said. "That's like claiming you need to first read *Hamlet* to understand it."

The slender muscles underlining her arms and shoulders contracted. "Why *Hamlet*?"

"What's the line? '*The glowworm shows the matin to be near, / And 'gins to pale his uneffectual fire.*' It's just as much of a reference, isn't it?"

"I could be losing it in my old age," Noah said, "but did you actually just quote Shakespeare at my pool?"

"This all seems like an unnecessary fixation with fire," Rebecca said. "Let's move on, maybe?"

"I'm only saying," I said, reddening, "it'd be just as valuable to thumb through *Hamlet* if you're trying to find helpful source material for *Pale Fire*. Which is to say, I guess, they're equally unimportant and you'd be lost reading either."

She looked at me so that I couldn't tell whether she was studying me or looking beyond me entirely. "*I'd* be lost?"

"No, of course not," I stuttered, "not you specifically, I meant someone would be—"

"I suppose you've read *Timon of Athens*, too, just for kicks?"

"No," I said, embarrassed. "Not yet."

"The Brooklynite next door," Rebecca laughed. "Shakespearean automaton."

"Christ," Noah said. "For papers I go to Sophia or Evan"—at this latter name Rebecca slapped him under the pool and Sophia looked away—"but now maybe I should be taking my talents across the street."

I was unsure whether to feel a twinge of pride at impressing them or a surge of embarrassment at revealing what I assumed to be the only thing less cool than hailing from Borough Park: being a lover of Shakespeare.

"Aryeh," my father called from the distance. He looked physically wounded finding me beside a bikini-clad Sophia. My mother trailed him, chatting with Noah's mother, a tall, well-dressed woman. "We're leaving now."

"Nice to meet you, neighbor," Noah said, eyeing my father.

"Well, then." Sophia offered her hand again. I took it, even with my father staring. "You're not overly dull to spar with, are you?"

"Neither are you." My voice wavered. Her hand was hot in mine.

"I'll be seeing you, Hamlet."

Breathless, I stumbled through something disjointed—an unnatural laugh, a hasty goodbye—and joined my parents.

—

RESTLESS DAYS FOLLOWED, DAYS SPENT unpacking, arranging my room, organizing my books. In Brooklyn, these books, nabbed at street fairs, thrift stores, dusty antique shops, were my escape. To master such works, I convinced myself, would be to achieve a sort of abstract intelligence, knowledge that softened melancholy, knowledge that isolated me from isolation itself. As a teenager, I'd allowed the piles lining my bedroom to multiply so that they spilled out into the rest of the house, overtaking the kitchen table or displacing some of my father's sefarim. "*Be warned*,'" my father grunted, evicting Roth from prime real estate in our new living room, cramming mishnayot back into our bookshelves, "*the making of many books is without limit, and much study is a wearying of the flesh!*'" And so, instead of exploring my new town, I busied myself with Hemingway and Fitzgerald, all the while allowing myself occasional glances out my front window at the mansion across the street, plotting furiously how I was possibly to overcome the impenetrable barrier separating me from the lives of Noah, Rebecca and the arresting Sophia Winter.

My opportunity came sooner than expected. Three days after the barbecue, I received an unexpected visitor.

"Sup, neighbor?" Noah said, nearly too large for my doorframe. "You busy?"

No one was home: my mother and father were each at their first day of work. I invited him in, offered him a drink.

"Have any Blue Moon?"

I imagined my father coming home from work and nursing a beer over light Talmud study. "Afraid not."

"That's all right. Water'll do." I served him a glass and joined him at my kitchen counter. "Nice place," he said casually.

"You should've seen my old house. It was half the size."

"That right?" He took a sip, looked about the kitchen. "You guys finished unpacking?"

"More or less." There were still a few small boxes lying around, but my mother had been superhuman in her effort to immediately tidy the house. My father and I had pitched in, following instructions when ordered, but mostly we loitered, organizing our belongings and acclimating to our new quarters.

"Enjoy yourself the other day?"

"Yeah," I said hurriedly. "It was great." A beat. "Was nice of you to have us."

"My parents love hosting. They say the house is a waste if we don't fill it with people." He said this without the slightest trace of arrogance. "By the way, Rebs said she enjoyed meeting you and to say hi."

"Same, yeah, she was really great."

"And how'd you like Sophia? Was quite the literary peacock dance you guys had."

I scratched my chin, trying madly to appear unflustered. "Yeah, that was—interesting."

"Extremely." He winked, took a long sip of water, wiped his mouth. "Anyway, I was wondering if I might take you up on that offer for essay help." I'd made no such offer, I nearly reminded him. "Have you written that *Pale Fire* analysis yet?"

I had, in fact. I was so eager for serious learning that I wrote it in July. "Yes."

"In that case"—he reached into his pocket and handed me folded pages—"mind looking this over? It's still kind of, you know, rough."

I unfolded the paper and gave it a glance.

"I feel really bad asking, it's just I need to make certain my grades are high off the bat, what with recruiting and all starting up. Plus Evan"—the name from the pool—"isn't around yet, he's in Europe or South America or wherever the hell he is, I can't keep track, and Rebs doesn't want me bothering Sophia, and Amir, well you don't know him yet either, but he can be a bit of a cutthroat, by which I mean he can be a massive cutthroat, especially now that application season is upon us. And it seems like you know this stuff cold—"

"It's no problem," I said.

His face lit up. "You sure? If it's a pain in the ass then don't worry. Seriously."

"I don't mind. I just can't promise I'll be any good."

"That I don't buy," he said, finishing most of his water and standing. I walked him to the door. "In my experience, people who quote *Hamlet* extemporaneously know a thing or two about smoothing out their buddy's paper."

"You really don't understand what sort of school I come from."

"Anything helps, really. The whole thing was over my head, to tell you the truth." He pounded my fist. "So, you busy tonight?"

"Um, no, don't think so."

"Why don't you come out with us? Lisa Niman's having a party. She's really sweet. Maybe you've already seen her around town? Her hair stands out, super red, usually dyed with streaks of purple or silver or something crazy like that. Rebelling against the whole ginger thing, she likes to joke."

"The what?"

"Sorry, I promise I didn't mean 'ginger' offensively." He paused. "God, your girlfriend is a redhead, isn't she?"

"What? No."

He laughed deeply, just like his father. "Rebecca likes to remind me that I have a special gift for inserting my foot right in my mouth. You don't, for the record, have a girlfriend, do you?"

This seemed profoundly unnecessary to ask. "No."

"Good to keep in mind. Come to think of it, maybe you should go for Niman?"

"I don't know," I stuttered.

He grinned. "Anyway, she has an open house tonight. Her parents are both chiropractors, and they're out of town at some chiropractor convention in Atlanta, which sounds much less believable when said aloud but she claims that's the story." He thought this over. "Whatever, unimportant. What's important is that Niman is having a party, and I thought this'd be a good way to break you in."

I scrambled for an excuse. Did I need to learn with my father? Help with unpacking? "Well, I—"

"No protesting. Come meet people."

"Yeah, but—"

"Great. You have your own car?"

I didn't. We had two cars shipped from Brooklyn, an old Honda Civic and a Nissan Versa, one for my mother, one for my father. I never minded this, seeing as I rarely drove in New York—where would I possibly go, save the library?—but figured showing up on bike to this party would be absolutely socially unacceptable. "No," I said, ashamed.

"Cool, you'll ride with me. You do own a cellphone, don't you?"

"I do."

He handed me his iPhone and had me punch in my number. "Great. Eight o'clock?"

"I—what do I tell my parents?" I asked before I could help myself.

The famous Harris laugh. "Tell them you're with me, or that you have an ice cream party or whatever you guys did in Brooklyn." He slapped my shoulder and headed back across the street.

—

"I'M TELLING YOU," MY MOTHER gushed over dinner, delighting over her first day of her new job, "these kids are just radically *different*."

My father helped himself to another ladleful of meat sauce. "What does that mean?"

"Well, for starters, they're light-years ahead of the fourth graders I've always taught, even though these cuties are only in the second grade. That's not hyperbole, Yaakov. Light-years. The way they read, spell, do long division. Half of them know where they want to go to college and have political opinions. I mean, did I ever even have a fourth-grader at Torah Temimah who knew the name of the president?"

"Shlomo Mandelbaum," I said, twirling my pasta. "He definitely knew what was flying."

"Good point. That's one, then."

"Interesting," my father said. "It's very important to understand the secular world. But surely there are trade-offs. Probably they can't learn Chumash as well, for example."

"I don't know," my mother said. Her fork was down. "I wouldn't be surprised if they did, especially if their parents think it counts as speaking a foreign language. They've had tutors from the time they were born. They're almost too precocious. They're angels when it comes to schoolwork, though they really dislike davening. I had one kid try punting a football during Alenu. I don't understand what that's all about."

"By the way," my father said, still chewing, "I booked reservations today."

"Reservations for what?" I asked.

"For Meir's bar mitzvah. Norman's been pressuring me to book through some travel agent he knows."

"Probably because he gets a percentage of the transaction," my mother muttered. "That *ganef.*"

"Probably," my father agreed.

I chewed the inside of my cheek. "But—what if I have something I can't miss in school?"

My father frowned. "In school?"

"Yes."

"We have time," my mother said. "You can always cancel if you really need to."

My father nearly choked on his seltzer. "Cancel on his first cousin's bar mitzvah?"

"Let's just play it by ear, that's all." My mother passed me a plate of mashed potatoes, ignoring the look on my father's face. "Ari, fill us in on your day."

"It was fine. Uneventful. I'm going out tonight, actually."

"Oh?" My mother looked pleasantly surprised. "With whom?"

I took a swig of water. "The kid across the street."

"Noah, you mean?"

"Yes."

"He seemed really nice, didn't he, Yaakov?"

My father ruminated over his plate. A smudge of meat sauce colored his chin. "He did," he conceded. "But these are different sorts of people."

My mother frowned. "And that means?"

My father shrugged innocently.

"Really," my mother continued, raising her brows, "I'm curious what you're implying."

"I mean," my father said in his monotone, "that Noah Harris is a long way from Shimon Levy."

"Well, that's silly. He seems perfectly mensch-like."

"Different places encourage different values. You said it yourself— the kids here are light-years ahead."

"I was referring, clearly, to their academic abilities." My mother returned her silverware to her plate. "So I disagree."

"And the davening stunts?"

My mother continued cleaning without looking up.

"Tell me, Aryeh," my father said, resting his gaze on me, "where are you off to?"

I shrugged. "Not sure," I said, which wasn't altogether a lie, though it was the first time I'd ever offered my parents so much as a mistruth. "Noah wants to introduce me to classmates."

"How downright devious," my mother said under her breath.

"And the girls," my father asked, "from the barbecue?"

"What about them?"

"Will they be there?"

"I don't know," I said, reddening.

"Of course they will," my mother said. "And Ari should meet them. He's going to be spending the year with them, isn't he?"

My father revisited his spaghetti with unbroken concentration.

"Cynthia was telling us about Noah's girlfriend," my mother said, "a lovely girl he's been dating for years."

"Her name is Rebecca," I said.

"Strange to think they can love so young." She looked away from the table, fingered her ring. "Who knows? Perhaps they can."

—

ALMOST EIGHT. I WAS SITTING anxiously in my room, door closed, flipping through Noah's paper. Finally, my cellphone rang.

I sprang from bed, peeked in the mirror. My thick brown hair was matted and unruly, my sneakers worn and sexless, my button-down replaced with a creased white polo, making my standard black-and-white ensemble slightly more palatable. Why, after many years of neurotically maintaining a clean-shaven appearance, had I picked today to experiment with sporting scruff? Why did the corners of my eyebrows insist on undergoing a slight vertical ascent? Would it be biologically impossible to gain even one-tenth of Noah's muscle mass? Did others suspect they, too, owned a fundamentally unrecognizable face, one people consistently failed to remember? Unsatisfied with what I saw, I took a deep breath, hid my tzitzit in my pants and emerged from my room.

"Imma?"

She was sprawled on the living room couch, reading another selection from the *New York Times* Best Seller list. The usual: self-help and educating children. "Abba's at mincha." She said this without looking up.

"Noah's outside. I'm heading out."

She hesitated. "Ari?"

I opened the front door. "Yes?"

I waited for a reminder to behave, to be home early, to daven ma'ariv. Instead, she gave a knowing look. "Make sure you have a good time," she said quietly. "It's more important than you think."

Noah's black Audi hummed softly in my driveway. Rebecca was in the passenger seat. I considered briefly whether this sight was a mirage. Timidly, I approached.

He rolled down his window, flooding my driveway with electronic music. Rebecca leaned over him to greet me, lowering the radio volume. "Ari!"

"Hop in, bud," Noah said. "They'll make room."

In the back sat two boys. The one on the far side was skinny and pale with slicked light brown hair, a thin nose and large, black-rimmed glasses that seemed especially expensive. He wore a crisp Oxford shirt and fitted, pale-gray jeans. "Greetings," he said, nodding haughtily. "Oliver Bellow."

The other boy—"Amir Samson, nice to meet you," he said, actually offering his hand—was fair-skinned with a thick beard, thinning brown hair, coal-like eyes that became black slits when he smiled and thick eyebrows that gave him the permanent impression of a faint frown. I couldn't tell if he was Latin or Mediterranean: he had large, white teeth, a square-shaped face, high-arching cheekbones and a Romanesque, slightly crooked nose. He and I were the only ones wearing yarmulkes.

"Yo, shove over," Noah barked. "Make space."

"Oliver, move to the middle," Amir said. "You're smallest."

"Not where it counts, Amir," Oliver said. "That dishonor falls on your lap, so to speak."

Rebecca turned in her seat to face me. "I'd say they're not typically this annoying, but they absolutely are."

"Maybe I'll just take the middle," I said, cringing at this glare of attention.

"How generous of our guest," Oliver said, as I awkwardly sidled my way between them. "Wait, aren't we getting Evan?" That name again.

"Nah," Noah said, "he's not home yet."

Rebecca changed the radio station to 99 Jamz. "When's he coming back?"

"This week, isn't he?" Amir said. "Thursday or Friday?"

Oliver yawned, putting his legs against the back of Noah's seat. "Where's he now?"

Amir played with his beard. "You don't know where your overlord is?"

"I don't recall."

"All that weed affecting your memory?"

"He's in Spain," Noah said. "One of those travel programs."

Oliver gnawed at his cuticles. "People in Spain are supposed to be breathtaking, did you know?"

After too long of a pause I realized I was being addressed. "No, can't say I did."

"Knock it off, Oliver," Rebecca said.

Oliver didn't look away from me. "Have you been to Spain?"

Amir snorted. "Suddenly Oliver is worldly."

"Nope, never," I said.

"Where do you vacation, then? The Maldives, maybe? Sukkot in Israel? Passover in Greece?"

"You're an ass, Oliver," Amir said.

"And you're balding, Amir," Oliver said.

Amir took out his phone and scrolled mindlessly through Instagram, double tapping a post by some college advising firm. "Rebs, now you see what I mean when I say there's something wrong with him?"

"I'm pretty sure she saw it a long time ago," Noah said. "Like, in second grade."

"What? I'm just trying to become acquainted," Oliver said. "Anyway, yes. Evan. Spain. He must be on some rampage."

Rebecca glared through the rearview mirror. "Don't be a pig."

"Oh, lighten up. You're just defending Sophia," Oliver said. This caught my attention. I looked around uneasily. "For the record, may I note no one's forbidding Sophia from doing the same. I'm definitely not. Far be it from me to overstep my boundaries."

"Stop fantasizing," Rebecca snapped. "It's repulsive."

Oliver winked at me. In response I pursed my lips.

"Where was she this summer?" Amir asked, changing the subject. "I haven't seen her in months."

"Abroad," Rebecca said. "But she just got back."

"Abroad where?"

"Kenya."

Amir frowned. "Wasn't she doing, like, interventional cardiology research or something at U Miami? Her dad's friend has a lab?"

"Yeah, but that was late June," Rebecca said. "Then she went to Kenya."

Amir cracked his knuckles absentmindedly, painstakingly. "What's in Kenya?"

"Volunteering at some institute that teaches music to orphans. Something like that."

"Orphans and music, huh?" Amir shook his head. "Great, that'll dance right off the résumé."

"Here they come, ladies and gents," Noah announced, "the rat race! Look, against all odds, there's Amir Samson leading the pack!"

"Fuck off," Amir said.

"Chill, I'm only kidding," Noah said, pulling into a driveway. "Anyway, pipe down. We're here."

Oliver glanced at the house. "Am I the only one down to punt this and hit Three Amigos?"

"Cut it out," Rebecca said. "Be well adjusted for once."

Four cars were parked outside the house, which was average-sized, at least in comparison to the other homes I'd seen, all still decisively larger than anything on my block in Brooklyn. The house was quiet, much to my relief. In fear, I'd envisioned deafening music, pools of vomit, half-naked bodies.

Oliver knocked. He carried a small backpack, adorned with the Miami Heat logo. "Drugs and booze," he said, returning my stare.

The door opened halfway, revealing a short, freckled girl with fiery red hair that was, sure enough, slashed with streaks of blue.

"Hello!" she said, fawning over the sight of my companions at her door. After a moment, her gaze rested confusedly on me. "Do I know you?"

"This is Ari Eden," Noah said, stepping to my side, slinging his arm around my shoulder. "He's with us."

Her blank stare evolved into a smile. She offered her hand. "Lisa Niman. Nice to meet you, Ari."

"You too."

"Very touching," Oliver said. "Inviting us in or what?"

She opened the door wide, stepping out of the way. "Everyone's out back."

There were about a dozen people in the backyard. They sat on folding chairs, circling a tiny pool and smoking from a translucent hookah. Oliver surveyed the crowd, mumbled his dislike for the clientele and proceeded to probe his bag for a pre-rolled joint, which he then stored behind his left ear. "You blaze?"

I gave a puzzled look, which he returned.

"Do you smoke marijuana?" he repeated, slower and more enunciated, as if I spoke a foreign language, which I suppose I did.

"Ah, right. No, thanks."

He handed me his backpack. I could feel a bottle inside. "Then make yourself useful by holding this for me." He turned to Noah and Amir. "Quick session?"

Amir retreated several feet, anxious to avoid being seen with the joint. "Funny."

"Yeah, sorry, bud," Noah said, waving his large hands. "Basketball season."

"It hasn't started yet."

"For me it has. Started training last month."

"God, I can't wait for Evan to come back," Oliver said, shaking his head in disgust. He took the joint from his ear and faced the group. "Any takers?"

Two boys stood. "Baruch Hashem," Oliver said. "Was nervous everyone spent their summers getting neutered." The two of them—

one blond and Hispanic, the other bespectacled and flat-nosed—trailed Oliver to the side of the house. Following Noah's lead, I found an open seat, keenly aware of everyone's stares. Sophia, I noticed, wasn't present. The anticipatory whirling in my chest subsided.

"Everyone," Noah said authoritatively, clearing his throat. "Meet Ari Eden. He's just moved from New York."

I nodded politely, gave a regrettable wave. There were brief, disinterested smiles, then nothing. The girl to my right, however, extended her hand. She was blond and had a long, thin nose and eager eyes. "Gemma."

"Ari."

"Nice to meet you. You just moved here?"

"Yes."

She eyed me skeptically. "Wow. But you're not, like, in a semicha program or something, are you?"

"I'm not."

"Isn't there one in Coral Gables?"

"I wouldn't know."

"It's just, you know, the way you dress." She gestured at my clothing—baggy khakis, my ill-fitting polo. Others, it seemed, followed some sort of unspoken uniform: slim-fit jeans, white sneakers, V-necks or T-shirts bearing some defiant graphic.

"You mean I'm unfashionable?"

"Sorry if that's rude."

"Fair enough, I'm only kidding. You should've seen me before I changed into this outfit."

She smiled charitably. "So how do you know Noah and the boys?"

"I don't."

"You don't?"

"I mean, I've only just met them."

"Oh. And what about Evan? Where is he anyway?"

"I hear that name a lot."

"Yeah, but who doesn't, right? Like, he's Evan Stark. Where'd you say you were from—Upper West Side?"

"No. Brooklyn, actually."

"Hm." She surveyed her phone for texts. "Well, people from New York *definitely* know him."

"I don't."

"How's that possible? He's the smartest kid in school. They say he has an IQ of, like, I don't know, one hundred and ninety."

"That's—impressive."

"Yeah, teachers are always in awe of him. Apparently he's best friends with the principal. Not to mention the fact that he used to date—"

"—we've never met," I interrupted.

Her face fell. "Oh."

"But I am neighbors with Noah," I said, trying to combat her disappointment.

Boredom receded slightly from her eyes. "Well, Noah's the best. Everyone *loves* Noah."

"Seems that way."

"No, I mean it. Literally everyone."

"I can see why."

"You know he's captain of the basketball team? He's, like, historically good."

"Figures."

"Runs in the family, I guess. His sister plays college volleyball. But anyway." She inched closer. "Are any of the rumors true?"

"What rumors?"

"I don't know, there are a bunch. Like, that they once threw Rolexes into the ocean. Or that their dads—well, not Amir's, obviously—have trade wars. Okay, yeah, they're probably made up, people say crazy things, but who knows, right?"

"Really," I said politely, "I couldn't tell you about any of that."

"It's just they're . . . well, exclusive, you know? Normal people don't just show up to a party with them, is what I mean, especially if"—she sized me up—"if you've just moved to town, let's say."

I took no offense at this insinuation. She was right: a half minute of conversation was sufficient to uncover the extent to which I was categorically unexceptional. During those first days in particular, I often imagined how I must have looked to others, those for whom social capital was a direct function of wealth, wit, beauty and romantic achievement. Picturing myself as an external onlooker, I watched as I sat there with Gemma, fumbling for words, dabbing at sweat stains. From the comfort of this secondary self, I enjoyed two novelties: my proximity to normalcy and my association with exclusivity.

I looked over at Noah. He was gesticulating madly, telling some story with Amir's help. Rebecca was perched on his lap. Those around him were laughing wildly. The hookah arrived at Gemma. She took a long, exaggerated puff before passing it my way. I declined. "I don't smoke."

"Neither do I," she said. "This isn't smoking, so."

"It's not?"

"You don't get high." She puffed again and thrust it toward me. I waved her off once more. "Suit yourself," she said crossly. "It's not carcinogenic."

Oliver reappeared suddenly, standing over us with painfully red eyes. "Eden?"

"Yeah?"

"My bag?"

I picked it up from the ground and handed it to him, feeling the weight of the bottle inside.

"Care to join me for an ill-advised number of drinks?"

Gemma launched herself to her feet. "Of course."

Oliver blinked impatiently. "I meant you, my new friend," he said, fixing his attention on me.

Gemma gave me a jealous glare.

"No," I said, nearly stuttering at this alien proposition, "I don't really—"

He rolled his eyes, turned to the others. His interest in me had dissipated. "Anyone trying to get plastered?" His words were well received: the people around me took last drags of the hookah, and we all shuffled into the kitchen, where Oliver passed around the Jose Cuervo from his backpack. He nudged a red cup into my chest. "Drink up." He smiled stupidly, eyes glossed. "If Amir indulges, so can you."

"Ignore him." Amir grimaced from a shot. "He can be an asshole."

Oliver took a long gulp. "Between you and me," he whispered when Amir's head was turned the other way to greet someone, "I'd be on crack by now if I were Amir. It's no wonder he drinks."

"Pardon?"

"His family situation. His mom, his grandpa. You'll see." Oliver raised his cup and left me.

Two girls sauntered over. The first, short with straight brown hair, wrapped an arm around Amir, completely ignoring me. The other was taller, fairer, her hair a blondish-red. She regarded me with momentary interest. "What're we drinking?"

"Nothing, actually," I said.

"Oliver's tequila," Amir said.

The girl with her arm around Amir snatched his cup. "Oliver's got good taste."

"Highly debatable," Amir said. "And easy on the gulping. We don't want a repeat of last week."

The blue-eyed girl laughed. The shorter girl slapped Amir in playful protest.

"Ladies, this is Ari Eden. Ari, this is Lily," he said, gesturing to the shorter one, "and Nicole," gesturing to the other, whose smile conveyed palpable disinterest.

Lily tossed the empty cup aside and grabbed Amir's hand. "Let's get refills?"

Amir gave me a final nod and allowed himself to be led away. This left me with Nicole. I stared, bit my lip nervously. A few moments ticked by. I tried a feeble smile. "Nice to meet you," I said, finally, wincing at how high-pitched my voice sounded.

"Yes," she said, her voice—low, sweet—trailing into silence, as if dissuade me. She stood on her toes until she spotted a friend. "Ex-
　 me a moment—"

Red-cheeked, hair on end, I watched her leave, praying no one had seen. Sure enough, I felt a clap on my back. My ears filled with familiar laughter. "Lord, that was excruciating."

Rebecca, standing with Noah, grabbed my hand affectionately. "Leave him be," she soothed, scolding Noah. "And don't mind Nicole, Ari. She's always been a bit standoffish."

A charged hush descended over the room. At the kitchen doorway stood a bearded, middle-aged man, stout and sloppily dressed, arms folded across his chest.

"Shit," Rebecca said. "Isn't that Niman's uncle?"

The room froze, eyeing him cautiously. Niman, dumbfounded, let out a pained squeal, but her uncle only went on staring. The rest of us stood in perfect stillness, camouflaging from a predator. Then, on cue, in stumbled Oliver from the bathroom, drunk, squinting, breaking the silence with an enormous belch. "What happened to the music?"

"Oliver!" Rebecca hissed. "Come. Here."

Oliver laughed, walking up to Niman's uncle. "Who the fuck is *this* guy?"

"Leave." The uncle shook with rage. "I advise you to—"

A moment of horror as we watched Oliver slowly raise his cup and, before Niman's uncle could finish speaking, dump its contents over the uncle's head. Reflexively, the uncle swiped Oliver with the back of his hand, sending Oliver stumbling. "Out!" he yelled, surging to life, tequila dripping from his raggedy beard. "Out or I call the cops!"

An avalanche of cups, a great exodus toward the door. Noah grabbed Oliver, who cursed drunkenly and staggered about, a bright-red handprint tattooed across his right cheek, and steered him away. Outside, we raced to the cars. Rebecca seized the keys from Noah, whom she deemed too drunk to drive, and we piled into the Audi.

"Wait," Noah said as Rebecca started the engine. "Where's Amir?"

Screaming from the front of the house, Niman's uncle had Lily and Amir by the collars and was attempting to throw them off the property.

"Get off me," Amir yelled, struggling to loosen the uncle's grip. Lily, hair tussled, went bright with embarrassment.

"In my brother's house!" Niman's uncle shouted. "In my own brother's house!"

Suddenly, Niman, a blur of flaming hair, launched her diminutive frame onto her uncle's back, allowing Amir and Lily to break for the car. Amir slid over my legs toward Oliver while Lily squeezed onto my lap, slammed the door and yelled for Rebecca to drive, all without giving me so much as a backward glance. Invisibility suited me.

I rode in silence, inhaling the rich leather of the Audi's interior, astonished at what I'd witnessed: smoking, drinking, an adult striking a teenager. It was past one when I walked through my front door. I removed my shoes outside, tiptoed to my room. In bed, I considered the long way from Brooklyn, imagined Shimon's reaction to finding Lily on his lap. As I drifted into sleep, I thought of Socrates reminding Simmias that a simple way leads to Hades.

—

I WOKE EARLY TO ACCOMPANY my father to shachris. I was sleepy-eyed in the car and said little, grateful for my father's silence. We sat in the back of the sanctuary, a change for us, considering my father insisted on claiming the first row in our Brooklyn shul, and wrapped the straps of our tefillin around our biceps and foreheads. My father, talis over his head, asked whether any of the boys with whom I was out the previous night were present. I shook my head. During Shemoneh Esrei, while my father swayed and I studied the glass-stained mosaics lining the sanctuary—a celestial ladder, a divided sea, a variegated coat—I noticed Amir shuffle quietly through the side door. He had his arm underneath the elbow of a beefy, elderly Israeli who maneuvered with a cane. I was floored: Amir, a few hours after being caught with Lily, now doubled as a ghost from my old life.

Amir was still bent in prayer when minyan ended, so I couldn't catch his eye. I pointed him out to my father as we left. He smiled to himself and seemed, in some small way, more content for the rest of the day.

—

I SPENT THE MORNING EDITING Noah's paper. It was, at best, mediocre. I fixed grammatical errors, struck a particularly far-fetched suggestion about Shade's sexual proclivities and then deposited the paper in his mailbox. Later, as I sat by my pool, revisiting my own work—I realized, with alarm, that the start of school was marching closer, only days away now—my cellphone rang.

"Hello?"

"It's your favorite neighbor."

"Hey, Noah."

"The edits were fantastic. Really a game changer. I have to thank you again."

"My pleasure."

"I can totally pay, by the way."

"Pay?"

"Yeah, a lot of people don't do this for free."

"No, no, that's okay."

"You sure? You know, you could really charge for this. People would pay good money if you started ghostwriting essays. You've got skills."

"I think I'm good, thanks."

"All right, well, if you change your mind let me know. I could spread the word."

"Right," I said uncomfortably. A mosquito landed on my arm and attempted to steal my blood. I crushed it against my skin. "Thanks."

"So," he said, "how'd you sleep after the big night?"

"Fine," I said, opting not to mention my nightmare of a cartoon version of Uncle Norman chasing me with an ax.

"Glad to hear. We're hitting the beach now. Be outside in ten."

—

HE ARRIVED WITH THE ENTOURAGE: Rebecca in front, her hair braided, one of Noah's oversized muscle shirts over her bathing suit; Oliver, donning chrome-red sunglasses, and Amir, shirtless, in back.

"Know something," Amir told me as I climbed in and took my place in the middle, "you're the only other kid from school I've ever seen attend minyan."

"I didn't think you saw me."

"He's intense when he prays, isn't he?" Oliver said.

"Sorry if my praying upsets you, Oliver."

"Don't be," Oliver said. "I just think you're a fascinating dude."

"How's that?" Amir asked.

"Boys," Rebecca said, "let's not." Noah switched lanes, cutting off the car behind us, which honked madly. Oliver and Amir, in unison from opposite ends of the back row, stuck middle fingers out the windows.

"You're an enigma, that's all," Oliver continued, rolling up his window. "Ari, tell him he's an enigma."

"Really, can we not start this please?" Rebecca called from the front, fidgeting with the air-conditioning. "And leave Ari out of this."

"Why am I an enigma?" Amir said.

"Because you're out with Lily, and then you scamper to minyan in the morning."

Amir resumed that anxious knuckle cracking. "Does no one else think Oliver's a bit too obsessed with me?"

"Don't be so sensitive. I'm just explaining things to our new friend—right, Ari? I mean, wouldn't you say you're kind of confused about how things work around here?"

"Nope," I said quickly, yielding to a sudden urge to examine my fingernails. "I mind my own business." In truth, of course, I did not quite understand how faith functioned in this quasi-secular world. Noah and Oliver, for instance, despite the fact that they attended a yeshiva high school, had not yet worn yarmulkes in my presence.

(Amir, for his part, currently had his head covered with an aqua Dolphins bucket hat.) Such behavior in Brooklyn would have been unfathomable, and yet here it appeared perfectly normal. And so while I wondered to what extent their families maintained kosher homes or observed Shabbat, I understood that, though perhaps never articulated formally, selectivity functioned as the organizing principle of Zion Hills's breed of religiosity. Here, apparently, one enjoyed the luxury of embracing mitzvoth deemed enjoyable or meaningful while neglecting those deemed burdensome or outdated. Shimon, my former rabbis, even my father would scoff at such freedom of choice, would lament a Jew unilaterally discarding centuries of tradition. I, however, was beginning to recognize the value of adhering to ancient rituals without sacrificing participation in the modern world.

Oliver smiled. "Is that right? So if I asked you, for example, whether you would turn on your bedroom lights during Shabbat, you'd say . . . ?"

I cleared my throat. "I don't do that."

"But if I asked you whether Noah does it? Whether I do it?"

"That has nothing to do with me."

"It sure doesn't. But what would you *guess*?"

"Oliver," Rebecca said. "Enough."

"You're allowed to speak up, dude," Oliver said. "Nobody actually cares."

"Look, I really don't know," I said.

"Do you think Amir does it?"

"Does what?" I asked.

Oliver shrugged. "Violates Shabbat."

Amir opened his mouth to say something but decided against it. "No," I decided, avoiding Amir's gaze. "I guess not."

Oliver smirked. "Well, allow me to break it down for you. Here are the *rules*, as actually practiced. On Shabbat, we don't drive, we don't work, but maybe we send a few texts or brush up against the TV so that the Heat game magically comes on. No meat out, Heaven Forbid, but go ahead and stuff your face with dairy, especially if you're on vacation and no one's looking. Do we really believe in the Flood or in the splitting of the sea or in, I don't know, Balaam's talking donkey? Maybe we do, maybe we don't, but either way we're sure as hell going to make sure you understand it's imperative that you drop several years of what's basically college tuition to ensure your kids learn these stories and develop the very same ambivalence!"

An awkward pause ensued during which I stared self-consciously out the windshield. Rebecca shook her head, returning her attention to her Twitter feed. Noah lowered the music slightly. "Jeez, Oliver," he said, "have you been FaceTiming Evan for lessons or something?"

"Say whatever you want," Amir said, rubbing his exposed shoulders, "but just because you're too shallow or too stupid or too, I don't know, too depraved to appreciate the complexities of Orthodox life doesn't mean it doesn't have depth."

Oliver raised his hands in peace. "All I'm saying," he said drolly, "is that Modern Orthodoxy is quite the experiment."

The beach was breathtakingly hot: great beams of sun, the sand a blinding white. Rebecca picked a spot for us near the waves. It was my first time at a real beach and I was in a slight daze. Two women to our left were facedown, topless. Oliver squeezed my shoulder blades as I averted my eyes. "Welcome to the land of flesh, tzadik," he said. *If only Mordechai were here to see this*, I thought.

Noah and Rebecca waded into the water. Amir, Oliver and I hung back, sprawled on towels, staring at the cloudless sky. Soon, Oliver grew bored and pulled out a carefully concealed baggie, some rolling paper and set to work.

"Risky," Amir warned. Oliver scoffed. He finished rolling, licking the ends so they stuck together, and then admired his craftsmanship. He lit up and took a masterful drag, leaning lazily on his skinny elbows, hacking up a lung. When he finished he extended the joint my way. I shook my head, turning my nose at the smell.

"Mr. Samson?"

Amir, head buried in a book, refused to look up.

"Right," Oliver said, tapping the jay with his forefinger, ash falling to sand.

We sat in silence. Noah and Rebecca had drifted so far out they were specks against a linear blue. After some time, Amir joined Noah and Rebecca in the water, leaving me with Oliver, who was busy retching pillars of smoke.

"Oliver," I said, watching Amir voyage farther and farther into the ocean, "you know what you were saying at Niman's party? About Amir's family?"

"Sorry, officer, I don't recall." Oliver covered his face with a towel. "I say lots of things about Amir." A small fixed-wing plane grumbled overhead, pulling along an advertisement for some club in Coconut Grove. "Good place," he said, gesturing above. "Want to go tonight?"

"I don't think so."

"Ever been clubbing?"

"Can't say I have."

He made a show of burying the remains of his joint. "Give me enough time, I'll make a degenerate out of you."

I readjusted my yarmulke, the black velvet scorching in the sun. "Yeah, let's hope not."

"You were asking me something?"

"Amir was in shul this morning with an older man. Who was that?"

"His grandfather. Bit of a frightening dude. Yom Kippur War hero. Led some famous tanking expedition, then moved to America and went to MIT and became an architect or something."

"He lives with him?"

"Yeah. Kind of a weird situation. Amir's dad took off when we were younger. Nice guy, but decided he didn't want to be Orthodox anymore and moved back to Tel Aviv. Pretty sure he's in touch with Amir's older sister, but Mrs. Samson doesn't let Amir have anything to do with him. She's no walk in the park, Mamacita Samson, let me tell you. She's a spitfire, to put it mildly. Rides Amir hard. Like, real hard. Like, he-doesn't-go-to-the-bathroom-without-consulting-her hard. She's the reason he'll go to MIT. Well, she and the legacy of Grandpa War Hero, who moved in after his son bounced. Some tale, huh? Remind me to major in history if I ever get accepted to college."

"So it's the three of them? And the grandfather is . . . Amir's mom's ex-father-in-law?"

"Yeah, but do yourself a favor and don't bring this up to Amir. He doesn't really talk about his father."

We fell back into silence. Soon enough, drowsy from the heat, we nodded off.

When I opened my eyes again I found two faces over me: one sun-soaked with bleached-gold hair, the other uniquely pale. In that warm, oozing realm between waking and sleeping I watched these faces—hazy, provocative—with a dreamy smile. Then, in a cruel moment, the fog burst.

"Hamlet?"

"Sophia," I said too quickly, jolting upright, immensely relieved I'd kept my shirt on. "How are you?"

The blond stood silently, eyes drifting between her cellphone and me.

"Sorry to wake you," Sophia said dryly.

"Just resting my eyes." I leaned forward, stiff from sand. Sophia was wearing a short, black sundress. Her friend, tall and slender with a rather absurdly toned stomach, wore a crocheted white bikini. Sophia strained her neck toward the sky, now smudged with clouds. The sun had slipped away.

"This is Remi, by the way," Sophia told me. "Remi, this is— Aharon?"

"Ari," I said, humiliated she'd forgotten my name. "Ari Eden."

"—Ari. He's just moved to town and he likes his Shakespeare."

Remi paused. "He likes his beer?"

"What? No," I said. "Shakespeare."

Smirking in acknowledgment, Remi returned to her phone.

"Nice to meet you," I said.

She gestured at Oliver, who snored loudly. "Smoked himself unconscious?"

"He, well—"

"I'm aware of his bullshit. It's why I dumped him." Remi lowered her phone. "Can't expect much else from the boy. It's what he is, after all. A boy."

Noah, Rebecca and Amir stumbled from the ocean. On cue, a loud crack overhead.

"Let's bounce," Amir said, gathering towels.

"Must we wake him?" Remi asked. Oliver's chest moved softly up and down.

"I'm totally cool with leaving him," Amir said. "It's only rain." An electric bolt to the west. "Fine. And minor lightning."

Noah shook him awake. Oliver rubbed his eyes groggily. "Remi?" he said, that wispy smile returning. "Always pleasant waking to your face. How was your summer, doll?"

"Divine," she said. "Yours?"

He got to his feet, pulling on a vintage Alonzo Mourning Heat jersey. "Little this, little that."

"I see."

"London, was it?"

"Paris," Remi said, already reabsorbed in her texting, I decided not to share the fact that I'd been outside the country but once—for the funeral of my father's father in Jerusalem.

Oliver got to his feet, rolled his towel. "Parisian admirers?"

"A parade."

Oliver stretched his limbs. "Sounds about right."

More thunder, followed by chill, summer drizzle. We hurried to the lot, the girls ahead, Oliver limping behind. Sophia and Remi threw themselves into a red Porsche while we loaded into Noah's Audi. I nearly laughed at the absurdity of this scene: two sports cars, each likely worth more than my house; a cast of wealthy strangers; me, tzitzit thrown over my T-shirt, lagging behind, fleeing from a beach, a real beach.

"What'd you think of ol' Rem?" Oliver asked when we were settled in the car.

"Well," I started, aware she was his ex-girlfriend.

"Go ahead, say it," he said, nestling back into sleep against the window, "she's a goddess."

Amir laughed. "You screwed up, Oliver. You know that?"

Oliver closed his eyes. "Eh."

"Her father's rolling in it," Amir told me. "Made a fortune in bio-tech and now cryptocurrency. He's on CNBC all the time."

"Crypto, dot-com mania, Dutch tulips. It's all speculative, if you ask me. Bubbles waiting to burst," Oliver mumbled, half-asleep. "Nouveau riche shit. That's not real money." The Porsche zoomed in front of us, soaring into the falling rain. Noah revved his engine, lurching after it, snaking through traffic.

I rode with my cheeks against the window, staring out at the Florida sun shower, replaying the sight of those hyper-realistic faces against the sky.

—

THAT FIRST SHABBAT WAS QUIET. Over dinner we discussed the Parsha: "Shoftim opens by instructing us how to appoint the right king," my father said, eyes closed, swaying slightly, using that singsong voice reserved for Torah study, "but why do we ask for a king in the first place?"

"To be like our neighbors," my mother said, distributing gefilte fish. "To blend in with everyone else."

My father brandished his pointer finger. "A great sin, forgetting who we are."

After dinner, my father and I learned while my mother read on the couch, eyeing us with contentment. We woke at seven the next morning for minyan, being that my father insisted on praying early, while his mind was half-dreamy, while most other shul-goers were still asleep, and then we returned home for another silent meal. Following bentching we sang briefly—I hated Shabbat singing but hummed intermittently, out of some vague sense of duty—until my parents retreated drowsily to their bedroom for a nap, leaving me to read on the living room couch.

As a child, I suffered through a recurring dream. I stood at the mouth of a cave, rolling a boulder back and forth. Something about the sound of that boulder scraping the ground triggered a neuropathic inflammatory response: fever, cold sweats, nausea. I despised these dreams, feared their production of what I imagined to be some combination of physical and psychosomatic cytokines—small, confused proteins tasked with destroying an infection that neither my body nor mind knew to be quite real. But the most intolerable symptom was the sensation of being frozen in time. My movements blurred, my thoughts unspooled too slowly, all sounds adopted a sunken pitch. Even the mere recollection of these dreams, while sitting in Gemara shiur or riding my bike, was enough to dredge up that feeling of being paralyzed in time, leaving me pale and clammy.

The dreams, probably the result of prepubescent migraines, stopped in my early teens. And yet, throughout my adolescence, I often felt time resume that insufferable creep. My mother never fully understood what I meant: from her perspective, my progression from infant to brooding young adult had occurred too quickly, leaving her unprepared for her only child's departure from her house. Shabbat was thus our shared antidote. For my mother, Shabbat suspended time, providing a moment to breathe, to reflect. For me, Shabbat restored equilibrium. We went to shul, we ate together, we sang and, for twenty-five structured hours, time resumed a more bearable pace. I grew up finding beauty in Shabbat for precisely the opposite reason that Eric Fromm and most Jews loved Shabbat: once a week, I had the chance not to overthrow time, but to slip happily back into its shackles.

After havdalah—my mother holding the candle above her head, my father dipping his fingertips into the wine, his pockets, behind his ears—I received the call. Oliver's parents were in the Hamptons, which meant Oliver was throwing a party. Would I come? I agreed.

Good, Noah said, they needed a designated driver. I was being used, but I was still flattered to have been invited. Besides, I reasoned, driving meant I wouldn't have to fumble for an excuse to stay sober. It was foolproof.

I was changing when my father knocked. He looked me over, frowned. "Going somewhere?"

"Yes."

"In that shirt?"

I'd replaced my white button-down with a navy polo. I craved color, had grown tired of snide black-and-white comments. "I'm just going to Oliver's," I said, shrugging, conjuring artificial nonchalance.

"Who?"

"Oliver Bellow."

"The one from shachris the other day?"

"No. Different kid."

"But the name sounds familiar."

"Like the writer."

"What?"

"Nothing."

He paused, snapped his fingers. "Bellow. It's all over shul. Big donors."

"Yeah, I mean, I wouldn't be surprised."

"Ba'alei chesed, then? They give a lot of tzedakah?"

"Sure."

This calmed him. "I'm not used to you leaving so often." I thought about my nights in Brooklyn: moping about my house, reading until my head ached, dozing early, on occasion attending a school oneg or, if we were feeling particularly adventurous, going for pizza in the attempt to spot Bais Yaakov girls. "But I trust you, Aryeh." He nodded, smiling faintly. He kept nodding as he left my room.

—

SOMEHOW OLIVER'S HOUSE WAS EVEN more impressive than Noah's: Victorian-style, high ceilings, a small fountain in the driveway. There were about a dozen cars outside, all parked at hazardous angles. Music swelled inside.

"His dad's a big shot," Amir explained as we walked in. "Would you believe he manufactures rocking chairs?"

"Rocking chairs?"

"Apparently they're in super high demand in, like, Cyprus. He's got some manufacturing monopoly there."

The front door led into a living room with tremendous open space and floor-to-ceiling windows looking out onto the pool. The furniture had been relocated, replaced by long folding tables to allow for chaotic games of beer pong. In the center stood a mountainous keg. There were at least sixty people in the house. It was oppressively hot and I was wild-eyed with fear. I'd braced for what I hoped would be, at worst, a party only marginally more intense than Niman's, but this was another level. Too-loud music, pockets of rowdy friends congregating in the corner and dancing, glancing from the corner of their eyes, waiting to be joined.

"C'mon," Amir said behind me. "Let's find Oliver."

We pushed our way into the kitchen—more precisely, Noah and Amir pushed, and I clung desperately behind them—where we found Oliver standing atop the marble kitchen counter in oversized sunglasses and a red, satiny bathrobe. "My boys!" He rushed toward us, nearly taking a nasty spill. Noah steadied him. "Noah," he said. "Noah, here, here." He handed him his bottle.

Noah gave a throaty laugh, put the bottle to his lips, passed it to Rebecca.

"You two," Oliver said, pointing at Noah and Rebecca. "Drink, and I . . . I want you to go upstairs into my own room . . . no, on second thought, make that my brother's room . . . lock the door, and make sweet, athletic babies, will you? Will you do that?" He wobbled about the countertop. "Will you let me adopt one?"

"Jesus." Rebecca gestured at his robe. "He thinks he's Hugh Hefner."

"Jay Gatsby," I said.

"What?"

"Gatsby."

She shrugged. "Can't hear you over the music," she yelled, pointing apologetically to her ears. Noah grabbed her hand, gave me a wink and led her from the kitchen. Amir, I noticed from across the room, had already located Lily. I was alone.

I wandered helplessly, snaking through the crowd, ignoring stares, sidestepping dancing bodies and puddles of beer. Tassels from my tzitzit strings, I realized, hung out over my rear; I crammed my limp tail back into my pants, only to scold myself for feeling such embarrassment at being spotted wearing tzitzit. I found no one to speak to and, eventually, drifted up the grand, freshly waxed staircase. It was quieter on the second floor, a good ten degrees cooler, which did wonders for my throbbing headache. As I breathed in relief, leaning against the bannister and overlooking the crowd, I made out, of all things, piano notes. I paused to listen: the piece was precise, confident, restrained. Slowly, I made my way in search of the music. I tried one door, bolted shut, frantic moans from within. As I floated down the hall the music changed, the notes becoming repetitive, louder, lower, that sense of calm giving way to frenzy. At the end of the hall I found a dim-lit study, door ajar. Careful not to make a sound, I pushed gently and peered through. At the center of the room sat Sophia, hunched before a grand piano, neck craned close to the keys, hair flying wildly from side to side. Her long fingers attacked the keyboard at unnatural angles, striking the same pattern over and over until, after a half-minute, she allowed her right hand to fall to her side so that her left, curled into itself, rested alone on the far side of the piano, pressing softly, discharging whispers.

I squeezed through the crack in the door. Sophia had her back to me, her body tense, regal. For a moment I thought she'd finished, until her right hand, limp at her waist, leaped violently at the keyboard. Her head swayed in hyper speed, her hands airborne, dancing savagely. I moved closer to see her face. Her eyes were shut.

The music stopped. She straightened, spotted me. A dazed blackness left her eyes. She looked as if she were recovering possession of her body.

"I'm really sorry," I said, embarrassment flooding my face. "I heard music and just—"

She forced a breath, combed her fingers through her hair. "It's all right."

I examined her mouth, her eyes, her jaw. She looked at me without recognition, as if she were still lingering somewhere in the privacy of her music. "I—I didn't mean to startle you," I said.

"You seem to be the startled one."

"What *was* that?" I asked, after a beat. "Did you make it up?"

"Not quite. That was something called Beethoven."

"Name rings a bell."

"Sonata 23 in F Minor, *Appassionata*, with a little twist."

"Right, the *Appassionata*, was it? Thought it sounded familiar."

She stretched her neck before returning her attention to me. "More literary than musical, are you?"

"Yeah," I said, "that's definitely fair to say."

"Sit." She ran her hands beside her on the bench. "Unless you prefer to hover awkwardly with your mouth agape."

I sat. My left arm grazed her waist. A surge of physical intimacy rendered me temporarily light-headed. "You're an incredible pianist."

"How kind."

"I've never heard anything like that before."

"Have you heard any classical music before?"

"Well, no, not really," I admitted. "But now I wish I did."

"Most people don't have much of an appreciation. Mr. Bellow lets me use this piano since nobody else touches it, which is just tragic. Gorgeous, isn't it?"

To be polite, I placed my palm on the surface of the piano. "How long have you been playing?"

"Since I was four. When I asked for lessons my parents were ecstatic—wonderful for the well-rounded college applicant, right?

They've grown less enthusiastic lately. Now they discourage it, in fact."

"Why would they do that?"

"I've become too good."

"That's a bad thing?"

She turned to look directly at my face, eyes unflinching. "My parents want their daughter to be a doctor who, charmingly enough, plays piano at an Ivy, then exclusively at dinner parties to amaze the occasional guest. They're less interested in raising a starving artist."

"I see."

"It's created mild tension in the Winter household." She closed the rack, folded her fingers over it. Her nails were painted white. "So, I've agreed to do both."

"Both?"

"I won't stop playing," she said, "but I'll go to med school."

I resisted a sudden urge to admit I'd searched recently for her on Facebook. Pictures of her at a recital, at a family vacation in Aspen, at Rebecca's sweet sixteen, at her brother's bar mitzvah. Pictures of her offering imperturbable smiles, pictures of her wrapped around her parents, pictures of her looking off, candidly, into remote sunsets, oblivious to the fact that this moment would be preserved in the sarcophagus of the Internet and accessed one day by someone she met briefly at her friend's boyfriend's pool. Thinking about my unauthorized glimpse into some stratum of her inner life was momentarily destabilizing. "Impressive."

"But let's ask the more pressing question." Her eyes flickered with amusement. My ears began to feel very hot. "What are you doing here?"

I stared down at the piano keys. "I needed a breather."

"At this party, I meant."

"Oh. Good question."

She leaned back, our shoulders brushed. My cheeks burst into flames. "So," she said, "you've come up here to escape the revelry below?"

"I could accuse you of the same."

"Go ahead. I'm not evading that fact."

"I'd like to leave altogether," I said.

"Together?"

"No, I—altogether." I ignored her smirk. "At least I wanted to until now."

"I'm flattered. Noah brought you?"

"They needed a designated driver."

A slight lull. "Who's they?"

"Well, Rebecca," I said. "Amir, too."

"Oh." Her face lightened. "That's it."

The door flew open and in wafted Remi, drink in hand, avoiding my eyes. "Sophia," she said loudly. "Jesus, I've been looking everywhere. I had to barge into that other room with those—noises."

"You thought that was me?"

"Obviously not. I was just curious who it was. And it was juicy."

"Somehow I suspect you knew exactly where I was."

"Well, I can't say I'm not alarmed to find you with *him*," Remi said flatly, looking at me with distress.

"I clearly hear you," I mumbled.

Remi rolled her eyes. "Sophia, join me in the restroom, will you?"

"You really need me to accompany you?"

"No. But I'm extracting you from an unpleasant situation. Come, silly pianist. It's urgent."

"I'm okay, I think, Rem—"

Remi grabbed Sophia by the wrists. "You trust me? Let's go."

Sophia laughed, allowing herself to be dragged from the piano. "Okay, okay. Sorry, Hamlet. I wish you the best of luck."

I sat a while longer, still stunned by the music, which for some reason made urgent the fact that I had no business being at this party, nor any real hope of being accepted by these strangers, unless I was providing a convenient favor: editing a paper, driving after a long night out. My headache returned, the air made heavy again. I was conscious suddenly of how alone I was, how alone I'd always been.

"The look on your face calls for a stiff drink."

Someone holding two nondescript red cups entered the study. He was tall, his face unshaven, almost wolfish, his nose sharp and small. He had a spectacular tan, one that made his teeth gleam, and muddy, heavy-looking eyes. His gaze—piercing, defiant—stood out most.

"I'm all right, thanks," I said.

He smiled. "Not a drinker?"

"Not really."

"Neither am I," he said, proceeding to drain most of his cup. "Don't believe I've seen you before."

"I'm new."

"Really? It's not too often that we're given fresh blood." He looked me over. "How does a newcomer find himself alone upstairs in the midst of a riotous Oliver Bellow party?"

"I wasn't alone."

His gaze lingered on the piano. "She plays beautifully."

"Sophia? How'd you know she was here?"

"Intuition."

"Yes," I said. "She's quite good."

"Quite good?" He smiled darkly. "My friend, she's a *prodigy*." He paced the room, studying the paintings on display. He lingered before the one above the piano. A man, smiling vacantly, grasped at a woman in a flowing pink gown, floating uneasily above his head. "Unsettling, isn't it?"

Emerald shades. A bluish-white sky. Treetops in the distance. The man had a harsh, burnt face. The woman, horizontal, arms spread into a crucifix, had her mouth pursed tight. "I suppose," I said. "But pretty."

"It appeals most, I've always thought, to those at home in the uncanny. Those with enough courage to travel great distances from ordinary life." He smiled to himself. "Do you know what I mean?"

"Don't think so, no."

He turned from the painting. "Leon Bellow's favorite, or so he claims. Familiar with it?"

"I'm not."

"*The Promenade*. It's a Chagall."

"Oh."

"You don't know Chagall, do you?"

"Art isn't really emphasized where I'm from."

"Where's that? Antarctica?"

"Borough Park."

Another long drink. "Chagall is worth learning. I suspect you'll see a lot of him now."

"Why's that?"

"Everyone has a Chagall."

"Not my family."

"Tell me," he said, eyes narrowing. "How do you know Sophia?"

"I don't, really."

"Surely well enough to be allowed to hear her *Appassionata*?"

"I sort of stumbled in." After a pause: "How'd you know what she played?"

"I heard fragments," he said. "Down the hall."

"You're friends, then?"

"We've known each other a long time." He drank further, gazing expressionlessly, waiting for me to speak.

"Shall we go downstairs?" I finally asked, desperate to get away, taking the initiative to stand.

We ambled through the hall and down the staircase to rejoin the party. I felt the hot air descend upon me again, sweat returning to my back.

"So." He observed the crowd, which seemed to have increased substantially since I'd disappeared. "Would you say you're tight with Oliver?"

"I'd say we're loosely acquainted. I was brought here."

"By whom?"

I scanned for Noah, to no avail. "That guy," I said, finding Amir in the crowd. He was wrapped around Lily, making out against a wall.

"Amir?"

"Rebecca and Noah, too," I said, trying to prove myself.

"Harris?"

"He's my neighbor." I offered my hand. "Aryeh Eden."

"How biblical. Do you have an English name?"

"I don't really use it."

"But it exists?"

"Yes," I said cautiously. "Andrew."

"Andrew Eden," he said. "That'll do."

"And your name?" I asked after a few confused beats.

"Evan Stark," he said, finally accepting my hand. "The pleasure is mine."

"Oh. I've heard of you."

"And I've heard you're quite the Shakespearean. What's your favorite play?"

I bit my lip, attempted an expressionless frown, unsure whether to feel a burst of kinship or insecurity. "Why?"

"I'm curious."

"Uh. *Antony and Cleopatra.*"

"*'Give me my robe, put on my crown,'*" Evan said. "*'I have immortal longings in me.'*"

I stared for a moment. "What made you say that?"

"What do you mean?"

"That quote. Why'd you say it?"

"I don't know, I've always liked it. Gets at what it means to be human, how we have to pine for things." He looked at me with amusement. "Why do you ask?"

"Nothing, no reason," I said, opting not to mention that the very line had featured prominently in my application essay, had indeed served as my title. "So what's yours?"

"*Lear.* But nothing comes close to the sonnets."

"Really?"

"My mother read them to me when I was a child," he said. "*'Nor Mars his sword, nor war's quick fire shall burn / The living record of your memory. / 'Gainst death, and all oblivious enmity / Shall you pace forth.'* Probably it was weird to find that kind of thing soothing before bed, right?"

"Yeah," I said, aware I was being challenged, though I didn't grasp why. Unsettled, I again scanned the crowd for a glimpse of Noah, eager for someone—anyone—to drag me away. "It was."

"Have a drink." Evan offered me a cup, this time with more force. "The way you're looking around is making me anxious."

"No, I—"

"Come on, Eden. To new friendship, emboldened by liquid courage."

"I'm driving."

"Who isn't? One drink. It's rude to refuse. By the time you leave you'll be perfectly sober."

I took the cup, raised it to my lips.

"Wait," he said, stopping me. "You'll need to make a toast."

"A toast?"

"We're not savages, are we?"

"I don't know any toasts."

"And you claim to be a man of letters. Nothing?" He shook his head. "*He who makes a beast of himself gets rid of the pain of being a man,*" he recited solemnly, raising his cup before finishing what was left of it. I took a deep breath and gulped, throat burning as I drank. "Know that one?"

"No," I said, eyes watering.

"Never neglect Dr. Johnson." He pushed my cup toward my chest. "Finish it," he said, and I did. "That should loosen you."

"What was that?"

"Homemade cocktail." He grabbed two Keystone Lights from the hands of a passerby. The boy turned to say something but, registering who had stolen his beers, decided not to object. Evan handed me a can. "Relax, enjoy, be yourself."

I opened the beer, drank with him. He asked where I was from, what brought me to Zion Hills. Things were becoming hazier, the room condensing into an indeterminate shape, illumined in vertiginous light. I tried walking it off, shaking my head.

He finished his beer, tossed it to the floor. "Feeling okay?"

"Sure," I said, ignoring the growing fog. When I looked up I saw two girls wandering our way. Through my internal vapor, I was still made aware of Sophia's pale beauty. I didn't care about Remi, standing beside her. Something about Sophia—light-dazzled eyes, sharp gaze, lips pursed haughtily—siphoned oxygen from my brain.

"Sophia," Evan said in a small voice, his face turned slightly pallid. He looked at Remi, at me, glanced about the room before returning to her. Their eyes met. They were alone before us. "It's good to see you."

She turned slowly, nodded, looking through him.

"How was—Kenya?"

"It was fine."

"When did you get back?"

A pause. "Recently."

"I see." More silence. By now I was too woozy to concentrate on what anyone was saying. I was focused, instead, on remaining upright. Finally, Evan plunged his hands in his pockets and nodded in my direction. "I've met your new friend."

"He doesn't look well," Remi said, chiming in, "does he?"

"He's fine. Aren't you, Drew?"

My name isn't Drew, I tried to say. Nothing came out.

Sophia eyed me suspiciously. "What's wrong with him?"

I was in a cold sweat, glassy-eyed, the music receding into the background, elastic, disorienting. "Nothing," Evan said. "He had one drink."

Sophia looked me up and down. "Why does he look as if he's—" Her tone unnerved me. I wanted to ask what she meant. Instead, I examined the indents of my palms. "He wasn't like this before."

Evan shrugged. "I don't know what you're talking about."

"This is what you do?" she said. I was aware now, to my sedated dismay, that I'd become an object of her pity. "Corrupt everything in your radius?"

"Sophia." The way he said her name made her fall silent. Evan, himself, appeared momentarily startled.

She shook her head and, without giving me a second glance, slipped away.

"Well, then." Evan gave me a look. "You good?"

The nausea was passing. I nodded, unsure what else to do.

Evan turned to Remi. "Let's get you something to drink."

Evan brought Smirnoff. By the fourth or fifth shot it was tasteless, at which point things began churning at a mind-bending velocity. We danced, music in everything, Remi's legs against mine. There was beer pong—Evan and Remi competing against Nicole and me—until Nicole, realizing we'd met at Niman's party, convinced me to chug our cups and some massive kid (Donny was his name?) slipped rear-first on the table, snapping it in half.

I was in a dark room, Nicole rocking against me, her hair falling over my face, our breathing warm and heavy. Soft lips, nimble fingers tracing my skin, the room spinning unbearably, walls closing in, the floor a black puddle, something disfigured on the wall, dipping in and out of consciousness. Panic gave way to desire, pleasure to heaviness. *I am falling*, I thought, *a boy from Brooklyn*. And then: my father's face in the window. I blinked, realizing where I was. I moved away, opened the door. She frowned and asked where I was going. I told her I was sorry and stumbled back into light.

—

WHEN I WOKE NEXT I knew only that I was not in my room and that the previous night was no nightmare. I sat too quickly but was forced to slink back down, overcome by an earsplitting headache. I closed my eyes, gave myself to the fear rising in my chest. Was I at Oliver's? Were my parents searching for me? I visualized a massive manhunt, spanning the coast of Florida. I forced deep, steady breaths.

I opened my eyes and tried sitting again, slower this time. I was in a nice room: clean, bright colors, trophies lining the windowsills, autographed jerseys of Dwyane Wade and Dan Marino on the walls. I massaged my temple and heard the sound of running water. My first instinct was horror: was I with Nicole? The nausea returned.

And then that distant sound of water stopped, giving way to throaty laughter. "First hangover?" Noah entered from a connecting bathroom. He wore only boxers and had a toothbrush in his mouth.

I nodded.

"Mazel Tov." He returned to the bathroom and spat. "Figured it'd be wise for you to spend the night and avoid your parents."

"What time is it?"

"Nearly two."

"In the morning?"

"In the afternoon," he called from the bathroom.

"Oh, God," I moaned, scrambling to my feet. I was wearing pants but had no idea where my shirt was. "I've got to get home."

"Relax." He came back, pulling a jersey over his sculpted body. The dizziness returned: blotches of red, swirled vision, my eyes smarting from sunlight. "I texted your parents from your phone to say you'd be sleeping at my house. You're good."

I exhaled gratefully and sank back down, trying to will away the nausea.

He handed me a bottle of water. "Drink this, shower, later we'll get you eggs and coffee." He proceeded to knock out several dozen push-ups, breathing steadily with each dip. "You're quite the drunk, you know that?"

I drank, blinked furiously, trying to piece everything together. "Thanks," I said, between furious gulps. Water dripped down my chin. "For helping me."

He sat up, rested. "What're friends for, if not dealing with your comatose, vomiting corpse?"

"I don't know what happened."

"Neither do I. Weren't you supposed to be our driver?"

"I'm really sorry."

"No worries, dude. We've all been there."

I opened my mouth, closed it, tried again. "Was it Evan?"

He moved to his drawers, pulling out NBA-branded socks and then applying Old Spice under his arms. "Was what Evan?"

"I think he gave me something." I gave my attention to Marino and Wade, allowing the question to hang delicately in the air.

"Damn right. He kept pouring shots. We need to teach you to say no, my friend."

"I don't mean alcohol."

"You smoked?"

"No."

"So what're you talking about?"

"I don't know, that first drink he gave me was this mix, and then Sophia said something about how I looked kind of—"

"Drunk?"

"Maybe, but I mean, I don't think so. More like I'd had something that was, I don't know, spiked or whatever?"

"Your drink? With what, like a Xanax?"

I shrugged. I had never heard of Xanax.

He sat on his desk chair, swiveled back and forth. "He wouldn't do that," he finally said. "At least not intentionally."

"Are you sure?"

"Sleep more," he said, rising suddenly. "I'll leave you to it."

—

I WAS THIRSTY WHEN I woke. I stretched—stiff, wobbly—and headed to the bathroom. I studied myself in the mirror: my hair was a ragged mess, my eyes red, my facial features incongruous, having drifted, the longer I stared, into a state of self-incoherence. I looked scrawny and worn. I dumped my face into the sink and checked the clock. Seven-thirty. Guilt boiled in my stomach, a lump formed in my throat: it was the first day in my entire adult life I'd forgotten to daven with tefillin. From the window I could see the sun beginning to fade, casting a quiet, orange glow over the Harris backyard. Below, Noah—

basketball jersey, white soccer shorts, a backward Nike cap—tossed red golf balls into the air and whacked them over his fence onto the golf course. I watched the balls soar higher and higher until they vanished into specks of red against the sky.

I wandered out of his room, down the spiral staircase, through the long hallways. I found my way into the kitchen, where, desperately thirsty again, I poured myself a cup of water.

"Hello, dear."

I nearly jumped. Cynthia was seated at the long kitchen table, flipping through a cookbook.

"Mrs. Harris," I said, my voice raspy. "I'm sorry I—"

"Oh, don't be. Help yourself," she said, nodding at the cup in my hand. "Can I offer you anything to eat? You're probably—famished."

"No, thanks, I'm fine. I should be heading out."

"You sure? I make pretty fantastic dishes, if I do say so myself, just ask my daughter. I'm allowed to admit that only because I'm a chef." She gestured at a row of books stacked neatly at the center of the kitchen table, all of which had her face plastered on the cover. *Kosher Kravings*. "I've written a few cookbooks in my day."

"Wow. But I'm fine, really, thank you."

"Feeling any better, at least?" She smiled knowingly. "Must've been a long night."

"Yes," I stammered.

"No need to look *that* ashamed, hon. I was young once. Plus you're much more polite in these circumstances than Oliver. You know Oliver, don't you?"

An image of Oliver, robed, tap-dancing on his countertop, came to mind. "I sure do."

"As you'd guess, he's a bit more rambunctious when he overdoes it." She laughed to herself. "You know, I just saw your mother a few hours ago."

"Oh, God."

"Don't worry, I covered for you. Said you boys were out golfing."

"Thank you, Mrs. Harris."

"Please," she said lazily, waving me off. "And it's Cynthia, that's not up for discussion. Now go find Noah. He's out back. But do me a favor. Hit some balls with him so that what I told your mother wasn't a lie."

I went out through the stained-glass backdoor. Noah turned, his club slung over his back. "Morning, sunshine."

I managed a weak smile. "Morning."

"Feeling all right?"

"Much better now."

"Good." He tossed another ball into the air and swung. His contact was impressive. The ball sailed into the distance. "You play?"

"Golf or baseball?"

"The toss is just an extra touch. We golf a lot, my dad and I. A client got him into it." He handed me his club, dropped a ball for me. "Not much golf to be played in Brooklyn, is there?"

"No. But that doesn't mean we were terrible at everything athletic." I lined up, swung, missed wildly.

"Yeah, I can definitely see that." He picked up another club from the grass and resumed knocking shots over the fence. "So aren't you going to tell me how it was?"

"How what was?"

"You know—with Nicole."

I took another horrible chop, sending the ball two yards. "Nothing happened."

"Nothing at all?"

"Well, yeah, some things."

"What sort of things?"

"Things," I said uncomfortably. "But not, you know, *the* thing."

Noah laughed. "It's not exactly rocket science, Ari. Want me to draw a diagram?"

"No, I—"

"I'm kidding, dude. Obviously I didn't mean *that*."

"Right," I said, red-faced. "I just meant that I kind of, I don't know, left in the middle."

Noah lined up, took another swing. "Wait, what? You're kidding." He looked me over. "Have you ever before, you know, done any sort of—?"

"No," I said embarrassedly.

He looked dumbfounded. "But you still just walked away? From Nicole? Nicole Honig? The person who wouldn't even talk to you at Niman's?"

"Yeah," I said, "pretty much."

He whistled, pointed his club at me. "Why in God's glorious name would you do that?"

I shrugged and finally knocked the ball over the fence.

—

THAT NIGHT I DREAMT I was in shul. A redhead entered the sanctuary, took my hand and guided me up a spiral staircase into dusk.

"Where are we?" I felt myself sinking deeper and deeper into the ground, though somehow remained upright on my feet—the sinking was occurring in my chest. I could feel the spell of unreality dissolving: I was aware that I was asleep, but knew with equal certainty that if I didn't wake now I never would.

She put a finger to her lips. "*Bind them as a sign upon your hand,*" she recited, eyes unblinking, "*a reminder between your eyes . . .*"

I woke in a sweat. For a while I stared at the ceiling, trying to fall back asleep but thinking instead of the day my father presented me with my tefillin. They had belonged to his father, had been smuggled into the Dachau concentration camp. My grandfather never missed a single morning of laying tefillin. My father hadn't, either, and I knew he never would. It took only several days in Zion Hills for me to break this chain.

I gave up and turned on my bedside lamp. *One who stays awake at night,* I couldn't stop thinking, *has forfeited his life.* I read until nearly six thirty, wiry shadows cast against my wall, until, just before daylight, I killed the light and succumbed to restless sleep.

—

THURSDAY WAS THE FINAL DAY of summer. I spent it in a frenzy, cursing myself for being so unprepared for the start of school, scrambling with my mother to purchase supplies and clothing. Kol Neshama's dress code was more lenient than I was accustomed to—a button-down of any variety sufficed—so we drove from store to store, searching for inexpensive shirts that were vastly cooler than whatever currently lined my closet.

"I like this." My mother held a striped, fluorescent green to my chest. We had wandered around the local mall into some place called Bohemian Terrain: dim lights, tinny music, posters of grim-faced guitarists. "It's on clearance. Want it?"

No one would have accused me of being a great dresser, though I had gained sufficient self-awareness to stop wearing only white button-downs on all occasions. So while Oliver and Noah looked as if they dressed each morning in strict accordance with a J.Crew catalog, I couldn't tell if the shirt before me was moderately fashionable or if it'd been selected by a color-blind mother recently transplanted from Borough Park. I crossed my fingers and went with the former.

"Perfect. Let's get out of here," she said, adding it to the rest of the cart and heading to the front to pay. "This place reminds me too much of my teenage years."

I poked around while waiting, running my fingers over shirts I couldn't afford, admiring a pair of sleek white tennis sneakers that I noticed Noah wearing. The music in the store was beginning to make my head throb.

"Hamlet?" From behind a mannequin stepped Sophia, so suddenly and wonderfully that, for a moment, I thought I was imagining her. Hermione, restored from statue to life, came to mind. *Bequeath to death your numbness, for from him / Dear life redeems you.*

"Sophia," I said, flustered, nearly jumping.

"So you don't like being snuck up on, do you?"

"I guess I don't take it as well as you do." I returned the sneakers to their place on display. "What're you doing here?" I asked stupidly.

"Shopping, believe it or not." Her amused arrogance had returned. All traces of her anger from Oliver's party were gone. She noticed the stack of green shirts beside me. "You're not buying *that* hideous thing?"

"Of course not," I said, cringing internally. "Just waiting for my mother."

"You shop with your mom?"

"Not usually," I said shamefully, immediately regretting having opened my mouth.

"Does she dress you in the morning, too?"

"I just needed some new clothing. For school."

"Indisputably."

"It's that bad?"

She eyed me up and down. "Unfortunately."

"If only you could've seen me in Brooklyn. My black hat was very avant-garde, actually."

"Did you really wear a black hat?"

"Well, technically it was a dark gray one. And it was only at my bar mitzvah."

Her phone buzzed but she ignored it. "Adorable."

"As you can probably guess, I'm pretty new to the whole shopping exercise."

"You should've asked me." She allowed me to consider momentarily whether this offer could possibly be real. Watching my head swim, she smiled slightly and pointed to a middle-schooler in the front of the store. "That's Harrison, my little brother. I'm preparing him for his first day of eighth grade. Handsome, isn't he?"

I caught myself in a half nod, unsure how to respond.

"Two girlfriends at camp this summer, or so my mother heard." She paused, tilted her head, looked at me funny.

"What?"

"About the other night." She lowered her voice. "What happened at Oliver's, I mean."

"Oh. That was—nothing."

"I don't think it was nothing."

"I'm okay, really."

"Well, I wanted to apologize."

"You didn't do anything."

"That's right. I walked off and left you there. Even though I had suspicions. And I heard things ended up being somewhat . . . unexpected. So, I'm really sorry if you were forced into anything uncomfortable—"

"Yeah, no. I mean, thank you but—"

My mother chose this moment to drift over. Unabashedly, though I suppose she didn't realize what she was doing, considering this was now only the second time she'd seen me within ten yards of a non-relative female, she swept Sophia up and down: her tight black jeans, the dim blue of her eyes, her unflappable self-assurance. "Hello," my mother said, innocently enough.

Sophia turned from me and offered a hand. "Sophia Winter. Nice to meet you, Mrs. Eden." I could tell she had a way with adults—confident, slightly standoffish, as if addressing an equal.

"You're in Aryeh's class?"

"Indeed I am."

My mother snapped her fingers. "And you were at the barbecue the other day, weren't you?"

"Good memory."

"How wonderful. I'm glad Ari is meeting such nice new friends."

"He's fitting in marvelously, you should know." She offered me a knowing look. I glanced away and cleared my throat. "Well, I need to finish with my brother, he's way too picky for a thirteen-year-old, but it was lovely to meet you, Mrs. Eden." She nodded, giving us her starlit eyes. "See you tomorrow, Ari."

Sophia left. My mother and I stood silently, embarrassed by the ordeal. "Well," my mother finally said, unable to stop grinning, "she's gorgeous."

I grabbed the shopping bag from her and walked ahead. "Should we go now?"

She nodded, pretending to ignore the look in my eyes.

SEPTEMBER

Endure that toil of growing up;
The ignominy of boyhood; the distress
Of boyhood changing into man;
The unfinished man and his pain

—Yeats, "A Dialogue of Self and Soul"

Orientation was on a dreary, end-of-summer Florida day: light rain, a chill in the air, the sky a bleak gray.

"Fitting weather," Noah grumbled in the car ride over. He had found me a block away from our houses, walking slowly, squinting through the drizzle, and insisted I get in.

The parking lot was chaos: music blasting, cars honking, bodies flitting in and out of traffic. We barely avoided a nasty collision, after some kid, in pursuit of a football, vaulted onto Niman's moving car, causing her to swerve violently within inches of the Audi's taillights. I watched friends reunite after long summers, underclassmen flirt shyly, strangers throw confused looks upon finding me in Noah's passenger seat. That itching, deep-seated unease from the Harris barbecue, the recognition of being hopelessly out of place, returned.

I had prepared to embrace this unease. Finally, I told myself, I had before me the opportunity I wanted. I could look upon unfamiliar faces and pretend to be anyone. I could be extroverted, easygoing, a tabula rasa. Yet when the moment came I failed, as I knew I would, to see myself beyond what I'd been until now: solitary, a formless presence in a foreign world. I accepted this in the way one accepts scientific fact—unfeelingly, without any resentment toward a truth that, though previously unrealized, had always existed.

We parked on the far side of the lot, next to Oliver. He was perched on the hood of his yellow Jeep, his eighteenth birthday gift from his parents, as he boasted shamelessly, and blaring Jay-Z.

"Did you just have a quick morning toke?" Noah asked cheerfully.

"I do what must be done to get by," Oliver said piously.

"You realize the day hasn't even started."

"Yup," Oliver said, nodding along to Jay-Z's voice. "Therein probably lies the problem."

Evan stumbled from the passenger seat, coughing. He shared Oliver's glassy-eyed look. My jaw tightened. Obsessively, I'd replayed the scene from the party, trying to determine whether Sophia's accusation held water or whether it was ludicrous, as Noah continued to suggest. Perhaps I had, in fact, simply drunk too much. It was my first time, after all, and it wasn't as if I could tell the difference between mixing too many drinks and having a mysterious substance slipped into my cocktail. I was trying my best to let it go, to assume that, even if Sophia were right, whatever happened could be reduced to bizarre miscommunication. Noah, sensing my turmoil, steered me from Evan and toward the building.

My previous glimpses of the school failed to convey just how spectacular the campus was in the flesh. I marveled, much to Noah's amusement, over the perfectly manicured lawns, the endless sports fields stretching into the distance, the way the building itself, in my eyes, resembled some sort of skyscraping cruise ship. A bulletin board in the lobby, showcasing a banner that read IVY LEAGUE ALUMNI, displayed pictures of beaming students being hugged by the same woman: short and slim, with implacably iron eyes. Noah dragged me along to the library, where we waited in line for textbooks.

"Let's see," he said, grabbing my schedule from my hand. "AP English Lit. AP Bio, I'm sure as hell not in that one. Same Talmud and Tanach. Elementary Hebrew? Don't you come from the Old Country?"

I shrugged. "That'd be Yiddish. My yeshiva didn't believe in modern Hebrew."

"But of course."

I pointed to a class on the bottom of my schedule. "What's this one?"

"J-Hip," he said. "Jewish History and Philosophy. Senior tradition. Mr. Harold teaches it—real sweet guy, super knowledgeable, passionate about the subject, but twenty years past his expiration date. Class behavior, unfortunately, borders on abusive."

Amir spotted us and forced his way over. He immediately requested our schedules and frowned as he vetted mine. Not that he had reason to worry: I considered myself intelligent, certainly well-read, but knew I'd benefited immeasurably from my lack of competition in Brooklyn and figured I'd been set back so irreparably by Torah Temimah that I'd be firmly out of Amir's academic constellation, if not light-years behind the average student. This dawned on him in a matter of moments. "You've never taken geometry?" He did a poor job disguising his relief.

We received our books—heavy, forbidding books that excited me but left me restless—stored them in our lockers and then were directed to another line for pictures. I took mine, smiling stiffly, aware of the stares I was receiving, mentally applauding myself for deciding against wearing the green shirt, and then watched as Noah and Oliver switched places for their pictures. ("Look at *you*, Ari!" Rebecca said, examining my picture in the photographer's camera, causing several heads to turn, which I suppose was her intention, despite my discomfort. "Who knew you'd be so photogenic? Those dimples? That cleft in your chin? That smile! We've got a diamond in the rough, don't we?") Our grade—one hundred and four students, over three times the size of my class in Brooklyn—was then ushered into the assembly hall, an enormous, regal room with velvet seats and humming lights, to join the rest of the student body. Girls were ushered to the right, boys to the left, though no mechitza went up. I followed Noah to the back.

Onstage stood a thinly bearded, dignified man with finely combed silver hair and a fierce but kind face. He was short and waiflike and wiped his nose with a multicolored handkerchief—red, white, blue, green, yellow, black—featuring the South African flag. "That's Rabbi Feldman," Noah told me. "Head of the Judaic Department. Bit of a disciplinarian, but really nice guy from Cape Town."

Rabbi Feldman waited for everyone to shuffle in and quiet down. The front row was conspicuously empty. "Harris," he called out in a sharp accent, his voice surprisingly emphatic for someone so skeletal, "please corral your row and move to the front." I stood immediately— it seemed an innocuous request—but realized everyone else was grumbling, rising reluctantly. Oliver, sitting to Noah's left, made a comment under his breath.

Rabbi Feldman raised his brows. "Pardon me, Bellow?"

"My apologies, Rabbi," Oliver said. "Please don't think I haven't missed you terribly." Our row broke into snickers. Biting back a grin, Rabbi Feldman politely warned Oliver to shut up.

We moved to the front, just a few feet from Rabbi Feldman. I noticed Gemma and a group of girls whispering, and then stole a glance at Sophia—noble-eyed, ebullient—sitting between Rebecca and Remi.

Rabbi Feldman cleared his throat and tried regaining his smile. "Welcome back, all. Wonderful to see everyone so—enthusiastic." He looked sarcastically toward Oliver, who gave an obnoxious thumbs-up. "The school is excited about this new year, as we think you all"— he gave the room an unconvincing wave—"are an extraordinary group. We're thrilled to have you as student leaders and to partner with you in making this year a success."

The back door burst open. In strolled Evan, whistling defiantly. In synchrony, the room turned to face him. Girls stared. Several junior boys leaped to their feet, as if standing for a rabbi. Sophia, I noticed, averted her eyes toward Rebecca, smiling unfocusedly.

"Surprise, surprise," Rabbi Feldman said, sighing into the microphone. "Mr. Stark, good of you to join us."

Evan took his time making his way down the aisle, wholly indifferent to the fact that several hundred pairs of eyeballs were presently glued to him. "May I note publicly, Rabbi, that summer was good to you?" Evan said. "You look really—sinewy. Was it that paleo diet I told you about?"

Rabbi Feldman held his stare and then, to my surprise, failed to suppress a chortle. "Don't believe I won't spend several weeks kicking myself for laughing at that. Freshmen, I advise you to refrain from emulating this young man's—pluck, let's call it. He's a poor role model. Impersonators shall undoubtedly fail to pull that off unscathed."

The room broke into giggles. Having caused as much commotion as he could, Evan took a seat in the row behind us.

"Swear to God," Noah said, turning to face Evan. "This kid gets away with murder."

"Where was I? Ah, yes, since you're all such fine, mature young adults," Rabbi Feldman continued, rolling his eyes, "we expect no behavioral issues, whatsoever, and trust you'll treat the school with the same respect with which you seek to be treated. Our seniors from last year were a fantastic group—"

"Deplorable bunch," Oliver whispered to Noah. "Did they even have a senior prank?"

"—and we expect similar cooperation and leadership from our current elder statesmen." He went on like this for a while: the key to the year would be building genuine respect between students and faculty, growing together, enriching both our Judaism and our secular studies. When he finished, he asked us to stand for Rabbi Bloom, our principal.

"The big boy," Noah whispered. "You'll like him. Smartest man you'll meet."

He was tall, slender, slightly bent, no older than sixty. He had an elfin face, steel-gray hair, detailed eyes that swept the room. "Ladies and gentlemen." His voice was low and thoughtful and gave the impression that he was speaking directly to you. "Freshmen and seniors, sophomores and juniors, welcome home."

"He still can't really get over himself," Evan muttered, smiling.

Noah nodded toward Evan. "He has a pretty deep-seated love-hate thing going on with Bloom," Noah explained. "Well, honestly, it's mostly just love. You'll see."

". . . it's my distinct pleasure to serve as your Head of School, at the forefront of our nation's Modern Orthodox high schools. I remember some twenty-five years ago, when we first labored to build this institution, I envisioned an academy where students would, in the deepest sense, enhance their instructors. Aristotle believed education, though bearing sweet fruit, contains bitter roots." He paused, surveyed the crowd. "With all due respect to Morenu Aristotle, I reject the notion that education should necessitate anything but excellence, in principle and in spirit. There are not, I'm sure you'll agree, bitter roots among *your* ranks."

My row wasn't listening. They were busy hearing Evan recount, through whispers, his mind-bending summer—girls in small Spanish towns, swims in the Tajo, breathtaking hikes in the Cordillera Cantabrica, the forty-year-old woman next to whom he woke on the side of a riverbank. Yet I was entranced. Rabbi Bloom spoke opulently and at a rabid pace, weaving the Judaic with the secular: John Adams' insistence that Jews civilized the world morally; Talmudic law as an intellectual forerunner of Lockean governmental theory; the difference between Marxist slavery and religious opportunity. Every word was in stark contrast to the broken English of my former rabbis. This, I told myself, was the opportunity for which I fled Borough Park.

"Fire is powerful," he said as he wound down. "But it cannot affect the inflammable. Set fire to glass, to bricks, to concrete, and nothing will happen." He looked us over, face by face. He had an intimidating way: not coldness, but intellectual urgency. "If, as students, you're refractory to inspiration, nothing will penetrate, regardless of how incendiary it may be." With that, we were dismissed, yet as we shuffled toward the exit, Rabbi Bloom again picked up the microphone. "Mr. Stark, Mr. Bellow, Mr. Harris and Mr. Samson, a word."

"Picking up where we left off," Noah said. "Early in the year for this, isn't it?"

Oliver patted my back. "Sing our tale, kid."

I headed for the door while they mounted the stage. I stole a glance at the four of them, whispering in a circle, and at Rabbi Bloom, who looked them over with quiet admiration. I allowed myself to burn, for a moment, with inexplicable jealousy, and then I left them alone in the grand room.

—

MONDAY, OUR FIRST REAL DAY of school, was gorgeous, everything dripping with sunlight, palm trees swaying in unison, the sky a glorious blue. I was even more nervous than I was on Friday. I'd spent the weekend considering the events of the previous month: I had fallen into a group in which I didn't belong, lied to my parents, neglected a morning of tefillin, drunk myself into oblivion, shattered shomer negiah and, potentially, been slipped some drug. After some deliberation, I emerged from Shabbat resolved to separate myself from these strange events, to regain a state of stasis. I had moved from Brooklyn with a desire to start anew, yes, but not like this.

"No way," Noah said as we walked into school, checking an announcement on the bulletin board.

"What?"

"This is hilarious." He ran his finger over the paper tacked to the board. "Look, this is the list of minyanim. There's the normal minyan, which hosts, like, eighty-five percent of the school, and then there's the Sephardic minyan, for our Mediterranean brethren. And then," he jabbed his finger at my name on the list, "last but not least, there's what we call the explanatory minyan, which is what we're in."

"I don't get it."

"Put it this way: it's easier to separate the good from the rotten. It's supposed to be educational, like remedial prayer, Davening 101."

I nodded. I saw where this was going.

"So the great irony is that this school placed its one Hasidic Brooklyn native in a minyan for apostates."

I didn't find this nearly as amusing. I'd been placed not by chance, I wanted to point out, but because of my association with him and his friends. "I'm not Hasidic."

"Fine. Semi-Hasidic."

I shook my head.

"Whatever the proper term is, then. How *do* you identify?"

I shrugged. "Frum. Jewish. I don't know."

"Anyway, don't look so offended." He bit back a grin. "It's a good thing."

"How is it possibly a good thing?"

"Because it's fun, we're all in it. Well, everyone except for Amir, of course, but that's to be expected."

"I should speak to someone," I said, "about transferring into the regular minyan."

"I wouldn't worry. Once the school realizes what they've done they'll toss you in with the uninfected in no time. They'll love you here, the rabbis."

Affectionately dubbed Minyan X, the minyan, which met in the science laboratory on the second floor, was every bit the travesty I feared. There were fifteen members, including Donny, the behemoth who splintered Oliver's beer-pong table, and the rangy, pug-nosed Argentinean from Niman's party ("Gabriel," he said warmly, shaking my hand). Oliver and Evan hadn't yet arrived; according to Noah, they routinely skipped davening to go for breakfast at some local, patently nonkosher diner. At the front of the room sat the supervising rabbi, playing Tetris absentmindedly on his cellphone.

"Rabbi," Noah called, steering me over, "this is Drew Eden, the new guy."

I shook his hand, restraining my desire to correct my name.

"Rabbi Schwartz," he said kindly, quickly pausing his game. He was short, middle-aged, gaunt.

"He's got like nine or ten kids," Noah whispered as we walked away, "hence the reason the poor guy always looks exhausted."

In Torah Temimah, kindergartners were taught to always daven with respect—or, at the very least, to remain quiet during prayer, lest they experience a rebbe's wrath. (Relics of Europe, our rabbis employed shouting as well as occasional ruler whippings; Rabbi Herenstein, in fourth grade, once flung Mordechai's digital watch, his beloved Chanukah gift, out of the window as a punishment. "Time flies," he had said with an unrepentant shrug.) By high school, we were so serious about davening that, much like the Levites racing up the Temple ramp, we'd jostle to reach the bimah first so as to win the honor of leading prayer. This minyan, on the other hand, would have had Rabbi Herenstein in tears. Electronic music blasted from portable speakers. Loud conversations began at Pesukei Dezimra and amplified steadily until we reached Alenu. Donny dribbled a basketball, others engaged in frantic attempts to finish summer reading, hardly anyone wore both the arm and the head components of his tefillin, settling instead for one. I took a desk in the back and, self-consciously, wrapped my tefillin, feeling heavy glances from around the room, as if I were violating a sacred code. Rabbi Schwartz looked up from his phone and realized I was waiting to begin; he turned beet-red, clearing his throat timidly. "Um, fellows, let's get going now, if you don't mind."

Our service was drastically redacted. Apparently the full version of morning prayers was overly burdensome, and so the school agreed to keep the entire affair to fifteen minutes maximum. Afterward, to fulfill the "explanatory" component of the minyan, Rabbi Schwartz spoke reluctantly about why it was important to pray, though hardly anyone listened. ("Prayer is an expression of gratitude," he said, ignoring the game of Texas Hold'em being held in the back of the room, "one that provides us with an opportunity to commune privately with the Master of the Universe.") When he finished, I asked quietly to switch into the regular minyan.

—

THAT DAY WAS A BLUR. Talmud was a double period with Rabbi Schwartz, who tried his best to pitch us on the wonder of Tractate Berachot. "Blessings," he droned, "are acknowledgments that we accept God as Creator of the Universe. But they also serve a second purpose. How, you ask?" No one asked. He cleared his throat. "By teaching us reflexive gratitude, to enjoy spiritually directed pleasure." In Tanach, Rabbi Feldman opened by discussing the Ramban's willingness to underscore the patriarchs' flaws ("for our key to becoming righteous people," he lectured in his wonderful South African accent, "is to understand that even the best among us are only human and therefore eminently relatable"). Hebrew, taught by Morah Adar, a seventy-year-old Israeli with unnaturally deep-dyed blond hair, was a particularly dull fifty minutes. ("Everyone, say *beit sefer*," she commanded in her thick accent. Oliver, beginning his fourth year of elementary Hebrew, replied with some dirty Hebrew word.)

She noticed my bewilderment. "*Atah chadash?*"

I waited as my brain translated slowly: Are you new? "*Kain.*"

"*Eich haivereit shelach?*"

"Er, *mah?*"

"*Eich—haivereit—shelach?*"

"It means *how's your Hebrew?*" someone behind me snapped. "Jesus!"

Morah Adar sighed, muttering on about American linguistic deficiencies.

After Hebrew came to a merciful close, Oliver dragged me upstairs to a nondescript classroom on the third floor and had me climb out the window to the balcony, where Evan, Noah and Amir were spread out on foldable beach chairs, eating lunch.

I peeked uneasily at the parking lot below, somewhat suspicious that I was being hazed. "We're allowed up here?"

"Yeah, Eden, of course," Evan said. "And they hardly mind when we smoke here, either."

"We'll have to get you a chair, Ari," Noah said. "Gio got these for us."

I took a spot on the floor, against the railing, and began unwrapping my food.

"First we'll have to initiate him," Oliver said through a mouthful of sushi, which he'd arranged to be delivered on his behalf to the front office, apparently despite being warned to stop such practice. "Beware, Eden, the last sucker didn't survive."

I looked at Oliver's sushi and then examined my own modest peanut butter sandwich with some repulsion. "I guess I'll take my chances."

"What's *that*?" Amir leaned suddenly toward Evan, who had removed a worn, leather-bound book from his backpack. "You didn't finish Hartman's summer reading?"

Failing to make eye contact, Evan returned the book to its place and zipped up his bag. "Just some commentary on Nabokov."

"Wait, really? Can I see that before English?"

Noah laughed.

"Relax yourself," Evan said without looking up at Amir. "You'd have no interest in this."

"Oh." Amir slunk back into his chair. "More philosophy?"

"Don't worry about it."

"I don't get how you read that shit," Oliver said, biting open another package of soy sauce. Black liquid squirted out, nearly hitting Amir. "I'd rather hang myself."

"Watch it!" Amir said, inspecting his shirt for stains. "Have respect for other people for once."

Noah took a long pull from a Gatorade. He wiped orange liquid from his lips. "Rabbi Bloom still giving you those books, Ev?"

"Here and there."

"What is it?" I asked.

Evan smiled, holding my gaze. "I don't think it's anything you've ever read."

Following lunch was J-Hip, which, true to Noah's earlier description, was a circus. Mr. Harold—six-six, exceptionally kind, minor wisps of hair still adorning his liver-speckled head—was in his late eighties and rumored to have once been drafted by the Rochester Royals. He'd been teaching variations of the subject for nearly forty years and, as soon became apparent, had absolutely no control over the class. By the Assyrian conquest, all pretense of order dissipated: Noah, the hood of his basketball sweater thrown over his head, was asleep on his desk while his iPhone screened *Breaking Bad* on low volume; Amir, scribbling notes halfheartedly, played tick-tack-toe with Lily; Evan and Remi flirted loudly in the back, where poor Mr. Harold's hearing did not extend. I sat stunned for a good deal of the class, heart breaking, though I found myself distracted by Sophia, who was whispering unhappily to Rebecca and glancing in the direction of Evan and Remi.

Geometry was an hour spent staring blankly at illegible graphs sketched by a thickset, awkward-looking man named Dr. Porter. "So not a single person knows the difference between a ray and an angle?" Apparently he'd once worked for the Department of Energy. Here he was blinking at our sullen silence. "Nobody at all?"

Nicole raised her hand. "Aren't they the same thing?" Her friends giggled.

Oliver, seated directly behind me, kicked at my chair as Nicole spoke. I grimaced, hot around the neck. Nicole and I had scarcely spoken since Oliver's party. I'd expected, at least initially, to address what had happened, yet she was perfectly happy, the one time she saw me, to offer only a curt hello. Confused as to the etiquette of such affairs—could it possibly be standard procedure, I wondered, to engage that intimately, only to pretend nothing ever occurred?—I turned to Noah, who advised that I respect Nicole's distance and follow her lead.

"Er, not in the least, actually," Dr. Porter said, bleary-eyed, giving a frail smile, looking as if he might very well burst into tears. "A ray is a line that begins at an endpoint and extends infinitely in that direction, while an angle is two rays with the same origin . . ."

After math, my head still spinning from vertices and parallel planes, I was approached by a stout, properly dressed boy. "Aaron Davis," he announced, extending his hand. I recognized him as the intensely bumptious kid in my Judaic classes who answered questions with a booming voice and excessive gesticulations. "Wanted to make a point of introducing myself."

"Ari Eden," I said gratefully. Most students were wary of me: either I was with Noah and the others, in which case people maintained careful distance, or I was on my own, in which case I was regarded as an alien.

"We have classes together, I see." He was dressed too sharply—he wore a tie and navy pin-striped pants—and had on ill-fitting, oversized glasses that slid off the bridge of his nose. "How are you enjoying your first day?"

It was great, I told him.

"Excellent. You seem to be adjusting well. From Norwalk, is it?"

"Pardon?"

"Or was it Waterbury? Somewhere in Connecticut, I know."

"I'm from Brooklyn."

"Oh, how quaint."

"Quaint? I wouldn't exactly—"

"Well," he said, straightening his tie. "I must be off to physics. But it was wonderful to meet you, a great privilege. It's like what Hamilton said, I'm sure you know, about the sacred pleasure of new friendship?"

As he strolled off, hands in pockets, whistling a Civil War tune, Oliver materialized from behind a locker. "Intolerable, right?"

"I don't know. I thought he was nice."

"Nice? Davis is a pretentious know-it-all obsessed with historians and Harvard, just like everyone else in his family."

"Oh. Well, when you put it that way."

"I'm sure he was plenty nice, though. Probably wants your vote."

"My vote?"

"For school president. Election season's starting, and Davis is a natural politician."

"I see."

"Evan can't stand him," he said matter-of-factly. "Not to mention that Davis and Amir are, like, eternal rivals."

"Competing for what?"

"Grades, awards, college, maximum dullness, becoming valedictorian. Everything, really."

"What about Evan?"

"He could be if he wanted. But he doesn't."

"Why's that?"

Oliver shrugged. "Evan doesn't care."

Biology featured the most bizarre teacher of the day: Dr. Ursula Flowers. "Yes, yes, an unfortunate name, I'm well aware, take a second to process and kindly move on," she snapped, scribbling her name with venom on the blackboard. She was silver-haired, muscular; a tattoo of what appeared to be a small, poorly rendered microscope was visible just above the collar of her shirt. "I guess that's what you get when your Hawaiian parents are good-for-nothing hippies nurturing unhealthy Disney addictions." On cue, she broke into a coughing fit.

"Are you okay?" someone eventually asked.

"Dandy," she wheezed, doubled over. She rummaged violently in her desk for tissues. "Get used to this, people," she instructed between shallow, frantic breaths. "Word to the wise? Never chain-smoke."

The class was surprisingly small: only seven seniors, the rest of the grade dispersed between AP Physics and AP Environmental Science. How I made it into this class I wasn't certain. At no point in my application to Kol Neshama had I expressed even a mild interest in biology. I decided I was fine with this, however, the moment I discovered Sophia in the front row.

"Ari," she said, arching her brows. "What a pleasant surprise."

I took the seat beside her, a risk that had me temporarily reeling. "Why is it you're always so surprised to find me anywhere?"

She looked me over, arranged her teeth into something resembling an amused, slightly patronizing smile. "Well, I didn't take you for a scientist."

"I'm not," I said, uncertain whether to feel insulted.

"Premed?"

"Nope."

"You're stalking me, is that it?"

"Enough flirting," Dr. Flowers barked, her coughing fit having subsided.

After a horrid hour of being berated about van der Waals interaction and the non-directionality of ionic bonds came English. Mrs. Hartman—tall, thin, severe, dressed in shades of black—walked in just as the bell chimed and, as the room fell swiftly into silence, carved a single word on the chalkboard in the most luxurious handwriting I'd ever seen: *tragedy.* "Why, as human beings, do we write and read and study and, at our most atavistic, *enjoy* representations of suffering?" Her eyes wandered slowly around the room. Amir, after looking about cautiously, offered his hand.

"Mr. Samson?"

"We're sadists."

"We're sadists. How so?"

"Er." He paused to think, surprised his first answer didn't suffice. "I'd say we have a natural desire to see others suffer."

"An intrinsic pleasure in witnessing suffering?"

Amir eyed Davis lurking. "Yes," he said uneasily.

"A fair albeit disconcerting theory. Others?" Silence again. "Is Mr. Samson alone in having a voice?"

"Catharsis," I spoke out, abruptly, just as Davis was winding up. Heads turned in place: the kid from Brooklyn had something to say on the matter of tragic literature.

Mrs. Hartman's eyes narrowed with interest. "Your name?"

"Ari Eden," I said, conscious of the stares I was receiving.

"And by catharsis you mean what, Mr. Eden?"

"That it purges us," I said. "Giving us the chance to release pity and fear."

"When do we feel pity and fear?"

"Daily," I said. "Our lives feel smaller than the lives of the Greeks. Less important, less grand. But still we feel sorrow, at least on a smaller scale."

I was aware of restless shuffling around me, yet didn't dare turn my head. Amir, I could tell from the corner of my eye, wore a gaping look. Sophia, to my delight, turned curiously in her seat, playing with her bracelet. Evan, directly to my right, watched attentively, nodding. He scribbled madly into his notebook before breaking into a self-satisfied smile.

Mrs. Hartman twirled chalk between her fingers. "Then tragedy to you serves a positive or negative social purpose?"

I thought of the solitary hours I'd spent in the Borough Park Library, absorbed in faraway worlds—whispers, daydreams, things golden and sublime—where form had been given to my loneliness. "Positive."

"And why's that?"

"Because it lets us experience what we'll never see ourselves."

Silence. People around me seemed impressed—Noah even shot me a furtive celebratory hand gesture—and I allowed myself to feel momentarily proud. Then Sophia raised her hand.

"Ms. Winter?"

"I disagree."

"With Mr. Eden?"

"Yes."

"Wonderful." A solemn smile came to Mrs. Hartman's lips. "Do elaborate."

"Tragedy doesn't save us." Sophia kept her eyes fixed firmly at the blackboard. "Tragedy doesn't enlarge our imagination or cast us in a nobler light."

"What does it do, then, Ms. Winter?"

"It flattens us. It turns us to dust." She straightened, her gaze returning calmly to Mrs. Hartman. "I thought that was important to note."

Mrs. Hartman nodded curtly. "Ms. Winter and Mr. Eden raise interesting points that allow us to begin our discussion of what makes up the bulk of the tragic and even epic canon we'll be studying this year, beginning with the *Iliad*." She went on to discuss the basic tenets of tragedy, the differences among the Greek, Shakespearean and modern genres. I listened with intense pleasure, enlivened by the thought that Sophia would approach daringly after class, challenging me with that downcast look, granting me her full attention. When the bell rang, however, Sophia hastened from the room.

—

THE REST OF THAT FIRST week flew by uneventfully. Each day I allowed Noah to drive me to school, joined him and the others for lunch on the third-floor balcony, sat near them in classes. I remained unhappily in Minyan X, Rabbi Schwartz shrugging apologetically when I cringed, and endured the sacrilegious rituals of my peers. I did the best I could, claiming the far corner of the room and sitting with my eyes shut, lacing my prayers with the shrill sounds of some DJ named Avicii.

I plunged headfirst into my studies. This was a necessity: to even survive academically, I reasoned, I'd need to become a serious student. I pretended I knew that three angles of a triangle summed to 180 degrees, stared stupidly when Dr. Flowers told us she wouldn't bother explaining covalent bonds, nodded along to Davis' recitation of the events leading to the storming of the Bastille. A sizable mound of homework was already piling on: a problem set for math, translations for Hebrew, a quiz in Tanach, an impending biology test. ("If anyone has any hope of taking the AP come May, we'll need to stay at this pace, and I won't allow anyone to hold us back," Dr. Flowers threatened, focusing her glare on me.) Still, I was enjoying the challenge, especially in English. I'd leave readings for the end of the night, after I retreated to bed, falling asleep to strange geometries of lamplight cast against my walls and images of burning Trojan citadels.

—

"YOU'RE COMING TO TRYOUTS TOMORROW night, right?" Noah asked at lunch, biting into a thick turkey sandwich.

"What tryouts?"

"For the basketball team. We're all on it."

"Are you any good?" Evan was perched on the railing of the balcony, raised above us. "I'd guess you're not."

I'd played basketball for a fair portion of my childhood. In Torah Temimah, I hovered around the top tier of my class, though this necessitated little more than competent dribbling abilities and mediocre hand-eye coordination. Our freshman year team practiced three times in six months and played but one formal game, an exhibition match against a local Chofetz Chaim. Mordechai, our best player, was forced to retire after his parents realized he was leaving mishmar early to shoot hoops. Our team folded shortly thereafter. "I'm decent."

"How decent is decent?" Oliver asked.

I hated when they studied me. I worried that, if they thought about it long enough, the sheer absurdity of my presence would eventually dawn on them. As it was, I overheard whispers in the halls, noticed faculty members gawking at the sight of the poorly dressed, wildly self-conscious Brooklyn expatriate climbing into extravagant cars with the likes of Noah Harris and Evan Stark. Such observations bothered me less, perhaps because on some level I enjoyed the strange phenomenon of having my private life differentiated from the anonymous ones around me. As someone who often neglected to muster appropriate interest in my own life, who failed to visualize what my face looked like and who felt incapable of imagining how it registered to other people, I found such limelight not entirely unpleasant, even during moments when I loathed that my reputation was becoming fixed to their lot.

"You're coming tomorrow," Noah said. "We've got three or four open spots this year. If it turns out you're trash, we'll tell Rocky you're useful entertainment. Good for camaraderie."

"Who?"

"Oh man," Oliver said, sifting through YouTube for highlights of Noah's junior year of basketball, "he's going to hate Rocky."

"Our coach," Noah said. "Few loose bolts, but stellar dude."

"He was a high school phenom," Amir said. "But tore his ACL during his freshman summer at Villanova. He did have a professional stint overseas, though."

Oliver laughed. "Yeah, in Scandinavia."

"You'll be wild about the man," Evan said, grinning nastily. "Especially if you have a taste for a wide sampling of physical torture."

—

THEIR DEPICTION OF ROCKY WAS grossly understated. Bald, under-sized—a self-proclaimed six feet that more closely resembled a Napoleonic five-ten—and heavily tattooed, Rocky was a vortex of energy, anger and ego, constantly moving, barking insults, snatching the ball at times to run the drill himself.

"Rocky, this is Drew Eden, the new kid," Noah said, bringing me over to shake hands.

Rocky grabbed my hand, his face inches from mine. "Got what it takes?"

"Pardon?"

"Do you have what it takes?" He crunched my hand until it began to ache. Noah motioned for me to nod.

"Yes, sir."

"I'm no 'sir.' I'm a fucking beast."

I extracted my hand. "Oh, right."

"If you don't have that same fire, the fuck off my court with you." He thrust a ball into my chest and sent me to the baseline to stand beside Oliver.

"Intense, huh?" Oliver asked.

Everyone around us began intricate stretching routines. I improvised by bending over toward my feet. "You enjoy this?"

Oliver shrugged, readjusted his shorts. "Honestly, I just chill on the bench."

Rocky blew his whistle, lined us up at center court and gestured for Noah to join him.

"He's obsessed with Noah, if you couldn't tell," Oliver whispered. "He's his all-time favorite player. Honestly, everyone's obsessed with Noah. He's Zion Hills's very own Swede. He's like, I don't know, freaking Thor."

"This is Noah Harris." Rocky paced back and forth, as if preparing soldiers for a military operation. "If you don't know Noah Harris, raise your hand."

No hands went up.

"Thought so." He flexed his arms. On his left bicep, I made out the silhouette of a rhinoceros and the Jordan Jumpman logo. "Who wants to tell me why we all know Noah Harris?"

Donny, from the opposite site of the baseline, raised his hand. "He's our captain."

"No, Donny, that's not fucking why. It's because he's the best player in this school, and when you're the best player in your school, you command respect. Why do I know this? Because I was the best damned player in my school, too." Noah turned pink. It was the first time I'd seen him look uneasy. "It's called working on your craft," Rocky continued, "mastering it until you earn respect not from everyone around you, not from your entire community"—the veins in his forehead throbbed—"but from yourself." He dropped his voice to a hoarse whisper. "That's what this game is, boys. That's the point of this goddamn life. Got that?" We nodded obediently, pretending this was even vaguely meaningful. "Good. Now, Evan Stark, Amir Samson, Gabriel Houri and, uh, fuck it, Donny Silver, step forward and face your teammates. This is our starting five. That means there are seven open spots. Nobody else is guaranteed anything, even if you were on the team last year, even if you consider yourself God's gift to this sacred sport. Even if your father is a major donor to this school, Bellow excluded. Understood?"

He divided us into groups, pushed us through drills: suicides, wind sprints, cone dribbling, layups in which we tried finishing at the rim as he attacked us with a large foam cushion.

"God damn you straight to the bowels of hell, Silver!" he screamed when Donny bricked his shot and tumbled to the floor. "If you don't have heart, there's no place for you here!"

I played poorly. I knocked down some jumpers—a random stretch of good luck, seeing how rattled Rocky made me—but I was slow and out of shape and managed to botch a fair number of the exercises, running the wrong route in one play and, in another, losing control of the ball and accidentally kicking it out of bounds.

"What the fuck is that?" Rocky roared, sending me off to run ten laps for "lacking purpose with the ball, on the court and, as far as I can tell, in life."

For the final twenty minutes we scrimmaged. This was my worst showing, considering how long it took me to lumber up the court—gasping, chest burning, mouth completely dry—and the fact that my random assortment of teammates was reluctant to pass my way. The part I enjoyed most was being taken out, as it gave me a moment to catch my breath.

At the end of practice, Rocky assigned the starters to play together. Donny, at center, was a train wreck, using his weight to ram us in the post but consistently bungling layups, much to Rocky's disgust. Evan was a stretch forward, a fantastic defender with an abundance of confidence who attacked relentlessly and made the right play over and over. Gabriel was small forward—a filler player, mostly, with little talent other than rebounding and running sets efficiently—while Amir played shooting guard, providing high-volume three-point shooting.

Then, at point, there was Noah, somehow exceeding all hype. He utilized speed and sheer strength, shooting from any distance and dribbling under his legs, behind his back and through defenders at a marvelous speed. He threw breathtaking full-court passes, dished through preposterous angles and pulled up on fast breaks, spinning in every direction to find himself uncontested under the rim. He was, without question, the best player I'd ever seen, but I was even more impressed by his demeanor. He was demonstrative and barked instructions, but never derisively, making certain to avoid dominating the ball and to comfort poor Donny after he was castigated by Rocky.

"Noah," I said in the car after practice ended, too sore to move but in awe of what I'd witnessed, "that was the most unbelievable—"

"Ari," he snapped, cutting me off. "I don't want that crap from you of all people."

Strangely gratified, I nodded and fell silent.

—

AFTER TALMUD THE NEXT DAY—a dull class in which we discussed *bein hashemashos*, that delicate blink of an eye when night enters and day departs—I heard my name on the intercom.

"Why would they call me?" I blurted stupidly, gravel-voiced, looking to Amir for help. "Is that bad?"

Amir gathered his things impatiently. "Relax. If you were in real trouble Bloom would probably call himself."

I made my way to the front office. The secretary, Mrs. Janice, a kindly, forty-something-year-old with a Southern accent and horn-rimmed glasses, directed me to a back office. I was to meet Mrs. Ballinger, Mrs. Janice told me, director of College Guidance. Confused, I walked up to the office and knocked.

"Enter."

It was a gaudy office: shelves lined with SAT aids and application guides (*Dream Schools, Part Two*; *How to Write the Perfect Essay and Avoid Shaming Your Family*), a bulletin board of banners (crimson, cardinal red, baby blue), every inch of every wall adorned with photographs of Mrs. Ballinger and bright-faced students, acceptance letters in hand. Behind a sparse desk, on which a single folder of documents was spread, sat Mrs. Ballinger: platinum blond, diminutive, middle-aged, sour-faced. She looked as if she'd been plucked from an Upper East Side prep school. I recognized her from the pictures on the Ivy bulletin board.

"Name?" she asked disinterestedly.

"Ari Eden."

"Take a seat." She motioned to a wooden chair, on which ROSS BALLINGER, HARVARD LAW, CLASS OF 2003 was emblazoned. "My eldest," she said.

"Oh," I said, blinking stupidly, attempting to rouse appropriate appreciation for this unsolicited fact. "Nice."

She pointed to a picture on the corner of her desk, in which she was being hugged by two girls and a boy. "Ross, Ashley, Zoe." I nodded with feigned interest. "Harvard, Chicago, Virginia," she rattled off. "Not too shabby, huh?"

"Right," I said, still struggling to understand why I'd been summoned. "Very cool."

"Before we start, your name is . . . Ari, you said? Or Andrew? I have conflicting information."

I frowned. "Ari."

She made a note. "Know why you're here, Ari?"

"No," I admitted, knitting my brows in discomfort upon realizing she was reviewing my Torah Temimah transcript. "Not particularly."

"That's perfectly fine. My name is Mrs. Ballinger. I get you into college." She smiled with pity. "Now, did you receive any sort of college guidance in your previous school?"

A small terror gripped me. I shook my head.

"I didn't think so, judging by its . . . methodology, let's call it."

"Is that bad?" Perhaps there'd been some grave error on the part of Torah Temimah that invalidated my entire educational history. I began wondering whether, technically speaking, the school was, in fact, even accredited?

"Everything's fine," she said. "Just seems they weren't exactly gung ho on college, were they?"

"Not really."

"As a point of reference, what percentage of the graduating class attends college, would you say?"

"Er," I stuttered, "a small one."

She glanced at her nails. "What kind of school is that?"

"An exceedingly religious one."

"Hm." She examined my transcripts once more. "The first question I should ask is if you're even interested in attending college. I'll tell you now that approximately ninety-nine percent of our graduates attend college. It'd be a clean one hundred percent if not for an unfortunate incident, which I won't get into now."

The truth was I knew virtually nothing about college. I'd heard, of course, of places like Harvard, I had some general familiarity with some of the New York schools and knew that my mother had, briefly, attended Barnard. Still, college was always a distant world, and for most of my friends it was a taboo topic, something reserved for those indifferent to serious Torah study. I suppose I fostered some general expectation that, eventually, I'd wind up at a local university, considering that both my parents had earned degrees, but this was something my family never discussed. "Of course," I said flatly, unwilling to reveal too much about the life from which I came.

"I hoped as much. And your parents?"

"What about them?"

"They're on board?"

"I believe so."

"So you've discussed it with them?"

"No," I admitted, "not exactly."

She frowned. "We'll have to sit down with them. Not to worry," she added, seeing my concern, "it's standard. I've already had preliminary meetings last year with our more ambitious students." I pictured Amir and Davis, flanked by scowl-faced parents, jostling to be first into her office. "The important thing at present is to get you thinking about which colleges you'd be interested in and which ones you'd have a shot getting into. Fair enough?"

"Fair enough."

"I should tell you, Ari, that I play hardball. I worked for twelve years in the admission offices of Duke and Brown. I have a fairly strong sense of the terrain, I avoid circuitous talk and I treat you like an adult. If you're not getting in somewhere, let's not waste our time."

I nodded, steeling myself for a bleak view of my future.

"To be frank, I don't think the reputation, or lack thereof, of your former school will do us any favors. I don't want to say your old classes and grades are . . . meaningless, per se"—she paused, tactfully—"but I assume they stand in stark contrast to the classes you're taking here. Would you say this much is true?"

"I'd say that's already been proven true."

She smiled pleasantly. "And how *has* the transition been?"

"Pretty good, thanks. I'm working hard."

"That's what we ask of our students."

"I'm taking honors classes," I pointed out.

"Which is laudable, plus great for your transcript. Upward movement: that's what I preach. Moving up is markedly better than moving down. Keep at it and let me know if you need help, will you? I want you to succeed here, so if some classes prove a bit of a stretch, we can always figure out . . . other accommodations. Sound good?"

I returned her half-patronizing smile. "Okay."

"Manage expectations, Ari. That's the goal. For all I knew, you could've marched in here and insisted on, oh, I don't know, Dartmouth!" She laughed, expecting me to join in, but stopped abruptly when I didn't. "No matter. So, we'll meet with your parents and start drawing up schools within your range. Good?"

"Yeah," I said. "Good."

"One last thing: the SAT. Have you begun studying?"

A dull ache came on in my temple. I was desperate, all at once, to be away from her collection of banners, from those glazed smiles on her walls. "I have not."

"Didn't think so. What about the PSAT? Have you taken that?"

"I—what is that?"

She sighed, glanced at her iPhone. "You'll need to start immediately on the SAT prep, dear, seeing as you should take the November test. In fact, here, take this name, it's a local tutor I regularly send students to. He's pretty affordable." She scribbled a name and number on a card, smiled sweetly while I looked it over and dismissed me from her office.

—

CONSIDERING MY MOOD, NOTHING SOUNDED less appealing than enduring an uncomfortable lunch on the balcony. I grabbed my brown bag from my locker and made my way to the cafeteria, resolved to find an abandoned corner and eat in silence.

The cafeteria, however, hardly made for a peaceful backdrop. An unruly line for hot lunch formed in front of Gio, the custodian, a short, well-built man beloved by the student body for the jaw-dropping jokes he delivered in a mix of Italian and Estonian. Rabbi Feldman chased down a freshman who had attempted to skateboard over a lunch table. Flirtatious junior boys flung yogurt at sophomore girls. I picked a mostly empty table in the far left corner, slumped down and unwrapped a particularly depressing tuna sandwich.

"New kid?" I looked up and saw a girl across the table, a few feet to my right. She had red-brown, bushy hair and reflective fawn eyes. Her face hovered inches from a physics textbook.

I wiped my mouth. "Pardon?"

"Sorry if that was rude," she said. "You are the new kid, though, aren't you?"

I blinked, nodded.

"Haven't seen you here before."

"In school?"

"In this cafeteria."

"Oh," I said. "Yeah, this is my first time eating here."

"Really? Where do you normally eat?"

I put down my sandwich. "You know, wherever," I said, deciding it was probably best not to mention the balcony.

She returned to her textbook with a smirk. "You eat on the third floor. Everyone knows that."

"Everyone?"

"Wouldn't you say?"

"You didn't even know who I was."

"Sure I did. I just didn't know if you were going by your Hebrew name or not." She picked up her mechanical pencil, bit the eraser. "Oh, come on," she said, rolling her eyes at the look on my face, "it's somewhat difficult not to notice when the sacred tribe of Stark adopts someone lifted from a Chaim Potok novel."

I attempted to conjure something trenchant. Nothing came to mind. Instead, I gaped.

"Kayla Gross." She put up her hand in an ironic half-wave. "So it's Ari or Andrew?"

"Aryeh, actually."

She laughed a harsh, deep-throated laugh that made her flushed face wrinkle. "So where are they?"

"Who?"

"Your guardians."

"Funny."

"They do look after you, don't they?"

I picked at the crust of my white bread, flinging pieces on the table. "Is that what everyone thinks?"

"How am I supposed to know?" She twirled her pencil between her fingers. "I hardly talk to anyone in this school."

"Why, what year are you?"

"I'm in classes with you, for God's sake."

"Sorry. The last few days have been a whirlwind—"

"Don't sweat it. You're not supposed to notice anyone outside your direct orbit, anyway. Isn't that how it works here?"

"I'm not really sure what you're driving at," I said, "but I'm not some puppet."

"May I ask the million-dollar question?"

"Go ahead."

"How'd it happen?"

"How'd what happen?"

"How'd you end up with them?"

"I don't follow."

"Seems like you do."

"They're my friends," I said, disappointed that I felt defensive over my inclusion in my new group.

"Of course."

"You don't believe me?"

"Why wouldn't I? Plus, it's not like I'm assigning any great weight to this, so you know."

"Weight to what?"

"A lot of people, you'll probably soon notice, will extend certain . . . attention, let's say, your way now."

"Right, any friends I make couldn't genuinely be interested in me. Who could possibly think that?"

"Yikes, didn't mean to hit a nerve there," she said. "I'm just saying that I'm personally not overly impressed with them. How you feel is your decision. But being your own person is acceptable, too."

I ignored her, picked irritably at my tuna. I considered leaving but didn't know where else to go. She, in turn, continued to sketch equations into the margins of her textbook.

When the bell sounded, she snapped her textbook theatrically and turned to leave. "Nice meeting you."

"Likewise," I said, hardly picking my head up.

"Sorry if I insulted you."

"It's all right."

"For the record, I liked your answer better."

I crumpled the Publix bag that held my lunch. "What're you talking about?"

"Sophia's was far too morbid for me."

I frowned, trying to remember.

"Hartman's class, on the first day. I sit four rows behind you," she said, gathering her things. "It was a relatively coherent theory for a boy with two names." She left, her bright-yellow backpack bouncing up and down.

—

ON WEDNESDAY, OUR CLASS WAS invited to "sunrise minyan," an annual tradition during which seniors bonded by enjoying an uplifting beachside davening service, followed by a catered breakfast. We arrived at six, dizzy with exhaustion, a thin mist in the air. Small spokes of light were just breaking through the dim-lit sky.

Davening, surprisingly, was pleasant. I'm not certain if this had more to do with the setting—the sky drifting from shades of dark gray to soft blue, light waves rolling against the shore, everything empty and remote—or with the fact that we were half-asleep. Rabbi Feldman spoke briefly before we began: about sensing divinity within nature, about the beauty of greeting God at the earliest possible time, about what you feel in your gut when standing at the ocean and pondering your place in the world. I spent davening on my own, lost in thought, unworried about being judged for expressing too much kavanah, something I had to consider each morning in Minyan X. It was the first time I'd experienced a fulfilling prayer service since moving to Florida.

Afterward, Gio drove up in a van ("Bellow, you stoned motherfucker," he said to Oliver when they were alone, "share the trees, I delivered damn balcony chairs, didn't I?") to provide bagels and waffles and glorious spreads of cream cheese and lox and rugelach and other unspecified gelatinous goods. Lighthearted touch football broke out. Rabbi Feldman quarterbacked a team of rabbis, including the diminutive Rabbi Schwartz, who on one play lost his footing and tumbled headfirst into the water, against Noah, Evan and Amir.

"Know something, Ari?" Rebecca and I sat off to the side on a soft patch of sand. We munched on waffles as we spoke. "These are those rare moments."

"What do you mean?"

"What they'll be telling us nonstop for the next nine months—

what they've already started telling us. About how this is probably the prime of our life, the year we'll look back on with a smile and with the wish that we enjoyed it a little more consciously."

I tore my waffle in half. "I'm fairly sure no one's saying that to me."

She laughed. "Oh, they will. And you'll shrug them off, just like I do, but they're right. Look around. We have our friends, our teachers, around us all the time, our family and siblings. No jobs, no real responsibilities. We'll never have this again, will we?"

"You sound really happy. It's nice, actually, to hear someone sound like that."

She touched my arm. "Don't make it sound so exotic, Ari. You'll start resembling that schmendrick." She pointed to Evan, who had just made a diving touchdown catch on a long ball from Noah and was now spiking the football and trash-talking Rabbi Feldman. "Look at him. He's been through a lot, of course, but he can be happy sometimes, can't he?"

After the game drew to a close, with Rabbi Feldman botching a reverse lateral Hail Mary, we were instructed to head to school for third period. Noah, Rebecca and I hung back for a few minutes, helping Gio and the rabbis clean the mess. When we joined everyone in the parking lot, Evan was standing in front of the exit, blocking traffic. Donny and several others encircled him. Cars lined up, honking, but Evan refused to move. He had Donny's car keys in his hands.

"Ev, c'mon," Donny said, making halfhearted efforts to swipe away his car keys. "I have to get going."

Evan grabbed Donny by his enormous shoulders. "Both your parents work, don't they?"

Donny gave a faint nod, his eyes darting from face to face, seeking help. No one intervened.

"So if my math proves reliable," Evan pressed, "your house is currently sitting there empty, begging to make itself useful?"

I felt an upsurge of sympathy for our friendly giant, reduced to stuttering by Evan's one question. Part of me hoped Noah would intercede, but he remained silent. "Maybe, uh, maybe we can hit your house instead, Ev?"

Seeing Evan's face darken, Donny immediately mumbled a hasty apology. Evan, in turn, returned the keys and, on his tiptoes, ruffled Donny's buzzed scalp before walking over to the Audi and taking what had been my spot in the passenger seat. When Noah, Rebecca and I walked over, Evan called out my name. "Eden?"

I blinked, uncertain why I was being singled out. "What?"

"I assume you're scampering back with Amir?"

I did, in fact, want to return peacefully to school, where I could slump into Tanach and listen drowsily as Rabbi Feldman lectured. It was a nice event, I wanted to tell him—why repay thoughtfulness by spitting in the administration's face? Despising myself, however, I shook my head.

"Really?" Evan said. "I'm shocked."

I watched as several cars pulled out of the lot. Sophia, I noticed, drove by herself. I could run over, ask to accompany her to school. Instead, I turned back to Evan. "Why's that?"

Evan looked at me with cold eyes, confident he was about to elicit the response he wanted from me. "You don't strike me as someone who participates in anything bold."

I climbed into the back seat, cursing myself. Evan, wearing that thin smirk, slammed his door.

—

BY THE TIME WE ARRIVED at Donny's there were some twenty people in the backyard, drinking and listening to the Minyan X playlist, which I'd grown to abhor. Oliver, having raided the kitchen, served screwdrivers from a rusty chaise lounge. "M'lady. Gentlemen. Eden. Can I interest anyone in a drink?"

Rebecca, Noah and Evan each agreed. I waved him off.

"Can we please try not finishing the juice," Donny protested, as if this were his biggest concern. He hovered over Oliver, giant sweat stains ringing the armpits of his gray varsity basketball T-shirt. Their height differential, in that moment, was inversely proportional to their power differential. "My siblings guzzle that stuff. My mom will be pissed."

"The bad news is that your momma will definitely be pissed," Oliver said. "The good news is it won't be because of the OJ."

Donny itched nervously at the spot of his head covered by his yarmulke. "Dude, it's, you know, expensive."

"Really? How much? Actually, sorry, know what? Have yourself a Leon Bellow cocktail, named for my semi-alcoholic father"—Oliver poured two extra shots into a cup and forced it into Donny's colossal hands—"and allow me to reimburse your family for their generosity." He rummaged in his wallet for four twenties, rolled them into a wad and crammed them down Donny's shirt. "Think that's adequate?"

Commotion overhead. Evan, shirtless, was scaling a ladder positioned against the exterior patio wall. He hoisted himself onto the roof until he stood over us, accepting drunken cheers. Slowly, he raised his hand for silence.

"Friends." He kicked off his Nike Roshes, which landed near Oliver's head. "Welcome to the final year." He ripped off his socks, unzipped his jeans and tossed them over the edge, watching his clothing drift below. Remi caught his pants, to further applause. Evan stood now only in Calvin Klein boxers. "Soon enough," he said, pacing the roof, "we'll gain independence. How thrilling. We've dreamed of it long enough, haven't we? We've imagined it since childhood, being old enough to no longer rely on parents and teachers and rabbis, to no longer accept living by rules devised by other people." I shielded my eyes from the sun as I stared up at Evan. Certain movements allowed his body to be swallowed by light, making it difficult to discern anything more than his silhouette. "But now that it's here, what will we do with it? Will we live, after all, like everyone else? Will we opt into precise replicas of our parents' lives? Will we perpetuate what's broken? Gossip, hypocrisy, greed, overpriced food, competition over cars and houses and tzedakah—everything we've been born into"—he paused again over the edge, arching his toes, peering down fearlessly—"can end."

"Jesus," Noah said beside me, "this guy knows how to ruin a good time."

"Blame Bloom," Oliver said indifferently, mixing another drink. "All that philosophy shit."

"Such freedom," Evan continued, now standing directly at the edge of the roof, "if we have enough courage, should be used to break boundaries." With that, he removed his underwear and threw himself from the roof, cannonballing into the pool.

Silence. When he surfaced, he treaded toward Remi, who had her feet dipped into the pool. He whispered something in her ear, causing her to refocus her gaze beneath the water. In an elegant motion, she rose and, basking in openmouthed stares, stripped off her clothing and dove into the pool.

A static charge persisted a moment longer, as the image of Remi White undressing replayed in everyone's minds. Then, on cue, a frantic dash for the ladder and for the water, clothing flying in all directions, lean bodies animated by transgression: Noah and Rebecca, hand in hand; Nicole, skirt around her ankles; Oliver, boxers over his head. He kicked over a Grey Goose bottle as he sprinted.

Bodies fell from roof to water, vodka bled near my feet. I stood motionless, unable to tear away my eyes as Nicole resurfaced, lowering my gaze at the sight of Rebecca. Snapping harshly to my senses, I slipped through the sliding glass door and fumbled through the house—wet footprints, spilled drinks, overturned chairs—to the driveway. Tanach had just started, I thought, attempting to erase what I'd seen, and if I could figure out transportation I'd get to class without being too late. For a crazed moment I entertained dialing my mother, only to imagine her greeted by Evan and Remi, gloriously nude. Battling the erotic panic building in my chest, I called an Uber.

The five-minute wait was agony. I resisted my growing urge to return poolside, kept looking over my shoulder to make certain no-body had realized I'd vanished; they hadn't, of course, which was worse. Finally, my Uber arrived: an older man with a grisly beard and Vietnam hat, reeking of rancid aftershave. I guided him to the Kol Neshama parking lot, in which he swerved frantically to avoid flatten-ing the security guard. I slammed the door, cutting off an unsolicited soliloquy, and hastened inside. As I signed in at the front desk, Mrs. Janice lowered her horn-rimmed glasses and unleashed a reproving look. Head bowed, I walked into Tanach thirty minutes late, sinking into the seat nearest the door.

Rabbi Feldman was making a point about Rashi as I walked in and so didn't address my lateness, though he did pause to glance my way. When I finally had enough courage to look up from the floor I saw how laughably empty the class was, about two-thirds unfilled. Amir was trying to catch my eye from the other side of the room, but I returned my gaze to my shoes, unwilling to draw attention. I sat through the remainder of the period like this, knots in my stom-ach, images of Nicole and Remi dancing through my head. When the bell finally rang, I sprang from my seat and disappeared into the crowded hallway.

—

THERE WAS A SLOW TRICKLE into school as the day wore on. Noah and Rebecca showed at the end of lunch. Lily snuck into the back of J-Hip. Remi stumbled in during math, smelling strongly of rum. By the end of the day, Evan, Oliver and Donny were the only ones absent.

I arrived early for biology, hoping to catch Sophia. "Look who showed," she said, taking the seat beside me, "Aquaman himself. Bring your Speedo to class?"

"You heard what happened?"

"More or less," she said. "I'm told it got slightly—risqué."

I blushed. "It was revealing."

"So who?"

"What?"

"Who'd you see?"

"Definitely more of Oliver than I'll be able to live with."

"And who else?"

I made a show of retrieving my textbook from my bag. "Oh, everyone, kind of."

"Was Rem—"

"Yeah, but I mean, *I* looked away."

Sophia's facial expressions remained unchanged. "You didn't enjoy the show?"

"I left right away."

"Don't tell me you deprived the senior class from seeing '*Hamlet's transformation—so call it.*'"

My face reddened further. "You'll be disappointed to know nobody saw '*my secret parts of fortune.*'"

She flipped through her textbook to our current chapter. Each page featured detailed handwritten annotations, accompanied by highlighted text. Her very handwriting seemed to conjure something bright inside my chest. "To be honest, I don't understand why you went in the first place."

"Neither do I."

"You could've driven with me, you know. I'm excellent car company."

"I wish I did."

"But you listened to him, didn't you?"

"To whom?"

Dr. Flowers burst into the room, slammed the door and launched into an unnecessarily hateful diatribe about triglycerides and fatty acids. Instead of pretending to pay attention, I allowed myself to become irrationally depressed from Sophia's last remark and to agonize over the prospect of disciplinary action. ("I do hope that anyone involved in today's controversy," Mrs. Hartman had said in her class, "prepares for a wrath worse than what '*brought countless ills upon the Achaeans.'*") With only twenty minutes left in the period, head aching from Dr. Flowers' voice, I heard Mrs. Janice's Southern drawl over the classroom telecom. *Aryeh Eden.*

Avoiding eye contact with Sophia, whose disapproval, I knew even without visual confirmation, was boring a hole through the side of my face, I rose and made my way to the office.

"Not for me," Mrs. Janice said, motioning across the hall. "This time it's the big guy."

Light-headed with anxiety, I walked toward Rabbi Bloom's office. Through the glass window I could see him waiting. I knocked.

"Come in, Mr. Eden."

I let myself in, stood meekly at his doorway.

"Please, sit." He motioned toward the conference desk in the center of his office. "Can I get you coffee, tea, water?"

"Oh. Uh, just water, please," I said, only to immediately wonder whether I was supposed to have politely declined.

He brought me a bottle from a small refrigerator hidden beneath his desk and took a seat opposite me, swiveling in his chair. "Do you like it here, Mr. Eden?"

I felt unexpectedly tense, bearing the weight of his undivided attention for the first time. "I do."

"Better than your old school in some ways, I'd imagine?"

"Yes."

"Surely it's not easy being new, though. There are—pressures here."

I nodded unsurely.

"I must say, you look fairly concerned to be sitting here."

"Somewhat, sir."

"My apologies, in that case. Truly, there's nothing to be alarmed about. I've been meaning to introduce myself, actually. I've heard some interesting things about you. Mrs. Hartman, for instance, speaks unusually highly of you."

"She does?"

"Your literary acumen, particularly in light of your background, is impressive. But I can't say I'm surprised. Your application essay was

remarkable. Perhaps the best piece of writing I've read from someone your age."

"Wow, I—thanks," I said. "Frankly, I'm kind of surprised you remember it."

He smiled and returned to his desk, rifling through a drawer for a
folder. When he found the folder, he opened it and passed me a page.
The final paragraph was highlighted.

The Sages utilize a unique calculus to determine how we orient
ourselves while praying. People in the east turn west, people
in the west turn east. People in the north turn south, people
in the south turn north. The blind, incapable of discerning
directions, focus their hearts toward God. Exiles visualize
Eretz Yisroel, Israelites Jerusalem, Jerusalemites the Temple,
kohenim the Holy of Holies. The Gemara thus institutional-
izes what we learn from Plato: the sting of longing cannot be
satisfied. "You think it's no use even dreaming of happiness,"
Tuzenbach asks, "but what if I *am* happy?" The Gemara's answer is emphatic: dreaming of happiness *is* all-important, even
if you are not happy. Happiness shall elude you, and yet you
shall pursue it. We never reach permanent happiness, but we
move steadily after its shadow, both physically and spiritually.
We creep closer and closer toward God, each time halving the
distance, but what we stand before is only an approximation.
We move to new places, we visualize new achievements, but
the yearning remains, because a life devoid of longing is not,
in the eyes of the Talmud, a life fit for a human.

Painfully self-conscious, I handed back the page.

"I'm not sure you realize this, but as a matter of policy we do not
typically accept transfer students beyond sophomore year. Our curriculum requires a period of trial and error, and so the arrival of
new students, after a certain point, causes disruptions and generally
makes for failure. As far as I'm aware, in fact, we haven't accepted

a single other senior transfer in at least a decade and a half. Did you know that, Mr. Eden?"

"Not entirely."

"Do you wonder why someone from a school called Torah Temimah proved to be the exception?"

I allowed my head to undergo a noncommittal rotation, neither nodding nor shaking.

He closed the folder and rejoined me at the conference table. "That essay reveals a sophistication of thought and a willingness to grapple with perplexing questions that extend far beyond your years. It made you too intriguing to pass up. And so far, I'd venture to say my impression of you was absolutely right." He crossed his legs. "I've been doing this a long time, Mr. Eden. Longer, frankly, than I care to admit. But, sitting in my office, facing the hallway, seeing you with Mr. Stark and Mr. Harris and Mr. Samson and even Mr. Bellow?" He leaned forward, placed both palms on the table. "I'd be lying if I didn't admit I'm fascinated."

Strange silence. I realized he had finished and now expected some response on my end. "I—I don't really know what you mean."

"I mean only that you possess what I believe to be extraordinary untapped potential."

"I imagine others might disagree." I thought, in particular, of Dr. Flowers and Dr. Porter. "But thank you."

"Most people are shockingly nearsighted, Mr. Eden. You learn that quickly in adulthood."

I glanced at a diploma hung in the far corner, nearly forgotten.

PRINCETON UNIVERSITY
hereby confers upon LAURENCE ISAAC BLOOM
the degree of DOCTOR OF PHILOSOPHY
together with all the rights, privileges and honors
appertaining thereto in consideration of the satisfactory
completion of the course prescribed in
THE DEPARTMENT OF POLITICAL SCIENCE.

Under the diploma was a framed poster:

> My guide and I went into that hidden tunnel;
> And following its path, we took no care
> To rest, but climbed: he first, then I—so far,
> Through a round aperture I saw appear
> Some of the beautiful things that Heaven bears,
> Where we came forth, and once more saw the stars.

"Students never fail to express shock when seeing that," he said, registering my surprise. "Teenagers fancy themselves smarter than the decrepit man behind the glass window."

"Sorry," I said hurriedly, "I didn't mean to be rude. It's just, where I'm from, my rabbis didn't often have—well, doctorates."

Rabbi Bloom smiled. "Perhaps you're not the only anomaly."

"Did you teach? In a college, I mean?"

"Once upon a time."

"Wow. In what field?"

"Political theory, mostly. I was an assistant professor for a number of years. And then, of course, I left the academy to build my own."

"Why'd you leave?"

"It was unsatisfying. Intellectually, I loved academia—I still do— but on an emotional level it felt divorced from something larger. I wanted Torah Umadda, the beauty of Western thought supplemented by a more spiritual sensitivity to the human condition. So, naturally, I went for the rabbinate, started this school and here I am all these years later—aging, withering, beating along to that same belief."

I pretended to sip at my water. "Do you miss it?"

"Certainly. And at times it's difficult not to imagine what life would've looked like had I remained on my original trajectory. My friends from my doctoral cohort have, largely without exception, gone on to achieve outstanding careers. Meanwhile, being princi-pal of a yeshiva high school, I'm sure you've noticed, can be a thank-less position. But it helps to be reminded why this is important, why Orthodox Judaism enriches lives, why rabbis can catalyze a lifelong impact in a way a professor cannot. And, to make the deal a bit sweeter, now and again you encounter exceptional thinkers who stand out, who make the whole thing worthwhile."

He stood, moved to his glass bookcase. "I've accumulated, along my journey, a wonderful assortment of books that collect dust, unappreciated as they are by most students. Unfortunately, until now, there's really been only one student who gave a damn about such things. I suspect, however, you might be the second."

Leibniz, Spenser, Locke, Chaucer, Hobbes, Rousseau. I blinked in awe, thinking of my own sparse collection.

"Do you happen to know that student, Mr. Eden?"

I picked at my fingernails. "It's Evan."

"We're quite fortunate to have an astonishing number of impressive minds here at the Academy. Top standardized scores, elite college acceptances, wonderful future graduate school and employment outcomes, all of which we track meticulously. But it's very easy for students, in the moment, to get caught up purely in their studies and their extracurricular commitments and their applications. It's rare to see someone take an active interest in the broader scope of things during their high school years. My point, really, is that I think you might be interested in finding intellectual companionship in Mr. Stark. In fact, you two might very well discover considerable overlap in your interests."

"Yeah, I, well—I don't think Evan would be too intrigued or flattered by that proposal."

Rabbi Bloom gave a soft smile. "Probably not, at least to start. But my unsolicited advice would be to avoid taking his detachment, let's call it, too seriously. He has a way of opening up eventually, once he's comfortable."

I thought of Evan flinging his naked body from a rooftop. "That hasn't been my impression."

"The year is yet young. You'd be surprised how things change. And I'd know, to speak candidly—Mr. Stark isn't particularly delighted with me at the moment, and from what I hear about today's events I don't think I'm especially pleased with him, either. But I also know this is temporary."

I didn't say anything. Rabbi Bloom moved through his bookcase. After a moment of consideration he handed me a book with a faded red cover and a worn spine. "Have you studied much of Yeats?"

"Uh, no, actually."

"Then you have homework. Drop by when you're finished. I want to hear what you think."

I left, confused, Yeats in hand.

—

BACKLASH OVER SUNRISE MINYAN CAME the next day. Almost everyone received a cut—which, as I learned, lost you half a grade point on the semester—for missing a full period, while Donny, Evan and Oliver also received half-day suspensions for failing to show at all. Somehow, I avoided any punishment, which may have actually been worse, as it fueled unpleasant rumors.

"What do you mean you didn't get a cut?" Evan asked, sitting on his usual spot on the balcony.

Oliver looked up from rolling his joint. "How's that possible?"

I was relegated to the floor. I still didn't have a chair. "I showed up for Tanach."

"True," Oliver said, "which, may I remind you, was mighty shitty."

"What do you care?" Noah unwrapped a high-powered protein bar. His mother had been making a big deal lately about him bulking up before basketball season. Personally, I didn't see how much more muscle mass he could gain, but I was also not someone from whom people sought bodybuilding guidance. "We should be happy he got lucky. I wish I got lucky."

Evan ignored this advice and turned back in my direction. "So I heard you talked to Bloom."

I frowned, uncrossing my legs. "You did?"

"What were you doing in his office?"

"He called me in."

"Why would he do that?"

"Just to talk," I said nervously. Amir looked up from his physics textbook to glance uneasily at Evan.

"About?"

I considered, for a moment, sharing Bloom's suggestion with Evan. I imagined we could have a laugh, lighten the mood. "Not much, really."

"How nice," Evan said, smiling coldly. "Did you talk politics? Social theory? Did he make you feel *special*?"

"Evan," Amir said. "Chill."

"Why is this a big deal?" I said. "He was just introducing himself to me."

"I'd be careful, if I were you." Evan accepted the joint from Oliver. "The man can be a bit of a liar."

"Jeez, Ev," Noah said, now working his way through a second bar. "What's with the new anti-Bloom aggression? Usually you guys are freaking inseparable."

"It's strange," Evan said, "that's all."

I leaned defensively against the wall. "What's strange?"

"Well, Eden," Evan said, "you're the only one to speak with Bloom, and coincidentally the only one who didn't get a cut."

"I really don't know what you're talking about. I didn't say a thing." This was true: I hadn't commented on Bloom's references to whatever was happening between Evan and him, nor had I even mentioned Donny's party. Unless agreeing to read Yeats constituted treason, I hadn't done anything remotely improper.

The bell rang, signaling the end of lunch. "That remains to be seen." Evan stamped his joint and climbed back through the third-floor window.

—

SUNDAY WAS MY FIRST SESSION with the SAT tutor. His office was on Lincoln Road, sandwiched between a run-down bar—grime-streaked windows, dozens of TVs broadcasting the Dolphins game, motorcyclists sitting aimlessly—and a trendy, well-lit breakfast place. I arrived early and considered loitering in the restaurant, taking in the white decorations and bustling crowd and frenzied waiters. Instead I walked several laps, reconstructing Yeats poems in my head.

I buzzed into the office and then knocked politely on a tarnished door that had the name A. BEARMAN plastered in faded paint.

"A moment, please," a gravelly voice called back.

I sat on the lone chair in the hallway, which apparently operated as a makeshift waiting room. After a few minutes, the door opened slightly, revealing a disembodied head. "Might you be—Ari Eden?" Bearman had a ragged beard, an impatient voice and enormous glasses that gave him large, startled eyes. He looked like a cross between an academic hipster and a disheveled drug dealer.

"Yeah, hi," I said, standing. "Mrs. Ballinger sent me."

"That jackass."

I raised my brows in shock, unsure if I'd heard him correctly.

"Only fucking with you." He opened the door fully. "Don't work yourself up."

"Right." I extended my hand.

He waved me off. "I don't shake. Personal sanitation policy." He allowed me inside and bolted the door. It was a claustrophobic room: bookshelves, sagging under the weight of too many encyclopedias, covered every inch of the walls; a menacing poster of Hitchcock filming *Rope* loomed over us; his desk displayed a strange assortment of items, from antique lamps and Marvel comics to *A Treatise of Human Nature* and a baseball mitt. Before his desk was a single wicker chair, where a girl sat scribbling in such desperate concentration she didn't so much as glance up when we entered.

"This is Donna. She's just finishing," Bearman explained, reaching for hand sanitizer and lathering meticulously. "Want some?"

"No, thank you."

"It's good stuff."

"No, really, I—"

"I must insist," he said, dousing my hands with Purell. "Let's see. She's got"—he checked a pocket watch—"seventy-seven seconds, and if she doesn't get eighty-five percent of the problems right I'll disown her. Don't need her screwing my averages, right?" He lumbered over to his side of the desk, leaving me to stand awkwardly as Donna, on the verge of a meltdown, finished.

"Time!" Bearman roared, lunging toward her to seize her pencil and snap it in two.

"I hate when you do that," she said, "as I've told you many times over."

"Test conditions must be simulated." He dropped the halves to the floor and scanned her test, mostly nodding, occasionally grimacing with exaggerated effect. "Donna, I am nothing if not merciful. You live to see another week."

"Enjoy this guy," she whispered as she left. "He's psychotic."

I smiled awkwardly, took her seat.

Bearman smiled, too. "A ringing endorsement, huh?"

Awkward silence as I tried determining whether he was joking. He crossed his legs.

"I have a friend who told me you were great," I said.

"Who's the lucky student?"

"Noah Harris."

"Noah Harris? The chiseled basketball Adonis with the impressively long hair?"

"The very one."

"You don't look like someone who'd know Noah Harris."

"So I've been told."

"Don't take it as an insult. Take it as—well, yes, it's almost certainly an insult." He shuffled through papers. "Have you taken a practice test?"

"No."

"Lazy. Would you say you're a math guy or an English guy?"

"Uh—"

"If you're neither, there is no more ideal time to admit so than the present."

"English," I said, trying to muster confidence.

"Never the math kids who come knocking. Very well. I'm guessing you'll want my spiel."

"Your spiel?"

He leaned back in his chair, swiveling back and forth. "You're ready to walk into some dingy office and fork over cash to a neurotic schmuck without so much as a sales pitch?" He began playing with his mitt. "I'm thirty-three, I went to Berkeley, I dropped out of three different law schools on three different occasions—never ask me about that. I've taken the SAT three times a year, every year, for the last nine years and have never scored outside the ninety-eighth percentile. I demand cash and no, I don't report all my income, sue me. Somehow I take home just south of one hundred and thirty a year, enough to get my mother off my back about burning out of law school and never marrying, not nearly enough to give me purpose. But who needs purpose? Satisfied? Lovely, let's begin." He handed me a practice test. "This is something I give all my clients, to gauge where you stand. See what you can answer."

I gave the math a cursory glance. What is the average mean of $5x + 7$, $8x-5$ and $3x + 3$? In a classroom of 50 students, 35 are male: what percent of the class is female? The equation $4x^2 - 7x - 10$ has how many distinct real solutions?

"Anything look familiar?"

"Sort of."

"Love the confidence."

"Fine. Not especially."

"What's your math background."

"Nonexistent."

"Excellent. For me, that is. Less so for you. I'll look great when I bump your score. What's your target, if I may ask? Which I may, considering I'm now your tutor, a very sacred position for the Greeks."

"I have no idea."

"You don't know much, do you? You remind me of myself in high school."

"Yeah?"

"Yeah, only a lot dumber. But with far less acne. So there's that."

"I'm thrilled."

"Go home, take this test and see if you can come up with anything. Next week we'll go from there. Capeesh?"

"Capeesh," I said stupidly. "But is that all we can do today—"

"Yeah, you have to get out now. My next client chews my ear off and I'd like to grab a burrito before he shows up."

—

SCHOOL SWUNG INTO HIGH GEAR. I received my first grade, a flat B on my math test, and threw myself into writing my first English paper, an analysis of the clash of Diomedes and Glaucus in the sixth book of the *Iliad*. Election season, meanwhile, intensified.

"Davis made a list of every freshman clique in the school, subdivided into tiers of influence to target swing voters," Amir ranted over lunch. "Is that not completely pathological?"

Davis, as it happened, was in the parking lot beneath us. He was lecturing at unsuspecting sophomores—"This is a delicate time for the trajectory of this school, requiring neoconservative leadership patterned after the inimitable Lincoln"—all of whom looked as if they wanted nothing more than to stop existing.

"Maybe it'll help," Noah said. "Everyone wants to hang themselves when he speaks."

"Yo! Davis! Shut the fuck up, will you?" Oliver, without my consent, grabbed the remains of my lunch and aimed for Davis. A marvelous throw: blots of tuna connected squarely with his forehead, splattering over his clothing.

"What in God's good name?" Davis wiped mayonnaise from his cheeks and scanned above until he spotted the five of us on the balcony.

"I think the two people least likely to do anything even remotely effective in this school are Davis and Amir," Evan said, ignoring Davis' shouts below.

"Right," Amir said. "Meanwhile you're a regular Machiavelli."

"Well," Oliver said, relishing the opportunity to goad Amir, "if anyone were to shake things up it'd be Evan, wouldn't it?"

"Don't fret, Amir," Evan said. "Bloom has no intention of letting me be president."

Amir scoffed. "Oh, he told you so, during your little meetings? Or maybe Schrödinger himself rose from the grave to tell you to follow your heart by running for president?"

Evan smiled. "Schopenhauer. Not Schrödinger."

"Schrödinger, Schopenhauer, Soprano, whoever the hell you read these days."

Noah laughed. "You think Bloom wouldn't let you, Ev? You're like his mini-me intellectual apprentice. His pride and joy."

"I don't know," Oliver said, peering over at Davis, "now that they've got their little lovers' spat thing."

"And for the record," Amir continued defensively, "it wouldn't work if you ran, it'd bite us in the ass. We'd cancel each other out and Davis would win."

Evan didn't blink. "Drop out, then."

"I should drop out?"

"It's not like you need it," Evan said.

"But *you* do?"

"This isn't for my résumé, Amir."

"Oh?" Amir forced a laugh. "Then what's it for?"

"I have my reasons," Evan said.

—

PLASTERED OVER THE WALLS OF the first floor the next morning were dozens of strange posters. Other presidential campaign posters were easy to ignore. Davis, for instance, had circulated images of his face superimposed over the bodies of political luminaries (Davis as a grinning Reagan, a solemn Lincoln, a brooding Hamilton), while

Amir had hung several bland SAMSON FOR PRESIDENT signs. These new posters, however, were impossible to overlook. Written on black paper in silvery ink was a simple inscription: THE REBELLION. I knew, at first glance, that this was Evan's doing.

Talk of the posters dominated the day. By the end of first period, the administration had ordered Gio to dispose of every mention of The Rebellion. ("Tell Stark," Gio said, cornering me on my way to class, "that I don't understand signs and also they're a huge pain in my huge ass.") The damage, however, was done. They were all anyone talked about.

"Yeah, the posters came from that crew," I overheard a freshman announcing to her friends. "You know, Stark and Harris and Bellow."

"You forgot Samson."

A third freshman, thumbing his nostril: "I think he's more of a— what do you call it? Consigliere?"

"You've been watching too much *Godfather*."

"That other guy's with them, too."

"Who's the other one?"

"The Hasidic kid," the first freshman said, pointing in my direction and lowering her voice. "I think they want to take down the school."

—

DR. PORTER HANDED BACK OUR second math quiz—I was down to a B-minus—and suggested I visit the peer tutoring service offered at lunch. So I did, making my way to the second floor, only to find Kayla, alone, picking at a large Greek salad, her nose in a book.

I stood at the doorway for a half-second, deciding whether to leave. I'd made it a point to avoid her since our last encounter, making certain to sit far away in classes. As I made up my mind to leave, however, she cleared her throat. "Your lunches are another flight up, if I'm not mistaken."

"Sorry. Wrong classroom," I said hastily. "I was looking for the peer tutor."

"How serendipitous."

"You're looking for the tutor, too?"

"I am the tutor," she said brightly.

"You're the tutor?"

"Don't look so shocked. It's insulting. Math, is it?"

I walked over and sat beside her, "How'd you guess?"

"You're more of a humanities type,"

"Does that make you a math brain?"

"It most certainly does not. I'm both."

"Lucky you." I took out my test, littered with red marks. I glanced at the book on her lap. "Artaud?"

"Ever read him?"

"No,"

"You ought to if you're to maintain your misunderstood literary persona. We can all use a little French avant-garde in our lives. Bump him to the top of your reading list."

I nodded, and then, to avoid further small talk, pointed to the first problem on my test—*find the length of X in this circle with four intersecting chords*—for which I'd received a whopping one out of ten points.

"Are you guys frightened?" she asked

I gave her a blank look. "How come I never know what you're talking about?"

"I'm obviously referring to Evan Stark's bid for presidency, and whether it portends civil war."

"Civil war?"

"You'll have to make the tragic choice between Evan and Amir, won't you?" She flipped her wavy, reddish hair. "Well, *you* won't bear that burden. But Noah and Oliver will."

"Maybe let's focus on math."

She nodded pleasantly, grabbed a pencil from behind her left ear and launched into a comprehensive explanation of circles and tangent lines, pausing now and again to give me looks I pretended not to see.

—

THE DAY ENDED WITH A surprise. As the final bell rang, Gio posted the roster for the basketball team. At the very bottom of the list was my name.

"Feast your eyes on that," Oliver announced, drawing circles around my name with a yellow highlighter. "Aryeh Eden, last and likely least, but nevertheless a member of the Kol Neshama Kings!"

"Well done, Drew." Noah gave me a celebratory smack on the back. "Time to start working on that left hand."

I'd already resigned myself to the fact that I wouldn't be making the team, and had done so contentedly: I could do without the time commitment, I figured, not to mention the pressure. Still, I couldn't help but smile, especially when Sophia congratulated me as she walked by.

"Look at that," Evan said, joining us. "Noah, had yourself a chat with Rocky?"

"Nah," Noah said uncomfortably.

"Right," Evan said, unconvinced. "Anyone see Amir?"

"He left."

"He hasn't said a word to me all day," Evan said.

"Yeah, well," Noah said, shrugging, "I don't think he's overjoyed with you at the moment."

"Shame," Evan said tonelessly, striding away.

—

THAT FIRST PRACTICE WAS PAINFUL. We started with fifteen minutes of running purposeless circles around the basketball court, and then, without grabbing water, received an expletive-laden speech about our potential ("I'm going to break each of you so that I can rebuild you with my own two hands"), our goals ("we'll win division, we'll win districts, we'll be the goddamn pride of this school") and, of course, the singular greatness of Noah Harris.

Only afterward did we get around to installing our playbook. "Our first game is in two weeks, right after the holidays. Learning my system is now officially more important than your schoolwork. Anyone have a problem?" He glared at us individually, pausing at Amir. "No? Excellent, I better not find out someone bitched to Ballinger."

We walked through sets, restarting after any minor mistake, running suicides when Rocky lost his temper. "Attention to detail!" he'd yell as we staggered through wind sprints. "No wasted fucking movements! Every fucking possession is fucking priceless! Fuck!"

I realized quickly that I had little value on the team. I did decently in the drills and for the most part managed to follow instructions without mishap, but contributed almost nothing during scrimmages. I scrambled irrelevantly, passed upon touching the ball, waited desperately for Rocky to mercifully end practice, which was already running a half hour late. My team went down early in our last game but stormed back frantically after Amir drained several threes in the span of two minutes.

"Attah boy, Samson!" Rocky thundered. "It's your fucking stratosphere, you hear me?"

Down one, Amir stripped the ball and found himself alone with Evan, who raced madly to steer him from the hoop. Amir, at top speed, lowered his shoulder and threw himself into Evan's chest, just as Evan leaped for the block, sending them crashing into a tangled mess. For a moment they remained on the floor, wrestling to unravel themselves, until they sprang to their feet, pushing and jawing, at which point Amir sized up Evan and socked him directly in the mouth.

Rocky, blowing wildly on his whistle, sped from the opposite baseline to separate them. He pried them apart and stood between them, gasping for breath, still making inadvertent sounds with the whistle. "What the fuck is wrong with you two?"

Evan spat blood, which he allowed to drip gently from his swelling lip to his white practice jersey.

"Want to swing at someone?" Rocky asked, vibrating with ad: line. "You guys know I get off on that. But then swing at an op not each other. Understand? Good. Because boy oh boy, I love this shit. Shake hands and go home."

—

AMID THE GROWING ELECTION TENSION was the fact that the High Holidays lurked around the corner. With Rosh Hashanah a few days away, the school announced that the annual selichot program—"Optional but heavily encouraged," Noah explained, "and painfully boring"— would be held Saturday night, and the focus of Judaic classes turned seasonal: teshuva, moral reformation, the necessity of prayer.

"*What is gained if I am silenced, if I go down to the pit?*'" Rabbi Bloom lectured at a school-wide assembly. "*Will the dust praise you? Will it proclaim your faithfulness?*' What we take for granted, what we ignore deliberately for much of our year, rises to the fore as we voyage toward Yom Kippur. When we don our *kittel*, when we spend day after day repenting, inching closer to God, when we fast and stand before our Maker, our hope is to transcend the fact that we are ashes, to reject our origin, to stake a claim in a higher dimension, to look God in the face. The beauty of Rosh Hashanah is not merely what we mindlessly refer to as renewal, which even the secular variant of the New Year contains, but the opportunity to affirm to ourselves, if to no one else, that we are, in fact, more than the dust to which we return."

Rabbi Feldman's class, too, was spent jolting us into thoughtfulness. "Everyone take one," he announced, bustling about the classroom to distribute colorful index cards. "Each of you should write one specific thing you want to improve in your life. It can be minor, like opening the door for people or making an effort to greet a friend, or it can be ambitious—say, committing yourself to praying each day or graduating from Minyan X."

Amir considered this prospect. "But who sees the card?"

Rabbi Feldman chortled. "Are you asking if this is graded?"

"Yes, actually," Amir said.

"~ards will be displayed in a school-wide project but will remain ~ous. And ungraded."

"What project?"

"Something the Engineering Club has been working on," Rabbi Feldman said. "They won an award from University of Miami for it, actually. It's absolutely delightful, the precision. You'll see for yourself."

Most people crumpled the card or debated the best sexual exploit to include. Yet Noah, I noticed, wrote thoughtfully and Amir, unsurprisingly, scribbled furiously. Even Evan was chewing the cap of his pen ruminatively. As the bell rang and the class rushed to lunch, I jotted the first thing that came to mind, folded my card and handed it to Rabbi Feldman.

—

THE PROJECT, UNVEILED LATER THAT day, was an intricate model of an ancient coliseum within a small city, stationed outside the school entrance. It was a large structure, the size of a giant outdoor chess set. The model stretched some fifteen feet in length and width, and its pieces were as tall as five feet high. There were replicas of buildings, of people, of cattle, all surrounded by massive pillars and walls and altars and gold-plated doors. An outer court, filled with figurines assembled in prayer, led into an inner court, which housed some sort of temple. Inside the temple stood a sanctuary, where small scale priests loitered, and then an innermost chamber. The architecture poked at my knees.

"What the hell is this?" Oliver asked, walking slowly through the model. "They can't be fundraising for a new school building, can they? I'm pretty sure my parents donated enough last time around."

"It's the Beit HaMikdash," Evan said. He knelt at the altar at the center, pointing to a figurine of a solitary priest. The kohen was equipped in full garb: a turban, an embroidered sash of purple, blue and scarlet, an ephod, a breastplate. The details were extraordinary: all twelve gems were carved into the breastplate. The priest's turban even featured the proper words—*Kodesh LaShem*. Holy unto God.

Covering the exterior walls of the temple were the notecards the school had circulated. *Judge everyone favorably. Marry Remi White. Find a passion. Try my hardest to believe in the Almighty.*

"Kind of creepy," Noah said, looking it over, "isn't it?"

"It's just a toy," Amir said.

I scanned the temple for my card: *What is this quintessence of dust?* "An ornate toy," I said.

Evan traced the details with his eyes, and then walked on. I would spend a lot of time over the coming months attempting to figure out which card was his.

—

ANOTHER RESTLESS SHABBAT. SMALL TALK, sweaty afternoon naps, light-headed reading. I was lying on the living room couch after lunch while my father reviewed the latest in our shared adventures in Gemara Bava Kamma. "Didn't Reish Lakish teach you're exempt from fire damage *only* when you transfer an ember to someone else who *then* fans it into a flame? Why is that so?"

I had my Gemara resting on a pillow beside me. A different book lay open on my lap. I didn't answer.

"Nu, Aryeh?"

"Sorry," I said, grabbing my Gemara again and absentmindedly tracing my fingertips over ancient words.

"Stay with me, Aryeh. Because the potential for damage in that scenario is not guaranteed!"

"Right, exactly."

Without looking I could hear Gemara pages being flipped angrily. "May I ask what is it you've been looking at nonstop?" My father gestured to the Yeats propped on my lap.

I poked my head up. "He's a poet."

"A poet? Are we not learning Torah right now?"

"Sorry, it's for school."

"You know, Aryeh, I'm very happy you're enjoying your English
much with that—what's her name? Mrs. Hararei?"

"Hartman."

"Yes. Hartman. But you shouldn't forget that a *bachur* needs to prioritize Limmud HaKodesh over secular studies."

"Actually, it's not for English class."

"Whichever class, it doesn't matter."

"Rabbi Bloom gave it to me."

My father stiffened in his seat. "The principal?"

"The one and only."

"Where does he come off giving that to a student?"

"Come off? I think it's wonderful he's worldly enough to be teaching things like poetry," my mother said, sweeping into the room, splaying herself on the opposite couch. "Plus, he's clearly taken a serious interest in Ari. He's impressed with Ari! You heard what he said about his application, his *rare* acceptance."

My father buried his face in his Gemara. "The rabbi circulates poetry, the silly basketball team pretends they're being paid to meet seven nights a week, the friends come and go late at night in ridiculous cars and don't wear yarmulkes outside of school and hardly ever go to shul. Is this a yeshiva? Which part of this education is a yeshiva?"

I smiled and returned my attention to "The Hero, the Girl, and the Fool."

—

AFTER HAVDALAH THAT NIGHT I waited to be picked up for selichot. Loud honking came a half hour later than I expected. I hurried into Oliver's Jeep before my parents emerged to investigate. "You had to honk like that?"

Noah, in the passenger seat, turned with an apologetic smile. "I told him to stop, Drew, but the idiot doesn't listen."

"Can we just get out of here," I said, unnerved at the sight of my mother peering anxiously from our front window, "before she comes to talk to Oliver?"

"Your lovely mother can have my ear whenever she pleases.

Whoops." He put the car in reverse too quickly so that the Jeep be-stowed a soft kiss upon the palm tree in my driveway. "I'm prolific with older women."

"Definitely better than you are with girls our age," Noah said. "Though that's not saying much."

"It's my fault they don't appreciate my advanced maturity?"

"Right, let's go with that." Noah checked the score of the Marlins game on his phone. "Shouldn't we scoop Amir first?"

"He said his mom wants him driving separately," Oliver said, de-liberately running a stop sign. "She doesn't like me driving him at night just because of that *one* little accident, can you imagine?"

"Before I forget," Noah said, twisting in his seat and pulling out a card from his wallet, "this is for you." He handed me what appeared to be a license. I shone the light of my iPhone over it: one Drew Car-raway, hailing from 770 Summit Avenue, Saint Paul, Minnesota. The picture was of my own face, the one taken at orientation.

"What the—?"

"Fake ID, buddy," Oliver said. "Be grateful. We had Amir hack the yearbook database for those professional headshots and I had a buddy hook it up. I figured it'd be a waste but Noah insisted on in-cluding you."

"I'm from—Minnesota?"

"Well, you can't be from here," Oliver said.

We went to retrieve Evan. It was the first time I'd seen his house, designed to resemble Miami Modernist architecture—sleek, mini-malist, tree-studded. A sculpture of enormous, clashing red triangles guarded his lawn. A black Aston Martin was parked beside a BMW.

I blinked at the house and cars. "So what's his family like?"

"Well." Noah's face dimmed. "His mother passed."

"Oh," I mumbled. "I'm so sorry to hear that."

"Yeah, pretty awful."

"When was this?"

Noah reclined his seat, stretching his cramped legs. "It's been—what? Nearly a year."

Oliver confirmed with a nod.

I played with the buckle of my seatbelt. "How'd it—happen?"

"She got really sick," Noah said.

"Nicest person you'll ever meet," Oliver added with uncharacteristic seriousness.

"And they were close, man," Noah said. "Extremely close."

"Does he have siblings?"

"Nah, Ev's an only child. His dad's never home. Hedge fund workaholic." And, after a slight pause: "Not an easy man."

Oliver scoffed. "Fucking understatement of the year."

Noah nodded. "Ev's been through some hell."

"If you ask me," Oliver said, running his hands over the steering wheel, "it's why he's doing all that weird reading shit."

I studied the triangles. Something about them made me nauseous. "What do you mean?"

"You know," Oliver said, "he's always ingesting some secret philosophical or religious or whatever book now, isn't he? I know it's pissing off Amir."

"I mean, it makes sense," Noah said. "He has the sort of brain that'd cope by turning to life's big questions, things like that." He strained his gaze through the window. "I know he can come across a bit harshly, Drew, especially when you're still getting to know him, but we can't underestimate how much he's hurting."

"Tell him about the Rosenbaum thing," Oliver said. "New perspective."

"When we were sophomores," Noah said, "there was a freshman who was a bit nerdy, super shy. What was his name?"

"Johnny? Tzachi?"

"No, it was . . . Mikey. Whatever, nice guy, just had a hard time transitioning into high school. Apparently he was getting picked on by older kids. I guess Evan was strolling down the hallway one day when he sees three or four seniors messing with Rosenbaum, moving shit from his locker, calling him stuff, whatever. And Evan calmly walks up to them, puts his arm around Rosenbaum and warns them—these are seniors, bear in mind, Ev's a sophomore—that, if another person so much as looks the wrong way at Rosenbaum, he will make sure their lives are ruined."

I spun my phone on my lap. "*Evan* did that?"

"Don't sound so surprised," Oliver said. "He's no bully."

"No, I just—so did it work?"

"Sure did," Noah said.

"Why'd those seniors listen?"

Oliver shrugged. "He's Evan fucking Stark. He could destroy them a million different ways."

"Point is," Noah continued, "I end up hearing about this story months later, since Evan never breathed a word. At the end of the year, Rosenbaum's mom shows up at school, pulls Evan out of a class-room and gives him a huge hug, in front of all these seniors, going on and on about how Evan doesn't even realize he saved her son's life. Anyway, that's random, and unfortunately the kid ended up switch-ing schools the next year, but you should know Ev's a good dude, deep down."

"Yeah, I mean, of course," I said quickly. "I never implied—"

"I know. But we grew up with Ev," Noah said. "And you're just seeing recent events. So I can't blame you for forming certain . . . opinions."

"I can," Oliver said, scrolling through his phone. "Damn, the Fish lost in extra innings. There goes two hundred bucks."

"He's different lately," Noah said, "I realize that, but I think griev-ing is the reason he's been acting a bit—I don't know. Erratic?"

I accepted this, pressed no further. We waited another few min-utes for Evan to emerge, lapsing into deferential silence, save for Oliver tinkering awkwardly with his SiriusXM stations.

"Eden," Evan said pleasantly, sidling next to me when he finally came out. I was struck with the impulse to offer belated condolences but nothing came to mind. He noticed my indecision, narrowed his eyes. "What's with you?"

"Not a thing."

Evan leaned toward Oliver as we began driving. "Have anything?"

"Does a chicken have lips?" Oliver rummaged in a compartment near his legs, forcing Noah to steady the wheel so as to avoid drifting into someone's front yard. He returned to the wheel with a baggie of weed. "Try this."

Evan took a lighter from his jeans, flicking it on and off. "Want the first hit, Eden?" He handed me the lighter: silver, rectangular, Cartier. Inscribed in faint cursive, just beneath the initials HLA, was a Hebrew pasuk: הֲלוֹא כֹה דְבָרִי כָּאֵשׁ. *Is not My word like fire?* "My maternal grandfather's," he said, allowing me to admire it. "Gorgeous, isn't it?"

"It is," I said, quickly returning it to his hands.

"Just a thought," Noah said, "but maybe you guys want to not be stupidly high while praying for repentance?"

Evan coughed his way through a hit. "Noah, remind me when you turned into Amir?" He blew smoke toward my face. "Was it when this guy arrived?"

Noah opened his window. Smoke released into the night. He gave me a look through the rearview mirror. "Jesus, Oliver. Can you actually see out the windshield?"

"Not really," Oliver said. "But maybe it's my eyes starting not to work, I don't know. This shit's powerful." He flicked the roach out the window.

We managed to arrive without incident, though I wondered if I'd worn down my molars from gritting my teeth throughout the ride. We were led by Rabbi Feldman into the assembly hall, where the seats closest to the stage had been removed, clearing space for students to sit on the floor in concentric circles. The lights were off; dozens of candles illuminated the room, casting pensive shadows. Onstage sat Rabbi Schwartz, equipped with a guitar, strumming solemn melodies. We joined an outer circle, endured the singing: Noah immediately began belting tunes (*"Achaynu Kol Beis Yisroel"*), and even Oliver was high enough to be reduced to respectful, albeit incomprehensible, humming. When midnight rolled about, Rabbi Bloom took the stage to offer a brief analysis of the Thirteen Attributes of Mercy before leading us into prayer.

The service concluded by one in the morning. Though normally I disliked Shabbat singing, I actually enjoyed the program and was experiencing a pleasant mixture of spiritual fulfillment and drowsiness. As we loaded into the Jeep, however, Oliver suggested assembling a crew and stopping at some nearby lake. I intended to decline and find another ride home, until Noah mentioned that Sophia would be accompanying Rebecca. Oliver began firing text messages. I shrugged in surrender.

It was a clear night, no clouds, the moon projecting aqueous spheres of light. Our group sat in damp grass by dark water. Evan disappeared, holding hands with a junior girl. Oliver was soon unconscious on a nearby bench, with people crowding him, capturing the sight on Snapchat. Noah and Rebecca wandered off into the trees, Noah giving me an encouraging head nod. Somehow, to my delight, this left me alone at the foot of the lake with Sophia, bathed in silvery lunar light.

"So that was all surprisingly tame in school," I said, attempting to break the ice, "wasn't it?"

"It was selichot," Sophia said. "What'd you expect?"

"I don't know. I guess I'm at the point where I'm surprised if they don't, like, break into riot at the first opportunity."

"You're not entirely wrong." She studied the trees. "Your friends do have a habit of occasionally resembling animals."

A light, unstrained pause. Moonlight fell through the branches above. "Can I say something weird?" I asked, mustering courage.

"I don't see why not."

"Your music."

"What about it?"

"It hasn't left my head."

She stared into the water, a faraway look in her eyes, her skin a raw white in the dark. "Pardon?"

"The *Appassionata*."

"Oh."

"It was really—haunting."

"I suppose all great pianists aspire for that kind of praise. To be awkwardly told they play haunting music."

"No, no, it was beautiful, of course, I only meant—"

She allowed her hand to linger briefly over mine. "I know."

"I hope," I said, holding my breath, "I'll be lucky enough to hear it again."

"Maybe a different piece. A happier one."

"I'd settle for listening to you warm up."

"There's a recital next weekend, if you'd like to come along. Unless you prefer your usual method of sneaking up on me while I'm practicing."

I stared helplessly at her thin lips, her slim wrists, her gold bracelet, her light-pinned eyes. "You have your own recital?"

"It's through the school. A fundraiser."

"But Kol Neshama asked you to perform?"

"They did."

"Well, that's pretty cool."

"Not that I had a choice."

"You didn't want to do it?"

"I don't like having decisions made for me."

"By Bloom?"

"By anyone. But God, no, it wasn't Bloom. My parents."

"I thought your parents didn't approve of you playing?"

"Not when it comes to going to music school and becoming a professional. But to be featured at a high school fundraiser?" She offered a brief, exasperated laugh. I was aware, watching her laugh, that I was experiencing a moment that would fundamentally alter the equilibrium of my life. I accepted this without question, even as I failed to understand it. "Now that's a great honor, they're convinced. That's prestigious. That's *good* for me."

"Good for you how?"

"Actually I'd rather talk about something else." She smoothed her shirt, regarded me with half-closed eyes. "Tell me about *you*."

"What do you want to know?"

"Give me a glimpse into that rich inner life of yours."

I waited for panic to set in at the prospect of being tested, but it never came. Being alone, vulnerable to her probing, was a rare opportunity to impress her. "Who says I have one?"

"You play the stoic card, but I'm unconvinced."

"Yeah, well, you're totally right," I said. "I'm actually fascinating when you get to know me."

She paused. "Do you miss home?"

I inhaled, cemented my tongue against the roof of my mouth. "No."

"I find that hard to believe."

"It's the truth."

"Isn't everyone supposed to love home?"

"Yeah, maybe. But I don't think I ever did."

She leaned forward, legs crisscrossed, hands on her knees. "What did it feel like there?"

Fierce, undefined longings. Incommunicable unrest. "I felt this overpowering sense of—of strangeness there," I said. "Almost as if I were, I don't know, unlived."

She picked at the grass near her feet. "That all sounds quite poetic."

"It didn't feel too poetic. But possibly that's my own fault."

"Strangeness, boredom—that's your own fault?"

"This is when I'm supposed to tell you that the mind is its own place, right? It can make a heaven of hell, a hell of heaven, a Zion of Brooklyn, a Brooklyn of Zion?"

She was startlingly close now, close enough to study the rhythm of her breathing, close enough to memorize the nexus of veins on her eyelids, close enough to inhale her perfume—vanilla, heady. "I have absolutely no idea what to make of you," she said. "Nobody does."

"People keep telling me that."

"Don't you know why?"

"I have my suspicions."

"It's because you don't belong here. Like I said before—you're different."

"That doesn't sound like an especially good thing."

"On the contrary." She pulled up more grass, allowed it to scatter, wiped her hands together. "I like your unbelonging. Don't you?"

"That depends."

"On?"

"Do *you* belong?"

"I used to think so. I always thought I'd miss home terribly when I finally leave for college." She organized her mouth into a wistful smile. She did so in a way that felt rehearsed, as if she'd practiced how best to appear natural, relatable. I was beginning to believe she had a way of transmitting emotions without actually being capable of feeling them. "It's a wonderful place to grow up."

"But you stopped believing that?"

Weak light scattered through black trees. "I think it's more that eventually we all need to get away."

"At least you have an escape."

"I do?"

"Yeah," I said, "music."

She shook her head, fingering her bracelet. "Did I forget to mention I have a strict rule? No psychoanalysis. Especially about my music. That's just way too . . . depressingly prosaic."

"Sorry, right, point taken."

"Anyway, music isn't for escaping. It's for, well—" She looked out beyond my body, focusing on something I couldn't see, even when I turned and tried. Moonlight hurled triangular fragments of light over her face. "For seeing things as they really are."

"That sounds kind of fitting," I said.

"Fitting with what?"

"The answer you gave in Hartman's class on the first day, the one you used to reject mine? About how tragedy doesn't purify broken things?"

"There you go. Likening my music to tragedy. Another surefire way to charm someone's heart." She rubbed at her eyes. "Well, we love what makes us miserable. Someone once told me that."

"Who? I don't think it was Shakespeare."

Twigs snapped behind us. Out from the trees stumbled Evan, the junior draped to his waist, one of Oliver's Grey Goose bottles in his hand. "Well," he said drunkenly, "isn't this heartwarming?"

Sophia's eyes settled on the girl, who returned her look with measured courteousness. "Hey, Jen."

Evan avoided my eyes. "This unlikely pairing again. You two must be becoming well acquainted."

"It's late," Sophia announced, rising suddenly to her feet. "I'm going to find Rebecca." Before I could mobilize, she slipped into the forest dark, leaving me behind. I looked at my phone. It was half past two. To be safe, I composed a text to my mom, claiming I'd be home soon, only to decide not to send it.

"Jen," Evan said, "have you met my new friend here?"

She hesitated briefly, looking at me with confusion before shaking my hand. "Jen Benstock."

"Ari Eden. Nice to meet you."

"Careful," Evan said. "He has a thing for girls I used to date. Isn't that right, Eden?"

Jen looked up at Evan. "What the hell?"

Ignoring her, Evan went on giving me a hard, drunken look. "Why do you think that is, Eden? Is Jen your type, too?"

Jen recoiled, releasing her hand from Evan's grip. For a moment, she looked up at him as if to strongly consider striking him. Instead, she stomped off into the trees, illuminating her way with her iPhone flashlight.

"Eden," he said, waiting until Jen's footsteps were no longer audible. He wore a glassy smile, fumbled to light a joint. He was drunker than I'd realized. I wondered what he'd remember in the morning. "A word of warning?"

I stood.

"To be loved by her," he said, swaying on his feet, "is to be impaled."

We waited in silence. Soon enough, Sophia reappeared with Noah, Rebecca and Jen in tow. Jen was slightly tear-stained and refused to say much to anyone but Rebecca, whom she knew from softball; I offered her a tissue, though this made me feel even more self-conscious. Noah and Rebecca, holding hands, seemed annoyed to have been interrupted. Sophia led us back, refusing to rest her eyes on anything above the ground.

Rebecca left her car in the school parking lot, and so she and Sophia piled into the Jeep with us to be dropped off. On the way back, Oliver stopped for gas and disappeared into the station, reemerging with a Gatorade and a large plastic bag of snacks. We drove to school in silence, Sophia breathing sharply beside me, our arms touching slightly, her very smell suffusing me with irrational happiness. When we arrived at the parking lot, Noah walked the girls to their car. As we watched the girls drive off, Oliver reached into the plastic bag and pulled out a tray of eggs.

"What the hell are you doing with *that*?" I asked, massaging my eyes, wishing I were already in bed.

"Take some," Oliver said, opening the carton.

I refused. "I don't get it."

Evan, however, grabbed the carton and threw open the door. Eggs in hand, Oliver and he walked to the entrance of the school. I heard Noah yell in surprise, and I stuck my head out of the window curiously just as eggs began raining upon the roof, the walls, the front door. *The Lord rained hail on Egypt*, I thought, *on every man and animal that has not been brought in.* Jagged shells littered the grass. Yolk bled from the model temple, oozing onto the pavement.

"There's blood in this one," Oliver cried, examining a cracked egg. Noah grabbed him before Oliver could wind up. He forced Oliver to drop his weapon and physically returned him to the Jeep. "What the fuck was that?" Noah yelled once they were all back inside the car. He urged Oliver to drive out of the parking lot as quickly as possible. "Why would you morons possibly do that?"

Oliver laughed hysterically. Evan, from the passenger seat, only smiled. "Rosh Hashanah is coming," he said. "We need reasons to repent."

—

GOSSIP IN SCHOOL ON MONDAY revolved around what was quickly being dubbed Night of the Yolk. Retribution, as expected, followed the sunrise minyan precedent. Oliver and Evan were summoned to Rabbi Bloom's office and each given a full-day suspension. Despite the school-wide chatter about the incident, however, Rabbi Bloom offered only administrative silence, allowing this latest incident to dissolve as some newer indignity arose. Noah was questioned, as were Rebecca and Sophia, given that we were all captured on the parking lot camera. Throughout the remainder of the day, as such, I prepared myself for interrogation. All day I waited for my turn. The call never came.

—

ROSH HASHANAH, FOR THE FIRST time in my life, was an uninspiring affair. In Brooklyn, the High Holidays were majestic, the prayers evoking reverence, or at least fear and trembling. I remember, as a child, standing beside my father, his talis over his head, his body shaking, his eyes closed. In those moments I considered whether he might be one of the *tzadikim nistarim*, the thirty-six hidden righteous for whom the world exists. I pondered this when he brought me into his talis, when he cried softly during Unetanneh Tokef.

This year brought no such awe. We sat in an overcrowded row in the rear of the shul. The air-conditioning was out. I gave my father the aisle, which meant I sat beside Mr. Cohen, a gruff, hulking friend of Eddie Harris, who bombarded me with stories from his youth.

"Got yourself a girlfriend?" He slung an arm around my shoulder. He wore far too much cologne.

I shook my head, my nose smarting, and fought for inches in my seat.

"But aren't you about Noah's age?"

"Yeah."

"Well, my boy here"—he pointed to the middle-schooler to his right, at the moment engrossed in a particularly laborious effort to probe his right nostril with his index finger—"has a girlfriend, and he's only in the sixth grade."

I lowered my siddur to my lap.

"Noah's girlfriend—what's her name? Michelle?"

"Rebecca," I said.

"Right, Rebecca, great girl, nice girl. Have her set you up."

"I'll consider it."

"Had myself several girlfriends at your age." A gabbai, patrolling the back of the sanctuary, unleashed a valiant shush upon Mr. Cohen, who reciprocated with furious fist waving until the gabbai slunk off in defeat. "Nerve of that guy. Remind me what I was saying?"

"I believe we were just finishing."

"Right, listen, if you manage to land yourself a girlfriend, take her on a picnic, but don't bring wine and cheese. No, sir. Bring M&M's."

"M&M's?"

"Green ones. Works like a charm, just ask my second wife." He elbowed my ribs, laughed too loudly. I turned red and glanced at my father, praying he hadn't overheard.

I spent the long hours this way, subject to Mr. Cohen's stories— the time he beat up a rival goalie, the time he accidentally snorted glue. When overcome with boredom I'd observe my scenery: Amir davening intensely beside his grandfather, whom people constantly approached, offering Gut Yuntif wishes; Noah snickering violently into Eddie's ear; Oliver asleep near the bimah, his father, a short man in a pin-striped Armani suit, popping a steady stream of Tic Tacs. I made out a glimpse of Sophia—simple white dress, straightened hair, grave eyes—on the women's side of the mechitza but failed to catch her attention. Much to my father's displeasure I brought along *Macbeth*, which we were reading for Mrs. Hartman, and leafed through it during slower moments. When the rabbi stood to speak I felt the need for air and wandered into the library, where I found Evan, a Talmud on his lap.

"Didn't expect you in here," I said, taking the seat beside him. "What a sight."

Annoyed, Evan scratched at his chin, his solitude disturbed. "Surely you didn't expect to find me out there?"

"I guess I thought you were home," I said.

"My father's the opposite of a pious man, but even he insists I attend shul during the Yamim Noraim. For appearances more than anything else."

"Right."

"Of course, he already left for the day. But what're you doing out of services? Hopefully not seeking relief from the marathon of prayers we subject ourselves to each year?"

"Everyone needs a breather." I put my foot up on a chair in front of me. "What's with the Gemara?"

He flipped back to an earlier page. "*Four things avert the evil decree passed by God on man*,'" he read. "'*Charity, prayer, change of name and improvement.*'"

"So I've heard."

"You're the Talmud chachum. What's your opinion?"

"On what?"

"That formula. Think it's real?"

I shrugged. "The first three seem a bit too good to be true."

"Agreed, as much as I hope they're effective antidotes."

"Why's that?" I asked. "Need some forgiving?"

He folded and unfolded the corner of the page of Gemara. He did this several times, before eventually tearing it off entirely. He rolled the paper into a ball. I watched with strange abhorrence. "I'm afraid so."

"What'd you do?" I eyed the page's deformity. It looked as if someone—something—had bitten off an inch.

"Something I'm not awfully proud of."

"I wouldn't worry too much," I said. Unwillingly, my mind replayed the bizarre occurrences I'd experienced since arriving in Florida. "We all have."

"This might be different, I think, from what you have in mind. Not that I feel guilty too often anymore. Thankfully, I've mostly rid myself of that."

"Of guilt?"

"Conscience is a dismal thing, Eden. Take last Yom Kippur." Evan dropped his voice, drew closer. "At that time, I was particularly displeased with the Almighty."

"Why?"

"For killing my mother." I recoiled, despite my best efforts, though managed to disguise my reaction in a forced coughing fit. "She was gone only a few days when Yom Kippur came around. And so, like the naïve boy I was, I tried exacting vengeance. I was in a state of blind anger and I wanted to make God feel me in any way that I could. But I don't want to be in that state anymore. I mean, do you think that's foolish? Believing we can make God *feel* us?"

I played with my tie, which was now too tight around my neck. My throat hurt when I swallowed. "What'd you do?"

"I settled on three small sins."

"Idolatry, adultery, murder?"

Evan smiled. "I'm a man of simpler pleasures. I went to Mass, I tried pork, did some other things."

I felt the need to tug at my collar. My Adam's apple throbbed. "You actually did that on . . . Yom Kippur?"

"Take it from me," Evan said. "Turns out those things don't make you feel better."

"But did they make you feel guilty?"

With some measure of sadness, or perhaps just a trace of nostalgia, Evan shook his head. "No. Empty, yes, but clean as a whistle, no guilt. Impressive, isn't it?"

"That's one way of looking at it."

"It's the only way of looking at it. Guilt is pointless. Guilt is our way of legitimizing self-cruelty. It's a basic human tendency to take pleasure in inflicting suffering, but seeing as we shouldn't inflict suffering upon others—and seeing as we cannot harm the divine, even if we wanted to—what do we do? We turn on ourselves. We make ourselves suffer instead. We feel guilt."

"Okay," I said, processing his logic, "but then why feel guilty now?"

He traced the spine of the Gemara with his fingertips. "Someone I care for has been wounded."

We sat in silence a few minutes longer. I didn't want to think about what this meant. Part of me, a small part, an ugly part, hoped he was referring to his family situation and not, say, a recent girlfriend, but I didn't think this was true. I surveyed the bookshelves, admiring some companions from my youth: Mesillat Yesharim, the Shulchan Aruch, the Mishneh Torah. Eventually I told him I was going back to pray.

"Enjoy yourself," he said, remaining seated.

When I returned the chazzan had begun wailing. *Who will live and who will die?*

Hidden under his talis, my father glared. "Where were you for so long?" *Who by water and who by fire?*

"Went for a walk." *Who will rest, who will wander?*

"You nearly missed shofar."

The shofar sounded long, defiant blasts. I tried thinking about guilt, teshuva, the destruction of the Temple, all the suffering in the world: genocide, poverty, terrorism, human rights violations. Instead, all I could think of was Macbeth, hearing the horns of war a final time, crying, *"My way of life is fall'n into the sere."*

OCTOBER

Surrounded by hordes of men, absorbed in all sorts of secular matters, more and more shrewd about the ways of the world—such a
person forgets himself, forgets his name divinely understood . . .

—Kierkegaard, *The Sickness unto Death*

On Sunday night, after an hour-long failed experiment with styling
mousse, I headed to Sophia's recital. The evening, advertised as an
exhibition of Kol Neshama's brightest musical talent, doubled as
an important annual fundraiser. Tickets ranged from one hundred
dollars to well over a thousand for our most esteemed donors—the
Bellows, the Harrises—though I procured a student rate of thirty-six
dollars. My mother tried accompanying me, eager as she was for anything vaguely cultural, but I convinced her it would mostly be a student affair, that I was better off attending with friends and that adult
ticket prices were, anyway, prohibitively expensive.

In truth, I wanted to go alone. I wanted, after our lakeside conversation, to impress Sophia, to be the conspiratorial eyes in which she
could find refuge when her parents proved overwhelming. Such hope
was delusional. I spent a solitary moment pacing through the model
temple outside, the Kohen Gadol observing me as I tried fixing my tie
and forcing deep breaths and guessing which notecards belonged to
whom (*Get into Michigan*; *Stop eating nonkosher pizza*; *Score 3 goals*

in soccer game). Then I walked inside to find her real friends—Remi, Rebecca, Noah—in attendance.

"Ari?" Noah excused himself from his parents at the cocktail reception, greeting me and examining my outfit and hair with an amused, almost paternal smirk. "So they let you in, huh?"

"It took some convincing."

He raised his glass. "What're you doing here?"

"Seemed like a cool event," I mumbled.

"Yeah, silly me," he said. "Forgot you're a die-hard classical music lover."

"And you are?" I asked stupidly, hands buried in my pockets.

"Hell no, though Sophia makes it tolerable. But Rebs said attendance was nonnegotiable. Obviously I'd rather be at the Heat game. My dad's client offered second-row tickets tonight."

"Right."

"Listen, I don't mean to dissuade you. Keep planting seeds, my man. You know that I applaud the effort." I reddened. He slapped my shoulder, straightened my tie for me. "For future Sophia pursuits, though, and all things cocktail related? Wear a jacket, yeah?"

Rabbi Bloom, from the center of the room, tapped a fork against his champagne glass and announced that it was time to wander into the hall. He looked at ease in a tuxedo, more like a college dean than a yeshiva principal. I imagined him in decades past, in his previous life, regularly attending such soirées. I wondered if he ever woke on certain mornings missing what he'd given up, experiencing those stabs of remorse to which my mother, I was certain, was not infrequently subjected.

"Mr. Eden." Rabbi Bloom caught me by the door and offered his hand. "Have you come alone?"

"Yes," I said, immediately irked that my presence at such an affair proved glaringly, perhaps laughably, conspicuous.

"Wonderful of you to support your classmate."

"The music's pretty good, too."

He readjusted his bow tie. "You've heard Ms. Winter perform before?"

"Only informally," I mumbled. "She was just practicing."

"Sometimes such sessions prove more meaningful than the real thing, don't you think?"

"Er, yeah," I stuttered, regretting having unnecessarily provided such information. "Maybe."

"And from what I hear, that's something of a rarity. Ms. Winter is rather private about her music. Not everyone earns that privilege."

"I got lucky."

He smiled faintly, as if registering useful data within an extensive mental filing cabinet. "In any event, enjoy the performance. You'll continue to find Ms. Winter most extraordinary, I'm certain."

My assigned seat was in the very last row of the assembly hall, next to the entrance. The hall had been transformed. Large TV monitors, positioned strategically around the room, provided detailed views of our pianist. A band of pale light shone beneath the piano. The lights were dimmed, making the possibility of Sophia spotting me, I realized, my heart sinking, wildly unlikely.

"Ladies and gentlemen." Rabbi Bloom took the stage, microphone in hand. "Thank you for supporting Kol Neshama and for joining us for what will undoubtedly be an evening of magical music." Light applause. "The Aseret Yemei Teshuva are a fitting time for this event. With Rosh Hashanah behind us, with Yom Kippur nearly here, we are tasked with self-improvement: through penitence, through charity, through prayer. Yet equally critical is the effort we put into self-reflection, for change hinges on both the spiritual and emotional hemispheres of our souls. It's for this very reason, indeed, that our Academy bears its name—Kol Neshama, Voice of the Soul. In this light, what better way to engage in self-reflection, in singing out to God, than through music? A soul moved to dance, whether in shul or in the concert hall, is a soul yearning for holiness. Tonight, I am confident, our neshamas will receive this opportunity to be given over to

music. Without further ado, I introduce a true virtuoso, our very own
Sophia Winter."

The room fell into abrupt silence as she ascended the stage. She
wore a blue strapless dress, hair pinned back, no makeup. Her face
was expressionless, her eyes vacant, as she made her way to the piano.
Ignoring the delayed, polite applause, she sat unnaturally, her back
perfectly straight. She studied the piano for half a minute, unblinking, the muscles in her neck straining. As the house lights dimmed
further and her hands hovered above the keys, a shadow crept down
the aisle, climbed over my knees and assumed the seat beside me.

"Evan?"

She began to play—softly, deftly, eyes closed. It was a soothing
opening, a slow tempo. The screens showed a close-up of her fingers
moving leisurely. Her nails were unpainted.

"I suspected I'd find you here." Evan wore a navy suit, no tie, his
hair gelled back. Even in the dim light, I could tell his eyes were red.

"Are you seriously high right now?"

He put a finger to his lips, nodding toward the stage. Sophia was
playing freely now, lingering over certain notes, allowing them to
reverberate through space, gradually adopting a feverish pitch, qui-
etude giving way to a fury of sound. I watched her hands convulse, fly
backward, dance arrhythmically. The older woman seated directly
before me drew sharp breaths and fanned herself.

She began a somber minor-key episode that made me feel physical, almost violent despair. "This is it, Eden," Evan said. I imagined
myself alone with her at the piano, sitting there while the external
world decayed. "The black pearl variation."

The variation seemed to stretch longer than the piece entailed. At
Oliver's party, Sophia appeared out of control, and yet here, detailed
in white light, she was restrained, even as soft tears leaked from the
corners of her eyes. Beside me, Evan hardly breathed.

The music lasted nearly forty minutes. When she finished, she
stood and, in a swift motion, delivered a single bow before gliding off
the stage. The lights returned: rolling applause, standing ovations,

dazed looks. Sophia hastened toward the side exit near the front of the room but was engulfed by her parents, her mother blond and heavily made up, her father lean and well dressed with what looked like newly gray hair and a habit of arranging his lips arrogantly as he searched the room. Wearing an unfocused smile, Sophia bobbed her head at admirers.

"My cue," Evan said, sidling from our row.

"What's with the weird entrance and exit?"

"Sometimes you respect when you're persona non grata."

I looked to the front of the room. Sophia was taking pictures with her brother. "She told you not to come?"

"I just don't think she'd be delighted to see me." The hardware in my chest, irrationally, felt lighter. Evan moved toward the aisle, only to pause suddenly. "On second thought."

"What?"

He pointed a dozen rows up, where Rabbi Bloom was conversing with someone in an expensive navy suit. The man had dark hair, a sharp jaw, a vaguely familiar coldness to his features.

"Who is that?"

"Don't recognize him?"

"That's not—your father?"

"The great Julian Stark," he said. "He doesn't know I'm here."

Julian whispered into Rabbi Bloom's ear. Rabbi Bloom, in turn, listened carefully, nodding on occasion.

"Are they friends or something?" I asked. "They look close."

"Bloom should have nothing to do with him."

I frowned. "Why are we watching this?"

"I want to see how Bloom reacts."

"To what? What are they talking about?"

"I have a feeling my father is about to make him an offer."

"What does that mean?"

"Long story," Evan said. I stood with him, staring blankly while Rabbi Bloom made a concerted effort to maintain an expressionless face as Julian whispered. After a minute or so, however, Rabbi Bloom began blinking unnaturally, almost as if in involuntary recognition. Seeing this, Evan nodded and turned away. "Need a ride home?"

"I walked."

"Why don't you join me for a drink. Maybe I'll explain then."

"I, um, I think I'll stick around a bit longer," I said, awkward at the thought of revealing my motivation for remaining behind.

Rabbi Bloom locked eyes with Evan. Blood drained from Rabbi Bloom's face; he whispered hurriedly to Julian and started in our direction. Yet Evan, without another word, disappeared into the exit, leaving Rabbi Bloom behind to struggle against the crowd.

I lingered awkwardly in my row, watching as the room emptied, hoping to catch Sophia on her way out. Davis, wearing oversized coattails, introduced me to his father, and I stood idly by as they worked themselves into a fiery debate over whether Watergate catalyzed the millennial obsession with high school internships on the Hill. I excused myself and tried inching toward Sophia, who briefly met my eyes from afar, but I was quickly swallowed by Eddie and Cynthia. Just as I finally broke free—after doing my best to offer handshakes, receive kisses to the cheek, present absentminded impressions of Zion Hills—Sophia was whisked away by her mother to meet a bald man in a garish suit. I conceded defeat and left.

—

WEDNESDAY AFTERNOON, FOLLOWING AN IMPROMPTU quiz on the Golden Age in early Muslim Spain for which I was wildly unprepared (Mr. Harold grinning vengefully when we turned our papers in), Mrs. Janice announced over the intercom that sixth period was canceled and that all grades were to file quietly into the assembly hall. Rabbi Feldman greeted us at the door, instructing us to quickly and respectfully find seats. Sitting onstage beside Rabbi Bloom was none other than Julian Stark, dressed in a pin-striped blazer, legs crossed, fingering his phone, whispering to Rabbi Bloom.

"What is this?" I asked Noah. I looked around the room for Evan. "What's he doing here?"

Noah fidgeted with his collar. "You don't know what today is?"

"No?"

"It's been a full year," Noah said, dropping his voice further. Julian, catching Noah's gaze, bent his head in recognition. Noah nodded politely. "Today is Evan's mother's yahrzeit."

Amir slumped into the seat on my left and leaned over me toward Noah. "How's this going to work?" he asked, covering his mouth. "This'll be excruciating."

"Yeah, well, not if he's not here," Noah said, still searching for Evan.

Finally, just as the room filled and Rabbi Feldman went to close the door, Evan and Oliver stumbled in, red-eyed and dazed. Evan stopped in place at the sight of his father. Rabbi Feldman, after hesitating momentarily, wrapped Evan—face slackened, body stiffened in surprise—in a bear hug before letting him pass.

"Good God," Amir said, clasping his neck, "they're high, aren't they?"

Evan and Oliver took seats in the very last row. Rabbi Bloom, upon seeing Evan present, finally stood, turned on the microphone and cleared his throat.

"Thank you all for coming," he said tenderly. He faced Julian, who nodded in approval. Rabbi Bloom turned back to his audience. "One year ago today, Zion Hills lost one of its most magnificent residents. Caroline Stark, wife to Julian Stark, mother to Evan Stark, was a brilliant woman: an accomplished physicist, a leader in the community, dedicated to gender equality, to human compassion, to learning and, above all, to family." I stole a side-eyed glance at Evan: tight-jawed, expressionless, eyes dark and unblinking. "Parsha Chaya Sarah emphasizes the ethics of grief. We are to come together, as Avraham Avinu did, *lispode vi'livkosah*, to mourn and to wail, to eulogize and to weep. Ours is a tradition that embraces the emotional vitality of the human spirit, that demands we reckon properly with loss. Gemara Shabbat teaches that attendees at a funeral are charged with shedding tears, and that such people are forgiven for all their sins. Why?

Because an emotional life doesn't just make us human, it solidifies our reality of being created Imago Dei, B'tzelem Elohim, in the image of God. As we learn in Gemara Sotah, worshipping Hashem—walking in His ways, cleaving to Him in all aspects of life—amounts to imitating Him. How do we do so? By emulating the Divine Attributes. By comforting mourners. By offering solace and love."

He surveyed the room. Handwringing, head bowing, gentle sniffling. Noah had his face in a tissue. Sophia had her face in her hands. Niman had been reduced to tears, despite my suspicion that she had never actually met Caroline Stark. Evan, however, remained perfectly stoical, even as Oliver, visibly panicking at the necessity of expressing some semblance of warmth, finally gritted his teeth and awkwardly placed his hand upon Evan's shoulders, only to immediately withdraw and mumble an apology.

"Later this year, you'll learn how Gemara Berachot describes Rav's vision of Olam HaBa: a world without earthly burdens, a world without hatred, a world where the righteous wear crowns and bask in kedusha. All those who knew Caroline Stark live with confidence that she is crowned among the righteous. For Caroline's life was always devoted to others. Before beginning her doctorate at Stanford, she spent two years in South America, building homes, planting crops, teaching children. As a scientist, she encouraged young girls to become involved in her field. Upon moving to South Florida, she was a backbone of the community, constantly volunteering with underserved students, even as she battled illness. She led an exceptional life and raised a brilliant and, above all, fundamentally good son"—a brief pause, his eyes on Evan—"of whom I am immensely and continually proud. Alcibiades, eulogizing his teacher, praised three things: Socrates' resolve, valor and originality. These three qualities, integral to Caroline's character, remain equally applicable to her son." The room tipped into sobs.

"To commemorate this yahrzeit, as well as all for which Caroline Stark stood, I now welcome Mr. Julian Stark for a special announcement." Rabbi Bloom pivoted toward Evan's father. "Julian?"

Julian stood rigidly, shook Rabbi Bloom's hand. He rubbed his clean-shaven chin, offering a diffident smile. "Firstly, thank you all for having me and, oh—" He pulled back, grimacing, realizing he'd spoken too loudly into the microphone. "Sorry. Okay. Thanks also, Rabbi Bloom, longtime friend of the family, for sharing such thoughtful words." He waited for a round of light applause. Eventually, catching on, we clapped clumsily, at which point he ungracefully cleared his throat. "I'm here to announce a new program I'm starting in memory of my late wife. These last years have been difficult, to say the least, for my son and for me. Caroline was sick a long time. She fought and she fought, but she was suffering and—well, now I know she is, at last, at peace." A strained smile: he squirmed on his feet. "Caroline was tremendously talented. I took the more lucrative finance route but she chose physics, because science was her first and most enduring love. She especially valued sharing this love with young women. And so, I think it's only fitting that I create the Caroline Stark Initiative to actively facilitate greater female participation in the sciences. We'll provide grants for research projects, mentorship from local college professors, summer internship placements, support groups, whatever. No expense will be withheld. That's—that's my promise in Caroline's name." He was enjoying himself now, loosening his posture, raising his voice over another round of applause. "This upcoming summer, additionally, we'll build a state-of-the-art science lab, named for Caroline." Even more applause, this time led by Rabbi Bloom, whose own gaze was averted to the floor. "My vision is to do everything in my power to ensure that Caroline's name lives on and that the causes she believed in—"

Julian fumbled the microphone. I twisted in my seat to see Evan storming from the hall. Whispers, people moving about in their rows. Oliver, blinking in confusion, tried mouthing to Noah, uncertain whether he was supposed to follow Evan. Julian, mortified, turned to Rabbi Bloom, who sprung to his feet, urging us to retake our seats. And then Sophia, eliciting sharp gasps, sprinted into the aisle and out the door.

—

WE DARTED UP TO THE balcony after the assembly's awkward conclusion—Rabbi Bloom hastily dismissing us, Julian lingering onstage, conferring furiously with Rabbi Bloom—expecting to find Evan, but he wasn't there. Leaning over the terrace, Amir pointed out the absence of the parking lot's lone Aston Martin. My heart hammered at the thought that Sophia had disappeared with him.

Noah checked his phone for a message from Evan. Nothing. "Think he went home?"

Amir shook his head. "Can't imagine he's going to want to face Julian right now."

"Jesus," Noah muttered.

I was still searching for signs of Sophia below. "Can someone explain what just happened?"

Amir looked uncomfortably at Noah and Oliver. Noah nodded at him. "There are . . . rumors, let's call them, about what happened between Evan's parents."

Oliver snorted. "Rumors? Let's not whitewash it. Julian's a piece of shit and everyone knows it."

"There was always tension between Caroline and Julian," Amir explained. "Even when we were little we could sense it. Stolen glares. Little remarks. Hushed conversations in the kitchen while we were in the other room."

"My mom was pretty tight with Caroline," Noah cut in. "Smartest person she ever met, my mom always says. She noticed things weren't entirely . . . cohesive in that house."

"I mean, you must've picked up on some of it during the speech," Amir said. "The crap about career choices? The implication that she looked down on him for his job? I don't know, just seemed like there was always resentment on Julian's part for being made to feel guilty or lesser or something like that."

"And you have to understand, Drew, that Evan and his mom were ᴇ this." Noah wrapped two fingers around each other. "Ev worshipped her. They'd do everything together, they'd have these long debates nobody else could follow. She was the perfect mentor for him, and that definitely drove a wedge between Julian and Caroline. And when Evan lost her? It shattered him."

"Think that's why Evan and Sophia broke up?" Amir asked. I examined my sneakers so as not to display the extent to which my face was suddenly reorganizing itself into a canvas of unjustified hurt. "Things were just . . . falling apart?"

Noah shrugged noncommittally and looked away.

"Bottom line," Oliver said, cleaning his fingernails, "Julian's an animal."

I glanced down at the temple, where freshmen were tossing a football from the inner to the outer courtyard. "What does that mean?"

"It means his wife was freaking dying and that sleazebag didn't even care," Oliver said. "He was sleeping with anyone he could, barely hiding it. Right in her face, in her last months, while she was sick as a dog. Torturing her."

Noah shook his head. "Ev never ever speaks about it, but we all know."

"And so for Julian to play the part of bereaved widower, trying to fix everything with money?" Amir combed his beard with his fingertips. "You can see why that'd send Evan over the edge."

"At Sophia's recital," I said, putting pieces together, "Evan got really upset when he saw his dad with Rabbi Bloom."

"He probably figured they were planning something," Noah said. "Must've been beside himself that Bloom would let Julian in like this."

"Maybe Bloom doesn't know about these issues?" I asked, feeling inexplicably protective of Rabbi Bloom.

Oliver laughed. "Bloom and Evan? There aren't too many secrets there. But money talks, Drew. I'll vouch for that firsthand. Offer a sizable enough donation, and maybe your kid isn't expelled freshman year for hot boxing the first-floor bathroom."

Amir frowned. "That was *you*? I knew it."

For effect, Oliver pulled a ragged joint from his pocket. "Build a lab, create scholarships—how can a principal turn that down in good conscience?"

"It's almost kind of hard to blame Bloom, isn't it?" Noah said, pulling at the ends of his long, blond hair. "Like, he knows he can do a ton of good with that money, even if he's got to grit his teeth and shake hands with that asshole. He's acting in the best interest of Kol Neshama. As a—what's the word? Pecuniary?"

"Fiduciary," Amir said.

"Right, that."

"But Evan blames him," I said.

"He expects real loyalty from Bloom," Amir said. "They've been so close for such a long time, I guess Evan's taking it as a personal betrayal."

Noah nodded. "So therefore Evan is making Bloom choose between him and the best interest of the Academy?"

"Well," Amir said, "Bloom's made his choice, hasn't he?"

Noah tugged at his Adidas socks. "So, like, the shit on Donny's roof? Or throwing eggs? All this is to get revenge on Bloom and basically just make his life difficult?"

"I guess that's why he's running for president," I said.

The bell rang. Nobody moved. "Family," Amir finally said. "It can really mess us up, can't it?"

—

ELECTIONS WERE HELD BEFORE SUKKOT break. It was a chaotic stretch, Rosh Hashanah bleeding into Yom Kippur, our classwork disrupted. ("How the hell will we get anything done with another holiday every five minutes?" Dr. Flowers thundered, as if we were responsible for the timing of God's revelations.) Presidential campaigns, meanwhile, reached a feverish pitch. Davis circulated a five-page manifesto ("A spectre is haunting Kol Neshama—the spectre of a lazy education . . .") and Amir began tutoring underclassmen in exchange for votes. Evan did little, though The Rebellion posters resurfaced on occasion, something he denied doing himself. And, just days before the race, a fourth candidate emerged: Sophia Winter.

"Sophia," I called out, catching her at the end of biology. "Rumor has it you're running."

She turned. "Why do you look so shocked?"

"Not at all, I—"

She tugged at the straps of her backpack. "I mean, I don't think this race needs to be a boys' club affair, do you?"

"Wait, no, of course not—"

"So," she said, daring me with her eyes, "what's the question?"

"Nothing," I said lamely. "I guess—I just didn't know you were interested in that. But I'm excited for you."

"Well, I've been convinced," she said briskly, breaking away to make her next class. "Now I want it." The thought of her sprinting after Evan made its way unpleasantly through my mind. When she arrived at the classroom door, however, she turned once more. "But Hamlet?"

"Yes?"

"You're voting for me," she said, disappearing into calculus.

—

ELECTION DAY. EACH CANDIDATE WAS to give a short pitch before the student body voted. I took a seat in the back of the assembly hall. Kayla, to my surprise, plumped down beside me. "All right if I sit here?"

"Yeah," I said, "of course."

"Lovely. Just wanted to be sure you're okay being seen with me."

"What're you talking about?"

She shrugged. "Sometimes I get the distinct sense you prefer speaking only in private."

I felt strangely ashamed at the prospect of having offended her. "I have no idea why you'd say that."

I watched underclassmen filter into the hall. Oliver walked by, stationing himself toward the front. He presented me with a look of severe disapproval when he saw I was with Kayla.

"See? That right there," Kayla said. "Kind of what I'm referring to."

"He's just being weird," I said unconvincingly. "He does that to me all the time."

"Sounds like a great guy. Real mensch."

"A mensch he's not, but he means well," I said, mostly attempting to persuade myself. I realized I sounded awfully like Noah when he was defending Evan. "At least I think he does."

"You know who I like? Amir. He's the only one in your group who acknowledges my existence, though probably because he wants to know my grades. But still. It's something. I think I'm voting for him."

"Yeah, I mean, he is great."

"Still. I have a slight feeling I know who you're supporting."

"*I* don't even know who I'm—"

"Ari, Ari." She patted my arm. "Please. You're voting for Sophia. That's the one certainty in this entire school. Not that it matters. It's inevitable he'll win."

"Who?"

"Evan, of course."

"Why do you say that?"

She looked at me as if I were stupid. "Don't you think?"

"I don't know."

"Look around the room. They love him, they fear him, but more than anything they want to be him."

I felt strangely deflated. I opened my mouth to object but stopped myself. It was true. Effortlessly brilliant, startlingly defiant and, as had quickly been established throughout my first weeks in Zion Hills, undeniably attractive: Evan, though intimidating, seemed almost universally revered. It was difficult to imagine him losing.

Rabbi Bloom ascended the stage and raised his hands for silence. "Quiet please, ladies and gentlemen, for the candidates to whom we owe respect. The rules are simple. Each candidate has three minutes to best represent his or her ideology. These speeches have been approved by the administration"—his gaze landed on Evan, sitting in the first row, as if to issue a silent warning—"and candidates are expected not to improvise. Lots have been drawn to determine the sequence of speeches. So, without further ado, I invite Mr. Aaron Davis to speak first."

Davis smiled broadly and raised his fist, despite tepid applause. Wearing an old-fashioned corduroy suit, he accepted the microphone and gestured for someone in the back to begin playing "Battle Hymn of the Republic" from an iPhone. "Ladies and gents of this fine institution, as literary editor of the yearbook, I stand before you today much like Lincoln did in Gettysburg . . ."

"Has he always been like this?" I whispered to Kayla.

"Put it this way," she said, leaning into my ear, "in third grade, he entered the school Purim costume contest as Henry Clay."

". . . as school president I'll seek knowledge, which, as is the case with all endeavors, requires a chemistry of Aristotelian virtues and an impeccable grasp of Tory political theory. I vow to sow virtue, not the mindless fun promised by my opponents . . ." He rambled on, undeterred by growing laughter, until Rabbi Bloom, watching for time, placed a forceful hand on Davis' back.

"Thank you, Mr. Davis, that was quite . . . rousing," Rabbi Bloom said, signaling for the hymn to be cut off. "Our next candidate is Mr. Evan Stark. Evan, we look forward to hearing your preapproved speech."

Evan rose slowly, glared coolly at Rabbi Bloom as he accepted the microphone and then broke into a smile. "With deep apologies to Rabbi Bloom," he said, inverting his pockets, "I've misplaced my speech and must instead speak from the heart." Small laughs broke out. Rabbi Bloom, standing at the foot of the stage, paled. "Let's keep this brief," he said, pacing about. "Initially I had no intention of running for president. I was content to watch others serve ineffectively—"

"Ad hominem!" Davis cried, leaping from his seat.

"—until I realized this would endorse a certain status quo." He trailed off, his gaze meeting Rabbi Bloom's. "And that's something I can't do. Why? Because our current way of life is corrupted. We attend a school supposedly dedicated to moral values. And yet, I ask you, what happens behind closed doors? How often do we see shuls turned into miniature kingdoms controlled by those seeking power? How often do we see dishonorable people achieve influence and piety through financial success while the righteous suffer and lose and—" He paused for a moment too long. At first I assumed this was merely for dramatic effect, until I recognized uncharacteristic vulnerability in his eyes. He looked, to my disbelief, as if he might cry. "And die of cancer," he said firmly. He took an extra breath, banishing that look of undisguised humanness, even as an air of cold shock settled over his audience. "How often do we witness the miracles we pray about three times each day? How often, may I ask, do we take seriously the notion that belief—real belief—ought to survive the crucible of doubt?

"And so, I stand before you without offering a commitment to liberalism or Torah or, for that matter, the administration. What I offer, what I will continue to offer irrespective of today's outcome, is resistance. Integrity. Action. And I do this because the Academy's operations should not be allowed to prove inconsistent with the basic religious values we've been spoon-fed all our lives. What I'm calling for is not simply transparency, but a new paradigm of authenticity. A paradigm in which we finally take matters into our own hands and make our own moral judgments. In which we expose all that is hypocritical—"

"That's quite enough, Mr. Stark," Rabbi Bloom said, snatching the microphone. But it was over: Evan, face blank, half bowing, had won the crowd. The room erupted into boisterous applause. It took several minutes to restore order, especially with Oliver springing from chair to chair, flinging confetti into the air. (Rabbi Feldman, finally, escorted him out.) Amir, legs crossed, turned green while he waited for the commotion to dissolve. Sophia, maintaining the intensity of her gaze, stared at her wrists.

She fought admirably. She likened the school to a sukkah, protecting and nurturing us while we adorned it. I tried catching her eye, though succeeded only in briefly meeting Rabbi Bloom's wandering gaze. ("Just *flawless*, isn't she?" Kayla whispered unhappily into my ear, her tone loosely accusatory. "Yeah," I told her, "actually I think she might be.") Amir, on the other hand, was entirely unnerved. Certainly he was equipped for leadership—he was intelligent, he was intensely responsible—but he was hopelessly overshadowed by Evan. He kept losing his train of thought, sputtering on with some lackluster analogy likening the Academy to ancient Egyptian architectural principles. He was still struggling to put it together when Rabbi Bloom mercifully called time. Amir descended from the stage with his head bent in defeat.

Voting stations were set up in the parking lot. I made my way to a booth, having quickly separated from Kayla, and found myself behind Amir at the back of the line.

"It was a fine speech," I said meekly. "Really."

Amir shook his head, biting his lower lip. "He ruined me."

I wanted to comfort him but couldn't think of anything effective. "I'm voting for you," I finally said, when it was my turn. It felt like the right thing to do.

He nodded, said nothing. I stepped into the booth, circled Sophia's name and waited for Noah by his car.

—

I WAS RELYING ON VACATION to catch up on the workload, which, with the onslaught of holidays, was teetering on disastrous. Dr. Flowers was attacking our curriculum at a breakneck pace—"Kindly do us a favor and leave if you don't like it," she'd warn, usually while staring forbiddingly in my direction—hurling us into the lovely world of fixed osmium tetroxide membranes. I retained little from these lessons, and would turn frequently to Sophia in desperation. "Dr. Winter," I'd burst out, hurrying after her in the hallways, dodging flustered underclassmen busy conducting double takes at the sight of me trailing Sophia Winter, "did you happen to catch that?"

Playfully, hiding a smirk, she'd accelerate her stride. "Which part, Hamlet?"

"How about every last bit," I'd say, panting to keep pace, breaking into an unabashed smile. "I didn't understand a single word."

In math, however, my grades were improving steadily under Kayla's guidance. My initial distaste for her had given way quickly to genuine appreciation. It was rejuvenating to befriend someone who also laid claim to neither unimaginable wealth nor unassailable beauty. Over lunches together we'd dissect recent gossip ("can you please explain how Evan hasn't been expelled or promoted to Head Ubermensch by now," Kayla joked, long after my math notes had been returned to my backpack) and throughout the school day we'd trade droll texts:

was just asked by remi y i didn't dye my hair.
or cut it. or just do something to "relieve
the aesthetic nightmare"—didn't know she
knew that word

> *Yikes. What did you say?*

that i'm auditioning 4 the role of simone weil

> *I suspect she did not find that funny.*

she blinked 4 several seconds & then told
me i'm much better off replicating simone
adamley's look

> *Who is that?*

from ferris bueller. girl who hears from
sister's bf's bro's gf etc. that ferris is sick.
astonishingly apt response, right?

> *I have no clue what you're talking about.*

good grief

Generally, I wondered why nobody else seemed to worry about schoolwork. Amir's work ethic was legendary, his extracurricular life equally impressive—he headed the Debate Society, founded the *Journal for Business Affairs*—and any anxiety on his part exclusively concerned how others compared to him. Noah hardly ever mentioned the workload, besides asking for my help on the occasional paper. Oliver, of course, cared little about so much as completing homework, shielded as he was by his parents' colossal annual donations. And then there was Evan, whose brilliance was unquestioned, even feared.

"Ev used to be first, you know," Noah once revealed during a car ride home.

Briefly, I touched my cheek to the burning window. "First in what?"

"The whole freaking class."

"Evan?" I knew he'd routinely receive A+ marks, even on tests he took while impaired, but his apathy rivaled Oliver's, making it difficult to believe he could sustain pace with the machinelike dedication of students like Kayla, Amir and Davis.

"Yup," Noah said quietly. "Up until, you know. Until his mother passed."

After a respectful pause: "What's he ranked now?"

"Dunno. Fifth? Sixth?"

"Wow." I didn't want to think about my own ranking. "Who's ahead of him?"

"Me."

"Really?"

"In my dreams. I know Davis is third. Amir, bless his little jealous heart, is second. Take a wild guess who's first."

I hesitated. My cheek singed.

Noah laughed. "Say it."

"Of course she's first," I said.

"Your girl's impressive. But I bet he could still come back, if he cared. Ev is frightening like that."

"What does that mean?"

"How his brain works," he said. "One day you'll see."

English was my lone bright spot. Mrs. Hartman had finally returned our *Iliad* papers. *An impressive start*, she wrote in thick, green ink. *I look forward to reading future work. Grade: A.*

"I knew I chose the right tutor!" Noah said, breaking into dance, thus infuriating Amir.

Amir ripped my essay from my hands. "An A," he hounded, "or an A-minus?"

"An A," I said uncomfortably, finally beginning to resent his academic hypersensitivity.

"But nobody gets an A from Hartman." He said so too loudly, in earshot of others. Sophia, standing several feet away talking to Rebecca, turned to observe me. I cringed. "Especially not on the first paper!"

"Well, I did," Sophia said, nodding in my direction. "But welcome to the club, Hamlet."

My mother was even happier than I was. To her, the mark validated years of effort, unappreciated by my father, to save my intelligence by making me seek refuge in the library. "I'm *beyond* proud," she said, overruling my objections to taping the paper to the refrigerator. I couldn't blame her for her enthusiasm, given that I gave her few other occasions to *shep nachas*. This paper, sadly enough, represented the first semblance of achievement we'd ever known, all the while assuring her that normalizing to Zion Hills—returning, in some way, to her life before my father—was still possible.

—

SUKKOT FELL ON SHABBAT. I spent Saturday sitting in the sukkah, agonizing over my biology textbook while admiring my mother's many decorations: dangling apples, clusters of flashing grapes, colorful paper chains, weathered Hebrew posters from preschool. Unlike Sukkot up north, where we sat cozily in pre-winter air, Sukkot in Florida bordered on torturous. Down here, as it turned out, confining yourself to prehistoric huts, with sunlight soaking through a bamboo rooftop, inspired little more than heavy perspiration, mutant-sized mosquito bites and, on balance, physical misery. Despite my father's insistence that we do everything in the sukkah ("*you shall dwell in the sukkah for seven days*,'" he'd scold, doused in sweat, flirting with heatstrokes, "dwell, not lounge, and that means eat, study, talk, sleep"), I gave up after a few hours and retreated for air-conditioning. I again tried studying on Saturday night, declining to join Noah and the others for drunk bowling, though ended up asleep before eleven, my twenty-pound textbook rising in harmony with my breathing. On Sunday, I skipped dinner so as to avoid my father, who wanted a definitive answer as to whether I was attending Meir's upcoming bar mitzvah. By nine, I conceded defeat at the hands of my geometry homework and shuffled across the street.

"Ari!" Noah answered the door with a Corona in hand. I submitted myself for a fraternal half-hug. "Where've you been?"

"Trying to work. Failing miserably."

"Dude, this is vacation. We're celebrating how our ancestors trekked through deserts! We're waving phallic symbols! You should be letting loose. You work too much."

"I don't work enough, actually."

"Well," he said, "now's a good time for a break. Parents are out and the girls are over."

Noah led me into the living room, where Rebecca was lying upside down on the enormous couch. "Ari," she said, grinning. "Greetings."

I pretended to turn my face upside down. "Hey Rebs."

She kicked her feet around in the air to right herself. "Excellent timing. We're looking to make moves."

"Who else is here?" I asked, already knowing the answer.

"Ms. Mozart is in the ladies' room," Rebecca said, immediately surveying my facial reactions, which probably did not disappoint.

"Want a beer, Drew?" Noah called from the kitchen. I could hear him digging raucously through his snack cabinet, which, once opened, typically vomited some assortment of chocolate, sour candies and half-vinegar-half-jalapeño chips.

A voice down the hallway: sweet, stomach-turning. "Doesn't beer ever repulse you? Maybe, just once, try a proper cocktail? Ah, Hamlet's here." Sophia emerged, her mouth assuming one of its sly contortions. She wore a white tank top tucked into jeans and her hair in a simple braid. Something in my chest somersaulted. "Decide what we're doing tonight. We're dying of boredom."

Noah returned from the kitchen, a bag of miniature pretzels under his arm. "They find my house boring."

"We can't *always* just lie around on your couch, admiring your mom's cookbooks," Rebecca said. "Though I could go for some of that banana cake from Yom Tov, if she froze any of it."

Sophia perched lazily beside me on the couch, bouncing her legs slightly so that her right knee, exposed in ripped jeans, rested gently against my left leg. "This is what becomes of us in adulthood? Supreme boredom? Drifting in and out of rooms, asking what we'll do tonight, year after year?"

"Hashem Yisbarach, I really hope not," Rebecca said. "Could you turn down the morbid tonight, Soph?"

Sophia turned to me. "Ari doesn't find me morbid, do you?"

I shrugged. "No more than the next guy."

"And for your information, life doesn't end at graduation." Rebecca gathered Noah's head in her lap, though only after flinging away the salty remains of the pretzels. "It just starts over, doesn't it, Noah?"

Sophia's knee stopped moving. I could feel it balanced against my calf, though dared not look down to see for myself. "Okay, Ari. Save us, please."

"Well, uh," I said, groping for an idea. I realized, pathetically, that I had no grasp whatsoever on what was considered fun. "Yeah, I mean, maybe we can—"

Sophia was smiling fixedly. "Aren't you supposed to be relatively articulate?"

I turned my attention to one of the room's glass cabinets, crammed with sky-scraping basketball trophies. How odd it must feel, I found myself thinking, to be so objectively *good* at something. "Not when I'm so rudely interrupted."

Noah yawned. "What about Ocean Drive?"

"Boring," Sophia said.

"Design District?"

"No," Rebecca snorted. "Please no."

"Fine," Noah said. "Should we bite the bullet and get a table at LIV? We can drop Oliver's name."

Sophia shook her head. "Absolutely not."

"Nikki Beach?"

Rebecca pulled on Noah's collar. "You really think Ari wants to go clubbing?"

I reddened but didn't argue otherwise.

"Cool," Noah said. "I give up."

"How about we get dinner and call it a night," Rebecca said.

"Not if it's that repulsive burger place," Sophia said.

Rebecca frowned. "I kind of like those burgers. So where, then?"

"What's the name of the Japanese one? Shalom L'Japan? Sushi Olam HaBa? Whatever its latest name is."

"I'm down," Noah said. "They have that all-you-can-eat deal."

"Do you really want mercury poisoning?" Rebecca said. "You're not having that."

"Watch me."

"I'll tell Rocky on you."

"Drew, end our misery," Noah said. "Vote for sushi or burgers."

"Nameless sushi it is," I said. "What Sophia said."

"You do know you don't need to agree with *everything* she wants, right?" Rebecca said.

Sophia took my hand, hoisted me from the couch. "Sure he does." Her hand felt smooth, warm. "Shall we?"

It was a cozy, almost upscale restaurant: white tablecloths, a discolored shade of red on the walls. We sat out back, overlooking a canal, surrounded by yachts.

"Let's take a boat out this week," Rebecca said absently, scanning the menu. "We never do that anymore."

"Remi's motorboat is fun," Sophia said. "We can take that."

We ordered a behemoth sushi platter and Noah, with the help of his fake ID, coaxed the waiter into bringing us Cabernet Sauvignon. Mr. Carraway, however, remained hidden in my wallet.

"So," Rebecca said, picking at a rainbow roll. "Where are the others tonight? That Three Amigos bar?"

"Probably busy with whatever degenerates do." Sophia held her chopsticks with impeccable form. I nervously dropped mine, submerging a piece of salmon-avocado in soy sauce. I tried probing for it, but the piece unraveled. "Hamlet, your sushi dexterity is appalling."

After we paid, the check considerably more expensive than I anticipated, emptying whatever was left in my wallet, Noah and Rebecca excused themselves to wander the docks. They left us with a wink.

Sophia drained the last of her wineglass. "Left alone again."

"What is this, the third time now?" I said. And then, stupidly: "It's a *chazakah*."

She smirked, leaning her head to the side, looking me over. "Finish your wine," she decided. "Then we shall walk."

It was cool and still out, a gentle breeze rippling the water. We sketched long circles around the dock, admiring the yachts, doused in bright, humming lights.

"Last we spoke, before the awfulness with the eggs," Sophia said, ending our silence, "you remember what I told you?"

"How could I forget?" I surveyed my outfit, wondered whether there was any possibility that it failed to register in Sophia's mind, which actually would have constituted a not insignificant victory, blending in among what was fashionably inoffensive. "You said I didn't belong."

"I'm beginning to rethink that."

"Really? I hope not."

"Why's that?"

I plunged my hands into my pockets. "You'll like me less."

Light poured off us, crowning Sophia in Technicolor. "You know

I saw you, right? At the recital. You left without saying hello. Nobody told you it's impolite to leave without praising the pianist?"

I laughed. "My apologies for being uncouth. The pianist was busy being swallowed by rabid fans."

"I appreciated that you came," she said quietly. "I did."

"Well, you were amazing. I'm glad I was there."

"Ari," she said earnestly, as if something pressing had only just occurred to her, "I don't even know what you're doing next year."

"That'd put you in good company," I said.

"You don't have ideas?"

"I'm not sure." I grimaced at how serious, how unnatural, my voice sounded. "I mean, college, I suppose."

"You suppose? Of course you'll be in college," she said. "You've begun applications, haven't you?"

I admitted I hadn't. This made her recoil. "You'll study literature," she said, chewing her lower lip. Pink-cheeked. Sharp-nosed. Misty-eyed. "Yes, perfect, it's decided, your say in the matter is no more. You'll go to a great liberal arts school, you'll study English, you'll write some ridiculous, overly idealistic dissertation on Nabokov's Hamletic anxiety of influence, dedicated to one S. Winter, and you'll veer far, far away from biology."

"That so?" My cheeks flushed. "You won't want me bothering you with science questions?"

"Good point. Okay, I'll allow a single biology class. But only the one."

"And what about you?" I asked. "What's your master plan?"

"Master plan? I seem like I have such a thing?"

"Yeah, actually," I said. "You of all people absolutely do."

She hesitated, though instinctively I knew this was for effect, that she absolutely intended to open herself to me. "I want to go to Juilliard," she said. "I've wanted to go ever since I was a little girl. But my parents want Penn."

"Why's that?"

"They met there. Fell in love there. Had their wedding there. It's where they want me to be a premed and meet my spouse, just like they did."

We stopped walking, peered silently into the water. Lightly, she ran her fingers through her hair. What I wanted was to confirm for her that this arrangement seemed unfair, particularly given the simple and indisputable fact that she was a singular talent. Instead, too neutrally, I asked: "So what'll you do?"

"I don't know."

"Well," I said, "you'll just get into both. Then you'll decide."

"I'm not sure I can."

"You don't think you could get into Penn?"

"I do think I can get into Penn." She said so confidently, though without haughtiness. Only people with absolute knowledge of their self-worth, I found myself deciding, are capable of appearing so effortlessly poised. "It's Juilliard I'm worried about."

"I don't think you need to worry. You're a prodigy."

She stiffened, leaning against the railing separating us from the water.

"What's wrong?" I asked.

"I despise that word."

"Really? If anyone ever called me a prodigy, I'd probably break out in dance."

A brief moment of wind tearing over water. Sophia shivered slightly. I wanted, more than anything, to hold her. "What makes you so confident in me?" she said.

"You're Sophia Winter." For weeks I'd been shouting her name in my head. In the safety of my interior life, her name conjured intimate worlds. It provided warmth, it induced euphoric helplessness. Her very name was an object of abstraction to which I tethered fever dreams I dared not pursue. Saying it aloud felt like relinquishing some secret.

"I'll end up in medical school," she said. "I know it. I'll end up like everyone else."

I prayed she couldn't see me reddening in the dark. "You're not like anyone else. Not remotely."

"My parents want me to be. I want to be. But unfortunately you're right. I'm not."

We walked onward again without speaking.

"What about your parents?" she asked, realizing I had either too much tact or too little audacity to challenge her previous statement. "What do they do?"

"My mother's a teacher," I said. "My father's an accountant."

"Really? I assumed he was a rabbi."

"He wishes."

She leaned toward me. Our hands, swinging at our sides, inadvertently brushed. "He's that religious?"

"He's extremely—serious, let's call it."

"But your mother?"

"Yeah, I mean, she is, too, though maybe not as much." Providing insight into my parents' spiritual lives would have been grounds for *kareth* back in Brooklyn. "She was raised differently."

"How was she raised?" Sophia asked. "The way we were?"

I tried imagining a childhood among my current friends. Would seventeen years of shared experience have altered my place in our hierarchy? Was it Brooklyn that made happiness feel permanently underemphasized, my relationship with my surroundings irreparably tenuous, or would I have felt such things, even worse things, living only in Zion Hills? What would it be like to unlearn loneliness? "You and I weren't raised the same."

She smiled knowingly. "Sorry, forgot for a moment." She clutched at her bare shoulders. "But they like it here, your parents?"

"My mom does," I said. "Actually, she loves it."

"I hear from Rebs that she's become fast friends with Cynthia."

"Yeah, she's pretty taken with her," I said. "The entire lifestyle here, really."

"What about your father?"

"I don't know." Then, rocking on my feet: "No, truthfully."

"And that's because—what?" she asked. "Because women wear pants? The school's coed? There's less Torah learning?"

"Yeah, partially. But I also think he misses being in a culture where everyone's constantly preoccupied with one thing."

"Fashion?"

I couldn't help but laugh. "Avodat Hashem. It's a difference in priority. Or obsession, maybe, I don't know. As in, do we consciously consecrate every element of our waking lives to growing closer to God, or do we live within a structure that allocates some time for worship, other time for existing in the greater world and then time for synthesizing the two."

She thought this over, though I sensed she was only pretending, that she had formulated a response immediately and was delaying for my sake. "Do you agree more with your mother or father?"

"I mean, coming here *was* a substantial culture shock."

"Certainly looked like it. But now?"

"I don't know," I said. "I guess I'm still figuring it out."

She grabbed my elbow so that we stopped walking. "I want you to tell me something."

"What?"

"Anything." Hands clasped together. Her right thumb probing her left wrist. Nervous blinking. "A secret."

"I don't have secrets," I said.

"We all have secrets. I want to hear something you've never told anyone."

I studied the discrete features of her face: her precise eyebrows, the faint lines in her forehead, the freckle below her left ear. I was so close to her that I could no longer really see her, so close to her that she was a blur of music, breathing, light. "My friends," I said quietly. "From Brooklyn. I don't like them."

Her look of utter calm disconcerted me. Should I ever receive the full glare of her attention, I knew then, I'd have no hope of hiding. "So?"

"What do you mean 'so'?"

She looked at me as if she were only peering into a mirror. "How long have you known them?"

"Only my entire life. They're supposed to be my best friends."

"People drift," she said, unimpressed. "Everyone drifts."

"But what if I never liked them," I said in a voice I didn't recognize. "What if sometimes I hated them. When I was with them I felt like I was by myself."

She looked at me, unblinking. "I know what it means to be alone."

A pause. "Well," I said, "your turn."

The night was beating heavily on us. Her gaze stayed on me, unfazed. "I wish this were a date."

The floor shifting beneath me, happiness ringing from all four corners of the earth. "I've never actually been on a date," I found myself admitting. I winced, waiting for the insult, but she remained still, observing gently. She was heart-wrenching, she was thoroughly unattainable. My knees, all at once, felt weak, as if I'd been walking for hours.

"I like that idea very much."

A couple approached from the distance, waving madly. "Thought we lost you," Noah called. "Let's get out of here."

—

"I APPRECIATE YOU COMING, PARTICULARLY during the holiday," Mrs. Ballinger said dryly. We were in her office, my parents on either side of me, everyone doing their best to smile sweetly. I'd been sitting in the dining room the night before, working through an unpalatable stretch of biology, when my mother interrupted to tell me the Academy had called to request a college guidance meeting.

"Must be a good sign," my mother said, beaming. "They wouldn't meet with just anyone, would they?"

"Actually they would," I said, imagining Mrs. Janice's Southern drawl on the other end of the phone. "In fact, they literally do."

"So. Ari." Mrs. Ballinger drummed her ring-laden fingers on her nearly empty desk. "You've had ample time to get acclimated since our previous conversation."

"Yes," I said after too long of a beat, realizing she expected her statement to elicit some response.

"And how have things been?"

"Better," I said evasively.

She peeked into a folder containing my grades. "Academically, too, you'd say?"

"For the most part."

My mother, to my left, shone with pride. "We're proud of how he's doing. I just have to say that, Mrs. Ballinger."

Mrs. Ballinger and I met eyes. "Yes," she said curtly. "Certainly be proud. Never an easy adjustment, particularly this late in the game. Still, I'd prefer to see some grades raised ever so slightly."

"Oh?" Now my mother looked distraught, as if she'd been told I was failing. My father, painfully polite, sulked silently. He had refused, at first, to attend the meeting, insisting that I ought to spend two years, at minimum, in a post–high school yeshiva before even considering pursuing a degree. This was what he'd done, he explained at length, and what the great majority of his family had done as well. My mother, however, won out.

"In biology," Mrs. Ballinger added quickly, recognizing my mother's distress. "That seems to be his most challenging class. His math has improved."

"But he did so beautifully on his English paper," my mother blurted.

Mrs. Ballinger smiled, amused. "So I've heard from Mrs. Hartman."

I perked up. "You did?"

"She told me at lunch the other day. She was highly complimentary, Ari. Unusually complimentary."

I felt a burst of gratitude for Mrs. Ballinger. My mother's face lit up once again, diffusing some atmospheric tension. Even my father nodded cautiously.

"Now. To the nitty-gritty." Mrs. Ballinger again surveyed my folder. "Have you begun considering particular colleges?"

We hesitated, nobody wanting to admit we hadn't so much as discussed a single school.

"Not extensively," I finally said.

"Not extensively," Mrs. Ballinger repeated. "Hm. And that means—"

I provided a meaningless shrug. "We've looked at only a few places."

She leaned forward at her desk. "And what have you in mind?"

"Somewhere with a strong liberal arts program," I said, echoing Sophia's words, impressing my mother. "I want to study literature."

"What's that?" my father piped up, unable to help himself. My mother countered with her finest death glare.

"Lovely," Mrs. Ballinger said, glancing curiously toward my father. "A premature decision, of course, but there are a number of wonderful liberal arts schools—"

"Which ones do you like?" my mother asked. "Stanford welcomes writers, don't they?"

"Stanford?" my father said. "That's one of those Ivies, yes?" I did a facepalm. My mother assumed a look of abject humiliation.

Mrs. Ballinger threw back her head, emitting a high-pitched, carefully restrained laugh. "That's really excellent, I'll need to jot that down for the book on college guidance I'm writing. But, yes, well, to your point, Mrs. Eden, I told Ari we'll need to stick to schools within the realm of possibility."

"Ivies are out of the question?" my mother asked, unable to disguise her disappointment. "All of them?" My heart broke, mostly for myself.

Mrs. Ballinger attempted an empathetic smile, only to pivot to an authoritative throat clearing. "Nothing is certain in admissions. It's all one big crapshoot. That said, I've been doing this twenty years. I've seen how things work."

"I see," my mother said, looking now to the carpeted floor.

"Legacy can help. Where did you two go?"

"Well," my mother said uncomfortably, "I started at Barnard."

"Excellent."

"But I transferred."

"To where?"

"Stern College."

"Yes, less helpful for Ari's cause."

"But I did earn a degree from Teachers College—so there's some legacy, isn't there?"

"Well, probably not much, to be brutally honest." Mrs. Ballinger shuffled papers. "And you, Mr. Eden?"

My father regarded her with unnecessary defiance, as if she were the person most responsible for tarnishing his son's mind with toxic secular ambitions. "Yeshiva."

"Yeshiva University? A great option I'm going to push for."

"No. I mean I went to yeshiva first."

"Oh. And afterward?"

"Queens."

"Okay, got it." She slid a paper across the desk. "I've prepared a list for you to research. I've organized schools by categories—reaches, possibilities, safeties." *Yeshiva University. The New School. Brooklyn College. Baruch.*

My heart sank. "Thank you."

"Let me also note I'm well aware of the difficulties in selecting a college as an Orthodox Jew. Finding the right campus with kosher food and prayer services and a social life and weekly Sabbath options—the whole nine yards. Rest assured, I've been there, done that many times over and am here to help."

"Yes, well, thank you again," I said politely, slightly bewildered. I imagined someone like Oliver laughing at receiving a speech about how to locate a minyan on campus. Then I imagined a world in which I told my parents I'd be attending school in a faraway land without any access to kashrut. I couldn't envision their reaction. "I appreciate that."

"Absolutely," she said cheerfully. "Now, lastly. Your meetings with Adam Bearman? How have they been? Productive?"

"He goes every other Sunday, you know," my mother said approvingly.

"Yeah, mostly productive," I lied. Bearman had been anything but helpful: during our most recent session, he had me accompany him to pick up bagels. ("New environments sometimes bolster productivity," he reasoned. "Plus I'm hungry as shit.")

"Marvelous. I want you taking that November SAT."

I stood to leave. "Sure."

"A fine boy you have, Mr. and Mrs. Eden," Mrs. Ballinger said unconvincingly, dismissing us for the next family.

—

THE LIST BOTHERED ME. Never was I under the impression that I was on the road to major academic achievement. Until now, in fact, I'd never so much as thought twice about college. And yet, I couldn't shake my lingering disappointment. I knew I couldn't compete with my friends: Amir was hell-bent on emulating his grandfather and studying at MIT; Noah was beginning to flirt with recruiters at Northwestern, where his father ran track and field; Evan could write his own ticket. And I wasn't exactly opposed to the schools Mrs. Ballinger had suggested; for the most part, I hadn't even heard of them. What bothered me was the thought that this was it: a single year of exhilarating, brightly lit dreams, and then an immediate return to my old life— slinking back into my cupboard-sized Brooklyn room, falling back in with Shimon Levy, morphing slowly into my father. I could not bear coming face-to-face with a life I now knew I wanted, only to have to give it up.

I spent the remainder of the break this way: inexplicably crushed by college prospects, obsessing over my night with Sophia, stumbling halfheartedly through schoolwork. We had a couple of miserable basketball practices, and I met once with Bearman, who, after mocking me for observing Sukkot ("you mean to tell me you believe

God descended on our forefathers and beseeched them to shake tree branches?"), gave me a full-length practice test on which I didn't do very well. When I got home I told my mother my projected scores. For the first time in a long while she embraced me, hiding her look of sympathy. She insisted, with her arms around me, that I was the most intelligent person she knew.

—

WE WERE IN TANACH ON our first day back when we heard a gentle knock. Rabbi Feldman, mid-sentence, stopped lecturing on why we read about Ezekiel's valley of dry bones on Pesach. Rabbi Bloom hovered at the doorframe.

"Please pardon me, Rabbi." He cleared his throat officiously. "I was hoping to briefly borrow three of your students. Mr. Davis, Mr. Samson, Mr. Stark, a word, if you will."

Through the window I could see Sophia loitering in the hallway. Davis and Amir stumbled out, looking grim. Evan went last, wearing the ghost of a triumphant smile while making a concerted effort to avoid Sophia's eyes. A strange unease settled over us, even after the candidates disappeared from view.

After a few short minutes the door reopened. Davis, hands probing the pockets of his tweed sport coat, looked dumbfounded. Amir refused to lift his head.

"Where's Ev?" Oliver piped up.

"Quiet, Bellow!" Rabbi Feldman snapped, more from habit than from anger. He bore his own look of confusion.

Evan returned with the period nearly over, dark-blue eyes aflame. When the bell rang no one stood to leave. Rabbi Feldman dawdled, shuffling lesson notes. Eventually, biting back his own curiosity, he nodded and left us alone.

"Well?" Oliver said, breaking the silence. "Anyone have the decency to tell us what happened?"

Evan slung his backpack over his shoulder and headed for the door. "She won," he said, leaving the room.

—

"YOU DON'T *REALLY* THINK HE fixed it, Ev?" Noah was saying, looking skeptical. We were on the balcony, beneath a ragged, violet sky. A drizzle had begun to fall.

"Pretty implausible," Oliver said brightly. "Bloom loves you too damn much."

"I don't know why you guys are even remotely surprised." Amir was doing something where he'd pretend to receive a text, spin his phone over his legs and then repeat the process anew. "Did you think Evan Stark was capable of conceding defeat?"

Calmer now, stretching his legs, Evan shrugged. "My position remains unchanged."

"But, like, what's your evidence?" Noah asked.

"I know how Bloom works," Evan said. "I could read between the lines."

"Come off it," Amir said gruffly. "Davis, Sophia and I were standing right there. He didn't say shit."

"You were," Evan said, "until he dismissed you all back to class."

"So he had you hang back, alone, to hint at some conspiracy?" Amir on the floor, back against the wall, shook his head irritably. "Or maybe you expect us to believe he actually came right out and admitted he fixed the election against you?"

"Well, I wasn't alone at first," Evan said. "But yes. More or less."

"Ah," Amir said, laughing spitefully. "More or less. He communicated it wordlessly in your shared unspoken language, is that it?"

"What do you mean you weren't alone?" Noah asked.

"She was there, too," Evan said.

I kicked at an empty Zephyrhills bottle with my sneaker. "Sophia?"

Evan rummaged in his backpack for a joint. He lit, took a sharp drag, sent a jet of smoke in my direction. "That's right, Eden."

Noah glanced my way when he thought I wasn't looking. "Why would he want you there with Sophia, of all people?"

"Bloom, if you haven't yet realized, enjoys pushing me," Evan said.

Oliver laughed. "To try and get you guys to make out? Sorry, that was Freud speaking. I think I meant make up."

Evan blew more smoke. "Just understand that he wanted me to lose and her to win."

"But why?" I asked, more frustrated than I ought to have been. "What's his motivation?"

"To humble me. To challenge me."

Amir stood. "If this was actually fixed, what makes you think *you* would've won?"

"I mean, let's be reasonable," Oliver said. "You saw how the crowd reacted to that speech?"

Amir flashed Oliver the finger.

"Besides," Oliver continued, "Bloom knows he can't control Evan."

"Why Sophia, then?" Noah asked. "Why not Davis or Amir?"

"Because he knew it'd hurt," Evan said.

"Bloom's trying to hurt *you*?" Oliver snorted. "Get the fuck outta here."

"Maybe she just beat you." I found myself inexplicably on my feet. I resisted the urge to sit back down. "Maybe people respect her. Maybe they didn't want you."

Evan placed his palms in the air. "Maybe, Eden."

We were silent until the bell rang, concluding lunch. Amir moved for the classroom window. "I just have to say—did I not warn you? Did I not tell you this would happen?"

Evan blinked. "What you told me, actually, was that Davis would win."

"No," Amir said, "I told you we'd both lose. I asked you not to do it."

"And I told you I needed it."

"But why the fuck do *you* need it?" Amir shouted. Several sophomores in the outer courtyard of the model temple below glanced up at the commotion, only to duck off upon spotting Evan. "Tell us why."

Evan said nothing.

Amir clasped a hand around his own shoulder, trying to calm himself. "Tell me."

My shirt was darker. I realized with alarming indifference that it had started to rain.

"Don't you realize?" Evan asked. "Don't you realize what Bloom let my father do? What everyone in this fucking town let him do?"

Amir was quiet at first, as if considering this argument. "That's the thing about you, Ev," he said, after the pause, climbing through the window. "Somehow you've convinced yourself that you're the only one who's unhappy."

—

OPENING NIGHT WAS LATER THAT week. We played Richmond, a charter school with an historical basketball ineptitude.

"Remove their organs!" Rocky commanded in the pregame huddle. We circled him, as per his instructions, while he performed his best attempt at a war dance. He claimed this spiked adrenaline. "Pillage them!"

We were playing in Richmond's undersized gym, which was a good forty-minute drive from the Academy. My parents drove out to watch, despite my insistence it'd be a waste of time.

I was right. The game was uneventful. Noah started in marvelous fashion, scoring our first seven points and, on one play, blocking a shot deep into the crowd. It was over early, Noah making certain we led by a cool fifteen at halftime. I was the lone person not sent in for garbage time, even as I tried to guilt Rocky by catching his eye.

"Not worth worrying about," my mother maintained on the drive back. "It's only your first game. He's just preparing you."

I had my head against the window. "I did tell you I wouldn't play."

"Aryeh, at the end of the day, you don't really think this matters?" My father was in the passenger seat, visibly annoyed to have been dragged out in the first place. Basketball, he made abundantly clear, was Bitul Torah, a shameless waste of time. "My own son, surely, doesn't believe we're placed on this planet to put a ball through a hoop?"

—

AFTER ENGLISH THE NEXT DAY, a lecture about melancholy in *As You Like It*, I wandered into the library during a free period to study for an impending biology quiz. Seated alone at the back was Evan, hunched over a book, taking copious notes. I took the seat across from him.

He looked up, blinked. "Eden."

"Writing a paper?"

"Just a treatise," he said.

"That doesn't look like Gemara."

Annoyed, he lifted the cover: *On the Genealogy of Morality.* "Ever read it?"

"Can't say I have."

"And Bloom thought you're well read."

"I thought so, too. That's not for class, is it?"

"You sound disconcertingly like Amir. This is personal research."

"About?"

He lowered the book, looked at me daringly. "Would you say you're pretty interested in *yearning* as an organizing principle of human life?"

I remembered how he quoted from *Antony and Cleopatra* at Oliver's party and again found myself suspecting he had somehow read my Academy application essay. I frowned, mentally articulating my accusation, if this even constituted an accusation. It felt wrong to have my privacy invaded, but it felt worse knowing Evan might have gained access to useful information about me. I tried brushing away the thought. The scenario was highly implausible, probably impossible, and the mere mention of longing, especially given Evan's affinity for cryptic questions, was not itself particularly unique. "How do you know what I wrote—"

He put up his hand, cutting me off. "Whatever you're winding up about is unimportant, Eden. Just answer this. Do you believe in a supreme value?"

I chewed on the inside of my cheeks. My face felt flushed, as if I'd walked into an examination unprepared. "I believe in God."

"Okay, great, but whatever's at the root of God. Whatever God embodies. A single, all-encompassing good. The center of all things."

I took out my biology textbook, flipped through it. "I could probably be talked into such a thing."

"Now what if we *are* that value?" Evan said. "What if we are the ones who dictate meaning for our own lives?"

I looked back up at him. "Who's we? You and I? Humanity?"

"Self-interest." He spun his ballpoint pen through his fingers. "The will of a single human being."

"I don't think that's it."

"No? What, then?"

Protists are eukaryotic organisms. Protists are not classified as animals or plants or even fungi. "I don't know. Anything else. Charity. Love. Self-sacrifice. Raising children."

He shook his head. "Living without limits. Having the courage to say yes to yourself. Recognizing that human will, unleashed appropriately, defines value."

I smiled pleasantly. "I guess, to me, that's just not, I don't know, super convincing."

Evan stretched, arching his back. "Nietzsche rejects one of the basic human premises we hold most dear."

I glanced about the library, envious of all those engaged contentedly in trivial tasks, like actually completing homework or formulating sufficiently flirtatious text messages. "Which is?"

"The atomistic soul."

"You've lost me," I said.

"The classical idea of the soul—that it exists, that it animates our body. That it's something indestructible and indivisible. You believe in all that, Eden?"

"Sure." *Protists are typically unicellular. They exhibit structural and functional diversity.* "I think so."

"Nietzsche doesn't. Nietzsche thinks that whole idea should be forgotten."

"And you agree."

He dabbed his fingers with his pen, inking his fingertips with small, black circles. "For a while I did. But not anymore. Now I believe the opposite, actually."

"What's the opposite?" I asked. "The good old-fashioned immortality of the neshama?"

"Sure," he said. "To put it crudely."

"Do you also believe in Olam HaBa, then? Or whatever other version of eternity?"

Evan's phone, stationed facedown on the table, buzzed several times, but he ignored it. "It'd be comforting to believe in that, wouldn't it?"

"Yeah, I guess so," I said. "But if you believe in everlasting souls, don't you kind of necessarily have to believe in the afterlife?"

"Yeah, in some capacity," he said. "Maybe just not the one they teach in Brooklyn. Clouds of glory. A stadium filled with tzadikim. Shabbos multiplied sixty times over."

"I see. So what do you believe in?"

"I don't believe in a literal afterlife," he said, fingering his book. "Or, at least, a postponed afterlife. I think the whole business of eternity is available in the here and now. I mean, isn't it kind of strange, almost ugly, to imagine ascending into infinity—to do nothing? To sit quietly, obediently? Why can't immortality, divinity, spiritual fulfillment, whatever the hell you want to call it, why can't it be something we accomplish here on earth? We claim to want independence, but we're too damn frightened to seize it when it's staring us in the face. Why don't we just take it?"

I pressed my temple. "I—you're asking why we don't just take what we desire? Maybe because there are morals. Just because we have a soul and therefore the potential for godliness doesn't mean we can go around doing whatever we want."

Evan smiled impatiently, as if this was simply an exercise in leading me toward something I could digest in uncomplicated terms. "So instead?"

"Instead, hopefully, we do what's right."

"That's the thing." He rotated his head, making sure we didn't have eavesdroppers. "If we are, in fact, the source of our own values, then *we* are what's right. Those desires we're too scared to pull off? Well, by definition, they are profoundly moral."

"Yeah, that's just . . . that's ridiculous."

"Why's it ridiculous?"

"I don't know," I said. "How about because we have good and we have evil?"

"Good and evil, virtue and sin, mitzvah and aveira. Those are tired terms, Eden. Objectivity just reinforces the old way of thinking, the way that makes us defer and deflect. But the real heights? Those are what we find in between."

"Like what?" I asked. "What are the real heights?"

"How about being able to move toward your self for once, not away from it."

"Yeah, well, sounds to me like embracing that inner self thing might be kind of dangerous."

"Something can be true in the highest degree and still be dangerous, can't it?"

I was beginning to feel nauseous. I wished I'd never joined him.

"Take the sun, Eden."

"The sun?"

"The more you see," he said, matter-of-factly, "the more your vision is destroyed."

"Sounds like a pretty dumb analogy."

"Apply it to God, then. Complete truth obliterates. Think *Raiders of the Lost Ark*."

I stared blankly.

"Right, I forgot, you're an empty vessel, you've never seen a movie. Okay, in terms you'd grasp? Think Lot's wife turning to look. Orpheus turning to look. The men of Bet Shemesh gazing into the Ark. Uzzah touching the Ark. The list goes on, but always it's the same: you see God and you're destroyed."

"Not everyone," I said. "Not Moshe."

"Precisely." Evan slapped the desk hard enough to receive a scowl from the librarian. He nodded his apologies. "Not the *exceptional*. They aren't harmed." He lowered his voice to a careful whisper. "Our ability to survive intense truth—and this is the trick, Eden, follow me here—our ability depends on *the strength of our souls*. And the strength of our souls is proportionate to how much truth we can withstand. So, how do we know? How do we know how much we can take?" His eyes were blue, eerie. "It's a fucking question, Eden," he said, after our uneasy pause.

"I don't know, Evan."

"We test ourselves. We see whether we're destined for that kind of freedom."

"And how do we test ourselves?"

"I'm still perfecting some details."

"Yeah," I said, "why do I feel like that's . . . well, kind of a worrisome thought?"

"It's not worrisome at all," he said, speaking to himself through me. "All we have to do to test ourselves, really, is to suffer. And relax, Eden, don't give me that look. I'm not suggesting self-flagellation here. I'm mostly referring to, I don't know—shedding, let's call it."

"Shedding?"

"Yeah, making a sacrifice. Getting rid of what we love. We're all stuck to something, imprisoned to someone, but if we get rid of it?" Evan shrugged. "We'd unleash ourselves."

"Great, I think I've heard enough." I began gathering my biology notes to go elsewhere, anywhere. "But I am super happy to hear you're now, I don't know, a full-fledged ascetic."

"Believe me," he said. "Most people find it hard, getting rid of everything. Not everyone, though. Not me. And not you."

The library lighting was making my eyes sting. I crammed my textbook into my backpack, desperate to get away from him. "Do me a favor, Evan? Leave me out of your weird fantasies."

"Just answer this, Eden. Answer it honestly, no pretending. Did you find it hard to leave home? To say goodbye to everything you knew?"

"That has nothing to—"

"Of course it does. You and I, we're accustomed to solitude. That's an asset, because it brings us closer to what I'm trying to do. But it's the few who do matter that make shedding nearly impossible."

I stood, turned to leave. "I don't know if this is all theoretical daydreaming or if you're actually . . . planning something," I said unsurely, "but if it's the latter, maybe just—don't."

Evan smiled coldly. "What choice do we have? Otherwise we'll spend our whole lives yearning."

—

READING IN BED LATER, STARING out through my window at the limpid night, I thought more about what Evan had said. He was right: I was habituated to solitude. Or, at least, I had been for much of my life. But he was wrong to insist I craved loneliness when, in fact, I hated the disease. I liked having friends, real friends, and I was growing to appreciate the person I was around them, even when it meant accepting that I was dangling in a world in which I'd never fully belong. I liked community. I liked the comfort of confiding in people. I liked feeling, for the first time, rooted in kinship, anchored to something concrete and familiar, no longer constantly adrift. Whatever plagued Evan, whatever crisis cornered him into isolation, had nothing to do with me.

To affirm this thought, I rolled over on my side, reached for my phone and, inhaling deeply, called Sophia.

She answered on the first ring. "'*How does my good Lord Hamlet?*'"

"Hey," I said, taken aback she'd answered so quickly. "I'm not calling too late, am I?"

"You think it's appropriate to call at this hour?"

"I, uh—" I checked my bedside digital clock. "Shoot. I'm sorry, Madam President."

Her mirthless laugh. "It's nine-thirty, Ari. I was joking." I imagined her lying in bed, ankles together, textbooks piled high, moonlight trickling over her. "What can I do for you?"

"Yeah, I—just a quick question. For school, I mean."

"Oh, for school? How surprising."

"What—you don't think I like talking to you?"

"I think you *love* talking to me," she said. "You love it so much you make up excuses to do just that."

"Excuses?" I was thankful she couldn't see the color of my face over the phone. "Wow. What an accusation."

"Poor kid. You're probably madly conjuring homework questions this very second, sitting there in your pajamas—"

"Pajamas? Whoa, who says I wear pajamas?"

"My apologies," she said, laughing slightly. "Hate to be presumptuous."

"I happen, for your information, to be wearing a highly trendy outfit."

"I'll be the judge of that."

"Basketball team sweatpants. Nike. Sponsored by the Bellows, no less."

"You're right, undeniably sexy. And your shirt? Don't leave me hanging without a complete image."

I glanced down at my chest. "No shirt."

"You Casanova. Trying to seduce me?"

I put my phone on speaker. "It's not working, is it?"

"Why the sudden loss of confidence?"

"Did you like it?"

"I like when you're yourself." This somehow ordered neurotransmitters to dispatch throughout my body a sensation of tingling that was neither pleasant nor unpleasant, just the tingling of someone coming to life. "Anyway. Probably enough phone sex for tonight, right? Let's calm you down. We don't want you too riled before bed."

I grasped my hair with my fingers. "Right, of course."

"So what was that urgent question?"

Far-off chirping. Iguanas, I figured, the sort that tended to congregate in Noah's backyard, slipping through the golf course fence, scaling his roof, migrating across the street when they felt like slumming. "Uh," I said, quickly opening my notebook, searching for something adequate, "yeah, so on the practice quiz, number forty-seven, the one about organizing the vessels from highest to lowest carbon dioxide concentrations—"

"—pulmonary arteries and right ventricle, left atrium and, yes, pulmonary veins."

"Oh. Wow. Cool, thanks." I paused to pretend to scribble notes. "You didn't need to look that up?"

"Nope."

"You have a pretty impressive memory," I said.

"I've been told. Any other pressing questions?"

"No, that's perfect. Really helpful, actually."

"I can tell. Well, then, I'm returning to the piano. Sleep well, Hamlet." She hung up. I fell back on my pillow, the sound of her voice, in that moment, enough to overcome anything Evan could say to me.

—

TWO DAYS LATER, WE WERE greeted at the school's main entrance by the following poster:

עַד מָתַי מֵאַנְתָּ לֵעָנֹת מִפָּנָי שַׁלַּח עַמִּי וְיַעַבְדֻנִי

It wasn't harrowing until I recognized that silvery ink. It was a harmless phrase, though somewhat esoteric divorced from context, a line that might appear on a Tanach test. Yet that Evan had selected it gave it a strangely sinister quality. *Until when will you refuse to humble yourself before me? Send my people, and they will worship me.*

The sign stayed up longer than expected. Gio assumed it was an inspirational Torah quote the school was promoting—"I can't read this fucking language, what you want from me?"—while the Judaic faculty figured one of the rabbis had posted it for a class.

"Isn't it a bit obscure?" I asked Evan during davening. It was one of the rare times he'd bothered to show up at Minyan X. When Noah and I arrived, Evan was wandering the room, huddling people together, drawing worried looks from Rabbi Schwartz.

"And kind of creepy, bro," Noah added. "What's with all the creepy shit lately?"

"It's for Bloom. Don't worry about that," Evan said. "He'll get it."

"Okay," I said, curious whether Noah found this as odd as I did or if my library conversation with Evan had rendered me slightly paranoid, "but what's it for?"

"I have something planned for third period," Evan said. "Something big. Spread the word. I expect compliance."

Noah laughed. "You expect compliance. What the hell does *compliance* mean?"

Evan turned away. "It means you follow me when I leave."

—

WE WERE SITTING IN TANACH, listening to Rabbi Feldman drone on about a little-known instance in Joshua in which God split the sea, when Evan stood. Rabbi Feldman paused to give him an amused look. "Rear-end cramp, Evan?"

Evan didn't answer. He was staring level-eyed at the front of the room.

Rabbi Feldman frowned. "Everything all right, Ev?"

Evan stepped forward slowly.

"Evan?"

He turned to face us, nodded and then, without explanation,

walked out of the classroom. On cue, the majority of the class followed.

"What in the world?" Rabbi Feldman growled, veins in his temple throbbing.

I turned to Noah. He stared in confusion, only to shrug and join the walkout. Unsure what else to do, I closed my notebook and trailed along. Amir, begrudgingly, came, too. Davis remained alone in the classroom.

"Halt!" Rabbi Feldman threw open the classroom door and yelled into the hallway, where we marched steadily and in menacing silence after Evan. "Get back immediately!"

Hallway doors opened abruptly, students pouring out to join us. There was Oliver, leading a battalion from the classroom to our right, and Gabriel, a room full of juniors in tow, emerging from the classroom to our left. Out of the staircase appeared Remi, herding seniors—Rebecca laughing in bewilderment, Nicole recording the event on Snapchat—until the first floor overflowed, bodies merging in line behind Evan, himself wraithlike and refusing to meet anyone's eyes. In my peripheral vision I saw Sophia lingering in the stairwell, watching gravely.

We followed Evan through the long hallway, past the front office, past Rabbi Bloom's glass windows—behind which he stood, arms folded over his chest, blood draining from his face—until we were outside. Evan continued marching through the basketball courts, where teachers pleaded for us to stop. Evan kept moving, undeterred, even as Rabbi Schwartz was barreled over, until he reached a large bush just off the soccer field. I looked about in disbelief. There were at least a hundred and fifty of us standing obediently, eyes dilated with adrenalized reverence.

Evan took in our silence before raising a fist. "Two choices," he called out, his face dark. "Rise above a broken system or be crushed by it. Submit to yourself or fail to discover whether you'll ever be exceptional." This was met, absurdly, with thunderous applause. He dug into his pocket, pulled out his lighter, flicking it on and off. "To the rebellion," he cried, holding the lighter to the bush, allowing it to catch fire. "My friends, your burning bush," he said, orange sparks at his elbows. "Let this be your divine voice."

Wild cheering. Sacrilegious flames. I remember the white circles in Evan's eyes, the smell of burning shrubbery, wisps of smoke rising heavenward, Rabbi Bloom and Sophia and the others, hundreds of yards away, watching us bow before Evan Stark.

—

DURING MY FREE PERIOD THAT next day, I tucked Rabbi Bloom's Yeats under my arm and, making certain no one saw me, knocked on his door.

"Mr. Eden." Rabbi Bloom looked up from a pile of papers and motioned for me to join him at the conference table. Looking worn and bleary, he eyed the book. "Tell me about your time with the schizophrenic seer."

"I loved him," I said. "I came to return it and to thank you."

"I'm glad to hear that, Mr. Eden. Some people are fatally disenchanted by Yeats' revolutionary intensities, not to mention all the cyclical talk."

"The gyres?"

"The gyres," he said, "and those tricky phases of the moon."

"Yeah, they were—odd," I said. "And pretty hard to get through, actually."

"I advise you refrain from subjecting yourself to reading *A Vision*. Pure mystic torture." He leaned toward me. "But you made it out the other end of the wormhole. What was your favorite poem?"

"'Adam's Curse.'"

"A noble choice as any. Why so?"

"I liked the interplay of narrative voices," I said, trying to remember key phrases I sketched mentally while walking to his office.

"And which voices would those be?"

"Two stand out to me. One is the fearless poet and then the other I guess is what I'd call the weary lover."

"Congratulations," he said, "you've discovered Yeats' much beloved anti-self." He reached across the table for his book and flipped distractedly through it. "I presume you recognize that term?"

"Yeah, it was all over the place," I said. "Other selves, antithetical selves, Daemons."

"*When I come to put in rhyme what I have found, it will be hard toil, but for a moment I believe I have found myself and not my anti-self,*" Rabbi Bloom recited from the book. He looked up at me, smiling cautiously. "What do you think Yeats meant by all that?"

"When he puts it that way," I said, leaning on the table for momentum, "I guess the anti-self is something almost, I don't know, aspirational. You're dissatisfied with the current image of yourself, which feels maybe inadequate or too nebulous, and so as a remedy you picture another self, a superior life, one attached to excellence or virtue or, in this case, to art." Abruptly I trailed off, wondering if I'd overdone it.

Rabbi Bloom, however, nodded earnestly. "I like that, Mr. Eden. I daresay you have a knack for this sort of work."

"Well, I wouldn't mind if that's true," I said. "I've got to be good at something."

"Being a tad behind, coming from your old school, is no crime. Certainly it shouldn't diminish the confidence you should have in your capabilities. Have more assurance in yourself. You're a fine thinker with a lot of potential, as I believe I've pointed out."

I felt unreasonably pleased with myself. "Thank you."

"Now, of course, the follow-up. Why the fascination with the anti-self?"

I rubbed a hand on my knee. "Right, so I think Yeats was essentially suffocated by consciousness and by, I suppose, the burden of being his own—"

"Yes, yes, quite so, Mr. Eden. Certainly Yeats suffered from internal fracturing, often to the point of unintelligibility. But what I mean to ask is why *you* are so taken with the anti-self?"

"Oh." I blinked. Now, I could tell, he was, in fact, studying me, waiting for a specific answer. "Well, maybe in a way that's not entirely dissimilar from Yeats," I said carefully, "I find it comforting to reimagine myself."

Unself-consciously, refusing to allow myself the internal humiliation of actually processing what I was doing, I envisioned myself, suddenly, as Evan. In this reverie I was slightly taller, slightly tanner, slightly more muscular. I had a sharper nose, I had a more interesting cut of lips, I had hair that no longer curled into thick confusion but instead framed my face to be angular and striking. All symptoms of my depersonalization were gone. People could look at me now and I could hold their gaze. People could meet me now and remember what I looked like. I could glance into the mirror now and mentally reconstruct what I saw hours, days, weeks later. I was not some reflection of a reflection. I was Evan.

"Precisely. It's what we all need, and we need it desperately, this ability to remodel our world, to be recast poetically, to constantly make and unmake ourselves. It's part of having an identity, part of coping with being human. Most people, most serious thinkers, at the very least, cannot lay claim to a single vision of the self, don't you think? There are gains to be made when what we are in the flesh comes into conflict with what we *think* is our true being. In this way, our chronically unfulfilled daily self can sometimes grasp parts of that ideal reality toward which we aspire."

A moment of polite pause while I pretended I didn't have an immediate question. "But do you think too much self-division can be— well, dangerous?"

A look of concern passed over his face. "In what way?"

"I guess theoretically you could lose sight of your true self amid many other artificial selves."

"Not if there is no *true* self. Not if we're always in flux, always evolving." He folded his arms. "So, the task is to find balance. To let both selves, all selves, live together, clashing in harmony."

"So how do you do that?"

"One way, perhaps, is to find your anti-self *externally*."

"In another person, you mean?"

"In dreams, illusions, experiences that drag you outside the confines of your self. But yes, at an extreme, in another human, someone to whom you're linked, even as that person resembles quite your opposite." He made a show of shutting the book and sliding it toward the other end of the table. "If you can find an anti-self, you can achieve a sort of harmonious self-expansion, a oneness within the power of your mind."

"So you'd become divine, in a way."

"Perhaps. But anyway, that's enough mystical metaphysics for now." He walked to his bookcase. "So would you enjoy another assignment? I won't be offended, just saddened, if you tell me our conversation served only to bore you."

My head spun in uneven circles. "Yeah, definitely, if you don't mind."

He grabbed a book, slid it toward me. *The Sickness unto Death.* "In keeping with current themes but exposing you to existentialism. It's a bit more affirming, I hope you'll find. Plus, Kierkegaard, at the very least, wasn't a fascist."

Gratefully, I placed the book in my backpack.

"May I ask, by the way, how you're finding Minyan X these days?"

"It's, well . . . chaotic, as per usual."

"Maybe," Rabbi Bloom said, stroking his chin, "it's high time to break you out. Clearly you've no business being there."

"I'd very much not object."

"So here's an idea. I propose we make today's meeting something of a regular occurrence, just for a little while. If you promise to daven on your own before school—"

"—of course."

"Wonderful. Then why don't you come see me when Minyan X meets? We can use the time to discuss your readings. How does that sound?"

"Perfect," I said, standing, making my way toward the door. "Thank you, Rabbi."

Rabbi Bloom leaned a hand on his the table. "For the slightest moment, you know, I thought you came in to discuss another self-appointed seer."

"Sorry?"

"I'm referring, of course, to yesterday's excitement."

I blinked, immediately wondering whether it'd all been a guise, whether I'd erred showing up. "Oh. No, I—"

"I've never seen something like that, Mr. Eden. Something so—disturbed." He paused. "*And what rough beast, its hour come round at last / Slouches toward Bethlehem to be born?*"

I only nodded, unwilling to offer anything self-incriminating or, worse, incriminating of Evan. Surprisingly, Evan had received only a one-day suspension, for the minor sin of committing arson on school grounds.

"Mr. Eden?"

I hovered at the door, waiting to be released. "Yes, Rabbi?"

"Do be careful who you follow into the dark."

—

"MEIR'S BAR MITZVAH IS NEXT Shabbat," my father reminded us at dinner. "You'll be able to go home with us, won't you, Ari?"

I had been avoiding answering this question for weeks, offering a wide array of halfhearted excuses: homework, essays, group projects. In truth, I couldn't bear the thought of standing in our old shul, attempting to make Shimon, Mordechai and Reuven understand the incommunicable—the sight of Remi White nude, for instance, or hearing Sophia play the piano. How could I explain what it was to curl tefillin around my fingers, to curl my fingers around Nicole's body, to curl tefillin around my fingers once more? How could I explain what it was to change but remain unchanged, to enjoy the perverse thrill of experience but still bentch after meals and undulate during Shemoneh Esrei and pull tzitzit over my shoulders each morning? To return to Brooklyn, even for forty-eight hours, would be to force myself to reckon with a tension I did not want resolved. "I don't think so, Abba."

He set down his utensils. "You don't think so?"

"It's just that I've got important tests coming up," I said, which wasn't a lie. "Plus my second game is Saturday night."

"Your game?" He frowned, rubbing his chin. "You realize Meir is your cousin. Your *first* cousin."

"I can't just miss it," I said after too long of a pause.

"He made a commitment, joining the team," my mother said. She spoke in an oddly unanimated voice. "Besides, traveling will interfere with studying."

I bobbed my head too animatedly at this suggestion.

We three drank in a moment of awkward silence.

"I'm sure Norman will understand, Yaakov," my mother finally said, playing with the rim of her glass.

My father nodded distantly. "So I'll cancel your ticket."

"I'm sorry, Abba," I said.

"You'll be all right alone?" my mother asked, shifting gears with a tone of finality. "Should I ask Cynthia if you can stay over with Noah?"

"No, I'll be fine. It'll give me time to study."

Dinner concluded without further discussion. Soon enough, my father gathered his plate and disappeared into the kitchen to wash dishes.

"He seems pretty angry," I said.

My mother dabbed at the tablecloth with a wet napkin. "Just slightly disappointed. Give him time."

"I *am* sorry, you know," I said, uneasily. "I do realize it means a lot to him."

"Does it mean a lot to you?" She asked this without making direct eye contact.

"Meir's bar mitzvah? Or going back in general?"

"Either. Both."

I shook my head. Now we were each avoiding the other's gaze.

She gathered the rest of the dishes. "It'll be strange to be back," she said. "I don't think I'm looking forward to it."

—

THEY CAME LATE FRIDAY NIGHT. I'd already eaten—my mother, worried I'd starve, left behind an enormous amount of food—and was sprawled on my living room couch, reading drowsily. Just as my eyes were beginning to grow heavy, Kierkegaard a potent sedative, I heard knocks.

I jolted awake, rubbed my temple. I tried ignoring them, but they began ringing the doorbell. I threw open the front door. "It's freaking Shabbos!" I hissed. "Don't ring the bell."

"Sorry, but how long were you going to make us wait?" Oliver stepped inside and brushed past me. "It's inhumane."

"I was hoping you might give up," I said irritably.

"Sorry, Drew," Noah said, following Oliver. "Thought maybe you passed out."

"No," Evan said, "I knew you were just ignoring us."

"Can we blame him?" Amir asked, the last one in.

I locked the door. I was grateful, at least, that Oliver hadn't brought anyone else.

"So. This is the humble abode, huh?" Oliver surveyed my living room, holding a bottle of Jameson. "About time you invited us over."

"I didn't invite you," I said.

"Real hospitable, Eden," Oliver said. "And after all the times we've hosted you, no less. After you and Nicole desecrated my poor brother's room!"

My neck burned. "No one else is coming, right?"

"Just your favorite four schmucks, no need to fret." Oliver found his way into the kitchen. "Where are your shot glasses?"

"You really ingratiate yourself, Oliver," Amir said.

I lingered at the kitchen entrance, hands attached to my pockets. "Why would we have shot glasses?"

"Silly me," Oliver said. "I assumed all parents drank as much as mine." He made a fuss throwing open cabinets, eventually finding dust-laden wineglasses above the stove. "These'll do." He lined them up, poured gratuitously.

"No, I'm not drinking," I said meekly, as Oliver gestured at the shot designated for me. "I'm still groggy—"

"You're absolutely drinking." Evan pushed a glass in front of me. "On three. One, two—"

We threw them back. I closed my eyes, tried not to choke, grabbed a handful of Pringles to mitigate the burning. There were more shots, each precipitated by bawdy toasts. I stopped refusing. The kitchen, soon enough, became slightly slanted.

"I'm starving. Have any grub to share with dear drunken friends?" Oliver found his way into my refrigerator, removing options that caught his eye. Schnitzel. Potato kugel. Mayonnaise.

Noah descended on the refrigerator, too, helping himself to a sizable stack of leftovers. "Hear that sound, Drew?"

Amir and Evan were arguing loudly at the table. Something about re-enfranchising felons, I think, or maybe Second Amendment rights. I wasn't paying attention. My head wasn't spinning exactly but had acquired alcoholic warmth.

Noah stuck his head out of the refrigerator. "Drew?"

"Did I hear what?" I asked, rubbing my eyes.

"Someone's at the door," he said, chin stained with mustard.

Oliver walked over to the table, poured himself another shot.

I grabbed his shoulder. "You said no one else was coming."

Oliver frowned. "I said that? Doesn't sound like something I'd say."

"Oliver."

The knocks again. Oliver wiped his mouth with the back of his hand and gave a large, drunken grin. "I do apologize."

Cursing, I hastened from my kitchen, slapping my cheeks to sober myself. I peeked, carefully, through the peephole. At the door, to my disbelief, were Rebecca, Remi and Sophia. I swallowed hard.

"We bear gifts," Remi announced. She handed over two bottles of Smirnoff and sidestepped around me, following the voices into the kitchen.

Rebecca studied my face, cringed. "You didn't know we were coming, did you?" she asked. "Oh, God. Don't kill me, Ari. Noah told us to come."

Noah emerged from the kitchen, red-cheeked, grinning stupidly. "That's what Oliver claimed you told him?"

"Look at you. Already drunk?" Rebecca delivered a peck to my cheek and a light slap to Noah's. "Too much to ask for you to wait?"

Sophia entered last. She allowed Noah and Rebecca to disappear before pulling me aside. Our bodies were inches apart. I tried not to think about this. "He isn't here, is he?"

"Who?"

She glanced down the hall. "Evan."

Her pointedness surprised me, but the impact was dulled by the brunt of the shots. I nodded.

"I don't want to see him," she said.

My heart soared. I could count her eyelashes. "You don't?"

"We can leave." She lowered her voice again. "Clearly this was a hoax, I can steer them out—"

Her whispering appeared to complicate my cognitive abilities. I shook my head. "Don't worry, I don't want to see him, either," I said. "Stay a while with me, it'll be fine." She pursed her lips in thought but eventually allowed me to lead her to the kitchen, where Oliver continued pouring, demanding that the girls catch up. Sophia gave Amir a hug. She and Evan nodded.

"To our friend, alcohol," Oliver announced. We raised our shots. "Cause of, antidote for, all our many problems."

We moved to the living room and, with the exception of Sophia, who sought refuge on the couch, took turns ripping the bottle. Oliver and Noah proposed toasts—to Sophia's presidency, to winning on Saturday night, to the ghost of Oliver's and Remi's relationship, to burning bushes and sunrise minyanim and what Noah termed "weird-ass rebellions." My living room began whirling at a frightening speed. I excused myself for the restroom, where I bowed before the toilet, contemplating the relief of vomiting. I came out, drifted into my room and found Remi on the floor, knees against her chest. "Remi?"

She looked up mournfully.

"You okay?" I asked.

"Just fine." She tried standing, fell back to the floor. "This your room?"

"Sure is."

"Kind of sparse."

"Decorated it myself, thanks."

She held a picture of my parents and me, taken at my elementary school graduation, which she found beside my bed. My parents had their arms around me. I stared blankly into the camera, clutching a blue siddur to my chest. "You're not smiling."

"Yeah, I tend to forget to do that."

"You don't smile much in general," she said.

"Listen, I'm working on it."

"You should do it more."

"Duly noted, thanks for the tip." I rocked slightly on the balls of my feet. "I'll keep that in mind."

"Don't you think you have a reason to smile?"

"Whoa," I said, "guess we're getting personal."

She frowned. "You flirting with me?"

"No, I—well, I don't know. I'm pretty sure I'm not."

"I wouldn't go for you," she said, shrugging.

"Yeah, that's actually perfectly okay with me, Remi."

"You could probably use some more self-confidence."

"Couldn't hurt."

"I mean, you have nice teeth, if nothing else." She threw the picture at my bed before I could stop her. I tried intercepting it, but to my relief it landed on my pillows. "So, what do you think Evan's deal is?"

I kicked at a stack of books on my floor. "Why do people keep bringing him up?"

"Who else?"

"Nobody," I said. "Never mind that."

"Well." She threw her head back, then returned it to an upright position. "I was looking for him."

"In here?"

"I guess. I don't know, I'm pretty drunk, to be honest."

"He's probably in the living room, where every other person is." I offered my hand, eager to remove her from my room. "Let me take you."

She held on to me but didn't budge from the floor. "Ari."

"Yeah?"

"We've spoken before?"

"You and Evan? I'd certainly say so."

"No. Me and you."

"Oh," I said. "Uh, minimally would probably be a generous answer."

She went on holding my hand. "You don't want to be friends?"

"Sure I do."

"Are you extremely shy or extremely stuck-up?"

"You just said I needed more self-confidence."

"Yeah, socially. But sometimes it feels like you're shut off. Like, I don't know, you think you're smarter than other people. Or you're above everything else or just not interested."

"You think *I'm* like that?"

"I guess what I mean is I don't know if you're a little bit cold and emotionless."

"This is—fairly unexpected criticism." I was taken aback that Remi had spent enough time contemplating my existence to actually formulate an opinion of me, but even more so that I could be perceived as anything other than introverted, out-of-place, insecure. How strange, I thought, feeling the weight of the alcohol again, for external life to exist in diametrical opposition to the life in your head.

"I give good drunken therapy. So we should speak more, shouldn't we?"

"Yeah, okay."

"Start now, open up. You like Sophia."

I was far too dizzy to blush. "I might."

"Want to know a secret?"

"That's okay. You don't have to tell me one."

"But it's about Sophia," Remi said in a high, drunken voice. "I think she thinks you're cute. Kind of handsome, actually."

This was enough to throw me, even in my current state. "She said that to you?"

"But you think she's *beautiful*." She laughed, pulled her hand away. "Everyone thinks she is."

"She is beautiful."

She looked up at me, dazed eyes sharpening, a finger tracing her retroussé nose. "But do you think there's something else about her?"

I didn't answer.

Her breathing slowed. "I do. I think she's sad. I don't know why, but she is." She paused. "It's why she won't drink much, I think. Like, for a while she didn't drink anything at all. So she won't lose control, maybe." Remi blinked heavily, licked her lips. "Okay, turns out I don't feel too well," she decided, her head falling back to her shoulders. Quickly, I grabbed the wastebasket from under my desk and looked away as she was sick. "Hold my hair," she commanded, midway through her retching.

I obliged, kneeling beside her. When she felt better she had me lead her back into the living room, though only after making me swear not to tell anyone what I'd seen. *Game of Thrones* was on mute. A dragon was annihilating several hundred people but nobody was watching. Evan held the Kierkegaard. "Where'd you get this?" He had it opened to the front cover, where a faded *L.B.* was traced.

Admitting I'd been studying with Rabbi Bloom felt, in my current state, inexplicably self-defeating, akin to surrendering a secret on which I might, one day, desperately rely. "Nowhere."

"Right. Well, just so you know, I was given this once, too." He closed the book, returned it to the couch. "Tell him not to forget that loss is a more important step for the self than God."

It became difficult to focus my eyes. Noah and Rebecca slipped into my backyard. Evan and Remi grabbed one of the bottles and, as I'd later discover, locked themselves in my parents' bathroom. Oliver and Amir raided my food cabinet, guzzling jellybeans. I stood around, dimly, wondering how it'd come to pass that I occupied a new home in which intoxicated strangers ran wild.

"Hamlet?" Sophia was snapping her fingers in the airspace above my head. "You all right?"

I closed my eyes, steadying my vision. I piled jellybeans into my mouth. Pale blues, bright oranges. "Don't I look good?"

"You look green."

I scattered jellybeans to the floor. "I should really stop eating these."

She looked me over once more. I felt an irrational urge to explain that I'd presented an inaccurate version of myself. This is not, in fact, who I am, I wanted to tell her. I am someone else entirely. I do not know what has happened to me. I do not quite grasp where I've gone. "You look almost as bad as you did at Oliver's house."

"I'm not," I said. "Drunk, that is."

"I respectfully disagree."

"What do I look like drunk?"

"Sad. Sloppy."

Nausea boiled in my stomach. "I didn't want them here," I said quietly.

"I know."

I leaned toward her. "I'm happy you're here."

"Absolutely, and that's our cue to get you to bed."

"No," I objected incoherently. "Actually, what I want is—"

I was on all fours, heaving a pool of colors. Evan was laughing, Oliver recording a video on his iPhone, my cheeks glued to the wet tile floor. Remi held my hand in solidarity, and then I was in bed, my ceiling spinning into the dark, Sophia's voice fading in and out.

—

IT WAS NEARLY TWO IN the afternoon when I woke, sunlight streaming through my window and hurting my eyes. I was lying over untouched sheets, half dressed, a fierce headache coming on, an awful stench coming from the wastebasket. I washed my face, changed and made my way into the kitchen where, to my astonishment, Sophia sat drinking coffee and reading *The Sickness unto Death*. "Really dull stuff," she said without glancing up. "Thanks for leaving me all morning with such shoddy reading material."

I sat beside her, trying to figure out what she was still doing in my house. My heart pulsed with possibility. Had she slipped in this morning to check on me? Had she never—

"I slept in the living room, for the record," she said, seeing my mind racing. "With Remi."

"Remi's here?"

I peeked into the living room. Sure enough, Remi was splayed out on the couch, blond hair blanketing her face.

"She was even worse than you," Sophia said. "So it was either letting her hibernate here or bringing her to Noah's."

"I was that—rough?"

"You did regurgitate an ungodly number of jellybeans."

"Yikes."

"And I was forced to undress you. Had no choice. You know, to get you to sleep."

I blinked frenziedly, turning outrageous shades of red.

"Relax. I kept you decent the whole time."

I looked around the kitchen. I had a hazy memory of Oliver sketching his name in ketchup on the table, but now it was spot-free, the bottles and general mess all gone. "Did you clean this all up?"

"What choice did you leave me? It was utterly appalling in here."

"Thank you," I said hoarsely.

"You owe me." She stood, started making coffee. "You should've seen this disaster. I found an avocado in the bathroom sink."

"An avocado?"

"I'd double-check the house before your parents come home, if I were you. Make sure vegetables aren't floating where they don't belong." She handed me coffee. "How're you feeling?"

"Like an enormous idiot," I said.

"I believe I've emphasized this previously, but you can't let them overpower you like that."

I sipped too quickly, scorching my tongue. "My parents are going to kill me."

"You'll survive because they won't find out. I cleaned too well." She sat beside me. "Where are those jet-setting parents of yours, anyway?"

"They've jetted all the way back to Brooklyn."

"How exotic."

"It's my cousin's bar mitzvah."

"You didn't go?"

"Told them I had too much work." I took another sip, the pounding in my head lessening slightly. "Truth is I didn't want to."

"Why not?"

"I just can't go back right now."

"Do you hate it here, too?"

"Not yet."

"Phone the local media," announced a cool voice behind us. "I just woke up in Ari Eden's house." Remi, whimpering, massaging her forehead, strolled in. "I need strong coffee, Soph. Generously tinged with vodka. Eden, not a word from you about any of this, ever, or I'll send videos from last night to every rabbi in Brooklyn." She took a mug from Sophia and, ignoring me, sat down, sipping slowly.

We sat awhile, drinking in silence. I stole glances at the curve of Sophia's fingers, at the corners of her mouth as she returned to reading. Eventually, Remi felt well enough to leave. I thanked Sophia again, walked them out and then returned to my room, collapsing onto my bed.

NOVEMBER

Since nor th' exterior nor the inward man
Resembles that it was

—Shakespeare, *Hamlet*

I spent the early-morning hours before the SAT tossing in bed, trying to surrender to sleep. I stared at the red numbers of my digital clock, my room stuffy, listening to the whirling of my fan, acutely aware of time passing. Around four-thirty I nodded off into an unsatisfying, dreamless trance.

At six-thirty I gave up. I davened quickly—*please help me, God,* I whispered throughout Shemoneh Esrei—took a hot shower, attempted push-ups to get my blood pumping. I found my mother in the kitchen, scrambling eggs. While I ate, my mother quizzed me on vocabulary words—*Junoesque* ("an imposingly tall woman"), *perambulate* ("the ability to walk"), *cicerone* ("a guide for sightseers") until I decided the exercise was pointless. My father was already at early minyan and cared little that I was taking the test, but my mother continued to hover, insisting I was prepared, refusing to listen to my objections. I said goodbye and met Noah in the driveway.

We arrived at school to find the majority of our grade loitering nervously near the model temple. Donny was asking Amir how to solve some geometrical equation. Noah was distracting Rebecca and Remi by suggesting racy words that might appear on the test. ("Lubricious, anyone? Or how about: Good Lord, aren't Amir's rugged looks simply titillating?") Oliver disappeared to hit a joint. Davis was hunched over on a bench, plugging something into his calculator at a rapid clip, glancing about guiltily. Evan was silent, inspecting the tips of his pencils.

Eventually, Dr. Flowers waddled outside, coughing, reeking of smoke. ("Unfortunately for all parties involved, I'm in no economic position to forgo proctoring.") She led us into a double classroom on the first floor, arranging our seating so that there was an empty desk between every seat. She placed me on the right side of the room. "Hope this goes better for you than our last quiz, Eden," she said, which was a fairly distressing comment, considering she hadn't yet returned that examination.

When the clock struck eight she began pacing gravely from desk to desk, glaring at anyone with whom she made eye contact. "All right. Welcome to the test that realistically determines your earning potential. It certainly did mine. For the next four hours, you will be tested on your reading, problem-solving and writing skills. This test is a national, accredited . . ." She read on in her rasping voice, pausing twice for violent coughing bouts. Whenever she turned to face the opposite side of the room, I noticed, Amir stole glances at his supposedly sealed packet. "Well," she concluded, "I guess I wish you luck. You may begin."

The opening section was the essay:

Literature often correlates suffering with character development. Assignment: Can sorrow and growth be linked in everyday life? Plan and write an essay in which you develop your point of view on this issue. Be certain to support your stance by utilizing logic and examples derived from your personal experiences, literary awareness and academic studies.

I read the prompt twice. The close of "Crazy Jane Talks with the Bishop" came to mind: *For nothing can be sole or whole / That has not been rent.* I thought about my conversations with Evan, about how being incomplete somehow allows certain people to long for transcendence, to escape present solitude and sadness by absorbing themselves in something patently extra-human. "We modernists," I began writing, conscious of the way my mind was surrendering itself to some sort of automatic trance state, "live without glory, without adventure and, largely speaking, without much in the way of formal meaning. How is it, then, that we achieve real heights? We tear apart some essential aspect of ourselves." I continued on in this way, wondering all the while whether I actually believed what I was writing. Was it true, in my experience, that "gradations of suffering result in a kind of moral allure"? In Evan's case, perhaps it was: his wound, whatever it was precisely, did prove somewhat cathartic, insofar as it lent him an aura of tragic grandeur. Indeed, wasn't Evan's loss integral to the way we looked up to him? No one vocalized this, but in my eyes it was true: his unhappiness, the sheer boldness of it, the singularity and marvel of it, gave him power over us. In my own case, however, I knew my social and religious deficiencies were just that, not sources of dignity.

I finished quickly. Pleased with what I dredged up, I spent a few minutes translating my hieroglyphics, hoping the graders would be able to decipher my penmanship. Then I waited, listening to Amir scribbling feverishly behind me.

Soon, Dr. Flowers sprang from her desk, calling time. Niman, sitting in front, tried erasing a smudge, sending Dr. Flowers into a rage.

"But I—I wasn't writing," Niman protested, her voice small, helpless. "Just erasing."

"Not after I call time," Dr. Flowers snarled. "Expect a notice of ineligibility from the College Board. Now get the hell out!"

During our ten-minute midway break we congregated in the bathroom to illegally debate answers, Amir looking sick every time he and Evan disagreed. Verbal was easy, though in a moment of distress I confused *mausoleum* with *moratorium*. Math was not. Starving and generally depressed about my college prospects, I guessed on several trigonometry questions. I tried calming myself by cursing Bearman for his unhelpfulness and reminding myself that the mere fact that I was here had to constitute some moral victory, given that my Brooklyn friends would never take this test. This did little to boost my spirits.

"What's the lowest you can get?" Oliver asked on the way out. "I'd like to know."

—

NOAH WAS DRIVING ME HOME from school on Monday when his phone rang.

"Babe?" Noah yelled, too loudly, into the speakers. "Hey, you're on with Drew."

"Oh—hi Ari."

I felt the need to clear my throat, as if that'd help solidify my presence. "Hey Rebs."

"You guys still in the car?"

"Yeah, just left," Noah said, speeding ahead of a slow driver. "What's up?"

"Listen, did either of you know what today was?"

"Uh, I know it's not our anniversary," Noah said, giving me a fist bump. "So I'm definitely in the clear."

No laughter from Rebecca. "Evan didn't say anything?"

Noah raised the volume slightly. "About?"

Rebecca coughed on the other end. "Apparently today would've been Caroline Stark's birthday."

Noah and I got quiet after that. "Oh," Noah said. He started driving a bit slower.

"I think it'd be a good idea if Ev wasn't alone right now," Rebecca said. "He could probably use you guys."

"Yeah, I'll call him," Noah said. "See if he wants to come over or something."

"Actually I think he's at Grove Street right now."

Noah frowned. "Grove Street Cemetery?"

"Yeah."

"So you're saying what?" Noah asked. "We should just show up there?"

"I don't know. Maybe that's best?"

"Wait," I intervened, "Rebs, how do you know this?"

"Sophia told me. This was her—idea." She paused, apparently taking a long sip of water. "I guess she remembered from before or Evan told her or something . . ."

We hung up, dialed Amir and Oliver. Neither had heard anything about this from Evan but both wanted to come along. Noah turned the car around and went to retrieve them. Oliver, to our surprise, was waiting outside his house with a bouquet of orchids.

Nobody said much on the drive. The sun hadn't yet set but it was noticeably cooler out. The cemetery was a short distance away. There were only a few cars in the parking lot; operating hours, it seemed, were ending soon. Amir spotted the Aston Martin in the far corner of the lot, under a palm tree, parked as unobtrusively as an Aston Martin could be parked.

It was a large cemetery, overrun by *Bucida buceras* and *Ficus aurea*. The front gate had Hebrew words carved into it:

אֲנִי מַאֲמִין בֶּאֱמוּנָה שְׁלֵמָה, שֶׁתִּהְיֶה תְּחִיַת הַמֵּתִים.

I believe with perfect faith that there will be a revival of the dead. We wandered until we found a figure reading with his back against a tombstone. We approached slowly without calling out, so as not to startle him. Perhaps he didn't hear us, perhaps he only pretended not to, but he didn't glance up in acknowledgment until, at last, we stood over him.

"Hey, bud," Noah said. "We figured you could use some company."

Oliver walked over to the plot, placed his flowers. The tombstone was large but unassuming—dark granite, with Caroline's Hebrew name written in elegant lettering. Oliver placed his hand on Evan's shoulder and then returned to where we stood.

Evan studied our faces. He was clear-eyed, he was calm, there was no evidence he'd been crying. He opened his mouth to say something but stopped himself, opting instead to nod. "You have no idea how much I miss her," he said, finally, breaking his gaze from our direction. "Every—every minute of every day."

We four sat on a bench, facing Evan in silence. Implausibly enough, he looked genuinely grateful for our presence. There was nothing else to say: I was floored he had, even momentarily, actually allowed us to see him in a state of weakness and knew he had no intention of sharing anything further. After a few minutes, Evan went back to reading—a tattered copy of Shakespeare's sonnets. A framed picture had been set down beside the tombstone: Evan, no older than five or six, with his arms around his mother, bearing those same burning-blue eyes. I couldn't help but think about how it takes something as true and irrevocable as death to finally lay down our masks. I kept staring at that picture until I felt a hot pressure building in my eyes. I blinked it off and looked away.

—

I TOOK THE FLOOR FOR the first time all season Tuesday night against Plantation. It was a ludicrously lopsided game, with Noah dropping twenty at the half. By the start of the fourth we led by nearly thirty, at which point it became socially unacceptable to continue to play our starters, and so, after giving me a worried look, Rocky cursed under his breath and threw me into the game. I was thrilled, though embarrassed by the way the starters, joined especially by Eddie and Cynthia, cheered too effusively when I checked in. Oliver, decisively high, made a point of getting me open looks, and the result was the best scoring output of my brief and unremarkable career: eight points, on four of seven shots. After the buzzer sounded, Rocky begrudgingly permitted Noah to hand me the game ball.

Despite enduring the slog of games in which I made no appearance whatsoever, my mother was absent that night, due to the elementary school's parent-teacher conferences. (My father, as far as I knew, had no clue I even had a game.) Even more depressing was the fact that Sophia, who attended only our biggest games, given her lack of interest in basketball and her considerable extracurricular commitments as president, wasn't present, for I'd been hoping, at long last, to demonstrate to her some shred of athletic competency.

During Rocky's postgame rant I learned that, in addition to holding the same title in scoring and assisting, Noah was now Kol Neshama's all-time rebounding leader. His family was heading to a late-night celebratory dinner. Amir, as such, offered me a ride home with his mother and Oliver.

Mrs. Samson was short, with heavy features and hardened eyes and her hair in a neat bob. I couldn't tell whether she spoke with an Israeli or Colombian accent. I thought back to what Oliver had told me about the Samson family dynamic and felt a peculiar surge of admiration for the job she did raising Amir.

"So, Amir," Mrs. Samson started as soon as we were on the road, "what was with that embarrassing shot?"

Amir looked up from his phone, giving Oliver an anticipatory glare through the rearview mirror. "What now, Ma?"

"The third quarter—look at this schmuck! *Estúpidamente!* A curse on your household!" She swerved to avoid a driver drifting out of his lane. "In the third quarter you took a dumbass shot in traffic."

"Why are we discussing this?" Amir asked. "Did we not win by a million points?"

She released her right hand from the steering wheel, swatting in Amir's direction. "You think that's how your ancestors fled persecution? With that attitude?"

Oliver leaned over toward the front seat. "Mrs. Samson, if I may, in your son's defense . . ."

"Don't start, you *shovav*." She slapped now at Oliver's hand. "Sit quietly or I'm calling your parents."

"You've been calling my parents nonstop for, like, fifteen years," Oliver said. "Haven't you noticed they stopped answering the phone?"

She turned her eyes on me in the rearview mirror. "Ari, forget that *loco* next to you, he's trouble."

"He keeps me on my toes," I said.

"So nu? I hear a lot about the impressive new friend. How do you like school?"

"It's great," I said politely, "thank you."

"*Yafeh meod*. And next year?"

"Ma," Amir demurred, though without much force, "leave him be."

"Next year remains to be seen." I moved uncomfortably in my seat, shivering slightly from the air-conditioning. It was the first time I'd actually sweated in a game-worn jersey.

"You know where you're applying?"

"No," I said.

"He's as lost as I am, Mrs. Samson," Oliver said.

"Nobody in the history of Zion Hills is as lost as you, Oliver. So listen, Amir, I was talking to Sabba. We think we should speak to his friend with the connection to the editor at *Haaretz*—"

"Ma, I told you I haven't yet finished that other project."

Mrs. Samson, realizing she was about to run a red light, slammed on the brake. "But I told you to finish! I told you Sabba wants to go to his friend and his friend can go to MIT—"

Oliver pulled out his iPhone and began videotaping. He didn't even bother containing his laughter.

We pulled up to my house. I sprinted from the car, ears ringing, the game-used basketball tucked proudly under my arm.

—

"SO," KAYLA SAID THE NEXT DAY, throwing open the classroom door, hair bouncing wildly, "you've managed to survive the wicked SAT."

I plopped my textbook on the desk. "You're late."

She took the seat beside me in the empty room and pulled out her lunch, one of those Greek salads she always ate. "When did you start keeping time?"

"I'm very reliant on my tutor," I said. "Sue me."

"Can't blame you, not when your tutor is this good." She leaned back in her chair, put her feet up on the desk. She wore beat-up Converse sneakers, streaked with yellow and red designs she added herself with markers and splashes of paint. "Debrief me on the test."

"It was okay."

"Okay? Not exactly what a tutor dreams of hearing."

"Don't flatter yourself," I said. "You weren't my SAT tutor."

"That's right. You decided to pay that maniac instead." She dug into her salad. "Well, I'm glad you didn't think it was *disastrous*."

"Yeah, well. When are you taking it?"

"I've already dealt with it."

"Figures. And I suppose you did quite well."

"Of course I did."

"Such modesty," I said. "That's great, though. Where are you applying?"

Kayla shrugged, chewed a mouthful of lettuce.

"At least I'm not the only one without direction," I said.

She laughed, flicking a piece of a tomato in my direction. "Oh, I definitely know what I'm doing. I'm just not telling you."

The door swung open. In walked Remi and Sophia. Remi, registering the scene before her, blinked in amusement. "What's *this*?"

I straightened quickly, as if I'd been caught doing something illicit. "Hi."

"Sorry to interrupt." Sophia smiled slightly, raised a brow. "I left a folder here from second period."

"Not at all," I said, "we're just, uh, studying."

Remi raised her iPhone's camera and snapped what I hoped was a selfie. "Are you?"

"Yes," I said.

"For what exactly?" Remi pressed, surveying whatever picture she had taken.

Kayla cleared her throat. "Geometry."

Remi had her hand on her hip. "That right?"

Sophia grabbed her folder from a nearby desk. "Look at you, Hamlet. So studious. Can't get enough tutoring, can you?"

"It's just—" I said, paling.

"Right," Sophia said, exiting. "Best of luck to you both."

"Eden," Remi said, hovering at the door.

"Yeah, Remi?"

"You have a tomato slice on your lap."

—

"RAV SHIMON BEN YOCHAI TAUGHT that God provides three gifts to Israel, all of which are received through suffering." It was late morning on Monday and we were sitting in Gemara, the room warm and drowsy. Even Rabbi Schwartz looked to be struggling to stay awake. "Anyone know what these gifts are?"

"Cars, money and Hamptons mansions?" Donny said.

"Life, liberty and the pursuit of a good SAT score?" Noah said.

"Sex, drugs and rock and roll?" Gabriel said.

Rabbi Schwartz gave us the impression he might very well break down and weep. "The answer I was looking for, actually, was Torah, the Land of Israel and the World to Come."

A soft knock at the door. Rabbi Bloom stood quietly, eyes narrowed. "Rabbi Schwartz," he said, "hate to interrupt, but I need to borrow a few of your students." He motioned politely to Evan, Amir, Noah and me. We followed in silence, avoiding eye contact with each other. We hadn't done anything wrong, at least as far as I was aware. I feared he'd somehow learned about the exploits at my house, though this seemed implausible, albeit petrifying.

He sat us around his conference table and offered tea. Only Evan accepted. I'd become strangely accustomed to the inviting solitude of my secret morning meetings with him—perusing his library, discussing poetry, philosophy, politics—which he'd ended only a few days earlier with the assurance that we'd find time in the near future to continue such conversations. In those meetings, moving from Kierkegaard to the likes of Blake and Aristotle, I discovered a real teacher, the rebbe I'd never found back home. The thought of reverting to quiet bystander, secondary, as always, to Evan and the others, was unbearable.

Rabbi Bloom took his seat at the head of the table. "I had an idea over the weekend and I want to hear what each of you thinks."

His door flew open without a knock. Oliver meandered in, whistling, those horn-rimmed glasses rendering him sharp-eyed.

"Mr. Bellow. Glad you could join." He motioned for Oliver to sit beside me. "I was just about to explain that I began this year with no small problem. I anticipated that, as seniors, you'd enjoy feeling, shall we say, unfettered." His gaze rested on Evan, though Evan didn't blink. "As it turned out, I was painfully right. Now I'm in something of a bind, because there's a pattern emerging here. Each troubling incident—what occurred at the Silver residence, for example, or the egg assault, to name a few—features this very cast of characters."

"Wait a second," Amir cut in, "we weren't all—"

Rabbi Bloom raised his hand for silence. "We can all agree, Mr. Samson, that certain individuals might *incite* more than others. But in that same vein I think we can similarly agree that the five of you, relative to the rest of your peers, constitute a common denominator. Others in my position—indeed, others in this very school—would not tolerate such alarming behavior. Many, in fact, would recognize this pattern and promptly nip it in the bud, here and now."

I looked, out of the corner of my eye, at Evan. He seemed perfectly calm, as if this speech were intended for someone else entirely.

"College, to be frank," Rabbi Bloom continued, "is the last thing I want to hold over your heads." I winced, realizing that, save for Oliver, who cared so little that he hardly counted, I alone did not have the comfort of knowing I'd inevitably attend some spectacular school. As if reading my thoughts, Rabbi Bloom turned to me. "Mr. Eden and I have been meeting on occasion. I'm not certain you've realized."

Amir frowned. "You have?"

"Yes," Evan said, smiling. "We've obviously noticed."

"And you've been curious about these meetings, Mr. Stark?"

"Nope. I have a solid sense of what you're doing."

Rabbi Bloom traced the corner of his desk with his hands. "Your friend is a hungry thinker, I'm sure you know. I've been offering him enrichment."

Amir looked aghast. "Enrichment?"

"Rest assured, Mr. Samson, it's purely extracurricular. But what I want to do now is extend an invitation to the rest of you."

I scratched my chin, realizing why Rabbi Bloom had abruptly canceled our meetings.

Noah chugged a red Gatorade. "An invitation to do what?"

"To join. You're all capable thinkers, arguably our finest—"

Amir looked at Oliver, blurted out a laugh. Oliver, in turn, offered his middle finger. "If this were really for our finest thinkers," Amir said, "then you'd bring in the actual top five instead of . . . this lovely assortment."

"This guy," Oliver sighed. "Always with the rankings. Ever met someone prouder of being second best?"

"I'm just wondering whether Sophia or even Davis—"

Rabbi Bloom crossed his legs. "Is it your preference to include Mr. Davis? I assumed you'd enjoy excluding him."

At this, Amir fell silent. Oliver snorted.

"So what's the deal here?" Noah asked. "This is basically, like, a book club?"

"Of sorts, Mr. Harris," Rabbi Bloom said. "Let's call it a book club centered on life's pressing questions, disguised as innovative discipline and designed specifically with you five in mind."

Oliver twitched in his seat, readying himself to stand. "Yeah, but no thanks, Rav. This is mighty generous of you and all, but I'm already up to my ears in reading."

"I've been teaching for quite a number of years, gentlemen, longer than I care to admit. It is my professional opinion that you may very well be the most irreverent bunch I've ever come across."

Noah laughed. Amir looked devastated. "Oh, stop it," Oliver said. "You're making us blush."

"My suspicion, however, is that your irreverence has as much to do with doubt, let's call it, as it does personal unhappiness." Rabbi

Bloom removed his glasses, wiped the lenses. I looked around our circle. Evan, eyes to the floor, gave a slight nod, as if he'd been waiting patiently for this sentiment to finally be shared. "So, scoff at your own risk. You're free to make your own decision, of course. I warn you, though, that if you decline to participate I will be forced to consider more traditional forms of discipline if presented with continued misconduct."

Evan smiled. "How did our forefathers put it while God threatened them into accepting the Torah by holding Mount Sinai over their heads? Na'asch V'nishma."

"But our other classes?" Amir asked. "How will we make up the work?"

"You wouldn't need to," Rabbi Bloom said, "if your commitment proves sufficiently serious."

"So," Evan said, "just to make sure we understand: you basically believe you can show us some great texts and magically fix us?"

"Actually, that's right, Mr. Stark. I do believe I can fix you."

Evan stood and offered Rabbi Bloom his hand. "When do we start?"

—

APPARENTLY THE BIGGEST EVENT OF November was Remi White's birthday. For the last several years, Noah explained, the Whites rented Miami's newest nightclub, access to which was otherwise virtually nonexistent, for a lavish celebration: bottle service, photographers, cage dancers, B-list celebrities with whom her father did business. "All the stops," Noah raved. "Ice sculptures, DJs, open bars."

Invitations had been mailed—heavy, cream-colored letters requesting a formal RSVP—which, despite my best efforts, I wasn't able to intercept from my mailbox.

"What's this?" My mother held an enormous rose-gold envelope displaying Remi's initials in elegant calligraphy. "A bar mitzvah?"

"I'll take that, thank you," I said, trying to grab it from her.

She opened the envelope. "Remi Alexandra White's eighteenth

birthday celebration, hosted at Elation in Miami? What in the world is Elation?"

I shrugged.

"Sounds . . . tawdry."

"Tawdry? It's the most upscale place in Miami."

"I thought you didn't know what it was?"

"I, uh, I've heard rumors."

She studied the invitation some more. "So which one is Remi?"

I thought about how Remi had vomited on the very floor on which my mother and I now stood. "You haven't met her," I said.

"Who are her parents?"

"Don't know. Her father's some mogul."

"Oh, right. I think Cynthia's mentioned them."

"Yeah. Anyway, it's supposed to be fun."

She hesitated, her maternal instincts running a quick analysis of the prospect of her son attending a birthday party in some Miami nightclub. "I think I should probably discuss this with Abba."

I tried projecting calm indifference. "What's to really talk about, though?"

She didn't answer. She read the invitation yet again.

"Abba doesn't believe anything other than Gemara is appropriate," I said, pressing further.

My mother looked up from the invitation to give me an uncharacteristically choleric look. "Aryeh. Don't mock him."

"I'm not."

"Then what are you saying?"

"I'm saying," I said, after an uneasy pause, "that he regrets leaving Brooklyn. He doesn't want any other life, and you know that better than I do."

I watched her look about the living room, evading my gaze. She looked at our shelves of seforim. She looked at our framed family pictures. She looked at the couches and dusty lampshades and discarded Shabbat shoes and miscellaneous self-help books that she loved and a misplaced pair of reading glasses and a lonely argyle cardigan. With tired eyes, she looked at all these things that combine to make a family.

"Imma," I said, deliberately pressing a nerve, "you like it here, don't you?"

"Of course I like it here—"

"Know why?"

She frowned. "Tell me why, Aryeh, since you have everything figured out."

My phone hummed in my pocket. We both pretended not to hear it. "Because we're a different breed than he is. We're adapting. We relate to what's here. He just—he doesn't have what we have in us."

A horrified look of recognition passed through her face, only to dissolve into blankness.

"I'm sorry," I said hastily. It was the first time we'd ever quarreled even slightly. "I didn't mean—"

"You're absolutely right. I did want something different," she said. "I wanted you to finally push yourself in a classroom. I wanted to see you make friends you could actually tolerate being around. I wanted you to, *chas v'shalom*, have some innocent fun for once. I wanted you to experience romance. I wanted you to realize a larger world takes place outside the four walls of the Beis Medresh. And you know what? As your mother, I wanted to see you become just a drop *happier*." At this I blushed, without quite knowing why, as if she'd exposed a secret we'd never previously acknowledged. "Don't forget that I took on Abba's life, I wasn't born into it, and so yes, maybe it is complicated and unusual, maybe I do still miss some things. Things I want for my kid. But if any of that comes at the expense of seeing my one child give up crucial parts of himself? I won't want any part of it ever again." She handed me the invitation and left the room.

—

WE BEGAN WITH LUCRETIUS.

"Epicurus believed unhappiness was the fault of the gods." Rabbi Bloom spoke softly, differently from how he usually lectured, as if returning to a life before Kol Neshama. We were seated around his conference table with copies of *De Rerum Natura*. "Godliness is something we humans naturally oppose. What, for Epicurus, is the central root of our resistance?"

"Fear," I said. "We fear God's wrath."

Rabbi Bloom nodded. "And can we be blamed? We suffer misfortune and tragedy and loss, all at the hands of the divine. Isn't it natural to be scared? Hence Epicurus' mission: to remove fear and therefore chip away at human unhappiness. To do so, to convince us we need not fear God any longer, he set out to prove that divinity remains wholly indifferent to our virtues and sins. What was his proof, Mr. Samson?"

"Atomism," Amir spat back.

"By which he means?"

"That the universe as we know it," Evan said, cutting in before Amir could answer, "materialism, our senses, everything tangible, has little to do with God."

"Precisely." It was strange seeing Evan and Rabbi Bloom interact in this non-adversarial way, teacher and student. It was, I imagined, the norm before Evan's mother died. "The mixing of elemental particles created our world, not the will of God. That was his argument, and this is where Lucretius comes in, to make this idea—that we exist by virtue of natural laws, divorced from the intervention of Supreme Beings—attractive enough to ease our prodigious unhappiness. His purpose, in other words, was to set us free."

Evan gnawed at his pen. "But isn't that where he goes wrong?"

Amir snorted. "You *would* question Lucretius."

"I mean it," Evan said. "Acknowledging that we fear God, setting out to free ourselves from Him—I think that part is right. It's good insight."

"Thanks for your approval," Amir muttered.

Rabbi Bloom sipped tea. "So what troubles you, Mr. Stark?"

"We can't free ourselves by removing God," Evan said. "That wouldn't work."

"But why not?" I asked. "If one were to legitimately believe that God had no role in our development—"

"Because whether God participated in creation doesn't matter." Evan removed the pen from his mouth and began jotting illegibly in his notebook. I craned my neck to try reading over his shoulder but could make out only a series of jumbled phrases. *NECESSITY OF SEEING. IGNORING/VENGEANCE→INEFFICACY.* I noticed Noah trying, too. "Once you concede even the peripheral presence of some divine manifestation, whatever that might mean, you're toiling in vain by ignoring it. It'd be like closing your eyes, willing away the world and thinking that it actually worked, that everything melted away."

"Then I think you realize the alternative, Mr. Stark," Rabbi Bloom said.

"Yeah, I do," Evan said. "Turning toward God, not away. But to do that, of course, you'd first need to actually believe."

"Well, yes," Rabbi Bloom said, "that does strike me as rather crucial."

Evan chewed further on his pen. "So then let me ask you this, Rabbi. Have *you* ever doubted God?"

Rabbi Bloom didn't blink. "Hasn't every sentient person?"

"You know what I'm asking. Has your doubt ever made you consider giving it all up? Do you reason with creeping suspicions, or do you ignore them?"

Rabbi Bloom paused, stirring his tea with a plastic spoon before closing the book before him. "How about this? I'll answer with a story."

"Finally," Oliver said, slapping Noah's back. "We have an easier time with stories."

Rabbi Bloom pushed away his teacup. "What do you gentlemen know about Pardes?"

Amir frowned. "Pardes? Like, the method for Torah study?"

"It's also a myth," I said. "From the Gemara."

"And what do you remember about this myth, Mr. Eden?"

I thought back to a fourth-grade mishmar with Rabbi Herenstein, whose shiur on the topic, though hazy now in the annals of my memory, had reduced Shimon to tears. "That it's bleak."

Rabbi Bloom loosened his tie. "As Mr. Samson alluded, the word *pardes* is an acronym. There's Peshat, the surface level. There's Remez, the allegorical meaning beneath the literal. Derash, the midrashic meaning. And, finally, Sod, the esoteric, granted through revelation. Together, these make up our four dimensions of knowledge."

"So far, doesn't sound like much of a story," Noah said.

"The story," Rabbi Bloom continued, "involves the four who entered Pardes, the paradisal orchard of Torah knowledge. Some claim this was purely allegorical: as in, the rabbis exhausted the four levels of study to unlock the deep secrets of the Torah. Others, like Rashi, insist it was a real journey embarked upon by the four holiest men alive."

"This sounds kind of important, actually," Oliver said. "How have I been in Jewish day school for eighteen years without hearing about this until now?"

Rabbi Bloom cleared his throat. "First to enter was Shimon ben Azzai, an expert judge so consumed by his devotion to Torah study that he neglected the sensory world, even refusing to marry. In Pardes, he gazed upon the secrets of the deep but was unable to bear the revelations of this higher world. Shimon ben Azzai looked at God and died.

"Next to enter the orchard was Shimon ben Zoma, master of Halacha, responsible for many of the axioms we use today. Ben Zoma became obsessed with the opening chapter of Genesis. Creation was all he thought about, to the point that he was accused of voyaging outside the limit of what's permissible to contemplate. He suffered terribly for whatever he saw and left the orchard insane."

"Could be a fair price," Evan said quietly, "for learning the secrets of God."

"Third was Elisha ben Abuya, who afterward went by *Acher*— 'Other One.' Acher's one of the most intriguing figures in our tradition, and perhaps the least understood. Little is known of his youth or career, but we do know that his downfall was his love for learning. Acher, you see, was enamored of worldly things, things forbidden to him—horses, wine, architecture—but most of all Greek philosophy, so much so that he'd stash illicit works in his clothing while in the Beit Midrash. When Acher entered the orchard, he abandoned everything and left a heretic, destroying the plants of the heavenly garden, as the Gemara tells us. Most interpret this to mean he not only surrendered his faith but actively participated in rebellion by luring away the youth from Torah.

"Last, of course, was Rabbi Akiva, Rosh LaChachamim, chief of the sages, humble shepherd-turned-giant through painstaking dedication to Torah. He's the one on whom history looks most fondly. His biography is legendary, taught to every child in yeshiva. Rabbi Akiva, like his companions, saw God, and yet he survived unscathed. And so, of the four who entered the orchard, all of whom were generational leaders, all of whom were dazzlingly holy men, only one managed to leave untouched."

Silence fell over us. "Wow," Noah said eventually, straightening in his chair. "Heavy stuff."

I watched Evan transcribe a flurry of notes. "What did Acher see to make him stop believing?" I asked.

"The Gemara," Rabbi Bloom said, "says he saw Metatron—"

Noah held up a hand. "Wait, who's Metatron? A divine robot?"

"The archangel," Amir said, "the heavenly scribe who records all human actions."

"Hopefully not all our actions," Oliver said, elbowing Amir in the ribs.

"But doesn't God take care of that kind of stuff?" Noah asked. "Recording our actions, who will live, who will die, who will get Christmas presents?"

"Not if God's busy," Oliver said. "Or taking a midday nap."

Rabbi Bloom kneaded his left temple. "Mr. Bellow, a modicum of respect."

"Sorry, sorry." Oliver lifted his palms peacefully. "For what it's worth, I do think it'd be a well-deserved nap."

"Anyway," Rabbi Bloom said, shaking his head, "Acher saw Metatron sitting, despite the fact that only God is permitted to sit in Heaven. And if Metatron could sit, Acher reasoned, perhaps there existed two gods. For this, he was given sixty lashes of fire and all of his merits were erased."

"Jeez," Noah said, "doesn't that seem like overkill?"

Amir itched his eyelids. "Yeah, I mean, *everything* was erased? What happened to divine justice?"

Rabbi Bloom offered Amir a smile that fused admiration with pity. "And what, pray tell, are the tenets of divine justice?"

"I don't know, how about fairness?" Amir said.

"Reward," Oliver said, flicking a paper football at Amir.

"Goodness," Noah said.

"Forgiveness," I said.

"Retribution," Evan said.

Rabbi Bloom played with the spine of his book, opening the front and back covers until they cracked and then returning them to a resting position. "A heavenly voice announced that all humans are allowed to repent, except for Acher. And that, I'm afraid, was divine justice."

I tugged at my collar. "Just because he *questioned*?"

Rabbi Bloom moved over to his shelves and rummaged around, returning to the table with the Kuzari. "'*The third fell into bad ways,*'" he read when he found the page, "'*because he ascended above human intelligence and said: "Human actions are but instruments leading to spiritual heights; having reached these, I care not for religious ceremonies."*'"

"Nietzschean," Evan said. I didn't look Evan's way. Neither did Rabbi Bloom. Evan blinked. "Okay, I'll ask it, then. Why Rabbi Akiva? What made him special enough to see God but leave unscathed?"

Rabbi Bloom rapped his knuckles against the table. "Unfortunately, Mr. Stark, the Gemara provides no such answer."

Calmly, Evan placed down his pen and scanned over the pages of his notebook. "Then *you* need to give us an answer. What did Akiva do to survive?"

Rabbi Bloom leaned forward, focusing his attention only on Evan. "I wanted you to hear this for a reason." He removed his glasses, biting the temples. "This story teaches us two things. It reminds us that, even while we stumble through the duller side of conventional expressions of religious observance, even when we don't feel the burning need to attend minyan or keep Shabbat or wait between eating meat and dairy, a higher realm does exist. Which is to say, never lose sight of the grander depths. But at the same time, it also reinforces an equally critical lesson: don't chase too obsessively after those higher realms. Don't discard the smaller but equally vital parts of Judaism in favor of supernatural myths, because without our basic rituals and customs and structures, without our daily love for and connection to Hashem, we are left with nothing but blind visions."

A few moments of silence, until Evan slammed shut his Lucretius. When Rabbi Bloom remained quiet, Evan stood from the table. "You didn't answer my question and you know it."

"Oh?" Rabbi Bloom said, allowing Evan to walk out. "Didn't I?"

IN THE END, MY MOTHER never mentioned Remi's party to my father. When the night came, I told my father I had a basketball game. To this, he nodded indifferently and returned his head to his Gemara, failing to notice as my mother slipped me pocket change, a move I interpreted as a conciliatory gesture. I wore my only suit for the occasion—navy, embarrassingly frayed—at the behest of Noah, who strongly advised me not to dress the way I usually did.

Elation was in the lower lobby of a resort, everything marble, white, glimmering. There was billowing smoke, a ceiling covered with mirrors, red fur on the couches, silver stages for dancers, walls lacquered in metallic gold, tables decked in glossy-red fabric, a massive glass bar at the center of the room. Only half our grade had been invited—"It's a pretty exclusive event," Oliver told me while working on his third cocktail, "which begs the question: how the fuck did you get in?"—and there were dozens of people I didn't recognize: French girls Remi knew from summers in the Côte d'Azur, wealthy cousins with that distinctive, sharply upturned nose, a former third-string Laker.

The night began formally, with a fleet of stretch limousines fetching us from a central location—Rebecca's house—but, quickly enough, devolved into a drunken affair. The bartenders, influenced by Mr. White's generosity, showed little interest in our age, circulating a constant flow of sparkling champagne and mixing exotic drinks with names I'd never heard of: Maiden's Prayers, Gimlets, French 75s. Deafening music started soon enough, but I remained on my own, nodding along, sipping an Old-Fashioned.

Nicole, in a sleeveless blue dress, materialized next to me. "Always on the side, huh?"

"Yeah, but as you can probably tell," I said, watching Noah and Rebecca dance, "Remi hired me to be the life of the party."

"Wow, congratulations. That must be a pretty big promotion for you."

"Yeah, I thought so, too," I said.

"What's that?"

"I said I thought so, too," I yelled over the music.

"Oh." She offered a polite smile. "Right."

People shuffled by, fighting for access to the dance floor. We remained in place, contorting our faces into what we hoped might be non-awkward expressions. "I'd ask you to dance," I said eventually, trying to combat how uncomfortable I felt, "but I don't exactly know how."

"How to ask or how to dance?"

"Apparently they're not mutually exclusive."

Nicole put out her hand. "I'll let you drag me to the dance floor."

"You're cool with me making a fool out of both of us?"

"It's your skin on the line, not mine." She took my drink, finished it herself and deposited it with a stray waiter. "Come on," she said, steering me into the chaos, "pretend it's the Hora."

I allowed her to lead me, tried not to focus on the way Amir executed effortless spin moves with Lily. Against my better judgment, I attempted to imitate Amir and succeeded only in elbowing Nicole in the ribs. "Sorry about that. Apparently I wasn't exaggerating entirely about my skills."

"I can see that." Nicole frowned at the way my hands hovered clumsily around her waist. "Somebody should probably teach you how to move like a normal human."

I readjusted my positioning. "How's this?"

"Literally not any better."

"Awesome."

Someone—Donny, it seemed—bumped me from behind, sending me crashing into Nicole's chest. She blushed. "You're really such a natural."

"Listen, Nicole," I said, deciding this was as good an opportunity as any, "we never really had a chance to talk about—"

She shook her head. "Nope. Not doing this."

"But I never said sorry—"

"—sorry for what?"

"I don't know. I just feel kind of weird we've never even, like, acknowledged the whole thing."

Another grimace. "Eden?"

"Yeah?"

"You're squeezing my waist a little too tightly."

"Shit, sorry."

Her hand retreated from my shoulders. "Is it true you're hooking up with her?"

I stopped in my tracks. The spike of someone's heel landed on my foot, crushing my big toe. "What?"

"The quiet girl with bushy hair. Katya?"

"Her name's Kayla," I said, trying to move my poor toe, which I could feel bruising.

"Someone said they saw you in a classroom together at lunch." She drew away slightly. "Is she here tonight?"

"No, I'm not seeing her, I just—" Out of the corner of my eye, I finally found Sophia: black fitted dress, hair straightened to fall in a precise line on her shoulders, earrings dangling from a long, golden chain, eyeliner rendering her gaze dark and brilliant. She was off to the side, speaking with Evan, who wore a tuxedo and a red bow tie. My blood thinned.

Nicole's hand was at her hip. "What're you staring at?"

The lights in the room broke in green flashes, making it difficult to tell what Sophia and Evan were doing. Screaming? Laughing? "Sophia."

"Sophia Winter?"

"Indeed," I said, slightly humiliated at the way my interest in Sophia registered to Nicole as absurdly beyond the pale of reason.

She gave a soft titter. "Eden."

"What?"

"I'm not sure you're exactly her type," she said, smiling to herself.

"What's her type?"

She shrugged. "It's always been Evan. Still is, by the look of it."

The music stopped. The DJ announced a surprise video in Remi's honor, giving Nicole a chance to slink away. A theater-size screen descended from the ceiling, featuring split-screen collages of Remi through the years: as a newborn, a toddler at the Eiffel Tower, a flower girl, a teenager posing in a one-piece bathing suit. After a few self-absorbed minutes the video ended and, dutifully, we applauded Remi: skintight, black designer gown; cerise lipstick; exquisite blond curls; a single pearl swaying from her neck. She and her father, an imposingly tall man with comically chiseled features, danced to Sinatra's "The Way You Look Tonight," after which the remaining adults trickled out. The dancing restarted, the DJ imploring us to again "get wild," and I grabbed two drinks, scanning for Sophia. After several nerve-wracking minutes, I spotted her in the back and fought my way over.

She was alone. Purple ropes blocked off the section. I sat beside her, handed her a drink. The pulsing green lights made it feel as if we were moving in slow motion. "Fancy yourself a VIP?" I asked.

"Don't you?"

What does yearning look like? Studying her face, I thought not of desire but of need. This, I told myself, is what it looks like when an old life is shed and a new one begins. "I'd say you're easily the most important person in the room. So yeah."

"You wildly overrate me, Hamlet."

"Are you all right?"

Airy, defiant eyes. She put the drink to her mouth and took the smallest sip one could take. "Don't waste your night worrying about me."

"I just—I saw you with Evan." The buzz from my drink amplified, making the music pounding my eardrums deliquesce into unintelligible noise. "I wanted to see if you're okay."

She bit her lower lip, ran a finger around the rim of her cocktail. "Why were you looking at me?"

"Oh," I said, blushing. "That I can't much help."

This time she took a long drink. When she finished she wet her lips with her tongue. "How long have you had that problem?"

"I'm pretty sure it started the day I met you at Noah's pool."

The force of entropy: the music, the strobe lights, the bodies on the dance floor. Sophia in her swimsuit, at the piano, beneath the tree, bathed in lights beside the water. These were strong drinks. I wanted, desperately, to hold her hand. And then two people came crashing from the dance floor into our section.

"Shit." Remi, tousled, and Evan, bow tie draped over his shoulders. "I didn't know you were here," Remi said, raising her voice against the music.

Evan was sweaty, his eyes dim. He nodded curtly at Sophia and ignored me altogether. "Sorry." He put a hand on Remi's back and led her away. "Didn't mean to interrupt."

"Can I ask you something?" I said after they'd left. Sophia had returned to staring into her drink.

"What is it?"

"What happened between you two?"

Momentarily, Sophia tightened her eyes, making me immediately regret having opened my mouth. Then she stood, flattened her dress, held out her hand. "Are we dancing or not?"

I took her hand, confused, keenly aware of my heart throwing itself riotously against my rib cage. We downed our drinks and, lightheaded, made our way to the dance floor, bodies parting at the sight of the boy from Brooklyn with Sophia Winter in her flawless dress. I held her, drinking in sparkling vanilla, feeling the soft curves of her body, spinning in ambient light.

—

WE WALKED, BAREFOOT, TOWARD THE beach behind the hotel. She handed me her black heels. "There." She picked a deserted lounge chair at the base of the sand. Faint waves licked at our feet. The tide was coming.

We faced the ocean, lying silently on the chair, her head against my chest. There were wet drops on my shirt. I looked down at the crown of her head, overwhelmed by her tears, by the magnitude of our privacy. "What's wrong?"

"Have you ever made a terrible mistake?"

Being this close to her, feeling the weight of her body against mine, gave me a sense of physical pain in my chest. I imagined my years of loneliness as a long corridor, one door after another, a passage of empty chambers leading me to this night. "I've never done anything important enough."

"Ari." Her voice rang out hoarse, broken. "What's wrong with me?"

"What's wrong with you? Literally nothing. Sophia, I mean, come on, you're brilliant, you're incisive, you're freaking heart-stopping. You terrify me and you're fierce and honestly you're entirely . . . yeah, I don't know, alien, really, to anything I've ever thought I'd know. And yes, fine—you're beautiful." I forced myself, briefly, to look toward the water. Vocalizing all this immediately inverted whatever governed our previous dynamic. She had revealed weakness, and I had responded by revealing myself. "You make everything else hollow."

"Beauty means nothing." She rose, leaned forward drunkenly. "My beauty means nothing." I was close enough to feel her breath. She kissed me softly, coolly, before falling back into my chest. I sat delirious, frozen in the night, running my fingers through her dark hair.

—

ECCE DEUS FORTIOR ME, qui veniens dominabitur michi. That's what Dante, still a child, told himself when he first saw Beatrice. Behold, a god more powerful than I who will rule over me. *Heu miser, quia frequenter impeditus ero deinceps*—how often will I be troubled hereafter!

I decided not to tell anyone, not even Noah. Withholding this secret felt like hiding stolen artwork. I had access to beauty that nobody else could see, an image stored away that was thrilling enough to illuminate the darkest recesses of my life but that I couldn't actually reveal. I'd kissed the most powerful person I'd ever seen and no one knew. Still, there was a sense of fear: that Sophia, ashen-faced with humiliation, would claim the whole thing had been a drunken, colossal mistake.

On Monday, I walked in early to biology to find her waiting at my desk.

I hadn't heard from her all weekend, nor had I worked up the nerve to text or call. I stood there, hands probing the depths of my pockets, bracing myself. "Hi."

"Ari." She was high-toned, bright-eyed again. "I want to apologize."

A deep, exultant roar in my eardrums. "You want to apologize?"

"I know I was a mess," she said, pink-cheeked, contorting her mouth into a smirk. "But I swear I'm not usually so, I don't know, doleful. I had too much to drink, is all."

Desperate, physical longing. I resisted the urge to throw down my books and gather her into my arms. "I don't think you could be a mess if you tried."

"Yeah? What would you call the tears?"

I smiled. "The natural result of finding yourself alone at the beach with me."

"You're too kind. And way too self-deprecating. But I just want to say that what happened with us—it was the highlight of the party."

How many more times throughout my life span, I wondered, would I merit feeling such pure happiness? "It was?"

"Ari," she said sheepishly, allowing herself to smile, "I mean it."

"So if I were to, say, ask you out," I said, enduring an unfamiliar surge of adrenaline, "theoretically you might consider saying yes?"

Dr. Flowers chose that moment to barge in, slamming her purse on her desk, accidentally sending a pack of Marlboros skidding across the laminate floor. "Shut the hell up, because today we cover the wonderful world of gene therapy." I fell silent, took my seat, opened my notes. Sophia and I stared at each other, trying not to laugh. For the first time all year, I enjoyed every moment of biology, Dr. Flowers' wheezing and all.

—

WE SAW A MOVIE THAT Saturday night, some big-budget superhero thriller. It took me an anxiety-ridden hour to shave, to decide which shirt best matched my newly acquired slim-fit jeans, to apply just the right dosage of cologne, to attempt to tame my hair. (Winking, clearly informed by Rebecca about my plans for the evening, Noah came over to drop off a new product, demonstrating in painstaking detail how best to achieve consciously disheveled, swept-back hair. Shoulder-length blond locks, I discovered, surrendered to gravity much more readily than did the tangled mess occupying the top of my head.)

My mother darted past my room, only to retrace her steps. She wore a proud, teasing grin. "Who's the lucky lady?"

"What's that?" I avoided her eyes, dousing myself in Creed and focusing on my reflection in the mirror. Undeniably presentable, I was, for a moment, unrecognizable to myself.

She continued to linger at the door. "Come on. I've never seen you dress so . . . meticulously. The only logical conclusion is that there's a girl."

"Just going out." I changed shirts: a pale-blue Oxford that Oliver had grown sick of and had donated to what he affectionately dubbed "the Ari Eden emergency fashion fund, may Hashem guard his soul."

"Yeah, okay. Well, enjoy yourself. We can keep this between us."

After the movie—two hours of furtive glances at Sophia, who wore her hair down and occasionally returned my looks—we went for pizza.

"Well," Sophia said, biting into a mushroom slice, cheese hanging delicately from her chin, "it appears I've won."

I offered her a napkin. She slapped away my hand. "Won what?"

"Wasn't this your first date?"

I sipped my Coke. "No need to rub it in."

"No mockery, I just want feedback."

"Okay, I'll admit," I said, reaching for fries, "it wasn't nearly as painful as expected."

"How gratifying. I'm a fantastic teacher, aren't I? Maybe you'd even say I'm as talented as your other teacher?"

A brief coughing session as Coke traveled down the wrong pipe. "Kayla, you mean? That's nothing. Remedial math."

"'Poison in jest,'" she said. "I'm only kidding."

"For what it's worth," I added, "you should know that I'm happy, too. That you're my first, I mean."

"Happy? You should be inconsolably exuberant." An indeterminate smile, followed by a flare of hesitation. "So can I ask the difficult question?"

"Which one would that be?"

"Does anyone know?"

"Know what?"

"You haven't told anyone?"

"About—us?"

She nodded.

"No. I haven't."

"Not even Noah? Or Amir or Oliver or—?"

"Nobody." Pained silence. "Have you?"

"Maybe a slight hint to Rebecca," she said, "but otherwise no."

I found myself hoping she was lying. "You're not too embarrassed of me," I said, trying to appear at least half-joking, "are you?"

"Mortified." A light smile returned to her. I focused my attention on her lower lip. "I mean, just look at you. All cleaned up. Did they give you a makeover on my behalf?"

My hands flew to my hair. "It's way too much, isn't it?"

"No, you're cute. Actually, you don't realize how handsome you are."

"That's for sure."

"If only you recognized how people look at you."

"I know how people look at me. For the most part, it's pretty unflattering."

Sophia put her hand on my back. I could feel the outlines of each of her fingertips through the thin material of Oliver's shirt. "My oblivious Brooklyn boy."

We paid, drove home. She lived near Oliver and Evan, in a stately Spanish colonial with thick, stuccoed walls, clerestory windows, royal palms, a flush of bougainvillea. Her house was big enough to swallow several of mine.

"Well." She opened the car door. "Time for my nightly interrogation."

"About me?"

"I'm afraid not. They don't know about you."

"Oh," I said, unreasonably disappointed.

She undid her seatbelt, climbed out of the car. "They cross-examine me whenever I leave the house."

"Why's that?"

"They're—protective. They're looking out for me. I don't fault them for it."

"Of course," I said. "So what do you tell them?"

"I don't really go places I can't tell them about."

"That makes it easier."

"When I must, though, I'll spare details and tell them I'm out with Rebecca or some such wholesome thing."

"So what was your alibi tonight?"

"Babysitting."

"Funny."

"Tonight, I had a student council meeting, and then I was at Oliver's, using Leon's piano."

"Genius."

"They don't need to know I'm on a date."

I was clenching the steering wheel, doing so too tightly. "I know what you mean."

"Ari." Her voice was smaller now.

"Yeah?"

"I had a great time." She clasped the back of her neck with her right hand, that far-off, icy-gray flickering in her eyes. "Can we just— can we be clear about something?"

"Clear?" I smiled distractedly, glanced at myself in the rearview mirror: a startled stranger, pale, blinking gravely.

"I like you, Hamlet. I mean that. It's just, at the moment, I really can't handle too much—"

"What does that mean?" I asked this too abruptly, only to curse myself for the misery in my voice.

She leaned over the passenger seat. I made an effort to focus only on one portion of her face; taking in her entire image suddenly proved overwhelming. I examined her forehead, her clear skin, save for a single hint of irritation beneath the surface of her right temple, her thin, nearly imperceptible veins. "We need terms."

"Right," I said, "okay."

She avoided my gaze. "We should keep things concealed, at least until I feel like I've had enough time."

"All right. I won't tell anyone." A long, strained pause. "But what do you need time for?"

"To heal." She said so immediately, much to my surprise.

I restrained myself from pressing further. I was desperate for her, entirely impaled, as Evan had once warned. I was willing, sitting in the car, red-eyed, sprinklers erupting on her lawn, palm trees moving in the wind, my desire for Sophia approximating something like delirium, to accept waiting, to be used, to trade future hurt for present happiness.

We looked at each other for a few moments.

"Good night, then, sweet prince." She kissed me lightly and headed inside her house.

—

ICE-CREAM DATES, MINIATURE GOLF OUTINGS (she beat me soundly), trips to the beach, ice skating (I fell too often, spent most of the time clutching her arm), a visit to the Vizcaya Gardens: carefree, joyous nights away from schoolwork, parents, friends. It'd been several bright, windswept weeks, her warm hand in mine, her lips on mine, her breath on my neck, intense euphoria, intense restlessness, the feeling of being propelled through several days at a time. Still, I couldn't help but agonize over what drew her to me, couldn't help but wonder when she'd come to her senses. I was different from the others, I reminded myself. I was naïve, I was sincere, I was thoughtful, I was untainted. This last part had to be it: above all else, I was not yet broken.

Even harder than it was to accept that she liked me was accepting that I could have what I wanted most, that I could become, overnight, unequivocally happy. Believing so involved a certain logical absurdity, not unlike Moore's: certainly I could know I was dating Sophia Winter without believing it. It would be only a matter of time, I was convinced, before things detonated, and yet I was content to pay any price if it meant hanging on to her for however long I could.

—

WE MET RABBI BLOOM THREE times each week. After Lucretius, we darted from creationism to political theology, exploring the relationship between Modern Orthodoxy and normative ethics. We devoured readings, wrote brief papers, competed to stand out. Evan, to our collective disbelief, emerged as our group's most serious student, despite his reputation in our real classes. He never missed an assignment, he always had a notebook to record epiphanies at a breakneck pace and he had a habit of lingering, after the rest of us had left, to engage Rabbi Bloom in heated discussions.

"Why wear tefillin?" Rabbi Bloom asked in our most recent session. "What's meaningful about tefillin?"

"It's obvious," Oliver said, sipping tea, "we find the dyed hide of a cow super beautiful."

"Because God delivered us from enslavement," Amir said, rolling his eyes, "and we value daily reminders of the life from which we came."

"There's the organ idea," Noah added, "the one they preach in middle school, right before your bar mitzvah: the arm and the head are the two ways we serve God."

"Yeah, but personally I think we serve God with a third organ," Oliver said, "at least the righteous do, isn't that right, Rabbi Bloom? A little healthy dose of *pru urvu*?"

Rabbi Bloom listened to us echo everything we'd been taught: we need constant reminders of God's sovereignty, we savor beautifying the mitzvah, we take solace in accepting that there are commandments we are not permitted to understand. Then, in his quiet, severe way, he lectured on Kierkegaard's belief that unfettered freedom is true enslavement, that liberty comes at the price of binding ourselves voluntarily, that tefillin leaves marks on our arms to remind us we've been changed in a way that is more than skin-deep. I miss these rapturous sessions greatly, spots of time to which I still turn regularly. Even nowadays, I'll wake from a distant dream and, in that delightful corridor between consciousness and reverie, I'll hear his voice, envision the fire in his eyes as he went on about Hume and Kant and all the others in whom I may never again believe.

DECEMBER

Do the gods light this fire in our hearts
Or does each man's mad desire become his god?

—Virgil, *Aeneid*

The SAT came back on a Saturday, which meant I had to endure an entire Shabbat of anxious waiting. I passed time reading and, later, walking the streets, hoping to chance upon Sophia. I considered stopping by her house, so close was I to jumping out of my skin, though came quickly to my senses and decided instead to try Noah.

"Sup, bud?" Noah said, clapping my back as he answered the front door. "Why do you look like you've seen a ghost?"

"I feel like I'm waiting to see a ghost," I said, following him down the hall.

"Then you might not like what's going on in the living room," Noah said.

"What do you mean?"

We stopped in his kitchen so that Noah could grab me a Heineken, and then he steered me into the living room, toward the others. "We're checking scores."

"Look who it is," Oliver said, iPhone in hand. Evan, beside him, snorted to himself when he saw me. "We were just revealing Noah's score to the kehillah."

I sat on the couch, put the Heineken on the floor. Amir examined my face, as if probing for evidence of guilt. "You haven't looked, right?" he asked me.

I blinked awkwardly. I was still unaccustomed to having people around me violate Shabbat with such impunity. Watching Amir await my answer, I thought of how, in the fifth grade, Mordechai admitted he had turned his Walkman on and off one Friday night. It was electrifying, he insisted, urging me to try it. "Even if you don't like it, even if you never want to do it again," he reasoned, "you'll always know you rebelled *once*." I requested a week of deliberation, but when Friday night arrived I refrained, suddenly picturing Mordechai as the snake presenting fruit to Eve. Why he'd entrusted me with his secret was evident in my reaction: I'd been shocked but not horrified. Unlike Shimon and the others, I was capable of entertaining sin. For weeks afterward, I imagined myself as Rabbi Amnon of Mainz, flirting too closely with betraying God. "It's Shabbat," I said.

"I assume that's a no, to be clear," Amir said.

"It's a no."

"Well, if it makes any difference to a Beis Din," Noah said, throwing himself down beside me, "it wasn't technically *my* sin. Oliver went online for me."

I sipped tensely from my beer. "Yeah, not sure it works like that."

Noah laughed with some degree of guilt. "You don't think our sins are transferable? Like currency?"

"By the way, in my defense," Oliver said, opening a Budweiser, "I didn't check my own score. So, I'm pretty sure that means the sin remains Noah's. Eden, need me to check yours? I won't charge for the service."

"Nah, I'll pass, thanks."

"Suit yourself."

Amir inched forward on the couch. "Oliver, you seriously didn't check your score?"

Oliver raised his drink. "Heard that right."

"Why wouldn't you?"

"Does it matter what it says?"

"Uh, yeah. It matters a ton."

"For you," Oliver said, taking a swig. "Not for me, thankfully."

"What a privilege," Amir muttered.

Oliver shrugged. "To be so rich? Yeah, can't complain."

"No. To be so simpleminded." Amir turned back to Noah. "So did you get the score you needed for recruitment?"

"Yes, sir," Noah said. "The coach will be happy."

"Awesome. Congrats. What about you, Evan?"

Evan, silent until now, was lying on the other side of the couch, the *Wall Street Journal* over his face. "What was that, Amir?"

"How do you feel?"

"What you're asking is if you beat me," he said lazily from behind the paper. "And I'm not in the mood to play that game."

"Don't flatter yourself." Amir grabbed for an old copy of *Sports Illustrated* in an effort to appear nonchalant. "I'm just being, you know, polite."

"Wait," I said, unable to stop myself, "Amir, *you* checked?" Until now, I'd been grateful to rely on Amir holding out against our friends' routine trespassing of Halacha—failures to daven, violations of Shabbat, a pervasive indifference to keeping kosher. When aligned with Amir, I defended ancient customs with pride. Hearing he had checked made me feel suddenly alone.

Oliver laughed. "Judgmental much, Eden?"

Amir, shamefaced, began tearing through a LeBron James interview.

"But yeah, I checked for him, too," Oliver said, looking pleased. "Trust me, I tried stopping him, but the man simply couldn't wait. Such *tyvah*! I'm sure God understands. We get a few hall passes in our youth, don't we?"

"Leave the dude alone," Noah said. "Everyone has a right to make a personal decision. Anyway, Amir did pretty damn well. Big surprise."

"Yeah," I said, angry at myself for having such a difficult time suppressing my disappointment in Amir. "I bet."

Oliver leaped from the couch and headed to the kitchen. "I'd guess Evan still did better, though."

"Couldn't have done too much better," Noah said.

We exchanged looks, waiting for Amir to snap. "Screw it," Amir said when he finally did, tossing aside the magazine. "Let's hear it."

Evan didn't lower his paper. "We don't need to compare, Amir."

"Bullshit. You already know mine. Oliver probably told you."

"Nope. He didn't."

"Yeah, my bad," Oliver called from the kitchen. I heard him rifling through drawers, looking for a bottle opener. "He got a 1560."

Amir reddened. "Shut the hell up, Oliver!"

"That's very impressive." Evan dropped the paper to the floor, stood, stretched lazily. "Noah, please tell me Cynthia has leftovers for us."

"Come on, Ev," Noah said, "you're leaving the poor dude in suspense. Just look at him."

Evan walked toward the kitchen, pausing at the doorway. "You really need to know?"

Amir didn't answer.

"I beat you."

Now it was Amir visibly failing to stifle his reaction. He tried, rather unnaturally, jutting his jaw. This made things worse. "By how much?"

"Relax," Evan said. "It's enough."

"I want to know by how much."

"What does it matter?"

"Was it by ten?" Amir scratched at his scalp. He looked prepared to rip hair from his head. "By twenty?"

Evan still said nothing.

"Thirty?"

"Amir," Evan said, "none of this matters, I promise."

Amir gave an exacting, fake laugh. "You're going to tell me you got a perf—"

Evan left the room.

—

I CHECKED THE MOMENT MY father finished havdalah. Math was as expected—fine, perfectly unremarkable—though I did rather well on verbal, even better than anticipated. I told Sophia my scores the next afternoon. It was my first time visiting her house; she'd invited me to keep her company as she tended to her brother, since her parents were in St. Augustine, visiting Castillo de San Marcos. Her room was precisely how I imagined: whitewashed, dozens of recital plaques, her desk organized with schoolwork and a large calendar into which she inputted all elements of her day, her childhood upright piano against the wall. When I admitted my scores, after some pressing on her part, she kissed me gently, that faint thrill returning to my chest, only to pull away for her computer. "Forget Ballinger's list," she decided, typing furiously, overcome with the prospect of revising my fortune. "Where do you actually want to go?"

I put my fingers to my lips. I could still feel the taste of her lips. "But my math sucks."

"It doesn't *suck*, per se."

"Yeah? You'd be happy with that score?"

She twirled a finger through her hair. "No, I'd be inconsolable. But I'm a different story. For you it might not matter. We're selling you on English, right? On being delightfully right-brained."

"I don't think I've ever been called anything but half-brained."

She rolled over on her bed, putting her head against my ribs. "Provide names. Now."

"How am I supposed to know?"

"You don't have a single thought on where you want to spend the next four years of your life?"

Light-pink pillowcases. An endless row of perfumes. An old pic-

ture of Sophia at a piano bench. She was only nine and already had
a haunting superiority radiating from somewhere behind her eyes.
"Columbia," I blurted.

"Columbia?"

Iron gates. Low plaza. Alma Mater's outstretched arms, an owl beneath her robes. Hushed memories from my mother. The purported
epicenter of the world. "Yeah."

"Interesting."

"Interesting?" I said. "As in, yikes, Ari, you're clinically insane?"

"As in, wow, I'm admittedly somewhat floored by this secret ambition, but what a lovely idea."

I had a fistful of her sheets. "You don't actually think that."

"No, I do."

"Well, I mentioned it to Bearman."

"And?"

"He laughed in my face. Literally. A belly-deep laugh."

She rolled her eyes, continued to comb through admission statis-
tics. "What does that moron know?"

"A lot, I'd imagine."

"You're above their average verbal score," she said officiously.
"Which makes you viable." Triumphantly, she shut her laptop and
placed her head on my lap. "But Ari?"

"Yeah?"

"You wanted out of New York?"

"I wanted out of Brooklyn. Columbia had as much to do with the
New York I knew as London did. Columbia would be an alternate universe for me."

"You've visited?"

"Once. When I was really little and learning to read, my mom took
me to look at the library. She did a lot of things like that. She went
there, you know, for a bit. To Barnard."

"Why a bit?"

"Well, she became frum."

"You can be frum there."

"Highly frum, I mean. Brooklyn frum. My father frum."

She fingered one of her pillows, peeked up from my lap. "So you're telling me then that this has absolutely nothing to do with me."

My right hand was in her hair. "What does that mean?"

"In case I go to Juilliard."

I shrugged.

She sat up, held her socked feet in her hands. "I really don't think you should be doing this for the wrong reason. It's a big life decision."

"Yeah, I know," I said curtly. My hands moved away from her.

She nodded. "Columbia it is."

—

WITH SOPHIA'S ASSISTANCE I BEGAN the Early Decision application. She pushed me through a headache-inducing Proust Questionnaire— *Describe your favorite heroes in fiction; share your take on happiness*— and offered advice about the personal essay, on which she herself had been hard at work for several months.

"I can't believe you started in August," I said. "That's crazy."

"I didn't start in August."

"Oh. Okay, you're slightly more human, then."

"This is Kol Neshama, Ari. I started last year."

"Jeez."

"Don't look so shocked. Everyone did."

"Well, what're you writing about? I'll take notes."

"Aren't you supposed to be the writer?"

I moved closer to her, put my lips to her neck. She lifted her chin, almost reflexively. Seeing her body move in response to mine made me feel a weird sort of strength, one that was exciting but far-off, unrelated to who I actually was. "I want to know the story Sophia Winter told."

"Sorry, kid. It's a secret."

"I thought we liked sharing secrets."

She squeezed my hand, moved away slightly. "It's a little too personal," she said, and I didn't press further.

—

"ARI EDEN," MRS. BALLINGER SAID, surprised to find me unannounced at her doorway. "Been a while, hasn't it? How might I help you?"

I approached, handed her bulky forms. "Any chance you have a second to sign some application stuff?"

She flipped through the documents, eventually removing her glasses and rubbing down her eyes. "Have a seat."

I sat.

"So." She leaned backward in her chair. "This is a joke to you?"

I raised my brows. "I don't know what you mean by that."

"Mr. Eden, the way this works—the way *I've* built this to work—is no joke."

"Respectfully, Mrs. Ballinger," I said, attempting to maintain leveled deference, "I just figured I'd apply."

"You figured? Despite the fact that I made your stratosphere crystal clear?"

"You did. But then I took the SAT."

She fell silent, excavating my folder from her records. "Well, this is the very first time I'm seeing this," she admitted, surveying my scores, clicking her tongue. "And I can't say I'm totally unimpressed."

"Thank you."

"Actually, I can't deny I'm pretty shocked."

"Yeah, I was, too. Imagine what Bearman will say."

She sighed. "Still. I'm afraid my reservations remain."

"Look, I know my math is comparatively weak, but it's still pretty good and—"

She pushed my forms across the desk. "I won't sign these, Ari."

I felt my intestines tightening unpleasantly. "You won't?"

"I don't feel right about it."

"Okay, but I do," I said, frowning. "And I have nothing to lose trying."

"Nothing to lose?" She gave an aggrieved laugh. "It's not simply a matter of a math score, Ari. There are reputations at stake. There are students already in the running. There are networks I've built— painstakingly, over years and years, before I even arrived at this school. My students don't apply on personal whims with nothing to lose."

"Well, why not?"

"Why not? Because . . . because there's a system!" She balled her right hand into a fist, then quickly relaxed it. "A system much larger and more significant than one student. And not to mention the grim truth that not everyone belongs at an Ivy, Mr. Eden. It's painful, I know it, but that's just the way the world works."

I inhaled, exhaled, calming myself. "That doesn't seem right."

"Consult Rabbi Bloom if you feel that way," she said, playing with her wedding ring instead of making eye contact. "I'm sure he'd be delighted to discuss this with you."

"What does Rabbi Bloom have to do with this?"

"I certainly won't be the one submitting an administrative letter of recommendation on your behalf."

I snatched the forms and, to her surprise, rose from my chair. "I'll be back, then."

—

"YOU'RE KIDDING?" KAYLA SAID. We had taken our lunch out to the soc- cer field. I'd done well on my last quiz—I received an A, my highest grade to date from Dr. Porter—and Kayla had insisted that I reward myself by taking a break from tutoring. ("Rest assured," she said, "I still think hanging with you should count toward community service hours.")

I was on the grass, observing the noonday sky, cloudless, a sharp shade of blue. "Nope. Totally serious."

"Ari Eden, a Columbia Lion?" She clapped. "The prodigal son re- turns to New York!"

"How come everyone's reaction to this is utter disbelief?"

"Who's everyone? I thought it was a secret."

"Ballinger, for one."

"What? You expected her to dance you down the Columbia aisle?" She unwrapped her lunch, busied herself with drowning her salad in dressing, offered me a bite. I declined. "And what's with Bloom?"

"I had to go see him and get him involved, after Ballinger shut me down. And he came through for me. He overruled her."

"Whoa, he actually went against Ballinger? That's a pretty big deal, Ari," she said. "Clearly the man's impressed by you."

I shrugged. "Who knows? Maybe he's just being nice. Or taking pity."

"Come on. Obviously you've very much piqued his interest." She picked at her salad. "You seem to have that effect on people."

"Really? I'd say I tend to have the opposite effect."

"Always with the immediate self-effacement. Is that like a defensive mechanism or something? Does it get kind of old?"

"Nope."

"Whatever. All I'm saying is that usually Bloom's a difficult man to intrigue."

"Why do you say that?"

"I'm in the top of the class, and how often do you see me scurrying to his office for ever-so-pressing conversations, ancient books in hand?"

"Ah. I get it. You're jealous."

She threw a fistful of grass my way. "Hardly. Go ahead and enjoy your meetings, I don't care. Just be aware, is all."

"Aware of what?"

"Bloom's acted like this with only one other person since I started here."

"Oh, God. Don't."

"Who is Brother Stark, for five hundred dollars?"

"He likes Evan, too, so what?"

"I don't know," she said. "It's just a bit—curious."

"Not really. He thinks we have similar interests is all."

"You two have similar interests? Similar anything? I don't see it."

"With some topics, I guess. I don't know."

She plundered some of the pretzels I was eating. I watched her hand dig around in my Ziploc bag. Her nails were unpainted. Sophia's, nowadays, were white. "Okay, we won't go there. Anyway, what's Noah been saying about Columbia?"

"Haven't told him. Or my father, for that matter."

"Wow, both your paternal figures don't know."

"Shut up."

"Can I just say I really like the idea of you at Yeshiva University? I still think you should look at it."

"Right, fair. I know."

"Wait, what about your mother? She knows?"

"Yeah, she's ecstatic, actually. Convinced I'm getting in and making up for her mistake."

"Mistake?"

"Leaving Barnard."

She stretched beside me, twisting to her side. Her hair had been straightened into neat, red lines. She wore sunglasses and an asymmetrical smile. "So you've told your mother, Ballinger and Bloom. And somehow you've also elected to tell me. To what do I owe the honor?"

"Tutor-student confidentiality."

"Right. Well, it's an interesting group. You sure no one else knows?"

A plane passed overhead. I watched it evaporate into faraway blue. "No."

"No what?"

"No one else knows."

"Not Sophia, you're telling me?"

I stiffened, rubbed my eyes. "Uh, actually, she's been helping a bit." I knew, right away, what Kayla was thinking, and I didn't disagree. Sophia's excitement at my decision to apply to Columbia wasn't selfless. Turning me into a Platonic, Ivy League version of myself would obviously render me an infinitely superior romantic partner. Still, I didn't care if Sophia had ulterior motives. I'd spent so long convinced that I'd been ruined by Torah Temimah, barred from the sort of life accessible to my friends, that I was eager for an opportunity to re-shape myself. As it was, my every performance—on dates, in class, with friends, alone at night—was designed, rightly or not, to impress Sophia, to prove that I was, in fact, *worthy*. That I was someone who made her smile. That I was the kind of person with whom she could trade literary repartee. That I could offer dependability and suffi-ciently ambitious aspirations. I wanted her to see that I was the one she should choose.

Our gazes were now both directed heavenward.

"Why'd you lie about Sophia helping you?"

"I . . . I didn't mean it maliciously. I just didn't really think it was important."

She sat up, moving farther from me. "It's really none of my busi-ness. Whatever's happening between you two—"

"—nothing," I protested, my voice whiny, horrible. I fought off the urge to just admit what Kayla already knew. "Really, we're just friends."

She sat cross-legged, swaying slightly. "I just hope you're sure about what you're doing."

"Why don't you like her?"

Kayla glanced away. "I don't actively dislike her. I mean, I've known her since kindergarten, but I hardly actually *know* her."

"So then what's the issue?"

"Maybe she once did something that I don't, you know, happen to love."

I pulled up dewy grass. "What was it?"

She looked back toward me. "Nothing, it's extremely stupid, not even worth getting into."

"No," I said, feeling strangely defensive. "I—actually, I'd really like to know."

"In seventh grade," Kayla said, "my parents forced me to have this big bat mitzvah party, which of course was basically the last thing on earth I wanted to subject myself to. And yet, they pushed for it, they insisted it was an important part of growing up, something cute but misguided like that. Anyway, over time I come to accept it, I'm actually excited about it, believe it or not, there's pizza, there are drinks, there's the lamest DJ you ever did see stationed in the corner of the room. And, agonizingly enough, hardly anyone shows."

I cringed, opening my mouth to interject with something comforting, but Kayla waved me off. "It's fine," she said, "I expected that to happen anyway. But my poor parents made some calls to figure out how it was that they steered their daughter into such, you know, abject public humiliation, and what they uncover is that Sophia had some local, astonishingly unimportant piano recital that same evening and actually campaigned—no joke, campaigned!—for most of our grade to attend. As in, she literally messaged people making certain they wouldn't be caught dead, God forbid, at my bat mitzvah and that they'd instead come see her Royal Highness perform, because already at that young age her ego required devoted fans."

"That's—horrible," I said, blushing on behalf of both Kayla and Sophia. "I'm sorry that happened to you, really. But, I mean, it was so long ago and—"

"It was a long time ago, Ari, and it's highly probable that she's changed extensively and even feels remorse for having done that to me. I, for one, have certainly moved on from that stupidity. But if you're asking me if a character flaw signifies *anything*? Well, then I can at least tell you privately, friend to friend, that perhaps I just don't buy it."

"Buy what?"

She snorted. "I don't like that you're repugnantly spellbound. I don't like that you think she's some mythological sketch of human excellence. Number one in the class. Spectacularly popular. Musical prodigy—"

"She doesn't like that word," I muttered.

"What?"

"Prodigy. She doesn't prefer it."

She rolled her eyes. "Sophia glances your way, you think it's real, suddenly you overlook all else."

"Overlook what? What am I overlooking?"

"It's not for me to say, Ari."

"No, really, tell me."

"Ever wonder why she's descended on you like this? Ever wonder whether she just needs someone there for her at the moment? Why she's pushing you toward a certain school? Why—"

Hearing someone else vocalize all this made me nauseous. "You say it with such, I don't know, *disdain*," I said quietly. "As if I'm some embarrassment."

"You're no embarrassment, Ari Eden. That's the point. You just have the emotional intelligence of, I don't know, a walnut."

"Right. So in essence you think she's using me to get back at—"

"At what?"

"Nothing," I said. "Forget it."

"Don't you find it agonizing to be with someone you know wants someone else?"

I didn't answer. She laughed softly, picked herself up from the grass. "Just be careful, *Hamlet*," she said, slinging her backpack over her shoulders. She dusted her skirt and headed back into school.

—

WEEKS PASSED TORTUROUSLY. AMIR WAS a wreck, sullen, irritable, prone to snapping at any mention of applications. Evan decided on Stanford but boasted that he cared little about what admission officers thought of him and that he was applying mostly because it was as far away as he could flee. (Not once did he mention, as Amir pointed out to me, that he wanted to attend Stanford because his mother had done so.) Noah was characteristically even-tempered; we took his lack of nerves as a sign he had received some form of confirmation from the coach at Northwestern, though he never admitted this.

I felt guilty keeping Columbia a secret. I didn't know how to tell Noah without sounding pathetic or directly addressing Sophia's involvement. ("Columbia?" I imagined him responding, face wracked with sympathetic disbelief, "the fuck?") Still, I thought incessantly about my *swarm of dreams / Of inaccessible Utopia*—Gothic bells, long shadows cast from austere buildings, pillars and pillars of musty books. I longed for this in class, in prayer, in bed, visualizing a fictive life of world-class professors and Italian suits and secret parties and Anglican roommates.

The close of the semester, meanwhile, crept upon us, midterms looming ominously, teachers piling on work with regained enthusiasm. It was a difficult stretch: I avoided going out much, did poorly on a string of math tests, wrote an unremarkable paper questioning Don Quixote's religious extremism. ("Well crafted," Mrs. Hartman wrote in her luxurious green ink, "but lifeless. Come see me.") Even the discussions in Rabbi Bloom's class had soured somewhat, partly due to the unspoken feeling of application competition, partly because Evan appeared to be in a progressively worse mood, speaking up less, keeping his head in his notebook.

Sophia and I saw little of each other outside of school. Occasionally we went for quick dinners or walks in the park, but mostly we fell into a stretch of awkward texting. One Saturday night, after we saw a particularly horrid movie about a wayward youth's escape from California, I decided to address our stagnancy.

"Soph," I said, parking in her driveway.

"Yes?"

I turned off my car. "Is something wrong? You can be honest."

A soft stare. She had on a diaphanous, beige blouse and a clover necklace. She looked thin and pale. "Why do you ask?"

"I don't know." A car drove by with its high beams on, blinding us with light. "You seem distant."

"I feel distant," she said. "But I think it's just the season. The uncertainty of things."

"What do you mean? The uncertainty of college?"

"Yeah, among other things, I guess."

"I see." She pressed herself against me. I put my arm around her shoulder without quite knowing why. "Want to talk about it?"

"Actually, do you mind if I cry?" She did so before I could respond, but it was brief: quiet, restrained. She stopped to wipe her eyes, and it was as if she hadn't cried at all.

"Are you—you're sure you're okay?" I asked.

Sophia bit her lip, moved a strand of hair behind her ears. "I've been kind of afraid to play lately."

"Play piano?"

She nodded.

For a moment, the silence between words took on a sort of pulsating quality, filling the interior of my car with imaginary vibrations. "Why would you be afraid?" I asked her.

"It's just—my music right now is wrong."

"Wrong?" I watched the way she breathed. "What, so like writer's block?"

"Not really, no."

"Maybe you're just overdoing it," I said. "You probably need a break for a bit. You know, to recalibrate."

"No, it's not that." She looked directly into my eyes, blurring all components of my field of vision external to her face. "I'm not like exhausted or tapped out. It's more that everything's . . . darker. I can't get back my, I don't know, my weightlessness, if that makes sense."

I thought about what she had asked me that night on the beach, behind Elation. *What's wrong with me?* "What does darker look like?"

"It's hard to explain," she said.

"What about what you played at Oliver's? The, uh, the Passion."

Against her will, she broke into a smile. "The *Appassionata*, Hamlet."

"Right, sorry, that," I said. "Was that dark? Because that definitely worked for you, didn't it? And what about the school recital? It was—I don't want to say dark, per se, mostly because I know I'm clearly out of my element here and don't understand exactly what I'm talking about, but it was regal. Breathtaking, actually, Soph, that's the word. It was breathtaking."

She withdrew from me, leaning back into her own seat. "That's kind of the problem."

"Sounds like a good problem to have."

"My music's changing," she said. "And I think the darker sound is superior."

I removed my key, unnerved by how much Sophia sounded like someone else I knew. "My parents are away," she said, stepping out of the car. "Come inside and I'll show you."

—

SHE PLAYED THE *APPASSIONATA* FOR me in her room, the lights off, a single candle lit. I watched from her bed, heart in my throat. In the shadows cast by the candle she resembled a Caravaggio painting: a body swallowed by darkness but invaded by violent bursts of light that illuminated fragments of her face. When she finished, she gave a slight shiver but remained at the piano, facing the wall, head against the frame. "You see?" she asked, finally, in a small voice.

"Honestly? It's a bit intense but I think it's incredible. I really wouldn't—"

A sudden movement in the dark: her fist against the fallboard. A framed picture—Sophia as a seven-year-old, at her first recital—crashed to the floor. The glass fractured. "Oh, God, I'm sorry." Her voice was hoarse. I wanted to reach out, grab her, but I was rooted to her bed. She retrieved the picture, inserting the shards back in place, her face fissured into hemispheres. "I need something else for my Juilliard interview. Something original."

"And this isn't?"

"I want it to be traditional," she said. "The way I used to play. Something untainted, something that doesn't frighten."

Pools of spiky shadows. Thin rain against the windowpanes. She had her back to me. "When did it start changing?" I asked.

"Before you met me."

"What happened?"

She moved to the bed, sitting beside me, clasping her ankles with her hands. Sitting on her bed, our bodies touching, I felt feverish longing. I wanted to be possessed by her. I wanted her to relieve me of thought and memory and complexity. I wanted her to wound me. "Tell me what that piece made you think of."

"Actually," I said, "I thought of something kind of random."

"Good. Be completely honest."

"It was a line from *The Wild Duck*."

"Lovely. My art reminds you of schoolwork."

"Remember that moment toward the end, when Werle's eyesight is going and Hjalmar and Gina are talking about Fate? How it can be pretty ugly?"

"Mostly. What about it?"

"Hjalmar says something there"—I paused to get it right. "*'It is profitable, now and then, to plunge deep into the night side of existence.'* That's what I thought of—how sometimes we have to walk through the slope of darkness to get back into the light."

She folded her arms, put her blanket to her face, breathed steadily. "When you say stuff like that, you sound like another person."

"Who?"

"I don't know. Nobody in particular."

I took her left hand. Her bracelet slipped down her arm, and my fingers brushed against a delicate line of scar tissue just below her wrist. She jerked away.

"Well, what do *you* think of when you play?"

"Being completely alienated from the world. Keeping secrets. Hurting people you love and who love you." Her head was still covered by that hot-pink blanket. "Feeling so cold no fire will ever warm me, feeling as if my head's been taken right off, feeling as if none of it really matters anymore—tests, colleges, rankings, parties, childhood, normalcy."

"And what about when you finish playing? What matters to you then?"

She removed the blanket from over her head, the top of her hair standing from static, and moved her face closer to mine. I inspected the rings around her irises. "Do you know what they want out of me? Harmless perfection. Normal extraordinariness. That's what they want."

"You're the least ordinary person I've met in the entirety of my painfully ordinary life."

Blood pounded in my ears. She took my hands. I traced her veins. I wanted every part of her.

"What do you think it's like?" Her lips were very close to mine. "At the very end." Her hands on the back of my neck, her breath on my face, a stirring in my body. "Passing into nothingness. You think it hurts?"

"Maybe it's just a light going out." Grief closed in on us. She laid me on my back, hovered above me. I breathed heavily. "Like slipping right into the dark."

She blew out the candle, lowering herself on me, and we moved into the dark.

—

EVAN HEARD FIRST. WE WERE sitting on the balcony when his phone sounded. He frowned, curiously checked his email. After about a minute, still expressionless, he put down his phone, clenching his jaw.

"Well?" Oliver went for an unnecessarily large bite of his sandwich. "You're going to make us sit like schmucks?"

"That was the decision letter." Evan gave a half-smile, despite himself. "I got in."

There was a sudden rush of excitement. We stood, we congratulated him, even Amir hugged him. We talked about Palo Alto and brilliantly dyed Californian skies and how it'd feel to be separated from home by a country's worth of distance. When the bell rang and we stood to leave, I asked him, unthinkingly, whether he felt happy. I wasn't certain why I felt any need to voice this. It was an odd thing to question; I cringed as the words slipped from my mouth. While the others gave me hard looks, however, Evan didn't blink. "No," he said, putting one leg through the open window. Sadness settled softly in his eyes so that, for the slightest moment, I could no longer quite remember what it was about Evan that was particularly superior to anyone else. "Actually, I feel very alone."

—

THE REST OF THE EARLY Decisions came in rapid fire. Amir and Davis found out later that day, joining Evan as the talk of the school with respective acceptances into MIT and Harvard. Amir, we believed strongly, wept upon receiving the news—ducking into the first-floor bathroom to do so in private—while Davis paraded around with his grandfather's class ring, belting Crimson fight songs. School was in a frenzy, phones ringing in the middle of tests, cheers breaking out in classrooms, three different people tearing out from math to sob after receiving rejection emails, students hugging, teachers hugging, Mrs. Ballinger and Mrs. Janice dancing the Macarena in the hallway after lining people up for acceptance photographs. Noah, unsurprisingly, made Northwestern; Rebecca the University of Illinois at Chicago; Remi NYU. ("Her father sits on the board," Oliver complained with uncharacteristic indignation. "Can we even call that a moral victory?") I monitored my phone every few minutes to no avail, a sharp pain in my stomach, feeling the grim fear of being left behind.

Sophia hadn't heard back either by last period, and sat staring vacantly as Dr. Flowers lectured about the value of state schools. ("You think for one minute that my Disney-obsessed, cheapskate parents would in a million years let me flee Florida?")

"Is it true?" Sophia asked me abruptly, as soon as we were dismissed.

"Is what true?"

"About Stanford?"

I swung my backpack over my shoulder, looking at her with surprise. My faced hardened. "Yeah. He got in."

She nodded faintly, which made me feel sorry for myself. We said nothing further.

—

SOPHIA BROUGHT ME HOME AFTER school. She didn't feel like being alone, she said, so we sat anxiously in her room, attempting small talk, discussing the day's various acceptances. When the conversation trailed off I moved to kiss her. For a while we were on her bed, sheets untouched, Sophia on her back, breathing softly in my ears, legs wrapped around my stomach. Afterward we were quiet. I felt strange, disassociated from her, our world of intimacy disintegrating with each passing silence. I told her I ought to leave.

"To go where?" She asked this partly with disdain, partly with relief, lips pressed tightly.

"Home."

I loitered aimlessly around my house. I read some of Stevens' poetry, Rabbi Bloom's latest assignment, and tried my hand at some homework. After a half hour I gave up, unable to concentrate, and, brooding, joined my parents for dinner.

"Something wrong?" my father finally asked, mid-chew.

"Nope," I said.

"A lot of silent eating for nothing to be wrong."

"'All my life I grew up around sages,'" I grumbled, "'and I've found nothing better for a person than silence.'"

"He's tired." My mother widened her eyes probingly. "You know how hard he's working now, at the end of term." I responded with a subtle shrug, which made her frown into her glass.

My father, to his credit, remained unconvinced. A small part of me was flattered he'd noticed at all. "It's just, you haven't said a word all night."

For a moment, I considered admitting what my mother and I were waiting to learn. "We hardly ever speak," I said instead. "How can you tell if something is wrong?"

—

I DIDN'T FIND OUT UNTIL eight o'clock. I sat on my bed refreshing my email, my mother checking in every five minutes. The letter was heartbreaking: the admission committee met, grueling deliberation ensued; regrettably, they couldn't offer me a spot in the incoming class. I read it several times—blinking stupidly, eyes moving mechanically from top to bottom—and then closed my computer and laid on my back. My mother tried comforting me, told me it didn't matter, even as she failed to hold back her own tears, pecking my forehead good night and retreating hurriedly to her bathroom. Staring at the ceiling, I thought about the lonely, dust-laden hours I'd spent in the Borough Park Library, Shimon Levy's collection of stained shirts, the look Mrs. Ballinger would give me until, under the weight of exhaustion, I collapsed into a dreamless sleep.

It was nearly midnight when I woke. I turned, rubbed my temple, feeling groggy and generally sorry for myself. I shaved, washed, studied my reflection, then returned to bed and shut the lights. When I couldn't sleep, I fumbled for my phone and dialed Sophia.

Her tone was sharp, startled. "Hamlet?"

"Hi Soph."

"Something wrong?"

"No, I—sorry I didn't call sooner. Just wanted to know if you heard."

"You're sweet." She said so in a hollow voice.

"Well?"

"Yeah, I—I got into Penn."

I smiled on the other end of the phone. "Wow. That's so great. Really great news."

"Thank you, Ari." A voice called her; with her hand over the phone, she said she'd be only a minute.

"I'm very proud," I said.

She thanked me. We fell back into silence.

"I should go," she said, tonelessly. "I—my family's still celebrating."

"Yeah, of course. Go enjoy."

"But Ari."

"Yes?"

"You're not going to tell me?"

I sat still on my bed. "No, I—it didn't work out."

"Shit. I'm so sorry." Her voice had a baritone quality. "I am, really."

"Thanks, but it's okay."

"There are plenty of other schools. We can think it through together."

"Sure."

"I'll see you tomorrow. We'll talk tomorrow."

"Okay. Tomorrow."

"Have a good night, Ari."

"Good night," I said and hung up.

—

WE DIDN'T TALK THE NEXT day. I hardly saw her, in fact: we didn't have biology, she was surrounded by Remi and Rebecca and others bearing balloons and cakes adorned in blue and red and she darted from classrooms after the bell. Not that I had anything particular to say. But I felt an obligation to do something: congratulate her, seek her help, blame her.

The day was a blur. I was in a fog, avoiding Noah and the others, eating on my own, sitting mindlessly through class, staring at the clock. I didn't run into Mrs. Ballinger, at least, and for that I was grateful. During davening I sat to the side, unmoved to pray. Kayla found me during a free period, brooding in an empty classroom, pretending to do homework so as not to be disturbed.

"You stood me up," she said calmly.

"Sorry, I just really didn't feel like being tutored today."

"No, I get it. I'm useful, but a chore. Discard after use."

"Oh, come on. You know that's not what I meant."

"So you didn't get in." I couldn't tell if this was a question or a statement, so I didn't answer. For a slight moment she took my hand. Her fingers were surprisingly warm, softer than I imagined. "Their loss."

"Yeah, well, I'm not convinced."

"How'd your mother take it?"

"Poorly," I said.

"Are you going to tell your father?"

"I don't really see the point."

She lingered, waiting for me to talk more. "Would you like me to leave you alone?" she asked finally.

I felt a surge of irrational frustration. "Yeah, actually, I think I would like that," I said, immediately feeling ashamed.

She turned to leave, then paused, twirling her hair lightly. "It's funny. You didn't even ask."

"Ask what?"

She snorted, shaking her head. "I got into the Honors program at Stern College," she said. "I got the full ride."

—

TOWARD THE END OF THE day I peered into Rabbi Bloom's office. He was reading calmly. I knocked. "Thought you might be in," he said. "Take a seat."

I sat at the conference table. I waited for him to offer water or coffee or tea, but he didn't. "I'm sorry about our friends in New York."

"I shouldn't have applied. Deluding myself was a mistake."

"Self-delusion is almost never a mistake."

"Have you heard from Mrs. Ballinger?"

"A single snide comment this morning. I told her not to take such a narrow view of things. At any rate, I wouldn't waste your time worrying about that."

"Yeah, well, what else should I be worrying about?"

"Perhaps a plan B."

"I don't have one," I said. "My plan B is Brooklyn."

He shook his head. "I don't think I'll be allowing that anytime soon. Brooklyn's not the place for you."

"Where is?" I asked. "I don't have a place."

On the first day of fourth grade, Rabbi Herenstein taught us about *hashgochoh protis*, divine providence. Such is the extent of God's involvement in our lives, he insisted, quoting Gemara Chullin, that we do not even bruise a finger without the Heavenly Court ordaining it. At the time, I imagined a crowded courtroom, bustling with angels and biblical celebrities who cheered as we silly mortals stumbled about earth, stubbing our toes and learning to swim and falling in love and burying our dead. At the time, I found it comforting to think that we are never alone, that something higher steers our every move. Suddenly, though, I was bothered by this idea. Surely, in the sphere of metaphysical calculations, allowing me to experience profound happiness and relief couldn't be drastically more taxing than, say, having me jam my finger while playing basketball with Mordechai. What, really, was a Columbia acceptance to the Almighty?

"That's the whole fun, isn't it?" Rabbi Bloom said. "Finding out where we belong?"

—

I WENT WITH FLOWERS. UGLY flowers, the only ones they had late afternoon: fake pinks, yellowed purples, the whole thing giving off a bright discoloration. I wrote a card, a rather nice one, I thought. Her housekeeper Norma answered, looking me over with a confused look, opening her mouth to say something before stopping herself. She told me, sternly, not to come in. I waited—feeling stupid, holding the bouquet and the card, shifting my weight from foot to foot—until Sophia came down, still in school clothing, taken aback to find me at her doorstep.

I handed her my gifts. "I didn't get to congratulate you."

"Hamlet." She studied the flowers, quiet grief coming over her. "They're lovely."

"Actually they're kind of hideous. But they're something."

She closed the front door, stepped closer to me. "You're remarkably good to me."

"Yeah, well, you've been good to me, too. And I'm really happy for you."

"My family's eating dinner," she said, glancing uneasily behind her, "otherwise I'd invite you in."

"Nah, that's okay."

"Ari." Her voice was throaty, low. "I'm sorry, you know that?"

"Yes," I said. "Yes, I know."

She hugged me, kissed my cheek softly, slipped back through the door. As I drove off, I noticed a familiar black Aston Martin parked on the street, two houses away.

—

WE PLAYED BROWNSON THE FOLLOWING NIGHT, a Catholic powerhouse that regularly shipped players to the likes of Notre Dame and Florida State and Indiana and which, without fail, annually made mincemeat of us. By now my interest in our team had waned. We were 6–1, enjoying the greatest stretch in Kol Neshama history, but I'd yet to see the court for more than five minutes at a time and had grown accustomed to my familiar spot at the far corner of the bench, where I'd snack steadily on the cache of chocolate that Rocky reserved for hypoglycemia.

"Their best player committed to USC," Oliver told me during warm-ups. "Massive dude."

Rocky, already drenched in sweat, pumping out push-ups next to the scorer's table, rolled to his side. "Shut your ugly mouth, Bellow! You think we need cowardice right now?"

We traded baskets for most of the first half, Noah putting on a masterful performance to keep pace, though fell into a sizable hole by the close of the third. Their USC recruit—listed at six-seven, closer to six-ten—went wild at this point, wreaking havoc in the paint, dunking thunderously over Donny to close the quarter. We were the home team, but the crowd, our biggest of the season, still erupted seeing Donny splayed on the floor, blinking off a concussion. My eyes, however, went to Sophia, sitting with Rebecca in the top of the bleachers. I looked away before we made eye contact.

Oliver noticed what I was doing. "Forget her already, will you? Both of you should." Still wearing his warm-ups, he was helping me inhale chocolate. "All she does is crush people."

"What does that mean?"

"Whatever." He unwrapped a Kit Kat. "Forget I said anything."

"Seriously," I said. Someone on Brownson dunked on Amir, tipping the crowd into mayhem, but I missed it. "Has he—does Evan ever say anything about her?" I reached nervously for a miniature Twix. "Or me?"

"I'm not getting involved with this."

"Just tell me what you meant by that."

"Jesus, Eden. Don't sound so desperate. You and Evan both— you're moping, he's fucking weird about things lately. You see me broken up over Remi?"

Noah cut the deficit to two with a minute remaining, eliciting cheers of disbelief from the crowd and swearing from Rocky, who appeared to be on the verge of some quasi-religious awakening at the prospect of defeating Brownson. "This is it," Rocky told us in the huddle, his shirt somehow missing three buttons. "Win and be legends. You'll get girlfriends, statues, investment banking jobs. Just give Noah the ball and get the fuck out the way."

Donny inbounded to Noah with twenty on the clock, everyone in the gym, save for Oliver and me, on their feet. Noah stood at midcourt, watching time dissolve, the USC behemoth guarding him. With five seconds remaining Noah jabbed left, dribbled behind his back and then spun right, catching his defender off guard. He charged forward, right into the USC player's chest, crossed back and, feet planted firmly behind the three-point line, fired at the buzzer.

Chaos. Noah sprinted for the stands, Rocky ripped off his shirt entirely. Students rushed the court, tackling in celebration. Eddie Harris, waving one of Noah's old jerseys, planted an enormous kiss on Amir's mother's cheek, which for once lost its scowl. I approached the mosh pit, hovering at the edge, unwilling to get sucked inside. Noah was lifted into the air. I stood back and admired his glory.

Afterward, I followed my mother to the parking lot. As we pulled out, I saw Sophia exit a car on the unlit side of the lot, distraught, blinking tears.

My mother put us in park. "Isn't that your friend?"

"Yeah, actually."

"Think she's all right?"

I unbuckled my seatbelt, threw open the door and hurried back toward the gym in pursuit of Sophia. From the corner of my eye, I saw the car she had just left jolt into motion. Before I could process what was happening, I instinctively jumped aside, just as the car barreled dangerously close to where I'd been standing. It was Evan, eyes raw, head down. I watched the Aston Martin disappear into the night, and then I went back to my car and slammed the door. "Never mind that," I said, fixing my seatbelt, leaning back. "Let's go home."

—

SOPHIA WASN'T IN SCHOOL THAT next day. I moved about in a haze, conjuring awful images: Evan just behind her front door, laughing as I stood pathetically with flowers; Sophia, in tears, flinging herself from Evan's car. Several times I drafted text messages, only to delete them. are you coming in late? feeling ok? need anything? I couldn't bear seeing Evan, couldn't stomach the thought of questioning the implied meaning of his every word, and so skipped lunch upstairs. I attempted instead to join Kayla, who was stationed at her tutorial post and picking irascibly at a salad, a book opened at her desk.

"Hi." I took several cautious steps into the classroom. "Mind if I join?"

She looked up, glowered, returned to her reading. "Very much so."

"What're you reading?"

"Nothing you've read."

"Clearly you're still mad at me."

"Nope."

"Sure seems like it."

"I just don't have anything to say to you."

I nodded politely and left.

After lunch, we congregated in Rabbi Bloom's office, where we debated reasons for wearing tzitzit.

"They slap us in the face before we sin," Oliver said. "Like the dude, in the Gemara, climbing the ladder to visit the prostitute. Pretty useful, really."

"They equate with fulfilling all six hundred and thirteen mitzvoth," Amir said. "The gematria is six hundred, and the threads and knots sum to thirteen."

"They give us an extension of our body," Noah said.

"They teach us that the Torah, like the ratio of white to blue strings, is seventy-five percent comprehensible and twenty-five percent shrouded in mystery," Rabbi Bloom said. "And that there's a perfect chemistry to achieve in balancing these two ideals, so that we lean largely on the rational, dipping into the mystical only as a supplementary force of faith."

"It reminds us," Evan said gloomily, "that we have nothing lasting in this world, no cars or houses or careers or parents or children, only tattered strings."

"See?" Oliver said, leaning over to whisper in my ear.

When my turn came, I offered the first platitude that came to mind, neglecting to mention that it'd been several weeks since I last wore my tzitzit.

In English I was similarly silent, staring out the first-floor window at the model temple, failing to answer Mrs. Hartman's challenge to liken Joyce's vision of Parnell to Moses. "Are you sure you're feeling well, Mr. Eden?" Mrs. Hartman asked. *Bloom, are you the Messiah ben Joseph or ben David?* "You're uncharacteristically incoherent today."

Davis sniggered from the other side of the room. Evan glanced suspiciously in my direction.

I had a free last period, but instead of loitering around to ride home with Noah, as I usually did on Wednesdays, I left early and walked, despite the fact that it'd begun to rain. I was in no rush to be home and decided to detour, drifting about, walking along the lake. Before long the rain worsened. No one else was out. I was perfectly solitary, wandering the gray.

When I walked up to my house I found Sophia at my doorstep, head in hands. She sat unmoving, unaware of the rain. "I knocked." She said so without looking up. Her hair was soaked, draped over her shoulders in long strands. Raindrops fell softly from her nose. "No one was home."

The rain picked up, covering us in thick sheets. "What're you doing here?"

"Waiting for you."

The first time we were alone, at Oliver's party, I was delivered infinitely far from reality. That sensation only deepened each time I'd been alone with her since. Looking at her now, I was frightened I'd never again have her transport me away from the confines of my internal life. "Why?"

"So I can talk to you," she said.

"You should leave."

"You're angry with me."

"Please," I said. She didn't move. "Please leave."

Sometimes she had such cold eyes, I thought. Sometimes beauty dissembles exquisite sadness. "You really want that?"

"I don't know," I said.

"Hamlet."

"Where were you today?" I asked.

"I didn't feel like coming in."

"Are you okay?"

She motioned for me to sit on the step beside her, but I was frozen where I stood. Her drenched black shirt, clinging tightly to her pale skin, made her glow a luminous white within the rain.

I glanced down the street: no sign of either of my parents, though I knew they'd be home soon. "I need to ask you a question."

"I know you do." She spoke now with such unnatural calm, as if nothing that ever happened—to her, to us, to anyone—actually mattered.

"Are you together again?"

She didn't blink. "Absolutely not."

"He was at your house. He was there when it was supposed to be me. And then, in the car the other night, after the game, I—I saw you two." Voicing this reinforced several fundamental truths. I was foolish for living in negative capability. I was foolish for retreating into the blurred world she built for me, for ignoring that some force bound her to Evan. Keats describes two rooms in the "large Mansion" of human life: the antechamber, where we suppress consciousness, and the Chamber of Maiden-Thought, where we become intoxicated by beauty, only to discover heartbreak. I was now, at last, experiencing whatever darkness follows fleeting light.

Sophia looked up at me with iron eyes. "I don't love him, Ari. We're not together. We've—I've had to see him about something, that's true, but whatever . . . sinister thing you're imagining is wrong."

I loved her in a way I didn't think I was capable of loving another person, and still I wasn't what she desired, she who had given me everything, she who had given me nothing. "What do you need to see him about?"

"That's not a simple question," she said.

I wanted to hold her, kiss her, warm her. I wanted to kick down the door, carry her into my room, submit myself to her. Instead, I remained where I was, a safe distance away.

"When I tried warning you," she said, "from the very start, it was because I knew things were going to become complicated."

"Warn me about what? That you'd use me? That I'd serve as a project or as some easy distraction until you two found each other again?"

She stood, stepped toward me. It appeared I was shivering from the rain. "You need to understand—"

"Are you still going to see him?"

She closed her eyes, let loose quiet tears.

"I'll never be able to do that to you," I said, "will I?"

"Do what?"

"Make you cry."

For the first time in my life, I wondered whether happiness might somehow be beside the point. "You wish you could, don't you?" she asked.

I was so cold from the rain that I was beginning to feel light-headed. The enormity of what I wanted, of what I always wanted, frightened me. "I do."

She kissed me, taking everything from me so abruptly and violently that I nearly buckled. "I'm sorry, Hamlet." The last of light sinking into night: I could feel the ground shifting beneath my feet. Her lips broke away. She gave a faint smile, tore at my heart. She removed her hand from mine and wandered from my driveway, dematerializing into fog.

—

WE WERE IN NOAH'S BACKYARD, drinking, sending golf balls into the dark. It had been a solitary Shabbat, a solitary week. The weather had turned unseasonably cold: rain for hours on end, granite-colored skies, splinters of lightning, wet and treacherous roads. It'd been several days now since I'd found Sophia at my doorstep and we hadn't spoken since. I ignored her in class, even in biology, and she missed two more days of school, allegedly suffering from the flu. Evan, too, was absent one of those days, deepening my paranoia. I tried reminding myself of Sophia's initial warnings, so as to forgive her, and then tried convincing myself I'd been mistreated. Neither approach worked. The discoloration of Brooklyn, for the first time since I'd arrived in Florida, was seeping back into my life.

"What's with the silence?" Noah asked, whacking a ball into the black distance. "Everyone seems so pissed lately."

I sliced my ball, moving it four yards to my left, narrowly avoiding contact with Amir's temple. Amir wisely removed himself from my circumference. "Midterms?" he asked. "The weather?"

"Nah," Oliver said. "I vote girl trouble."

"Drew?"

I finished my beer, shrugged.

"Check out that attitude," Oliver said. "I think Eden's had too much to drink."

"What about you, Ev?" Noah asked.

Evan didn't look up. "What about me?"

"I don't know," Noah said. "You've been MIA every night this week. You skipped school on Tuesday. You don't answer texts. You've been as weird as Drew."

Oliver shrugged. "Like I said. Girl problems." Nausea surged briefly through my upper body.

Evan tossed aside his club. "Don't compare us."

"Who?"

"Me and Eden."

"What's that supposed to mean?" I said, mostly to my own surprise.

"Look at you," Evan said. "So alarmed to hear we're different?"

I kicked dirt in his direction. "On the contrary. I hope nobody compares me to you."

"All righty, then," Noah said, trying to defuse things. "Let's say we do something else now, huh?"

Amir leaned on his club. "Like?"

"I have an idea," Evan said. "Let's get Eden to smoke."

"Funny," Noah said. "Clearly you are pissed off."

I put down my club, walked over to Evan, a dull ache starting in my temple. "Okay."

"Okay what?"

I blinked in pain. "Let's do it."

Evan smiled, studied my face. "You kind of look like you want to fight me, you know that? You can punch me if you want to. I won't mind."

Amir cracked his knuckles. "I've been there, Ari," he muttered. "Might be worth it."

I considered the prospect. The notion of striking him, of making him bleed, was, for a moment, disturbingly appealing. I massaged my forehead. "We doing it or not?"

"I like the boldness," Evan said, "but we know you're full of shit, Eden."

I found myself inside, seated on the couch. Noah got the fan going and opened the patio door for a cross-breeze. Oliver disappeared into his car and returned with an obtrusive, yellowed sock from which he removed a plastic bag. He did his grinding and gave Evan the joint. Evan applied his lighter, took a long breath, cocked his head, blew out. Smoke billowed, fogging the windows.

Evan waved the joint in my direction. "Your move, Eden."

Things crashed over me: alcohol, Columbia's rejection, the way my chest seared at the sight of Evan, the thought that Sophia could be texting him at that very moment. I snatched the joint. Curious silence, everyone watching. I held it to my face.

I had no desire to smoke. The act itself bore no appeal, nor did the way Evan and Oliver typically functioned in the aftermath. I didn't know why accepting a joint from his hand would do anything to shift the balance of power between us. I knew only, in my semi-drunken state, that I refused to suffer another loss to Evan.

"Whoa, hold up a second," Noah cautioned, realizing that I wasn't joking. "Don't do something you'll regret."

"He won't," Evan said. "Like I said, he's too much of a coward."

"Ari," Amir said, looking as if he wanted to grab me and shake sense into me, "don't be a huge idiot. Do *not* take the bait."

Drunkenly, I inhaled.

"Holy hell," Oliver said. "Ev, you gave birth to a monster."

"That's it, hold a few seconds," Evan instructed. This reminded me of the way Evan first taught me how to drink, which just so happened to be the night he gave me that Xanax. I wanted to point this out, but my lungs were filled with smoke.

I held until my breath broke. I coughed violently, throat burning. I paced the room, trying to steady my breathing.

Oliver crossed himself. "Never thought I'd see the day. I'm a believer."

Noah grinned, shook his head. "Nobody tell Rocky." He took the joint from me and put it to his lips. "Because, for the record, this is definitely a mistake." I was still preoccupied coughing up a lung.

We looked at Amir now. Finally, cursing us, he accepted the joint from Noah. "I hate you people," he said, scrunching his face. The joint underwent several more revolutions until it burned close to our fingertips and Oliver flicked it to the coffee table, though Noah made him retrieve it and dispose of it properly. Oliver leaned against the couch and put his hands behind his head, eyes circular and bleary. "Now, we wait, boys," he announced dreamily. "Now we wait."

We sat quietly, sipping warm Yuengling. My throat was on fire, the smoke had worsened my headache, my vision was now strained, slipping out of focus, occasionally darkening around the periphery. A floating sensation snaked through my intestines. I thought I heard something, muttered incoherently to myself, drawing laughs. Amir—watery eyes, lopsided grin—was playing with a pillow, hurling it at the ceiling. Noah had the TV going. *The Magnificent Seven* was on. We watched without blinking.

Until: a small, whirling noise.

"Hear that?" I stiffened. "You guys hear anything?"

Noah's eyes fluttered. "Hear what?"

The actors in the movie uncoiled grotesque mouths. Were they inspecting me? A cold sweat came on. I forced away my eyes.

"You okay, Ari?" Amir snapped in my direction, whistled at me. "You're pale."

"Yeah, you kind of look like shit, dude," Oliver piped up. Noah was asleep beside him, his head on Oliver's left shoulder.

Evan glanced at me and then refocused his attention on the film. "He's going to boot."

I was standing, it seemed. "The bathroom."

Nobody answered.

"Where's the bathroom?" I repeated, nausea washing over me. The muted, faraway voice from my childhood migraines was back.

"Dude. You know where the bathroom is." Amir waved in no particular direction, shoveling popcorn into his mouth. "You've been here a million times."

After a terror-filled minute, I found the bathroom and, head spinning, vomited without closing the door. After some dry heaving I rinsed my mouth, washed my face. In the mirror I had the eyes of some other boy.

When I came back out Oliver suggested we go for drinks. Three Amigos, that hole in the wall they were always talking about. There I flashed my fake ID, clenched my beer, braving distorted colors and pulsating lights. Our waitress hovered over Oliver. I was desperate to sleep, my vision swimming, lights rearranging around me. Oliver left, waitress in hand, and I was home now, it was past three now, I was climbing into bed now, attempting to will away nausea, liquid words dancing around me. *The eyes are not here / There are no eyes here.* Images of Brooklyn: the three creaky steps leading into my house, the sound my bike made when I'd skid. The arch of Sophia's back, one leg beneath cold sheets, the taste of her neck. Kayla, storming from every room I was in. Noah in his pool, the water rising. Evan wandering through fields. An Aston Martin suspended in air. *Draperies of grief.* My parents fighting, silently, through their eyes. My rejection letter: the steps of Low Library, dwindling into whiteness. I am alone, I am alone, I am alone.

JANUARY

Evil and brief hath been my pilgrimage

—Browning, "The Bishop Orders His Tomb
at Saint Praxed's Church"

Oliver proposed spending a week in Key West during winter break. I was hesitant, given that I could neither independently finance this trip nor ask my parents for the money, but Oliver decided to book a swanky hotel on his own. "I don't do accommodations significantly worse than my house," he insisted, matter-of-factly. "So you don't need to pay me back."

I was excited for the trip, desperate as I was to distract myself from the fact that, in all likelihood, I'd soon be sitting in a cramped classroom of a local college, listening to someone drone on about how and why to read, my blood boiling at the thought of Evan loafing around Stanford. First, however, I had to suffer through midterms, none of which, save for English, went remotely well. (I didn't even complete biology; Dr. Flowers gave me a sympathetic look when she snatched my exam, as if observing a wounded dog.) That sense of purpose Sophia made me feel was gone. Having failed to wriggle my way into Columbia, I'd received my dreaded answer: the gap between everyone else and me could not be bridged, the future toward which I was hurtling could not be made less bleak. I'd begun smoking not infrequently, slipping out late, tiptoeing with sneakers in hand, locking the front door with my breath held. When especially high, I'd sit still and wait patiently for sadness or guilt or regret to come for me. Increasingly, however, I felt no particular emotion, only an absence of thought verging pleasantly on numbness. *Ah! When the ghost begins to quicken.*

My father, as expected, responded with a blank look when I announced I'd be leaving to Key West for a week. "What's in Key West?"

"It's a tourist spot, Abba."

"So there are shuls?" he asked. "There's kosher food? A kehillah?"

"I wouldn't be surprised," my mother said, clearly making an effort to convince herself. "Probably not a full-fledged community, but there must be—something."

"Yeah," I lied. "Of course."

My father remained skeptical. "And this is with Noah and the others, you said? The minyan guy and—"

"Yes, Abba. The usual bunch."

He played with his glass of water. "Even Bellow?"

I feigned defensiveness. "What's wrong with him?" I asked, only to immediately imagine how I'd feel if I had a child traveling with someone like Oliver.

My father shrugged, put his palms up. "Nothing's wrong. He's just—"

"Just what?"

"He's rowdy, Aryeh. It's not a . . . well, a quiet chevrah."

My mother sat silently, lips pursed, eyes to the floor.

"A quiet chevrah?" I repeated, forcing a laugh. I felt an unfamiliar upwelling of rage coming on. "Why would I want that?"

"All I'm saying, as I've said from the beginning, it's not your old friends," my father said. And then, with gruff self-satisfaction: "*Halevai!*"

"They'll be responsible," my mother said without lifting her gaze from the tablecloth. "They'll have fun."

My father scoffed. "Fun?"

"You never wanted that as a teenager, Yaakov? Freedom?"

"'*Never put thyself in the way of temptation,*'" my father said, translating the Gemara into English. "Even Dovid HaMelech couldn't resist."

My mother stood. "He's going." We all froze at this act of open confrontation. Glassy-eyed, my mother returned her stare to the floor; red-cheeked, my father kept his eyes on me in a vaguely accusatory fashion. Nobody said a word. I left for my room.

—

I LOVED THE HOTEL FROM the moment I saw the lagoon-style pools and oceanfront rooms. Oliver booked a suite at five hundred a night. "Early birthday gift from the parents," he said, changing into one of the white satin robes hanging in the bathroom closet. "I only do king-size beds."

We spent the afternoon in the ocean, drank heavily after dinner. When we were sufficiently drunk—Oliver had already vomited and smoked it off—we made our way toward Duval Street, epicenter of Key West nightlife, according to Noah. We ducked in and out of bars, Oliver buying drinks: shots of pale-blue tequila, Irish car bombs, bile-tasting vodka set aflame. A group of sophomore girls from Florida A&M picked out Evan from the corner of a cowboy bar. They matched me with a raven-haired twenty-year-old who told me she intended to become a horse veterinarian and had the habit of steering me with her hands. A local attempted to sit on Noah's lap; he sprang to his feet and into the bathroom with the same speed he pushed fast breaks. We passed a small, grime-streaked house, aglow with neon lights. Two women beckoned from the porch.

"Pricing?" Oliver yelled drunkenly, stumbling on his feet.

"Hundred an hour," one said.

"A bargain," Oliver said, nearly pitching over into a garbage can. He went for his wallet but Noah and Amir hauled him away.

The A&M group bought a table at the back of a club. Evan's companion took a vial from her purse and, her friends keeping watch, cut lines with her credit card. I watched with muted horror as she used a rolled-up twenty and passed it around the table. Oliver and Evan each accepted, snorting with violent, euphoric looks. Noah, drunker than I'd ever seen him before, considered the prospect for a moment until he snapped to his senses and relocated to the other side of the table to sit with Amir and me.

The veterinarian draped her arm around my shoulder. "Can I ask you something weird?"

"Yeah, sure."

"What's with that—thing?" She nodded at the top of my head. "The beanie."

"Oh." I grabbed my yarmulke and stuffed it into my pocket. No one else was wearing one. Amir had an MIT hat pulled toward his eyes. I felt exposed, suddenly, as if someone had stolen my clothing, as if I were sitting there with my jeans removed. "That's nothing."

"Fashion statement?" she asked, laughing.

I typed a text to Kayla: in KW, haven't yet been knocked out by Hemingway—how are u? "Yeah. Exactly."

She had more beer. "Don't you do this in school?"

"Do what?"

She gestured toward the other end of the table. I considered asking whether she assumed we were in college. "No," I said instead, checking my phone. No response from Kayla. "I don't."

"It's real good." She had beery breath. "Try it."

I excused myself for fresh air. Out front, Evan was leaning over the porch railing, facing the dark street, drink in hand. He didn't address me, I didn't address him. It took a moment to realize he was crying.

"Evan?"

He didn't turn. I approached the railing, seeing tears on one side of his face.

"You all right?"

He thumbed away whatever was left under his eyes—two or three quiet drops. "It's nothing." He rubbed at his nostrils. "Just that powder."

I didn't say anything as he moved back toward the entrance. The door opened behind me and I felt a surge of relief; I wanted to be alone, even briefly. Yet when I turned around, I saw that Evan had changed his mind and was still standing there. The tears were gone. I wondered if I'd imagined them.

"Know what, Eden?"

I took his spot against the railing. "What, Evan?"

"You're hiding what you are."

I could hear shouting inside as some DJ came onstage. "I don't know what that means," I said, "and to be perfectly honest, I'm really not in the mood."

He finished what was left of his drink. "You're an affectation. A fucking mask. Know why I think that?"

I didn't. I didn't know why my heart was pounding, either. I considered never drinking again. "Nope. But, uh, thanks for that, as always."

He set down his empty beer bottle to the floor. "Actually, I'm not saying that as a challenge."

"No?"

"What I mean is that"—Evan stopped himself, gently kicked over the bottle, which rolled toward me, coming to a stop at my feet. "Maybe I'm a bit too fucking gone right now, I don't know. But what I mean is that I wear the same mask you wear. I'm just as isolated from everything and everyone as you are. I'm just"—he coughed briefly, sniffed loudly—"I guess I know how you feel," he said, nodding. "Because somehow you might be the only person in my life who understands what it's like." He said this and headed back inside.

What did I have to show for my life? Eighteen years of minimal evidence proving that I was a real person, someone who wanted things, felt things, recognized emptiness. Sometimes I could hide, restructuring myself into a different person entirely. Other times I could not. I wondered if Evan, too, viewed himself as shapeless, flitting between anonymity and omniscience, capable of shrinking or expanding into nothingness.

Our night ended with a beach bonfire. Evan had slipped off with the girl he met. Oliver, meanwhile, was nowhere to be found when we left the nightclub. "He's fine," Amir reasoned, collapsing on the sand. "He'll show in the morning." Noah had enough after a while and went up to FaceTime Rebecca and steal Oliver's bed, leaving me alone with the veterinarian. It was close to three and I was beginning to sober; the idea of returning to the room made me feel unwell. She lit a joint and we walked along the water, barefoot, jeans rolled to our ankles. The water was black and cold. I thought about the last time I'd been to the beach in the dark. I thought about meaningless distances, about seas and heavens. I thought about Sophia's lips against mine.

"Something's wrong with you," she said, burrowing her heel into the sand, "isn't there?" She was coked, her eyes glossy red.

She sang beyond the genius of the sea. I wasn't listening. I was elsewhere, body not wholly body. "I think there might be."

"I think so, too."

"Sorry about that."

"Are we going to sleep together?"

I smiled pleasantly, too high, shook my head.

"There's a girl?"

We kissed, first by the waves, soon on the sand. We rolled into the water. The sky went black, flickering around the edges.

—

IT WAS A HAZY, TORPID stretch. We spent the daytime baking in the sun: parasailing, kayaking, deep-sea fishing (this last activity leaving me incredibly seasick, vomiting for hours from the side of the boat, the captain refusing to turn back). Save for Noah, who insisted on greeting sunrise by sprinting five miles along the ocean, we rose at noon, were drunk by one and remained so for the duration of the day, drifting from outdoor bars to buckets of iced beer to restaurants that went heavy on shots, particularly with Oliver tipping. We were in Cleopatra's Egypt, disposed to mirth, and in our idleness I tried my best not to think about Sophia or Columbia or my parents or any of the other changes under way in my life.

Food was the issue. There was nothing kosher in sight, and so for the first few days I joined Amir in subsisting mostly on canned tuna, peanut butter and pretzels. Growing tired of this diet, feeling a surreal sense of escapism in my surroundings, I decided to break kashrut for the first time in my life, much to Amir's disapproval.

"You all." He pointed to Evan, Oliver and Noah after I'd caved and ordered pizza instead of another soggy garden salad at one of our meals. "You've done this to him."

Noah, filleting an expensive branzino, grew silent. Oliver raised his glass.

Evan only smiled. "You're blaming *us*?"

I looked at the floor, feeling guilty, the way I did when my parents fought.

"This is our fault?" Evan said. "Because *you* don't seem to have any trouble resisting. *You're* still keeping kosher. This is Eden's problem."

"What I'm doing is not the point," Amir said testily. I swallowed the piece I was eating and placed down my slice.

Evan leaned forward. "Would you say Eden's stronger or weaker for doing this?"

"Forget it," Amir said, digging furiously into his salad. "I'm not doing one of your talks."

"No, seriously. I know you think we're corruptive, but it's just as compelling to argue that Eden's losing his morals on his own."

"Dude," Noah said, putting his hand on Evan's shoulder, "let's not upend lunch here."

"He did stop wearing a yarmulke all of a sudden," Oliver said, sipping peacefully at his piña colada. "Or are we just not acknowledging that?"

I reddened, gripped my fork. "I'm wearing a hat."

Oliver shrugged. "What about that girl? And have you been davening every morning?"

My scalp burned underneath my hat. "Fuck off," I said.

"Hey," Oliver said, "it's not any of my business."

"Point is," Evan said, "we can mock Eden, but that'd be near-sighted. It's the kneejerk reaction, the superficial takeaway, when really he deserves to be praised."

I looked up in surprise. "What?"

"Think about it. Here's someone who's been raised a certain way, right? Accustomed to a particular and rigid way of living. And yet, this guy *desires* things, even when they're incompatible with his lifestyle. So how does he respond? It takes time, some encourage-ment, but he seizes them, and this seizing is actually more morally attractive than if he'd simply conformed to custom. What does that Gemara say? Performing an action when you're obligated to do it yields greater reward than when you're exempt? Same idea here, really, just inverted a bit. We"—he motioned at Oliver, Noah and Amir—"were born into a sort of moral indolence, at least compared to Eden. We've been raised with all sorts of contradictions and hy-pocrisies. And so Eden actually should get more credit for breaking through because his barrier—the moral activation energy required, so to speak—is substantially higher than ours."

"There's definitely something wrong with you," Amir said. "This theorizing bullshit, it's . . . it's fucking peculiar."

Noah pushed aside his fish. "We were so damn close to a nice lunch."

"I'm with Noah," Oliver said. "Let's not Bloomify this."

"Last night, when you were passed out, Ev?" Amir said, clasping his hands together. "I couldn't sleep, so I went looking for some read-ing material. Know what I found?"

Evan didn't blink.

"I picked up one of your books, rifled through it a bit. Lot of notes in the margins."

"Which book?" Evan asked.

"Schopenhauer."

I bit my lip. "And?" I asked, after Evan didn't respond.

Amir shrugged. "Complete gibberish. Some shit about how Lucretius erred here or that guy erred there. Whatever, I don't know, it was basically the ravings of a lunatic."

"It's impolite to intrude upon someone's privacy," Evan said calmly. "Maybe I'll sue you."

Noah motioned to our waiter for the bill. "Cool, so anyone want to Jet Ski later? Think I found a good deal online."

Evan raised his Red Stripe. "A toast. To Eden, for being brave enough to submit to desire, for making a beast of himself to get rid of the pain of being a man."

I tried ignoring what Evan said, to no avail. He was right. I was wading farther from whatever I'd previously thought was my life. When my mother called that afternoon for the first time since I'd left, I didn't pick up, for after hearing what Evan said I couldn't bear fielding questions about what I was eating or if I was wearing tefillin or whether there was a shul nearby that corralled a minyan. And when later that night I nearly accepted the vial from the veterinarian, Evan's voice returned once more at the thought of where I was—on a beach at an ungodly hour, the last inch of a jay between my teeth, a half-dressed stranger dabbing at her nostrils. I was not the person I had been, nor was I the person I'd hoped to become when I left Brooklyn. I'd been filled, finally, with experience, and yet along the way I'd been emptied out. Eliot claimed poetic growth demanded "a continual extinction of personality," and this is what I began to feel during those evenings: an annihilation of something essential within me. My world had changed gradually at first, but now, almost overnight, it had changed seismically. If my ceremony of innocence had not yet drowned, it was shuddering beneath the water.

—

WE WERE ON THE BEACH on our final night, sparking a joint near the boardwalk, the drinking and smoking and general sleep deprivation weighing on me so that I ambled around in a fog. The wind blew forcefully over the ocean. I was trying not to shiver.

Oliver waved his phone, showing us a text. "The A&M ladies sent an address."

I didn't realize how high I was until I stood and heard an invisible crack, as if someone snapped their fingers in my ear. A sudden Doppler effect: light waves changing in frequency, cold nausea falling over me. I bent over, held my head in my hands, waited for it to pass. It didn't.

Noah, looking glazed, roused himself by slapping at his face. "You good, bro?"

Evan eyed me impatiently. "Don't start, Eden. Climb out of your head for a bit and just fucking enjoy it."

"I—" The moon above, full and fragile. The wind picking up. My teeth chattering. "Was there something wrong with that stuff?"

"Impossible," Oliver said, kicking sand in my direction as he ordered an Uber. "Evan picked it up himself."

A car materialized, whisked us to a beach house. I spent the ride with my face out the window, night made formless, dark swirls obscuring my vision, the ringing in my ears making me wince. The house swarmed with bodies: college students, locals, homeless people, an old man with a cane.

Pushing, yelling, dim corridors. My friends disappeared, I closed my eyes: I was alone, kneeling in the backyard, facing the ocean, vomiting into the grass. A woman was sitting cross-legged to my right, counting twenty-dollar bills, waiting patiently for me to finish dry heaving.

Ashen-faced. Flinching eyes. A mouth from Beckett. "How old are you?"

I wiped my mouth. "Eighteen."

She gave me her left hand—thin, veiny—and ran black nails over my cheek with her right. "Take these." She put two bullet-shaped pills into my palm. "They'll help." Explosions of gold, snakes falling from trees, the Tiger in the monstrous deep. I tried asking: who are you? Instead, I swallowed.

She told me to get up. It didn't seem to be something I could refuse. This time I asked who she was. She laughed. "Why do you ask my name?"

We went inside. Dizziness ossified into delirium: bare walls, soft carpets, cracks in the ceiling, my reflection in mirrors. She gripped tighter. White noise. Upstairs, a long hallway. I listened for the piano. Nothing. I'd like to turn back now, I told her. She was quiet.

She opened the door to a bedroom, revealing a circle of people on a bed, cutting lines on a hand mirror.

"Oh shit." Hunched over the mirror, Noah looked up in surprise, nostrils swollen, eyes bulging with guilt. Oliver and Evan were beside him. "Where, uh, where've you been, Drew?"

Evan, an arm around his A&M companion, eyed the woman leading me by the hand. "So you two found each other. I had a feeling you had it in you, Eden."

"I want to leave," I said again, this time to no one in particular. "I'm trying to leave."

One of the men on the bed stood, pointing at the girl and then at Evan. I squinted, tilted my head curiously; he was speaking Spanish, something about money, and seemed rather upset. Evan was yelling back. And then: I was on the ground. I'd been punched squarely in the mouth.

Noah was there first, in a singular motion leaping from the bed and toppling the man. I was horizontal, taking in the ceiling, something warm trickling from mouth to chin, thinking about how odd it was to be unable to lift my limbs. Someone threw himself on Noah; Evan punched him in the jaw. Noah and my attacker wrestled to my left. The woman fled. Oliver, from the bed, laughed, threw white powder into someone's face. I noticed blood on Noah's knuckles, I was hoisted to my feet, I was dragged out. We bolted down the staircase, found Amir outside—making out drunkenly with a woman who looked at least forty-five—and piled into the back of a loitering cab.

—

I NEVER WENT TO CAMP. Instead, my summers were spent cooped up in our small house. My trip to Key West, as such, was the longest I'd been away from my family. When I returned, I discovered a pained charge had descended upon the silence of my home. My parents scarcely spoke with each other, my father retreating into his study with a Gemara, ignoring my offers to join him, my mother alternating between venting to Cynthia and hovering over me in my room. They didn't reference the trip or the fact that my lip was slightly swollen. They didn't notice that I walked up my driveway bareheaded, that I nearly forgot to excavate my yarmulke from my suitcase before I went inside my house. I didn't acknowledge the guilt I felt from having plunged my parents into their state of enmity or from piling nonkosher food into my mouth or from carousing with the veterinarian. Above all, I didn't draw attention to the unmistakable sense of freedom I'd achieved, even briefly, while being on my own over the last few days. All this silence, at the very least, saved me from having to manufacture a week's worth of lies.

—

"MORAL INTUITIONISM," RABBI BLOOM EXPLAINED on our first day back, dividing us into factions for an impromptu debate, "is the idea that our natural inclinations are sufficient to guide us ethically." Amir and Noah, Rabbi Bloom decided, were to argue in favor of deferring to larger collaborative structures, like rabbinical tradition and government, while Evan and I were responsible for arguing that individuals ought to be left alone to adjudicate moral decisions. (Oliver was offered the chance to join either side or to provide a third approach. Respectfully, he abstained from the exercise.)

"So what you're telling me," Amir said, matched up against me, pulling irritably on his beard, "is that you're totally cool with allowing someone like Evan Stark to look inward for moral direction?"

"You're assuming he has an inside," Oliver chimed in, legs crossed. "That there's more than just, you know, endless black void down there."

"Well," I said defensively, annoyed by Amir's aggression, clearly honed through years of organized debate, "I'd argue that that's kind of a reductive way of framing what I'm—"

Evan put up a hand, cutting me off. "Eden, don't respond. Amir can't help that he's been subjected to moral weakness all his life."

Rabbi Bloom sighed. "As I remind you all too often," he said, sipping black coffee while he refereed, "let's refrain from ad hominem."

Amir snorted. "Believing *certain* people should not be left to their own devices—how exactly does that make me weak?"

Rabbi Bloom stroked his clean-shaven chin. "You know what? Let's return to before Mr. Eden was interrupted, shall we? Ari, how might you respond?"

"Well," I said, "I guess my position would be that we feel certain emotional impulses when we make decisions, and that these impulses are to be trusted, because they're just as important as logic or reason or anything else. Essentially, we should be able to go with our gut."

"So, in your estimation," Rabbi Bloom said, "it's as Hume would put it? Morality is whatever gives us 'the pleasing sentiment of approbation,' and immorality the contrary?"

"Actually, to a large extent, yes," I said, inordinately pleased with myself for eliciting Hume's posthumous approval. "I think that, when it comes down to it, we should be able to *feel* whether something is right or wrong."

Evan nodded with an indistinct smile, glancing at Rabbi Bloom before writing something into his notebook. Rabbi Bloom, however, didn't meet Evan's eyes.

"Isn't that kind of slippery, though?" Noah said. "Like, what if something feels right to me but wrong to you?"

Oliver waved at Rabbi Bloom in exaggerated deference. "If I may?"

"Please, Mr. Bellow. Enlighten us."

"Maybe I'm someone who not everyone always considers all too, I don't know, what's the word? Ethical, let's call it," Oliver said, "but don't some things kind of *have* to be objective? Like, yeah, call me old-fashioned, but cold-blooded murder is cold-blooded murder, right? It's wrong, however you slice it. I don't care where you are, I don't care how many books you've read, that's just plain, old sinful." I thought briefly, of all things, of Mordechai protesting against letting someone drown.

Rabbi Bloom looked around the table, waiting for someone to bite. After some hesitation, I did.

"No," I said quietly.

"No what?" Amir asked.

"I disagree."

Oliver whistled in amusement. "I don't know which Torah they teach in Brooklyn, Eden, but you're telling me you don't think murder is, like, universally wrong?"

"Of course *I* do," I said. "I know it's wrong and I can feel it's wrong. But I just don't think you can prove it. Objectively, I mean."

From the corner of my eye I saw Evan, to my left, nodding in approval. I didn't know whether to feel proud or ashamed. "Even I'll admit he's right," Evan said. "Because basically, the whole idea of one objective, universal truth is a bunch of bullshit."

Rabbi Bloom leaned forward on his elbows. "Mr. Stark."

"Sorry, but come on, think about it," Evan said. "Take Torah values. Religious law. If God is the epicenter of morality—if God *is* morality, then all of his dictums have to be moral, don't they?"

"I mean, no," Amir said, "that's not an accepted Halachic position, that's just you applying contemporary standards to an ancient and much more complicated system."

"Right," Noah said. "Plus, like, maybe God creates morality."

"Well, hold on." I wondered why I felt this strange urge to defend Evan. "Whether God *creates* morality doesn't really make much of a difference for this argument, does it?"

Amir frowned. "What? Sure it does. If God creates morality, then he's synonymous with morality."

Noah drummed his hands on the surface of the conference table. "Yeah, as in, God can create morality, put it into place and then chill. He can give us commands that are moral, or that have nothing to do with morality, or—"

"Again, that's all unimportant," Evan snapped. "You're missing

Eden's point. The details are irrelevant. Because whatever the Torah contains must be, at minimum, not *immoral*. But really, of course, that threshold is way too low. Embarrassingly low. Everything it contains should *be* moral."

"Mr. Stark," Rabbi Bloom said cautiously, "maybe let's tread carefully."

"Oh, please," Evan said, "now this is controversial? You're going to tell me that every last part of Torah is defensible on normative moral grounds? Slavery, corporeal punishments, Amalek—"

"We can't pretend to understand *everything*," Rabbi Bloom said. "There are things that exceed human comprehension, things that challenge—"

"Yeah, a lovely idea. But that's not just blind faith, then, Rabbi, that's lethally nearsighted. Because either certain commands are fundamentally immoral, in which case God is immoral, in which case we have ourselves a bit of an issue, don't we? Or, on the other hand, maybe such commands are not intended to last forever, are supposed to evolve, but then morality doesn't age very well. Pick your poison, because either way, doesn't that give us a collection of artificial, terrifyingly meaningless boundaries?"

"No," Amir said harshly, massaging his forehead with the intensity of someone attempting to untangle complex mental knots, "because, again, you're just applying incongruous standards. Like, what if human beings simply weren't ready at Sinai? God couldn't just impose crazy laws on moral cavemen all at once, laws we couldn't understand and that didn't make sense according to cultural and historical standards. In that case, God's way of transmitting morals is pretty genius. Gradual, steady, increasingly ethical."

Evan shook his head. "That's an appealing option to you? Is it any better to worship a God who can reveal Himself in miracles that shock society's historical and cultural standards but apparently cannot convince His own people to renounce indentured servitude? In my mind, we're better off just calling the whole thing like it really is."

Noah studied Evan's face. "Which is?"

"I see three options." Evan closed his notebook, smiling slightly. "Door number one: newsflash, God isn't moral. Door two: God didn't write what we think is our Torah. That's maybe our most palatable option. And then, there's lucky number three: God doesn't exist. I'll let you guys pick the winner. Kind of depressing, right?"

"Right," Noah said. "It is, if you actually believe that."

"Well, the good news is you don't have to believe that," Evan said. "Because there's a way out—cast aside this particular model of religion and embrace a completely new paradigm, one that doesn't reduce to three depressing dead ends."

"Yeah?" I said. I rubbed my palm against my neck. "So what is this new model?"

Evan hesitated, looking unsure of himself suddenly, as if he'd revealed more than intended and wasn't yet certain how to proceed. We waited for his answer but it didn't come. The bell rang; we stood, gathered our things. Amir, still in debate mode, too exasperated to make eye contact, hurried toward the door. Rabbi Bloom, however, stood in his way. "Given the nature of today's debate, which I think deserves a proper response, I'm going to request you each do some writing on the topic."

Oliver groaned, throwing back his head. "Haven't we written enough? Can't we make this a writing-free zone?"

"Unfortunately not," Rabbi Bloom said, "because to think well, as Orwell taught, we need to write well. And so to solidify these thoughts, I'd like you each to write a paper on this subject."

Amir pulled at his backpack straps. "On insane religious gibberish, you mean?"

"On whether you agree with Mr. Stark's hypothesis. You'll have free rein to come up with something innovative. Ten pages. Assume you'll receive feedback, and that the feedback will count. I'd like this to be some of your best work."

"How long do we have?" Noah asked.

"A week should be more than sufficient," Rabbi Bloom said, and then we left, merging into the crowded hallway.

—

I LOITERED OUTSIDE AFTER SCHOOL ended, waiting for Kayla. Sophia emerged, probably heading home after a student council meeting, and so I wandered into the model temple to avoid her. We'd been operating this way for weeks, observing each other not as strangers but as if we were separated by some formidable physical distance, even when only desks apart. I said hello and not much else in biology, evaded her looks in English, still found myself unwittingly jotting down her answers to Hartman's questions. *Machado wrong: no voluptuousness to misery. Why didn't Nietzsche know Dionysian only swallows you in madness?*

After a few more minutes Kayla finally left the building. She floated toward her car with her head down, earbuds in, books hugged to her chest, yellow backpack bouncing. When she spotted me reading the flash cards in the temple, however, she stopped short, grimacing. "Doing teshuva?"

"In a manner of speaking."

Kayla removed her headphones. "Is that right?"

"I've been waiting."

She continued toward her car. "For someone else, I hope."

"For you," I said, hastening to catch her.

Again she stopped, arching on her tiptoes. "What do you need, Ari?"

"To apologize again."

"Again? Maybe my memory fails me, but I don't recall a first time."

"I tried having lunch with you. Remember?"

"I remember you showing up with a sheepish look, expecting me to drop whatever I was doing to leap at the chance to join you, as if nothing happened. That I remember."

"How come you don't answer texts?"

"I'm not so into texts heavy on wit and light on remorse."

"Fine, you're right. I'm sorry, Kayla. I was a total asshole. I was selfish and unappreciative and too stupid to immediately make things right. I miss being friends. Does any of that suffice?"

She folded her headphones. "Yeah, that'll do. Even if I am a tad suspicious."

"Of?"

"Your motives."

"What does that mean?"

She grasped at the ends of her hair. "Is it a coincidence you're doing this now?"

"No. I'm doing it now because I miss you."

"Not because your math grades suck?"

"They've slipped, you'd kill me. But no. That's not why, I swear."

"In that case, yes, I'll allow you to accompany me."

"Home?"

"What? No, don't be overeager. Today's Thursday. I volunteer on Thursdays."

"Of course you do. Remind me where?"

"The homeless shelter. We're making sandwiches. You'll love it."

I spent the afternoon with her at the local chapter, dicing tomatoes, mashing tuna fish, wrapping whole-wheat sandwiches in tin foil.

"You really do this every week?" I asked, after we'd finished. I was busy scrubbing mayonnaise from my shirt.

"I do." She used her gloved hand to wipe a chunk of tuna from my left cheek.

"You're a pretty good person, you know that?"

"Yeah, well, it's the least we can do, right? This kind of thing makes you appreciate your privilege a bit more."

Removing my hairnet, following her to the parking lot, I tried focusing on things for which I felt actively grateful. I appreciated my mother. I appreciated my friends—Noah, at least, and Amir. I appreciated my ability to read and to write and to think. When this inevitably failed to inspire, I made a list of things I could appreciate more deeply: the intensity of my father's conviction, without which most people live entire lives; my experience with Sophia, however short, however painful, which expanded my capacity to feel; the fact that we'd left Brooklyn, that we had a moderately stable income, that we had a warm place to sleep, even if it was dwarfed by neighboring mansions. I knew such gratitude was crucial to deepening my general sense of happiness, and still I couldn't manage to feel anything more than abstractions.

"This was nice, wasn't it?" she said, unlocking her white Prius. "Kind of a refreshing change."

"I still smell like fish, not sure how refreshing that is."

"I meant, actually, that this is happening. That we're hanging out."

I climbed into her passenger seat. "We always hang."

"Outside of school?"

"What, you think I was avoiding you? I'm just busy, that's all. I've got basketball and schoolwork and—"

She reversed out of the lot, laughing. "I tutor, I head three different clubs, I volunteer and I have nearly a 4.0. If *I* have time, Ari, you have time."

"Fair, duly noted."

"It's just that—I mean, don't you feel that we have a lot in common?"

A hazy sundown: orange and pink shafts of light filtering through the car's windows, a flush of a breeze.

"Yeah," I said, "I'm a better dresser, maybe, but otherwise definitely."

"I'm serious."

We fell into some silence. I directed her to make a left onto Milton Drive. "Harris Manor, in the flesh," she said, whistling at Noah's house as she turned into my driveway. "Seems like it's gotten even bigger since the last time I was here."

"When was that?"

"Third-grade birthday party, probably. Something prehistoric like that."

I undid my seatbelt but we kept sitting there in her car. My parents weren't home. I felt acutely aware of the fact that we were alone, in private. Our bodies faced the same direction from separate seats, but we were close together, her right elbow grazing my left arm, unfamiliar desire stringing us together where we touched.

"I'm sorry for saying that before," she said, eyes fixed on my house. "I just—I guess I hate seeing you become someone else. I hated how you were basically, I don't know, embarrassed of me, like you were hiding me. Can I say that much?"

I didn't think about it. I grabbed her, leaned forward. It was pleasant: less heart-stopping than other kisses, though unexpectedly arousing. In ways I couldn't exactly define, actually, it felt right. She pulled back, laughing, wiping her hand, gently, over her lips. I went inside and set out to write the paper for Rabbi Bloom.

—

WALLOWING IN SELF-PITY, I'D ALLOWED the months after Early Decision to slip away. No longer could I afford delaying regular decision applications, I realized, the deadlines approaching rapidly. I submitted my paper ("Against Pure Reason," in which I made the case that imagination and emotion, not logic alone, lead us to truth), and Rabbi Bloom did a lot of nodding as he read it over, urging me to muster hope and begin the application process anew. So I did. With little left to lose, with nothing in the way of expectations, I locked my door, accessed the fee waiver secured by Rabbi Bloom and poured myself an inch of Jameson, which was leftover from that Friday night party I hosted unintentionally and which now resided in a shoe box in my closet. I started by listing every school I knew. I added schools I found online, random schools in interesting locations with appealing curricula and a focus on liberal arts. For good measure, I included Mrs. Ballinger's list. It was an eclectic megillah:

Cornell, Harvard, Stanford, Penn, Northwestern, Chicago, Yale, Princeton, Johns Hopkins, Brown, Dartmouth, Oberlin, Bennington, Queens College, Brooklyn College, Florida State, University of Florida, Emory, NYU, Miami, Bowdoin, Haverford . . .

I sipped whiskey, made cuts. Eventually, I settled on a preliminary fifteen and, light-headed from the whiskey, went to work. Shamelessly, I reproduced my Columbia essay, inserting the name of the school for each application. If a school had too many supplementary questions—*discuss a problem you'd like to solve; recount a failure; reflect on a time you altered a fundamental belief*—I scrapped it without hesitation. After little more than two hours, I'd submitted a dozen applications, drained another glass and shut my computer.

FEBRUARY

It is true that both ethics and religion aim at one thing—to raise man above the filth of the narrow self-love and bring him to the heights of love-of-others. But still, they are as remote one from the other as the distance between the Thought of the Creator and the thought of people.

—Ba'al HaSulam, *The Essence of Religion and Its Purpose*

have a question," Evan said.

It was a drab Tuesday. We were making our way, painstakingly, through *The Methods of Ethics*. Afternoon listlessness had overtaken the room: Oliver was too bored to muster sarcasm, Noah was sleepy-eyed from another extraordinary performance the previous night (seventeen points, ten rebounds, twelve assists) and even Amir, typically much too proud to admit something was difficult, especially if Evan understood it, was thoroughly lost. I'd been trying my best to stay alert, blinking away stagnant silences, resisting the soporific sound of rain streaming down the windows. Evan, meanwhile, had remained deferential until now, listening intently as Rabbi Bloom lectured, scribbling along the margins of his book.

Rabbi Bloom looked around the table before agreeing. "Go ahead, Mr. Stark."

"You told us to keep in mind whether Sidgwick helps our cause," Evan said slowly, "which is to say: does he lessen our religious doubts, our dissatisfaction with Orthodox Judaism and, by consequence, our personal unhappiness."

Rabbi Bloom twirled a spoon through black coffee. "So I did."

"Considering the energy in the room"—he gestured toward Oliver, whose head was buried in the fold of his right elbow—"I propose we move past reviewing Sidgwick's arguments and actually address this question."

"Very well," Rabbi Bloom said. "Maybe we're somewhat bogged down by the mechanics."

"I didn't make it past the first ten pages," Oliver said without lifting his head. "I'm man enough to admit it."

"Yeah, and I didn't even understand the SparkNotes," Noah said.

"For those of us who aren't up to speed," Evan said impatiently, "here's how Sidgwick leaves things. Of the three methods of morality—"

"—intuitionism, the idea that I can figure out moral rules on my own," Amir cut in, reciting eagerly from his outline. "Egoism, pursuing whatever makes me happy. And then utilitarianism: happiness for the greatest good."

Evan rolled his eyes. "Of those three, intuitionism and utilitarianism can coexist, whereas egoism and utilitarianism cannot."

"At least so far as he can prove," Rabbi Bloom corrected.

Evan straightened in his seat. "Well, that's the thing. He suspects egoism and utilitarianism *can* be squared. He just can't demonstrate how."

"So what good does that do in academic terms?" Amir asked. "If it can't hold up to analytic philosophy, it isn't rational."

Noah rubbed his eyes. "Well, *you* can't demonstrate God exists, right? And you still trudge along to minyan each morning."

"That's completely different," Amir said. "That's not logic, that's taking a leap of—"

"Shut up a second, will you?" Evan said.

Amir, predictably, turned hazardously red. "So he's running this class now? Does he *always* think he's running this class?"

Rabbi Bloom, looking very much like Evan, raised a hand. "Let's allow Mr. Stark to make his point," he said. "But cordially, please."

Evan looked as if he didn't even register Amir's reaction. "How do we reconcile self-interest and morality? We can't. Not without God. God, Sidgwick shows us, makes it work. God shifts the paradigm."

"Yeah, well, I still don't see it," Noah said.

Evan frowned. "Think about it. If we're bound by reward and punishment, then self-interest reorients to something beyond the immediate world."

"Sacrificing what *you* want in the pursuit of something quote-unquote *moral* is still in your best interest," I said, nodding along, "because you'll be rewarded for it in the World to Come."

"Exactly," Evan said. "So essentially, if God exists, doing what you want can still be considered moral. Really, almost anything can be made moral through access to God."

A pause as we absorbed this. I watched Rabbi Bloom's face darken.

"First of all," Amir said hotly, "let's note that *you* were the one denying God's existence pretty recently."

"That's completely false," Evan said. "If that's what you came out with, then the whole thing went over your head."

"Nothing's over my head."

Rabbi Bloom cleared his throat. "Gentlemen, please. Arrive at the point."

"Whatever. Secondly, what he's saying is cheating," Amir said. "You can't just resort to the supernatural, basically, so that things can make sense. That's not how pure logic works. Even Sidgwick says so!"

Evan leaned backward in his chair. "But Sidgwick didn't attend a yeshiva high school," he said. "He didn't wear tzitzit, he didn't pray three times a day, he didn't play Amish on weekends. Our whole lives are built on the premise that we believe in something outside of pure logic, so why wouldn't we use that same reasoning when it counts most?"

Rabbi Bloom pushed away his coffee, as if losing his appetite. "What's the upshot here, Mr. Stark?"

"The upshot is that God solves the equation. Without God, freeing the ego, the self, the force of your desires, is a dead end—we have to admit 'an ultimate and fundamental contradiction in our apparent intuitions of what is Reasonable in conduct.'" I flipped to the last pages of the book to find these lines, realizing Evan was quoting verbatim. Rabbi Bloom, judging by the look on his face, was equally impressed. "So in that sense, Sidgwick's totally right: divinity is what we can use to finally unlock our self-will."

"You keep talking about making your own choices and expressing your will and whatever else," Amir said. "But what does that even mean?"

"Our most basic human trait," Evan said. "The fundamental part of being alive. The desire to live, to find meaning, to have power, to do what *you* think is right."

Rabbi Bloom tried cutting in. "Perhaps let's pause and—"

"And so what I was saying," Evan continued, "is that Sidgwick's insight is all great and important, but he's still missing something pretty crucial, because he makes the mistake of postponing the fulfillment of self-interest *until* you're rewarded in Olam HaBa. What we need to do instead of waiting for the afterlife is achieve fulfillment on earth, in the here and now."

More silence. Amir looked horrified, but also as if he didn't quite know why. Noah and I fidgeted in our seats. Oliver played with his gelled hair.

"And how do you aim to do that?" Rabbi Bloom asked, after a brief interlude during which he proved incapable of meeting Evan's eyes.

"So that brings me to *my* question." Evan reached beneath the table for his backpack, pulling out an old, leather-bound book. "You believe in Kabbalah, Rabbi?"

Noah eyed the book, frowned. "That's not . . . the Zohar, is it?"

I'd never so much as opened the Zohar. My father, diligent Torah scholar that he was, forbade me from expending mental energy on

Kabbalah when I could otherwise devote myself to the more rigorous and pressing universe of Talmud.

"Whoa," Oliver said, cocking his chin. "Aren't you not supposed to touch that until you're forty? I thought it's, like, basically voodoo."

"Do I think it's much more than mystical rubbish?" Rabbi Bloom smiled politely. "No."

"But what if I found the morality offered by traditional Judaism to be restraining and unfulfilling?" Evan asked. "What if I thought it ignores your potential as an individual thinker?"

"In that case," Rabbi Bloom said, "I'd probably tell you that you don't understand traditional Judaism."

"What's not to understand? I've been living it for eighteen years."

"Judaism does not seek to ignore the self, Mr. Stark. It seeks to enrich it."

"But I very much disagree," Evan said. "Because the Judaism you teach here relegates the individual to an afterthought. It cares little about how you *feel*. It makes you fall in line and sacrifice everything and wait patiently for the next world, where you can finally earn it all back, where all that suffering actually amounts to something. But does it give a shit about the self? Does it have anything to say when you're alone? When you're betrayed? When your mother dies?"

Unidentifiable heaviness flooded Rabbi Bloom's eyes. "I know how . . . torturous your mother's ordeal was, Mr. Stark. And so if you decide ultimately to take that personal hell out on God, nobody would deny you that right. Nobody here can stop you from doing that."

Evan said nothing, eyes affixed to the Zohar. He rubbed his fingers together.

"But there are ways to heal," Rabbi Bloom said. "There are ways to find strength within faith, even when faith is shattered, even when faith reduces, at best, to doubt. Nobody ever ought to feel overlooked in the service of God."

"You don't get it," Evan said.

"What don't I understand?"

"I don't need platitudes. I've found my own way."

"A way to what?" Noah asked.

"I've been working on it all year. He's seen me," Evan said, pointing at me. A pit deepened inside my stomach, thinking of his ramblings in shul on Rosh Hashanah and in the school library, Nietzsche in hand.

"I don't know what you mean," Rabbi Bloom said, "and in truth, I almost don't want to."

Evan closed the Zohar. "I strongly believe that achieving fulfillment here on earth hinges on unleashing our capacity to become divine. In short? I think we should channel God to empower ourselves instead of allowing Him to crush us." I thought, for some reason, of that line from Henry James: *Just so what is morality but high intelligence?*

Amir scoffed. "So now you're, like—what? An esotericist?"

Evan shrugged. "I'm what *he* made me," he said, nodding at Rabbi Bloom. "What loss made me."

"Yeah, but, again," Amir said, "this is really sounding like a bunch of Kabbalistic nonsense. Like, are you going to tell us you believe in fairies, too? Goblins, maybe?"

"I'm obviously not talking about magic and monsters," Evan said. "I just mean, in a strictly Zoharian sense, that conventional standards require some . . . reexamining, let's call it. Because nothing's really evil absolutely, right? I mean, isn't that what Eden argued in our moral intuitionism debates? And wouldn't you agree, Rabbi, that anything, alternate realities included, can lead us to truth, even when they first appear off-limits?" Evan looked around the table and smiled. "It's like what Yeats teaches and Nietzsche teaches and whoever else teaches. What Shir HaShirim teaches: *Shkhora ani venavah.* I am dark, but beautiful."

—

EVAN HAD US MEET HIM at the lake Friday night, after our families finished Shabbat dinner. He wouldn't tell us why. I hurried through my meal, much to my mother's displeasure, interrupting my father's long-winded monologue on Parshat Terumah, which questioned what it means for God—*"Ain lo demut haguf, veaino guf"*—to seek physical sanctuary and dwell in our midst. I bentched to myself and told my parents I was going to Noah's for a classmate's birthday dessert.

When we arrived, Evan was lying on a bench, joint in mouth. His right hand fidgeted with a strip of scrolled white paper.

"What *is* that?" Amir asked, after Oliver promptly snatched Evan's weed.

Evan sat up, angling one leg on the bench. "This," he said, handing me the paper to examine, "is tonight's main attraction."

Cautiously, I unrolled it, straining my eyes in the dark. "It's blank," I said, turning it over.

Evan extracted a pen from his pocket. "Not for long."

"I don't get it," Noah said. "And my mom made slutty brownies tonight. Did I just give that up for nothing?"

"Dibs on leftovers," Oliver said, standing on his tiptoes to put his arm around Noah's shoulder. "Cynthia outdoes herself with those."

"Sorry, dude. Rebecca's family is over tonight, and her dad doesn't take prisoners when those brownies are served."

"Fuck me."

"Um, back to the issue at hand, maybe?" Amir cracked his knuckles impatiently. "What are we doing here?"

Evan took back his jay and blew large filaments of smoke into Amir's face. "I'm going to conduct an experiment I'd like you to witness."

Amir swiped the air in front of him. "Oh, cool. Are you going to perform some Kabbalah for our entertainment? Walk on water? Maybe pull a rabbit out of your yarmulke?"

"No, as appealing as that sounds. I'm going to write the name of God on this piece of paper and then cast it into the water."

Blank looks. Oliver retched, spitting phlegm into the grass.

"Think you're finally starting to lose it, buddy," Noah said.

Nervous laughter from Amir. "I mean, you're kidding, aren't you? Because I was definitely not serious about the Kabbalah shit."

"I don't think he is," I said, wondering why it was that I'd felt compelled to decline Kayla's dessert invitation and instead pay further testament to Evan's volatility.

Amir's laughter subsided. "And why the hell are you going to do that, may I ask?"

"To see what happens," Evan said.

"The full name?" I asked.

"All seventy-two glorious letters."

"My family does tashlich here, you know." Noah placed his hands in his pockets, swaying slightly. "Maybe this is a bad idea. Maybe it's, I don't know, sacrilegious?"

"Most things we do are sacrilegious." Evan twirled his pen through his fingertips. "But it's not like that's my intention. I'd say tonight I'm more interested in the question of, I don't know, of *worthiness*, let's call it."

I unrolled the sleeves of my shirt so that they covered my wrists. "You want to know if you'll be—what? Punished?"

"Okay, yeah, the more I think about it, the more I think you should punt on this little activity." Noah looked at me for support, but I shrugged. "This could curse us."

Evan stomped out the joint. "Since when do you believe in curses?"

"I don't know, I guess I—" Noah ran his fingers through his hair, pulling strands down past his neck. "I just feel like some things you don't do."

Removing the cap with his incisors, Evan took his pen and, with careful, ornate handwriting, sketched out seventy-two Hebrew letters in red ink. "I was generous enough to supply extra paper," he said, patting the pockets of his black jeans, "in case anyone wants to write their own?" Nobody moved, not even Oliver. Noah looked sick.

"Very well. You'll live vicariously."

Amir retreated a few steps. "And if we don't want to watch?"

"Then don't." Evan walked toward the water. "Then leave."

"Okay, I have to ask," Oliver said, glasses fogged from smoke. "So, like, what if this works? What's supposed to happen?"

"When Moshe did this," Evan said, "he split the Red Sea."

"And retrieved Joseph's bones from the water," I said.

Evan smirked. "Good point, Eden. Forgot that one."

"To be totally clear," Amir said, "you're actually telling us that this isn't some weird prank but that you actually intend to, like, perform a freaking miracle?"

"Well, no promises," Evan said. "I just want to try my hand. See if I'm . . . spiritually strong enough, I suppose, to receive divine revelation of some sort."

Amir nervously itched his beard. "I mean, guys, seriously, come on. How are we—how is this not really fucking weird?"

"Maybe what it takes to rise above ordinary life," Evan said softly, "is something shocking and dangerous. You know how rabbis always teach that holiness is associated with separation? Kohenim are holy because they're separate, the Beis HaMikdash is holy because it's separate, God is holy because He's separate? Well, follow that logic: divorce yourself from ordinary life and find yourself moving away from being human and toward something . . . I don't know, something thrilling and risky and very much divine."

Nobody responded. I wasn't taken aback by the content of this idea, merely the latest in a sequence of increasingly bewildering theories on Evan's part, but by the fervor with which it was delivered. Somehow I knew—somehow we all knew—that Evan, at last, was veering away from theoretical debates and into the realm of practical belief.

"You'd have to be pure," I said, finally. "Only the pure are supposed to use the hidden name."

"Let's pray, in that case, that I am." Evan kissed the paper and dropped it into the water. Noah turned away; I inched up the bank with Oliver and Amir, watching the white disintegrate under the stars. We stood in silence, long after the paper was gone. Finally, Evan cleared his throat and walked away from the water. "So that was anticlimactic."

"What'd you expect?" Amir asked. "Prophecy? Bubbles in the water?"

"I hoped the ground would swallow me whole," Evan said. "I hoped to meet Korach and the rest of his rebel army."

"Maybe you had the wrong name?" Oliver said. "Who knows what God's secular name is. Or maybe He has a middle name?"

"We shouldn't have done this," Noah said, to no one in particular. He kicked up patches of dirt, darkening his white Nikes.

"Now what?" Amir asked. "What'd that prove?"

Evan surveyed the heavens. Night air pressed against us. Dull moonlight shone down in silver glints. I was sweating. "Nothing."

"You're going to need a better experiment," Amir said, "if you're trying to prove any of your shit."

"You're absolutely right." Evan lit a second joint, a lone light in the dark. "I am."

—

THERE WAS A DRUG TEST at the end of that week. Mrs. Janice delivered the news, quite happily, over the loudspeakers: tests were school policy, selections random, cooperation compulsory. We were sitting in Mrs. Hartman's class when we heard this, scribbling a mock AP essay, an analysis of Rimbaud's "Delirium." (*Je croyais à tous les enchantements.*) Davis, seated several rows before Evan, turned in his seat and grinned wickedly. "You're done," he mouthed.

Evan flipped him off.

Cold sweat broke out on the back of my head. I glanced around: Amir turned green, Noah drummed pen over paper, Kayla gave me a look of urgency. Mrs. Hartman peeked up from grading essays. "Is there a problem?"

Davis sniggered from the far side of the room.

"Something to declare, Mr. Davis?"

"I think," he said, attempting to compose himself, "some dear friends may be in peril."

I spent the day holding my breath each time another student was summoned. Oliver, of course, was among the first wave. ("I told them not to bother," he said, shrugging, "to keep their little urine container and mail another bill to my old man.") Evan was summoned, too, along with Gabriel, Donny, Niman and, to her amusement, Kayla. ("It's fine," she said, "expected, really. They need to balance clear-cut offenders with someone unable to so much as identify the scent of marijuana.") Noah was a nervous wreck, insistent he'd lose Northwestern were he to test positive; when he was called he blamed Evan, rambling on about divine retribution for casting the name of God into the lake. I was increasingly nauseous at the thought of being tested, not because I was scared for my college prospects—I had none—but because I was desperately afraid of disappointing my poor mother. Drug usage, I knew, was something even my tireless advocate could not defend, and the thought of her fallen face was too crushing to bear.

The call came at the end of the day, as I was suffering through double biology. Dr. Flowers paused mid-sentence and frowned. "Better be clean, Eden. Good Lord, you better be clean as a whistle."

"Yes, well, I am," I said unconvincingly.

"Good." She played with her chalk, white dust landing on her blouse. "Because I'm guessing you're already skidding on thin academic ice."

I caught Sophia's eyes on the way out. She gave me a hopeful nod—hands at her side, those painted, frescoed eyes narrowed—but I made a point of avoiding her gaze.

Davis was the only other student in the office. I was greeted with a smirk. "Afternoon, Aryeh."

"Here you go, Mr. Eden," Mrs. Janice said, handing over a nondescript plastic cup, eyeing me suspiciously. "I'm sure you know what to do."

"I'll walk with you, old chap," Davis said, empty cup in hand, shooting Mrs. Janice an unrequited wink.

"Surprised they bothered testing you," I said, annoyed he was following me into the bathroom.

"What choice did they have? Would look odd otherwise, wouldn't it?"

"What does that mean?"

He clapped my back. "These tests are expensive. Helps when people donate to the cause."

"This is your family's idea?"

"Hardly their idea, per se," he said. "Though do we see anything wrong in bringing to the attention of the administration problems regarding the abuse of narcotics? It's our civic duty, after all."

"Civic duty. You're a jerk."

"Please." He held open the bathroom door. "Don't let this come between us. It won't really affect you, will it? I know your friends are . . . astonishingly delinquent, but you don't seem like the sort of fellow to get caught up in that, a guy from Teaneck."

"Brooklyn."

"Right, sorry. But I swear, truly, I'd no intention of harming you."

I hesitated at the doorframe. "You're after Amir?"

"Samson?" He scoffed. "Can't stand the guy sometimes, but I respect him. And I know him. He isn't foolish enough to be vulnerable. Stark, on the other hand?"

We approached the urinals. I took the one on the far left. Davis, despite an open row of urinals, took the one beside me.

"You really have to stand right here?"

"Come on, Eden."

"I can hear you breathing."

"A man's got a right to breathe. Don't be trigger shy on my accord."

I fumbled to open the lid of the container and listened to his whistling as we filled our cups, my heart pounding in my chest. We finished and went to wash our hands, setting down our samples on the counter. I ran water, splashed my face, felt as if I were on the verge of hyperventilating. The door flew open. In barged Gio, vacuum in hand.

"You two—back to class," he barked, plugging in the vacuum. "I got work to do."

"Just a moment, Giovanni, my good sir," Davis said. "We'll be right off."

Gio threw the vacuum to the floor. "What you say, Davis? Talking down to me? Talking shit?"

"Mea culpa, Gio." Davis raised his arms in peace. "But please. Are the profanities necessary?"

Gio threw his sanitation gloves to the floor. "You walk around, doing whatever you want? I tell you something, little shit, if you think you—"

"Now, listen here," Davis said, turning his back to me and jabbing his finger toward Gio's chest, "you can't talk that way to a student. My father—"

Allowing Davis to lecture on, Gio nodded, almost imperceptibly, at the two containers of urine at the sink. Staring in confusion, I realized what those head movements signified. I hesitated, despite Gio's frantic blinking in my direction, until, my mother's disappointment in mind, I switched the samples, just as Davis finished his diatribe and groped for the nearest cup.

"Okay, okay, you're right, Davis, very right, now get out, yes?"

"Yes, well." Davis took a deep breath, holding my cup. "I *will* be off, thanks very much." With that, he stalked away, humming some Harvard ballad.

"That guy, huh?" Gio glanced under a stall to make certain we were alone. "Not as bright as they say."

"Gio, I don't understand."

He stroked his chin. "Just take cup and be on way. My eyesight's bad. Cataracts. Didn't see thing."

"Seriously, how did you—"

"Christ." He grabbed the sample from the counter. "That story the rabbis tell? The flood and the guy praying and the boats come but he says no and keeps waiting and waiting until the bastard drowns? Where's help, he asks God when he gets to Heaven, I wait for You, I turn down boats? Moral of story, very practical, don't drown in own urine. Catch my drift?" He shoved the cup at my chest. Reluctantly, I took it, holding Davis' warm, yellow liquid. I gagged. "Not a word, okay? Hand it in, run to class." He swore in what I think was Italian. "They think I don't listen but old Gio listens. When boat shows up, get fuck in, don't ask questions." With that, he moved me out of the bathroom and slammed the door.

—

DONNY HAD A BIRTHDAY PARTY on Saturday night. He was permanently grounded for his role in what had transpired after sunrise minyan, but his parents took pity and threw a small, contained backyard gathering, inviting just the basketball team. There was cake, some ice cream. We milled around the pool, aware of the Silvers' inquisitorial looks, pretending we'd never before been to his house. ("What a lovely home, Mrs. Silver," Oliver made a point of exclaiming early on, much to Donny's mortification. "So tasteful. Can't believe I've never been over!") The party lasted fewer than two hours.

We were still hungry when it was over, so Evan suggested we try the late-night Israeli pita place. It was a small shop, two tables, tucked away in the far end of a dingy plaza. Next door was a neglected office with rusted windows and a lit-up sign that read: PSYCHIC VISIONS & READINGS.

"How does that place stay open?" Amir asked over a mouthful of shawarma. "Like, how has local government not shut that down?"

Tahina dripped from Oliver's mouth. "Why should they?" He didn't bother reaching for napkins. "It's a legitimate business."

"Yeah," Noah laughed, "no different from that brothel in Key West you tried checking out."

Amir shrugged, taking another bite. "In both places you pay to get screwed."

"Cute *and* clever," Oliver said, checking his phone. "You're not going to MIT by any chance?"

Evan pushed his plate toward the middle of the table. "Fuck it. Let's do it."

I frowned. "Do what?"

"Visit the psychic." Evan spun his knife absentmindedly. "It'd be fun to try."

"Makes sense," Amir said, watching the knife in motion. "Your idea of fun is re-creating the splitting of the Red Sea, so yeah. This is totally on brand."

Evan checked his watch. "Come on, it's not even midnight. We have anything else to do?"

Oliver tucked his phone back into his jeans. "Fine, I'm in. Gemma just canceled on me anyway."

Noah picked at the scraps of his baba ghanoush. "Gemma?"

"We've been hooking up."

"Since when?"

Oliver shrugged.

"Romance of our time," Amir said.

"Thought that title belonged to Drew," Oliver said.

Evan placed his palm on the table. Slowly, he allowed the knife to pass back and forth between his fingers. "Eden and whom?"

"Aren't you getting with Gross, Drew?" Oliver said.

"Dude," Noah said, "chill."

Oliver raised his hands in protest. "What? Simple question."

"Don't phrase it like that," Noah said. "And it's not your business."

"Sorry. Drew, are you not currently *seeing* Ms. Gross?"

Unsure how to answer, I nodded noncommittally, finishing my Sprite.

"Now that we've settled that important issue," Evan said, increasing the speed with which he stabbed, "are we ready to go?"

"Jesus," Amir said, cringing, "can you stop? I'm anxious watching you."

Evan went faster. The serrated edge, at the very end of the cycle, nicked his pinky.

Noah recoiled. "Shit, you okay?"

"It's nothing." Red drops pooled into the web between Evan's pinky and fourth finger.

We piled back into the Jeep and, the plaza looking sufficiently abandoned, broke out Oliver's stash. Y100 was on, playing Kanye, proclaiming itself Miami's number one hit station. The windows fogged. In the distance the streetlights glowed red.

When we finished, nighttime bent slightly, we pushed open the psychic's door. Beads rattled overhead, announcing our arrival. The office was nearly pitch-black, save for the glow of a computer screen, reflected through a back mirror. The room smelled vaguely of dead flowers and burnt incense. Under the mirror, I realized, was a woman at a desk. She was tan, with sunspots and leathery skin. A turban sat on her desk, beside her computer.

Evan approached her. "You open?"

The woman glanced up at us and swore in what sounded like Romanian. "You scared the shit out of me." She was wearing Beats, we realized as we stepped closer. She removed them and put her turban back on. "Apologies. I was doing some work."

"You're watching *The Office*," Oliver said.

"I'm studying astrology, actually."

"I literally see Steve Carrell's face in the mirror."

She swore again, minimizing the tabs on her screen. "Yeah, well. It was getting late. You boys here for a reading? Because I close at one."

"Your sign says two," Evan said.

"Tonight I'm tired, so. Quick reading but still good. Does that work? Perfect, take seats around my desk, yeah? You, strong one," she said, pointing to Noah, "bring that chair from the front and we have five. Lovely."

Noah dragged it over and we assembled before her. We could see, up close, that she had her nails painted black. She wore enormous hoop earrings and several low-hanging, fake-pearl necklaces. Astrology charts and hamsa hands and anti-vampire amulets adorned the walls. On her desk was a large bottle of wine, accompanied by a picture of a toddler.

"My son, Abner," she said, catching me looking at it. "But let's begin, yeah?" She screwed up her eyes. "When did we all last meet?"

Noah cackled. "What?"

"That's how I start."

"Oh, sorry."

She gave an irritated look. "You guys been smoking?"

Noah shook his head spiritedly. "Course not."

"Right. Well, want the usual package? Seventy dollars and I'll read your palms, ninety and I'll include tarot cards."

"Quick question," Amir said, leaning forward, "but do you by any chance know God's secret name?"

"What?"

"Never mind. I'm surprised they didn't teach that in witchcraft school."

"I'm no witch, kid, I'm a healer. Or a, uh, what do you call it, a possessor. A spiritual ventriloquist. Don't laugh, I studied hard for my degree."

"Your degree?"

"College of Transcendental Pursuits. Graduated with honors."

"Maybe we should apply there, Drew," Oliver said. "Where is it?"

"Online. Anyway. Cash or credit?"

"We're not interested in readings," Evan said.

My phone buzzed. A text from Kayla: haven't heard from u, so i'll bite: where art thou?

"No phones!" she barked. "Screws up ethereal waves. Also, no recordings."

"Sorry," I said, holstering my phone.

Evan dug inside his jeans for his wallet. "How much to talk to the dead?"

"That's what you want?"

"Can you do it?"

"Sure I can do it, but it's, you know, a rare thing. People usually want something—comforting."

Amir crossed his legs. "This isn't comforting?"

"Maybe. Maybe not. The future is one thing. The dead are unpredictable."

"Right," Amir said.

"Plus it's a little frowned upon these days, to be honest. But if that's what you want, I'll do it. It's more expensive, though."

"How much?"

She examined us, calculated how much she thought we'd pay. "Two seventy-five."

"Two hundred."

"Two twenty."

"Deal," Evan said.

Amir laughed. "I'm out."

"Yeah, same," I said. "I can't pay that."

Evan rifled through his wallet and handed her a credit card. "My treat."

"Okay, let's go," she said, putting on reading glasses to run the card. "Some ground rules. One, no refunds. Whatever you get, you get. I don't control the deceased, I'm just a conduit. Once a woman came in and had me rustle up her grandmother and then didn't want to pay because the old lady told her to screw off. Family squabbles are not my problem."

"Understood," Evan said.

"Second, summoning a spirit is very complicated. And it's much more complicated depending on when they passed. Once a body is interred, the spirit roams earth for twelve months, yeah? During those months it's much easier to summon, because the spirit is still restricted, whatever. But after that, the spirit is free and doesn't have to show up when I call unless it actually wants to give over a message. Got that?"

"Yeah," Amir said, "sounds super scientific."

"It's bad luck to insult a healer," she told Amir. "Very bad." Inhaling, she turned to Evan. "If he gets me pissed, I cannot perform with a clear head."

"Let her do her thing, Amir," Evan said.

"All right," Amir said, "go ahead."

"So, who do you want to talk to and did they die recently?"

We went silent, each thinking the same thing. The psychic frowned. "What's the issue?"

Noah passed a hand through his hair. "Ev?"

"I think it should be Samuel," Evan said.

I frowned. "Who's Samuel?"

"Like the story in Navi," Evan said. "When Saul is ignored by God and so asks the Witch of Endor to communicate with Samuel."

A look of intense relief passed through Noah's eyes. "Ah, okay. Yeah, I mean, incredibly random, but that works."

"Of all the people in human history," Amir said, "*that's* who we want to chat with?"

"What about that dude you love, Ev?" Oliver asked. "Freddy from Prussia? The Marvelous Mr. Frederick the Second?"

"That'd be Friedrich Nietzsche," Amir said, "of Germany."

The psychic lit a cigarette. "Don't know how I feel about that. He's a downer, I hear. Care if I smoke?"

"I'd much prefer Shimon bar Yochai," Evan said, "but I think it has to be Samuel."

"Why Shimon bar Yochai?" Noah asked.

"He wrote the Zohar." I looked up at Evan. "But this is why you wanted Pita Haven tonight, isn't it? So we'd end up in here for another experiment?"

Evan didn't blink. "Well, of course."

"Son of a bitch," Amir said, tapping his foot restlessly.

"It's getting late," the psychic said. "Let's make a decision, yeah?"

"Wouldn't it better prove your divinity if you merit summoning a *different* Samuel to shoot the shit?" Amir asked. "Like, I don't know, Samuel Clemens, let's say."

The psychic nodded. "I like Twain."

"Or Beckett," I said.

"Or Adams," Oliver said. "The real one or the cutie plastered on the beer bottle. Either works."

Evan shook his head. "Samuel the Prophet."

"Okay, Samuel the Prophet it is," the psychic said. "Beautiful. So we use a very strict procedure. When the spirit comes, show respect. Don't shout questions, don't speak out of turn, don't frighten it off. Only I can hear the spirit, but the spirit can hear all of you. Okay?"

"How convenient," Amir said.

She reached inside a drawer for a sheet of paper. "Pass it around," she said, dipping a quill into a bottle of ink, "and write your name and one question you'd like to ask our guest. Just one, since there's five of you."

I watched as Noah, Oliver and Amir each turned strangely quiet when receiving the quill and paper, avoiding eye contact, hesitating before writing. I went second to last. I tried, unsuccessfully, not to survey the questions above my slot:

1. Noah: I'm definitely supposed to marry Rebs, right? (College or after?)
2. Oliver James Bellow . . . will I ever make my parents proud
3. A.S.—should I forgive my father?

Horrified at the prospect of what I really wanted to write being revealed, to Evan or to the others, I asked instead whether I'd find a college I liked and hurriedly passed the sheet to Evan, who immediately wrote something down and handed it to the psychic.

She scanned the list, powered down her computer. "Let's begin," she said, putting out her cigarette and lighting a candle. Producing a kitschy goblet from underneath her desk, she began muttering incantations, picking up the candle and allowing five drops of wax to fall into the goblet before adding five drops of wine. Eyes closed, she swirled the cup. "Last part," she said, reopening her eyes. "Someone needs to make an offering."

"What does that mean?" Noah asked.

"Like a sacrifice."

"Here." Evan put his right palm above the goblet. He squeezed his pinky until he managed to extract five droplets from the coagulating wound.

Amir gagged. "That's disgusting. I really hope you use new cups."

"I maintain a very sanitary environment," she muttered. "Now listen."

"To what?"

"Shh." She blew into the goblet and stood. Her eyes closed. She opened her mouth to speak but stopped herself. "He's rising."

Oliver withdrew a piece of Doublemint from his pocket and placed it in his mouth with as much noise as he could. "Nice, what does Sammy look like?"

"An old man," the psychic whispered. "Wearing a mantle. But he's—he's not coming the usual way."

Oliver elbowed my side. "Not *coming* the usual way. Like that one?"

She stiffened, turning her attention on Evan without opening her eyes. "You didn't tell me."

"Tell you what?"

"What you were. Who you are," she said, speaking frenziedly. "And now he wants to know why you've disturbed him. He says you shouldn't have brought him up."

"Just ask the question," Evan said.

"The *questions*," Amir corrected. "All five."

She folded the paper into fourths and deposited it into the goblet. Then she lit another match and dropped it in, too. "He's angry," she announced, her voice rising. "He won't stop shouting."

Oliver grinned. "What'd we ever do to him?"

"You didn't obey! You broke the limits! You're becoming—yes, yes, I know—an adversary to the Lord!"

"Okay, okay," Amir said, covering his ears, "we get the act."

The psychic ignored him. "She says so, too, you know. She says to stop. You'll be ruined."

Evan blinked. "Who says?"

She was convulsing now, her limbs shuddering with such intensity that she knocked the picture of her son off her desk.

"Ask it!" Evan reached for her hand. "Should I do it or—"

An earsplitting screech as Evan touched her. Her head lulled back.

I thought for a moment that a vein in her temple would burst, showering us in blood. As it happened, though, she went silent, falling back into her chair, pale and panting. Just at that moment, her security alarm began to wail.

"Goddamn it." She snapped to, forced herself up. The alarm was deafening. I crammed my fingers into my ears until she had punched in her code, restoring silence. "Sorry," she said, slumping back down. "Happens randomly. Don't worry, cops won't call for at least half an hour. In case it's actually real, you know, so intruders have time to ransack the place."

"So," Amir said, "that was totally worth the money, huh, Ev?"

"As I said." She lit a new cigarette and reached for the wine. "Spirits are volatile. Never know what you're going to get. And they're possessive, no? They take right over. Did I give you a fright? Here, have wine, calm your nerves."

We sat a few minutes, sipping wine from plastic cups. Oliver shared her cigarette. Evan didn't drink, didn't speak. We drove off as a police car appeared down the street.

—

"SO THE DRUG TEST?" KAYLA asked, bent over her palette. She'd taken me to a contemporary museum in South Beach, where we'd signed up for a painting class. There was a room in which a rudimentary robot, equipped with three arms and no legs, performed the wave to a dystopian rendition of "Keep the Home Fires Burning." There was a room with a vintage film projector, rattling noisily, showcasing in rapid bursts the gestation of a human skull. By the time the class started I was nursing a modest headache.

"What about it?" I glanced over at the instructor, who was teaching us how to reproduce Frank Cadogan Cowper's *The Golden Bowl*. Kayla was a rigid fundamentalist, imitating every stroke, line and angle, the result surpassing the instructor's own work. Kayla had her maiden in a red turban and a golden, floral, bare-shouldered gown, eyes blue and piercing, brows lifted in unflinching defiance. Against a violet backdrop, the woman held out a golden bowl of votive fruit: grape vines, pumpkins, delicate peaches.

Kayla stole one of my brushes and, ignoring my protest, gilded her maiden's gown. "Are you worried about it, I mean?"

"You seem to think I should be."

"No, I'm just—I don't want to see you jeopardize anything, is all."

"I'm pretty confident it won't be an issue."

"What does that mean?"

"Nothing, let's just focus on painting."

"How can I focus with your monstrosity staring at me?"

"No art is monstrous." I twirled a thick paintbrush into the lower right section of my canvas. Yellow and red spots landed on our smocks. "Didn't you learn anything from the exhibitions?"

"In this case I disagree." She leaned her head on my shoulder to examine my canvas. By now, I'd surrendered any hope of following instructions and was entertaining myself by experimenting with an abstract blur: phosphorescent gold trapezoids, a metamorphosed bowl, eruptions of green light, objects resembling broken crowns. "And now, after witnessing you paint, I wonder what I see in you."

I saluted with my brush. "A misunderstood visionary, born too early. Tragic, really."

The instructor shuffled over. She gave an envious grunt inspecting Kayla's canvas but an alarmed gasp at mine. "What . . . have you done?"

Kayla smirked. "Enlighten us, Ari."

I put my hand to my chin, suppressing a laugh, avoiding Kayla's eyes. "Well, if you see here," I said, gesturing toward the upper left quadrant, "this is Judgment Day, of course, evoking the feeling of the celestial encountering sinful physicality. And here, just over to the right, is an ode to the Deluge—"

"—to the left, you mean," the instructor cut in, leaning over my shoulders, tilting her head at various angles, "here with the aquatic hues?"

"You'd think that's water rising," I continued, drawing muffled laughter from Kayla, "or the Ark, maybe, but no, this part to the right is more océanic in a surrealist sense, don't you think?"

I was given a death stare. "Not in the slightest. In fact, this is what I'd call a picture without meaning. But cruder sensibilities could perhaps see it in a . . . Kandinsky kind of way."

"Right, Kandinsky," I said. "Precisely."

The instructor frowned. "You speak eloquently for a person who's presented the world with such . . . well, filth."

Kayla pinched my cheek. "Don't get him started. He's an English student. He turns all sorts of garbage into poetry."

"Garbage?" I said as our instructor stalked off. "And you're going to tell me your incredibly detailed, objectively impressive painting is what—spectacular?"

"In every sense of the word."

"But what's so different about these two canvases, if you really think about it?"

"Yeah, what *is* the difference between Rembrandt and a preschooler's depiction of a smiling sun wearing sunglasses?"

"Fine." On my palette I married yellow to indigo. "What do you see in yours?"

"I'm not as talented in that department, Mr. Seer of Judgment Day."

"Which department? Literary criticism?"

"No, its close cousin, the department of bullshit."

"C'mon, you're the tutor. Show your student how it's done."

"All right." She pointed to the maiden's facial expressions. "So she's gorgeous, obviously. But her real power is her negative beauty."

"Now we're talking."

"I mean it. Look at her. She knows it just as much as I do. All that beauty, but she's paralyzed, alone, caged."

I swept my eyes over the woman. "Heavy stuff. I thought you were just going to comment on how she represents Demeter and fertility and the coming of winter."

"Quit showing off."

"Sorry."

"But you see what I mean?"

"Eh. I mean, maybe she is sad. But loneliness doesn't have to be some moral defect. It can be . . . part of someone's allure."

"Being self-absorbed, beyond the grasp of anyone else, you think that's attractive?"

"I think it's attractive to be a rarity." I observed her stance, her eyes. "And anyway, whatever she's missing doesn't matter. It makes her fuller, gives her suffering some dignity."

Kayla snorted, plunged the brush into the jar. Muddied colors rose to the surface. "I didn't paint her to have *dignity*. I painted her to possess her."

"Yeah, well, even so," I said, "it's still there. Her nobility or, I don't know, her magnitude. The feeling she's been wounded and yet once you've seen her you never go back."

"To what? Chasteness? Joy?"

I shrugged. "To whatever it was being only the person you used to be."

We fell into silence, pink with embarrassment, seeking refuge in the act of tidying up and signing our names in the corner of our paintings. In a sudden, erratic movement, Kayla snatched the smallest brush, dipped it black and sliced a dark dash down the middle of the bowl.

—

"FOUR FIFTHS OF THIS GROUP FAILED," Rabbi Bloom announced at our next meeting. He pushed away his copy of *Guide for the Perplexed*. "I'm not certain whether this means this class isn't working or if it's more pressing than ever."

"Don't take it to heart, Rav," Oliver said. "I fail tests on the regular. You get used to it, trust me."

Evan frowned. "Four-fifths?"

Rabbi Bloom stirred his teacup. "Sadly enough, Mr. Stark."

"How could *one* of us have passed?"

Oliver smirked, looking around the table. "Yeah, with all due respect, Rabbi, you're the only person in this room who'd show up clean. At least I assume you would. I'm not one to judge."

Noah placed a jug of Gatorade on the table. "So only some of us were tested?"

"Well, I was definitely tested," Amir said miserably. "My mom slapped me across the face when she heard the results." This reduced Oliver to a giggling fit, which he tried relieving by sipping on room-temperature water, only to spit up a mouthful.

Evan rested his gaze on me. "Eden?"

My face burned. Slowly, my friends turned their attention to me. "What?" I said.

"Well done," Oliver said, "but how'd you get fake urine? And why didn't you share?"

I looked, too quickly, to Rabbi Bloom, as if expecting a private answer to what I was thinking. "I can assure you that collections were held under sterile and controlled environments," he said officiously, pointedly ignoring my stare. "And in any event, it's hardly anyone's business whether someone else passed. I'd prefer you worry about the fact that you failed."

Evan laughed. "Hardly our business? Rabbi, please tell us how Eden can possibly be the only person in the clear? Why are you protecting him?"

I said nothing. Certainly I was grateful to avoid being caught, but to a large extent I shared their dissent, or at least their confusion. What I rationalized, at first, as a spontaneous favor on Gio's part now seemed increasingly suspicious. That Gio had somehow been directed to save me was implausible, and yet I couldn't shake the feeling that Evan's accusation was not entirely wrong.

"Gentlemen," Rabbi Bloom said, "this is serious."

"Well," Oliver said, "let's not be melodramatic."

"This school has rules, Mr. Bellow," Rabbi Bloom said wearily. "Abusing substances is no laughing matter. Experimenting with drugs for the sake of having fun is bad enough." At this Rabbi Bloom gave Evan a cautious look. "Experimenting for other purposes is materially worse."

"What about our colleges?" Noah asked weakly.

"We're forced to draft a letter detailing the violation. The letter will be held in our records but will not be released unless there is a repeat violation."

"Forced?" Evan gave a bitter laugh. "You're hardly forced."

"This institution has an obligation to disclose a pattern of disciplinary issues, Mr. Stark. I advise you refrain from such action if that concerns you."

When we were dismissed we went out into the parking lot toward Oliver's Jeep. Evan grabbed my shoulder before I could climb in, forcing me aside. "Want to tell the truth now?"

"I don't know what you're talking about."

"C'mon, Eden, no bullshit."

Briefly I considered admitting what had happened in the bathroom with Gio. But I didn't trust Evan, and I felt perverse gratification knowing he needed something from me. "What do you think I'm hiding?"

"If something's going on between you two," he said quietly, "then it concerns me, even if you don't understand why."

I shook him off. "Funny," I said, "because I'm pretty sure you're the one hiding something that affects me." I didn't mean to say these words, but I was happy I did. His face went white. I turned my attention to the perimeter of the model temple.

"Careful, Eden," Evan said. "You don't know what you're talking about."

I brushed away, joined them in the car. Inside they'd already moved on to discussing Purim costumes. It was nice out, though a bit overcast, the sky hazy-gray. Oliver dug around his glove compartment, exhuming a baggie of weed. "Shall we?"

"You're joking," Amir said from the back seat. "Tell me you're joking."

We hesitated. Then, ignoring Amir's moralizing, we smoked.

—

MORE THAN A WEEK WENT by and Purim was fast approaching. Growing up, Purim was my favorite holiday. Our community gathered in synagogue, twice, to recite the book of Esther, frolicked in costume, delivered gifts of food, enjoyed massive feasts. I loved the dancing in the streets, the shalach manot runs with my mother, the twenty-four-hour sugar high, the seudahs during which my father, refusing to drink more than absolutely necessary, would become flushed with wine and retreat early to bed. Torah Temimah actively encouraged us to dress up, though we were to choose strictly from biblical costumes, and to wander the neighborhood collecting tzedakah from drunken revelers. What I loved, I suppose, was Purim's energy: alien and seductive, a day on which my life, to my relief, no longer quite resembled itself.

I felt no such *ruach* this time around, anxious as I was about my future. Still, holiday preparation was in full swing. My mother was doing her best to impress Cynthia, assembling hundreds of hamantaschen, including but not limited to chocolate chip, apricot, prune, poppy and peanut butter. Kayla, meanwhile, dragged me to a local thrift shop in search of coordinated outfits.

"We'll need something literary," she said, rifling through a rack of secondhand costumes. "Any ideas?"

"Not really."

"And you're supposed to be Hartman's star?" She returned to her searching, hair whipping from side to side. "Personally, I'm torn between two."

"Which?"

"Being a suffragette," she said, "or biting the bullet and being Shelley."

"Shelley is cool," I said. "You can carry around an umbrella."

"I said Shelley, not Mary Poppins."

"For the west wind."

"Clever." She pulled out a Gothic Victorian-style dress and held it to her body. "But I meant the great Mary Shelley. The superior Shelley."

"Oh."

"This'll do," she said, examining the dress. "With a copy of *Frankenstein* in hand and some serious powder applied to the face."

"Brilliant."

"I'll let you be Percy. Look for floaties."

"Isn't that sort of weird?"

"What?"

"To come as the Shelleys?"

"It's a Purim bit, Ari, not a marriage proposal."

"I know, it's just—"

"Scared your friends will mock you?"

"I didn't say that."

A row of masks: monsters, aliens, centaurs, bloodstained zombies. I picked a small skull from a neglected shelf. "How about this?"

"Don't think that'll fit your head. Your ego's become too big." She disappeared into a fitting room with the dress. "But be my guest and try."

"No," I said, leaning against the dressing room door. "As an accessory."

"For what? A tomb raider?"

"It's Yorick."

She came out, frowning, in her dress. "You're joking."

I collected tacky medieval attire: hooded purple robes, black tights, a cheap crown. "It's great, see?"

"You have to go as Hamlet, Ari? Really? Can't you be the gravedigger instead?"

"It's literary, like you said. And I like it better than being P.B."

"Look, not to be harsh, but I really think your fixation with her is becoming slightly . . . unhealthy." She twirled in front of a mirror. The owner of the store provided an approving thumbs-up. "You're too hung up on her for your own good."

"Come on," I said, lowering my voice, throwing a suspicious glance at the owner without quite knowing why, "I'm not—"

She returned to the fitting room, changing into her clothing. "Could it be more painfully obvious who this is for?"

"It has absolutely nothing to do with her." She tossed her outfit over the dressing room door. It landed on my head. "It's just a funny costume."

"Dress however you'd like," she said testily when she emerged, rolling her eyes. The owner, ringing her up, gave me a sympathetic wink.

—

"WE ARE TO DRINK," RABBI Bloom lectured in his office the following day, "until we no longer remember the difference between Mordechai and Haman, so Rava tells us."

"That's why Rava is my hero," Oliver said reverently. "I'm very *machmir* on that."

"You're *machmir* on that all year," Noah laughed, "not just on Purim."

Even Rabbi Bloom allowed himself a momentary chuckle. "A simple dictum to drink yourselves into oblivion, an activity of which Mr. Bellow seems quite fond, is hardly aligned with Torah values. The danger of doing so, after all, is made apparent in the Gemara."

"The feast of Rabbah and Rav Zeira," I said.

Rabbi Bloom nodded. "Rabbah, Gemara Megillah tells us, drank himself into such a stupor that he accidentally murdered Rav Zeira, only to pray, successfully, for his resurrection."

"On-demand resurrection," Amir said. "What a convenience."

"When the next year came around," Rabbi Bloom continued, "Rabbah again invited Rav Zeira to his seudah. But Rav Zeira declined with the perfect response: 'Miracles do not happen every hour.'"

"Love it," Noah said.

"The point, of course, is that there's something deeper at play in a night of sanctioned drinking. Why are we encouraged to reach the point at which we do not know?"

"To set ourselves free from the everyday," Evan said. "To separate from ourselves and see things in a new light."

Amir bit at his fingernail. "Is this the Zohar speaking?"

"What sort of new light?" Rabbi Bloom asked.

"Alcohol is just another way to overthrow the burden of self-consciousness," Evan said. "To move beyond our usual restraints. If we drink properly, we can enter a reverie of sorts."

"We play characters, we drink, we step outside our bodies," Rabbi Bloom said. "We do all this to peer beyond the self. And it's cleansing, it allows for unique self-examination. But it's also much more. It's theater. It's when we tap into unfettered creativity, when we are swallowed up in something greater."

"It's when we feel divinity," Evan said.

"We do aim to feel kedusha. For when we're dressed only in our bodies, we have a harder time elevating our vision. During Purim, while confronting the national tragedy that nearly resulted in our annihilation, we break with the routine to which we've become accustomed. Such is the inextricable link between Purim and Yom Kippur. On both days, averted disasters, flirtations with death, give rise to a new relationship with divinity. On Yom Kippur, the Kohen Gadol casts lots to determine which goat will live. On Purim, Haman, may his name be erased, casts lots to determine the timing of his genocidal decree. So on both days, human life hinges on caprice. But on a greater level, both days, in aspiring toward maximal holiness, demand rituals that defamiliarize the world as we know it so that we can give ourselves to creativity and godliness."

"Jeez," Oliver grumbled in the hallway after we were dismissed, "here I was thinking that Purim was all about watching my father drink himself under the table. Silly me."

"Yeah, sort of ruins Purim for you, doesn't it?" Noah joked.

"No," Evan said. "Just the opposite."

—

WE HAD MEGILLAH READING IN SCHOOL. Amir, dressed as Danny Zuko—leather jacket, laughably tight pants, hair greased into place, sideburns elongated to the appropriate length—read for us in the assembly room. Rabbi Bloom, as Herodotus (monk's robe, fake beard, walking staff), presided over the service from the front stage. It was a rowdy reading, freshmen setting off sirens and shooting streamers at every mention of Haman, Rabbi Feldman, dressed as Waldo, chasing someone in a gorilla suit. Oliver, a sexy mailman, circulated flasks. Evan arrived as Harry Houdini, Noah and Rebecca as basketball player and cheerleader, respectively, Remi as Catwoman and Davis as President Taft stuck in the bathtub, rubber ducky and all. Sophia drew sharp breaths in a long, white sleeveless dress, embroidered in gold, with flowing silk attachments at her back and bright bracelets adorning her wrists and forearms. A golden, beaded tiara crowned her head.

"Who is she?" I asked Rebecca, attempting to contain my desperation, lowering my voice so that Kayla, to my left, wouldn't hear.

Rebecca smiled knowingly. "Athena. What'd you expect?"

After the reading, Evan, to our surprise, announced he'd be throwing a party. I'd still never been inside his house and figured his rift with his father would make any sort of hospitality unpleasant. Yet, as he explained in the parking lot, while everyone shuffled into cars and headed toward his cul-de-sac, his father was away on business, leaving him free rein over the house.

I convinced Kayla to join. She was in a sour mood, displeased I'd actually shown up as Hamlet, a move I was already regretting. Typically, Kayla declined my halfhearted invitations to join my friends, yet tonight, after some prodding, she agreed. She piled next to me in Oliver's Jeep, grimacing at the residual smell of smoke, her absurdly long dress folded over my lap.

Evan's backyard was perfectly standard for the upper echelon of my friends. At the center of a large swath of grass was a circle of stones, inside of which was a stack of timber, positioned into a ten-foot-high teepee.

"A bonfire," Evan explained as the backyard began to fill. He lit the center aflame and stoked the fire with gasoline. "Purim Same'ach to all."

Students from all grades attended, still in Purim garb, hauling packs of beer and bottles of vodka. It was a strange sight: Cinderella, Pacman, a Hasid, Mickey Mouse, James Bond all dancing around the fire, swigging from bottles, sharing joints. Oliver was playing music from outdoor speakers. Amir broke out a guitar he found inside Evan's living room. Having ensured the fire's vitality, Evan disappeared into his house.

"Want something?" I asked Kayla, taking her hand. She was surveying the backyard in disgust: binge drinking, smoking, several couples utilizing the cabana, a sophomore already sick in the garden. I was reminded of the way my father examined the layout of the Harris barbecue many months earlier. "Maybe let's get you a drink?"

"So this is what you guys do," she said, gravel-voiced. "Like, is this just another evening?"

"What does that mean?"

"You really drink this much, Ari? Because, to be honest, I'm pretty . . . horrified. This isn't *you*."

I dropped the nearly empty beer can I was holding and, twisting my foot, crushed it into the grass. "Not at all," I said, trying to sound light, jovial, kicking mud from my sneakers. "I never keep pace with these people."

Oliver approached, with Amir, Noah and Rebecca in tow. He was swaying on his feet, shirt removed, a handcuff dangling from one wrist. "You know," he slurred, pointing at Kayla, "I . . . I bet you still tell the difference."

I couldn't blame her for looking revolted: Oliver was gimlet-eyed, reeking of smoke, doused in sweat and vodka, his left nostril inflamed. "Pardon?"

He stifled a drunken belch. "Mordechai. Haman. Good versus evil. Ying and Yang. Methinks you're not drunk enough for Purim."

"I'm not even slightly drunk, thanks very much."

"Leave her be," I told Oliver, physically moving him aside. He nodded obediently, stumbling off toward another circle to recite the same line.

"Well, Kayla," Rebecca said loudly, clearing her throat and observing Oliver out of the corner of her eye, "it's nice to finally have you out with us."

"Yeah, I mean, we've been asking Drew about you incessantly. All these excuses?" Noah said, bottle in hand, trying to sound inviting. "We thought maybe he was hiding you or something."

"How funny," Kayla said, brushing away, "no one seemed to ask a year ago. Or a decade ago. Excuse me."

"Right, then," Amir said as Kayla stomped off. Rosy-faced from Svedka, he poured himself another shot. "Merry Purim, kids."

Rebecca elbowed my ribs. "You're not going after her?"

"I'll let her cool off," I said, finding myself another beer. As I stared off into the crowd, cringing at the prospect of dealing with Kayla, I noticed the patio doors to Evan's house burst open. A golden glint: dark hair, a tiara, a figure in white gliding through night. Before I could stop myself, I stole away after her.

"Sophia?"

She stopped abruptly in her tracks, her eyes—red slits, slightly puffy—tracing the ground. "Hamlet," she said, finally glancing up. "Been a while."

"Yeah, feels like it."

"Guess you're talking to me again."

"It's not like that," I said awkwardly.

She dabbed slightly at her right eye. "Really? You haven't been avoiding me at all costs?"

"Soph." I poured the rest of my beer onto the grass. "I don't really know what you expect from me."

We watched the stream of foam dissolve into dirt. I closed my eyes, visualizing her bedroom, the way she undressed. I wanted to remember what it was to kiss her. I wanted confirmation that our relationship hadn't existed only in the confines of fantasy. "That's quite an outfit," she said.

"Didn't think you noticed," I said lamely. Enormous waves of shame battered me: black, subterranean shame for my pathetically public display of affection, for standing with Sophia while Kayla wandered furiously, for losing Sophia in the first place.

"You didn't think I noticed you at the recital, either." Again, she swiped hastily at her eyes. "That feels like a lifetime ago, doesn't it?"

It did, I told her.

"You're here with her?" she asked, puncturing a stretch of silence.

"With Kayla? Yeah, I am."

She examined our surroundings. "Where is she?"

"Around. Circulating."

Creed Sublime Vanille. Downturned eyes. Bare, slender arms. My heart attempted its desperate exit through my throat. "What were you doing inside?" I asked.

"I'm leaving now."

I felt nauseous. My visual field temporarily threatened to disintegrate. "He's in there?"

"You should find Kayla," she said.

A great crashing from inside the doors: glass breaking against the floor. Over and over until, just as quickly as it started, it stopped.

Panicking, I moved toward the house. "What the hell was that?"

"Ari," she said, quiet fear in her voice, "leave it alone."

I tried the door, but it was locked. I hammered the curtained windowpanes, peered inside. No light, no sound.

A hand—gentle, flinching—on my shoulder. "Don't go in."

"Why not?" I turned to face her, but she had dissolved into the night.

A clear night, stars abound, rare for Florida. I was breathless, dizzy with anger. I reeled about, sweating from the damn fire—still burning, several freshmen tasked with adding fuel every so often—

and joined Amir in one of the cabanas, hitting a joint with Lily and Gemma. I accepted two shots from a passerby, gagged on the second, dumped the cup on the floor. *Pleurant, je voyais de l'or—et ne pus boire.*

I spotted Kayla across the yard, chatting spiritedly with a junior, another of her math students. My vision swam slightly, the landscape tilting so that it assumed a fatigued, sunken quality.

"Should probably go after her," Amir said, high-pitched. He passed the joint, his face frozen in a weed-induced, wide-eyed smirk.

I inhaled deeply. "Yeah," I said, rising, coughing, "I should."

"She's your girlfriend or what?" Gemma asked, contorting her face with distaste. And then, whispering to Lily: "Talk about a fall from grace."

Staggering slightly, I made my way across the yard, walking too close to the fire, around which people engaged in drunken simcha dancing. I loosened my robes, realized I was still carrying Yorick in my pocket. I rubbed his head and, gently, added him to the pyre.

A forceful hand on my midriff. Lips on my neck, a tongue probing my right ear. "Where've you been?" A low, seductive voice: the hair on my neck stood in place, my body falling limp. "Forgot about me?"

I turned. Remi, still masked, blond hair spilling over her black suit, held my body. "Eden?" She teetered backward, releasing my hand. "What the actual—" Her eyes narrowed in revulsion. "The fuck do you think you're doing?"

"What am *I* doing?" Goose bumps overtaking my arms, a feral stirring in my chest. "You grabbed me."

"I thought you were Evan." She rubbed her hands on her latex outfit, as if to disinfect them. *The voice is the voice of Jacob*, I thought, nausea building in my chest, *yet the hands are the hands of Esau.* "Jesus Christ. Just in the dark, from the side—you looked exactly like him."

I kept moving, my head spinning perilously, approaching Kayla at the edge of the backyard, nearly tripping over a sprinkler buried in the grass. "Kayla," I said, restraining myself from grabbing her hand, praying she hadn't seen me with Sophia or with Remi, "hi."

She nodded at her friend, who made a show of rolling her eyes in my direction before disappearing reluctantly. "About time, Ari."

"I'm really sorry."

"Where were you?"

"I got—distracted."

"You reek." She fingered her copy of *Frankenstein*. "It really is frightening. You're an entirely different person around them. I mean, you'd never in a million years act like this without them, would you?"

"I'm not," I said. "I swear. I didn't mean—"

She kissed my cheek, allowing her lips to linger over my skin. "I'm going to leave."

"I'll drive you home."

"Tell me you're joking."

"Why?"

"You're high, Ari!"

"Yeah, but hardly."

"Not to mention you don't have a car here."

"True." Running my fingers through my hair, trying to think on my feet, trying to sober. "So we'll walk."

"I've already called my mom."

Confused silence. We turned to find Evan—black tailcoat, magician's hat, shackles over his shoulder—striding toward the bonfire. He looked calm, as if nothing had happened behind those doors just minutes before, and carried a large, square frame, wrapped in a blanket. "Your attention, if you will," he called out. Bodies moved gradually toward the fire, encircling him. Evan set down the object and instructed Amir—incoherently high, too high to object—to play on with the guitar. "After Purim," Evan shouted, pacing before the fire, "we read of the Red Heifer in preparation of Pesach."

"What is this," Kayla whispered, "a sermon?"

Frenetic, drunken chords from Amir. "But on Purim, holiday of opposites, the Red Heifer, sacrificed to God as an atonement for our sins, finds its analogue in the Golden Calf, of all things, an idol, our most monumental sin. Why? Because purity and idolatry are two faces of the same coin. We must understand the relationship between what the Zohar calls leaving and returning, our urge to overcome this world and our urge to sanctify it. Now, seeing as we don't have enough gold lying around tonight, I brought the next best thing." He bent down, unwrapped the package: a small oil painting of a cubist bull, eyes crazed, legs splayed at excruciating angles, muscles rippling under its hide, a sword buried in its gray torso. "Our own bull," Evan said, hoisting the painting above his head. His eyes resembled the bull's: swollen, frenzied, pale-green in this light. "Our own way to mix kedusha and the sacrilegious, to purify ourselves through fire, to make ourselves a bit more worthy of seeing God. I hope my father doesn't mind."

"Jesus Christ," Kayla said, "is that a Picasso?"

"Behold," Evan yelled, tipping the painting into the fire, "the oneness that is hidden." The music beat on, people screaming, rushing the bonfire, offering contributions—costume accessories, beer bottles, dollar bills, Amir's guitar—our high priest at the center, watching Picasso turn to ash.

MARCH

I have a horrible fear that my heart is broken, but that heartbreak
is not like what I thought it must be.

—Shaw, *Heartbreak House*

was clearing plates after dinner one night when my father broke his
silence.

"Aryeh," he called, playing with his shirt collar. I stopped, lowering the piles of dishes I was carrying. "I have to ask you something, if
you don't mind."

I sat. My mother was in the kitchen with the faucet running.

He looked me over, chewing his nails. "Do you enjoy being here?"

My phone lit up with five texts from Kayla. I made a point of reading them before answering. "What does that mean?"

"I'm asking if you— if we— are better off in this place."

"Better off than in Brooklyn?" I placed my phone back down. "Well,
yeah, of course we are."

"You can say that so easily? Don't you think you've—changed
here?"

"Sure I've changed. But, I mean, in good ways, I think," I said, trying to contort my voice so that it sounded slightly more convincing.

"When Hashem tells Avraham *lech lecha*, what do you think He
intended for Avraham to become?"

"I guess a filicide, right?"

"What's that?"

"Nothing, sorry."

My father's face dimmed. I thought then of Jacob finding Joseph's bloodied tunic. Believing his son devoured by some beast, Jacob tears his clothing, dons sackcloth, refuses to be comforted by his other children. Rashi attributes Jacob's inconsolability to a metaphysical phenomenon: a person cannot find solace over someone still alive, for it is heavenly decreed that only the dead, not the living, are to be erased gently from the human heart. Seated across from him at our modest table, I told myself that this is what my father must have felt: an inability to accept what supposedly remained of his son, agony at being trapped in a liminal state in which I was still there with him, still his boy, and yet slipping quietly into another realm from which he could not save me. "He knew Avraham would change, of course," my father said, "because it's only natural to change when you leave your birthplace and discover new worlds. But He hoped—He expected— that any change would be elevating. An ascent in kedusha, after having overcome the obstacles of a foreign country. A going away from home *toward* yourself, not a going away *from* yourself."

I didn't respond right away, mostly because I couldn't properly muster the energy to rebut his subtle criticism, partially because I knew he wasn't wrong. "Whatever's happened here," I said, choosing my words carefully, "was probably bubbling beneath the surface the whole time."

This made him visibly distressed. "You can look me in the face and claim my son hasn't been replaced?"

"Abba—replaced by what, exactly?"

"I don't know. Someone I don't recognize."

"Maybe," I said, spinning one of the dishes before me, unsure why I felt the need to say this, "you just don't quite know your son."

"You could be right. Whatever's wrong is my own fault. It was my decision to leave. It was my decision to go with this job and take the security of it and not have emunah that something else would work out. It's just—I didn't imagine," he said, pausing ruefully, "what things could look like here."

"For me? Or for Imma?"

This brought silence.

"You're going to leave, aren't you?" I said.

"Do I have a real choice? This is no place for us."

"Imma wants to leave?"

He refocused his attention away from the table. "People take measures to fix what's broken. People make sacrifices for what's best."

"What about your job?"

He shrugged, gray-faced. He looked as if he'd aged substantially overnight, as if months of worrying over the fate of his family, longing for Brooklyn, distressing over money, shouldering the fragments of faith that had chipped away from the other inhabitants of his household had, at last, taken a toll on him. "I'll find another."

"I'm pretty sure you said there were no others."

"Then I'll be a janitor if it gets me out of Gehenem."

"Right. And me? Do I matter?"

"You matter most, Aryeh," he said. "You'll finish your schooling, but then you'll be an adult. The rest will have to be up to you."

I stood to leave. He remained at the table, staring at the walls.

"Remember," he said as I turned into the hallway. "*U'vimakom shi'ane anashim, hishtadel li'hiyot eesh.*" Strive to be human where there are none.

—

REMI THREW A PARTY SATURDAY NIGHT. She lived in a palatial Miami estate: two wings, four floors, land overlooking the intracoastal. The party was well attended—free-flowing drinks, earsplitting music—but I arrived irritated from bickering with Kayla. She'd refused to accompany me, had sworn, in fact, never to step foot at another of these events. Passive-aggressive discussions, hasty apologies, exaggerated sighs: I'd hung up on her and climbed into Noah's car. Within an hour, however, mostly everyone had paired off: Noah and Rebecca disappeared, Amir rekindled with Lily, Oliver slunk off with Gemma. So it was that I found myself alone with Evan in Remi's backyard, slumped beneath a massive palm tree, passing back and forth a bottle of Glenlivet nicked from Mr. White's study.

"Eden," Evan said, finishing a long sip, wiping his mouth with the back of his hand, "remember when we met?"

"How can I forget?" I took the bottle. "Actually, being drugged tends to have that effect."

"Apologies."

"You're not forgiven."

"Holding a grudge is beneath you," he said quietly. "Anyway, it was a mistake. I was—jealous. Defensive."

"What the hell were *you* jealous of?"

"Think about it from my perspective." He stole back the Glenlivet, twirled it in his hands. "I'd returned from abroad to discover everyone talking about how some stranger had been quoting Shakespeare to her at pool parties. And then, believe it or not, that very same stranger was sitting with her at the piano."

My neck burning, I dug a hole in the dirt with a fallen tree branch. Never before had we discussed Sophia so openly. At last, Evan had violated the unwritten rules of the game we'd been playing these long months. "Well," I said, trying to match his candor, "turns out you had nothing to worry about."

"I wouldn't say that." Drunken shouts poolside. Silhouettes launched from diving boards. Evan grasped at his neck, looking uncharacteristically ill at ease. "Anyway, to some extent it was my own fault."

"What was?"

"I should've figured you two would find each other."

"What're you talking about?"

"Nothing, I'm drunk. Forget it."

"Seriously. What'd you mean by that?"

"Just that if you and I had certain similarities, and if you were going to come to Zion Hills—"

I snapped the branch in half. "Enough with that, we're not fucking similar. And unless you're somehow responsible for my dad losing his job in Brooklyn, you have nothing to do with my family being here."

He stared off into the bay. "Can't argue with that."

"So what'd you mean?"

"Drop it, Eden."

I drank again. "You don't say anything without a purpose and we both know it."

Calmly, he rolled up the sleeves of his button-down shirt. "How is she?"

I snorted. "You're not seriously asking me that, are you? I mean, shouldn't *I* be asking you about her?"

"I was referring to your new situation. With the one who tutors you."

"Pretty sure you know her name. You've been in school together for . . . only twelve years?"

"Sorry," Evan said. "Kayla."

"Things are fine."

"Why didn't you bring her tonight?"

"She didn't want to come," I said. "Not after Purim."

His turn for the whiskey. "That's fine," he said, matter-of-factly. "You don't love her."

"Pardon?"

"You didn't stay with her tonight."

"Know what, Ev? Mind your own fucking business for once." The whiskey was taking its toll, but I didn't mind. "You don't know anything about us."

"I don't claim to, Eden. I just know you."

I forced a heavy laugh and, with effort, got to my feet, leaning against the tree for support. "You don't know shit."

"I know things about you because I recognize them in myself." He requested my hand. I pulled him up. "Bloom sees it. And I think *she* does, too, even if she won't admit it."

"Good for them," I said, despising myself for feeling waves of pride at this comparison, "but they're very wrong."

"We think similarly," Evan said, indifferent to my reaction. "We feel discontent similarly. We idolize our mothers, we have issues with our fathers, we're incapable of normal expressions of emotions, of loving easily, we've both been crushed by the same person. Why do you think Bloom's been trying so damn hard to force us together? Pairing us in our little sessions, giving us the same readings, keeping you out of trouble just to piss me off—don't you see that we're his, like, little fucking experiments? That he's been waiting to get his hands on *two* of us? That he likes to push us against each other?"

Strained silence. We stood staring at each other under the corona of moonlight.

"Evan," I decided to say, "are you okay?"

He rolled his eyes. "Think I'm unhinged?" He snatched the bottle from my hands. "Noah does. Amir has for a while now. Shit, even Oliver probably does, not that it'd bother him."

"Can you blame us? You've been acting—"

"Unstable?" he said.

"I was going to say deranged."

Evan took another substantial pull. "Definitely took long enough, but I appreciate you, Eden."

The shouts near the house died down. People returned inside. We were alone in the backyard. "Not what I asked, but glad to hear."

"Know why I like you?"

"I'm not sure I want to."

"That innocence everyone thought you had when you first arrived?" He smiled to himself. "That wasn't innocence or shyness. That was, I don't know, that was fucking *wildness* lying dormant."

"Wildness? What are you—"

"Wildness as in . . . alienation, let's call it. Having something deep inside you that's incompatible with the world you're in. Being in agony because you're dissatisfied with the basic rewards of order and pleasantries and the fucking—the *convenience* of unquestioned conformity to gray and lifeless things. Honestly, you're"—he paused, smiled again—"I guess what I'd say is that you're just as spiritually ruined as I am."

"Well," I said, after a few beats, "you really do know how to flatter a guy."

Evan put the bottle to the floor and pointed to a motorboat docked by the water's edge. "Forget about it. Let's just—I don't know, let's take the boat out. I've driven it with Remi."

"Sure you should be driving?" I asked uneasily, eager as I was for an escape from this conversation. The boat was sleek, fifteen feet long, big enough for three or four passengers. The name NESTOR was engraved on its hull.

Evan walked out to the water and undocked the boat. He climbed into the driver's seat, revving the motor. "I've driven in worse states."

Hesitating briefly, feeling stabs of drunken wretchedness, I threw myself into the passenger seat. In my haze I knew Evan was right: I was miserable, probably always had been, and I alone was to blame, not my parents, not Brooklyn, not my rabbis, not Sophia, not Kayla, not Zion Hills, not Evan. An immense, pulverizing cloud of loneliness descended upon me so suddenly that I began shaking. I told him to drive.

We shot into vaporous darkness. It was well past midnight. I put my feet up, folded my arms across my chest, feeling as if we were gliding through space. Wind ripped through us. I could feel my hair blown out, standing atop my head, the collar of my shirt against my neck. It was difficult to see ahead, but Evan maneuvered confidently. I finished the last drops of the bottle and deposited it in the water.

"I'll miss this place," Evan said thinly. He inhaled again, his face—angular, haunted—illuminated briefly by the flare of the joint.

"Florida, you mean?"

"I mean everything."

"I thought you couldn't wait to get out?"

"That's how you felt, right? In Brooklyn?"

"I did. It was a mistake."

"You aren't happier here?"

Again I took the joint. "I thought I'd be given a new life here," I said, coughing. "But I know now Brooklyn was never the problem."

Smoke spiraled from Evan's lips. "New life is a terrible thing to waste."

"Listen," I said, leaning forward. "I want to ask you something."

"Now's a good time."

"I want to know what happened between you and Sophia," I said. Something in my chest hurt. Devastating exhaustion came over me as soon as I said her name, an exhaustion I felt not in my body but somewhere beneath my skin. "I—I want to understand."

He looked away, one hand on the wheel. He went on sucking the joint until there was nearly nothing left, then flicked the remains into the bay. "Something bad."

I was on my feet. "Something bad? That's all you have?"

"Some things are better off unshared," he said calmly.

"I deserve to know." All we could hear: my voice, the engine. All else, for miles in each direction, perfect silence.

"If there's a single thing in this world I believe in," Evan said softly, "it's that we have no fucking idea what we deserve."

"God, not that bullshit." The moon, infinite and weak, folded in the distance. I returned to my seat beside him. "She wouldn't tell me, you know. Purim night, about whatever was happening in your house."

Evan increased the boat's speed. "I was . . . helping her prepare."

"For what?"

"Her Juilliard interview is in a few days."

I felt dizzy, forced my eyes shut. Instead of blackness, I saw strange green phosphenes. "I don't believe you."

"Don't envy me, Eden," Evan said. "You should never envy me."

"I still love her," I blurted, words tumbling out against my will, my voice hollow and far off.

His teeth were of a pure white in the dark. He took out his lighter, switching the flame on and off. "So do I."

I looked up to make out the jetties looming ahead: large, black, cavernous. "Let's just go back."

"We can't."

"I'm serious," I said. Evan was pushing sixty. Wind cut my hair. My limbs were freezing. The stinging in my face was turning to numbness. "Turn around."

"Can I ask you a question now, Eden?" Again he pushed the throttle, lurching us forward. My head snapped back and then forward against the dashboard.

"Ow, fuck!"

"What are your thoughts on Nadav and Avihu?"

"What?" I could feel my forehead swelling, a dim buzzing in my ears. I pressed my fingers to my head, checking for blood. "Jesus, Evan. Slow down."

"Humor me."

"What is this—another experiment?"

"Since the Sidgwick class, I've been wondering about them," he said, raising his voice above the surging wind. "About what it means to communicate with God on your own. About what it means to be worthy."

"Enough, Ev. For real. Let's just—let's go back."

"Just hear me out," Evan said. "You're supposed to be the other thinker."

"Know what? You were absolutely right before. I do think there's something very wrong with you."

We were skidding. The jetties weren't far off. "Listen to me," Evan said, "or I won't stop the boat."

"I'm fucking listening!"

"So Nadav and Avihu were allowed up Sinai, allowed to see God with clarity, and then?" He pushed forward, harder this time, nearly knocking us off our seats. "Then they were cut off."

Fifty yards away now. "Evan," I said, calming down, reminding myself he was trying to frighten me, "why are we talking about this?"

"Because I want to know your opinion, Eden. Why do you think they were cut off?"

"Why? Because they weren't supposed to offer the sacrifice." I clutched a hand to my forehead, which continued to bulge beneath my fingertips. I thought back to learning about Parshat Sh'mini in elementary school, about how Aharon, after being informed that his two priestly sons had been slain by heavenly fire for bringing an unsanctioned Temple offering, responds with silence. "It was an aish zara. A strange fire."

Evan threw back his head. "A strange fire," he said, laughing, "a strange fire."

Thirty yards. "I'll jump," I told him. "I swear."

"In Kabbalah, there's a belief in two warring forces in the soul," Evan said, eyes fixed on the jetties. "There's *ratzo*, our desire to free ourselves from earthly concerns so that we can cleave to God, and then there's *shov*, our desire to return to human life. Our whole lives, we go back and forth between these forces. So in my opinion? Nadav and Avihu weren't *cut off*. Just the opposite. They nearly won. They allowed their *ratzo* to overpower them, they overstepped physical boundaries, they stretched toward transcendence, they made a sacrifice. But guess what, Eden? In the end, they just weren't worthy. In the end, not everyone is strong enough or destined to see God."

I was inches from his face. "This isn't funny anymore. This is sick."

"Don't you want to see if we're like they are?" Evan asked. "Don't you want to see which of us is worthy?"

Ten yards.

"If you're the worthy one you survive," he said. "If you're—"

I lunged for the steering wheel. An endless-seeming moment: night pitching sideways, the curious sensation of being lifted from my feet. I didn't know whether I was vertical or upside down, the atoms in my brain felt as if they were being reshuffled, all I could make out were bands of electric lights. When the brightness dissolved I found myself beneath the water. Kicking, I broke through the surface, gasping for breath. Ringing in my ears, the chemical stench of gasoline and burning rubber, salt in my nostrils. I paddled several yards ahead, washing up headfirst in sand. Hot liquid poured from my ears to my back.

"Evan." A pathetic whisper. My throat cracked. "Evan."

Around me things were black, still, save for a small, crackling flame. Fighting to stay awake, the world spiraling on around me, I forced myself to think. I could see the boat, capsized, sinking into the water. I'd been ejected when we overturned, I told myself, launched into the water near the shore. And Evan? A body, only a few feet from where I landed, floating facedown in the water. Dark edges; my vision flickering. I could do nothing, and for a hideous stretch of time I intended to do nothing, my chin buried in sand, his body drifting peacefully. *Man: I halt/ At the bottom of the pit ... And shout a secret to the stone. Echo: Lie down and die.* If I succumbed, if I tumbled headfirst, longingly, into unconsciousness, leaving Evan Stark behind— who would know? Justice, the voice told me, justice if he drowns. *Man: That were to shirk the great work and then stand in judgment. Echo: Sink at last into the night.* Heavy shadows falling, my eyelids falling. I was close now, sliding gently into opulent twilight. And then I rose, stumbling back through the shallow, dragging him ashore, sinking to my knees, striking his chest, knuckles raw. *Man: What do we know but that we face one another in this place?* Breathe, breathe, breathe, until he arrived, a suited man on a shiva chair, the man with my unremarkable eyes. Hands together in prayer, he recited these lines, over and over:

> Is this the region, this the soil, the clime,
> Said then the lost Arch-Angel, this the seat
> That we must change for Heav'n, this mournful gloom
> For that celestial light?

—

WHEN I WOKE I FOUND myself in a hospital bed, an IV plunged into my arm. I blinked at the bright lights, realizing where I was. Sudden panic washed over me when I remembered. I tried throwing myself from bed.

"Aryeh!" My mother to my left, holding me down, soothing my forehead. "You can hear me?"

"Yes." My voice low, hoarse.

"My poor, poor baby. Don't stir." She grabbed my left hand, a look of tremendous relief coming over her. "How're you feeling?"

Strange discoveries: a machine blinked beside me. My right arm was in a large cast. My left arm was dotted in pinpricks. "Am I—all right?"

She nodded, still fighting tears, holding my head in her hands.

"I'm paralyzed, aren't I?"

"Paralyzed? God forbid. You're okay, Aryeh. You're going to be perfectly okay."

Briefly I wept—relief, exhaustion, misery. Then I stopped. "Imma."

"Yes, Aryeh?"

"Where is he?"

"Abba just stepped out for more coffee. He'll be right back. He's going to be so relieved, Baruch Hashem. I mean, we knew—"

"Evan."

She looked at my vitals. "He's in the ICU."

"He's okay?"

My mother shrugged, gently releasing my face. "As far as I know."

"I'm sorry." My voice cracked. "Imma."

Now she cried. She did so gently, hardly making a sound, into her hands so I couldn't see her face. I knew I ought to comfort her, but I didn't, the prospect of moving, of finding words, too exhausting. "Your father nearly didn't come." With some effort, I passed her a tissue. She dotted her eyes. "He's scared to see you. Scared to talk to you."

"That's okay," I said. "I understand."

"I think he's right, Ari," she said, nodding vigorously, blowing her nose. "Maybe he was all along."

"About what?"

"Leaving home. Coming here. What's best for you."

I closed my eyes, embraced the pain radiating from my arm to my shoulders, my shoulders to my neck, my neck to my skull. How could I not see that my father was correct? And what right did I ever have to consider myself inherently miserable? And how many parents or spouses or children or friends or coworkers or grandparents or rabbis or ministers or neighbors or acquaintances had occupied the seat on my which mother sat? How many sleepless hours had passed through these four walls? How many prayers had been unanswered? How many people, faced with illness, oblivion, had formulated lackluster end-of-life theories from this fucking bed? I opened my eyes again, I said nothing.

"What's happened to us?" she asked. I looked out my window, the curtains thrown open: early morning, hot and dry, a view of a towering, sleek-windowed corporate office across the street. "Are you unhappy?"

"Unhappy?" I tried stretching my legs. "Yeah," I said, my voice breaking suddenly, "yeah, I think I am."

Tears again, the feeling that some natural barrier between mother and child was being peeled away. "But you were always such a happy person."

I took her hand in mine. "No, Imma." I smiled sadly, I rubbed her arm. "Maybe I never was."

—

SOMEONE WALKING A DOG ALONG the water saw our wreck and called 911. My parents received the police call at one-thirty in the morning. The doctors found substances in our systems. Evan, as driver, was expected to face charges.

The hospital kept me for four and a half days. I was beat up fairly well, covered in bruises, in need of three dozen stitches on my forehead, chest and back. My right arm was fractured but wouldn't require surgery, assuming it healed properly. Dr. Friedman, a kind-eyed man with a bushy, gray mustache, stressed how lucky I was to even be alive, let alone walk away largely unscathed. A minor miracle, he called it. Plus, he stressed, I was in considerably better shape than Evan, who had an orbital fracture, his right leg snapped in three places and would have to stay a week and a half longer, at the very least. "But none of that would've mattered, of course," Dr. Friedman told me, "if he hadn't made it out of the water."

"Yes," I croaked, sensing the Vicodin kicking in, "I suppose."

"They say you dragged him out?"

Light as air, floating sluggishly toward the ceiling, lungs filled with helium. I tried nodding.

"Well," he said, patting my shoulder, leaving me to my oncoming narcotic stupor, "that young man owes you his life."

They told me I couldn't see him until I was discharged. I had little interest in doing so anyway. I couldn't imagine what I'd say to him. I had questions to work out, questions I pondered during welcome stretches of clarity between painkillers. He had nearly killed me; that was indisputable. His recklessness was deliberate, of that I was certain. To the police, there was little mystery here—two wild teenagers, drunk and high, making a grave mistake—but I was less assured. I couldn't rule out an accident; it was quite possible that his only intention was to scare me by skirting the jetties. And even if he hadn't intended to swerve, even if he'd been set on plowing into the rocks and breaking us into human fragments, perhaps it was the result not of malevolence but of combining substances with months of loss, anger, pain? The final option: he had, with a clear mind, intended to kill us, or at least to kill me, using me as some sacrifice while he jumped at the last moment. Lost amid those fluorescent ceiling lights, I struggled through these options, replaying the moments of the crash.

Noah, Rebecca and Amir visited daily. Noah brought cheer, Rebecca sweets—usually baked by Cynthia—and Amir updates on what I'd missed in class. Kayla came most days, too, hovering guiltily over me, making small talk with my mother, watching a movie with me or sitting silently while I dozed. I saw Oliver only once, though he claimed he'd tried coming when I'd been asleep. He was surprisingly quiet at my bedside, and presented me with a wrapped bottle of Glenfiddich. "Pretty nice beverage, if I may say so myself," he said. "Tried ordering a stripper, swear to God, but the insurance fiasco for a hospital visit? Real letdown."

Not many others came. Remi hadn't shown, I was told through Rebecca, on her family's lawyer's behest. Eddie and Cynthia sent fruit platters, Mrs. Hartman a collection of Blake's poetry, Davis an inscribed copy of Abba Eban's *My People: The Story of the Jews*. Donny popped in once, though I pretended to be asleep when he arrived, and left a basketball, signed by the team. At one point—hospital time an intolerable creep, one day blurring into the next—Rabbi Bloom knocked softly at my door and introduced himself to my parents, my mother regarding him with quiet reverence, my father with disdain. After a bit of small talk, during which he won over my father by adeptly fielding Shulchan Aruch questions, my parents left for coffee, leaving me alone with Rabbi Bloom.

He looked more worn than ever. His glasses, normally cleaned compulsively, displayed a collection of fingerprints. In his eyes I saw regret tinged with fear. "How're you feeling, Mr. Eden?"

"My arm's killing," I said. "But otherwise a bit better."

He picked up the basketball from my nightstand. "This is touching. Rocky must be beside himself losing two players so close to districts."

I shook my head good-humoredly. "About Evan, sure. But I'd be surprised if Rocky even realizes I'm absent."

He returned the basketball to its stand. "I'm told Mr. Stark's a bit worse off."

"Haven't seen him."

"No?"

"Not allowed." I frowned. "Have you?"

"I'm stopping in his room next."

"Bikur Cholim rounds."

"I'm also told you saved his life."

"That's getting out, then?"

"It's nothing to scoff over. *Whoever saves a life saves the entire world.*" I didn't answer this, and in the meantime he took the seat beside my bed. "Your poor parents," he said, crossing his legs. "They must have been worried sick."

"They've been fairly distraught."

"You realize how lucky you are, Ari?"

"The doctor reminds me every time he examines me."

"You shouldn't forget it. *Zichroo niflosav asher ahsah, mosav u'mishpitai feev.*" Remember His wonders, which He performed, His miracles and the judgments of His mouth.

"I know. I won't."

He attempted a cheerful smile, though ended up with a contortion that more closely resembled a mournful grimace. "Can I ask, Mr. Eden," he said, dropping his voice, glancing behind us to make certain no one was coming, "exactly what happened?"

The picture of the mind revives again: shrill laughter, jetties looming, an anonymous body suspended in the dark. I didn't answer.

"You can trust me."

"I can't decide," I said, my gaze resting past him, on the cream-colored wall.

"Whether you trust me?"

"Whether I understand what Evan was doing."

"What was he saying before the crash?"

"Deep things, crazy things. You know how he gets. Stuff about sacrifices. Nadav and Avihu. The ways he and I are alike." And then, after a careful pause: "Theories about you."

I felt another round of exhaustion coming on, struggled to resist. When he realized my eyelids were fluttering, he snapped to attention from his internal fog, straightened his jacket and stood. "I'll let you rest," he said. "We need to get you out of here in short order."

"I'd offer my hand," I said sleepily, erupting into a giggle, raising my cast, the head rush moments away, "but it's out of commission."

"Feel good, Mr. Eden." A doleful smile. He paused at the door. "I'll go save him."

A buzzing in my ears. "What's that?"

"—I'll go see him."

"Oh," I said, either to him or to myself, and then my vision descended into a haze of white.

—

SOPHIA CAME THE DAY BEFORE I was discharged. I'd already given up by then, having spent my first several days with my heart quivering at the sound of every visitor, rousing myself into consciousness with the hope that, if I'd only crack open an eye, Sophia would materialize in a burst of phantasmagorical light. When she finally did come, Kayla was reading beside my bed while I watched TV. My mother had left to eat; I'd told Kayla she could leave, too, but she'd refused.

Sophia knocked shyly, waited for an invitation inside. ("Not wildly unlike a vampire," Kayla would later put it.) When I saw her I smiled, unable to help myself. Her lips twisted, her hair in a tight bun, a soft, embarrassed look on her face. Kayla glanced up, frowned.

"Am I interrupting?" Sophia asked, eyeing Kayla.

I looked to Kayla. She shrugged indifferently.

"No," I said. "Don't worry."

"Know what," Kayla announced too loudly, leaping to her feet, "I think I'll step out for coffee."

"No," I said sheepishly, "no need."

"Suddenly I'm desperately craving caffeine."

"Well, it's good to see you," Sophia said politely.

"You as well," Kayla said, squeezing past her in the doorframe.

Sophia waited until Kayla's footsteps retreated down the hall. She remained at the door, chewing her lip the way she did when she was strategizing. "So, Hamlet."

"Madam President."

"I've been sent by Dr. Flowers to retrieve her star student."

"Tell her I miss her dreadfully."

She moved into the room, pausing before my bed. "You gave me a real scare, Ari, you know that? How are you feeling?"

"Been better. I'm sorry if that was—awkward."

"Only slightly." She took Kayla's seat. "You're something of a hero now, I hear."

"I sure don't feel it," I said, gritting my teeth at the throbbing in my arm.

"Everyone's talking about it. The myth of Aryeh Eden, pulling ashore his drowning shipmate. The very stuff of legends."

"I was wondering if you'd come." I wasn't sure what made me say this. The painkillers, probably.

"I should've been here sooner. It's just, I was out of town, and hospitals—they frighten me."

"Why's that?"

"They just do."

"So much for premed." I squinted, trying my best to ignore the ache spreading through my right arm. "Wait. Your audition."

She maintained her look of expressionlessness. "How'd you know?"

"Evan," I said, watching the color drain from her face.

"I see."

"So how'd it go?"

"Well, I think. I mean, I hope. I literally got back last night. I would've told you it's just—we weren't exactly speaking."

I blushed slightly. "What'd you play?"

"Something new."

"I haven't heard it, have I?"

"No. A recent breakthrough."

"Must've been stunning," I said. "I have no doubt."

"Thanks, dear Hamlet."

"When will you hear back?"

She shrugged. "Could be anytime."

"And if you get in?"

"Then I guess we celebrate."

"What do you do about Penn, I mean? Don't you have to go because of Early Decision?"

"Let's not get ahead of ourselves. We'll deal with that if it actually happens."

"It'll happen."

"As always, I appreciate your unwarranted confidence in me." She paused, allowed herself a long breath. "Listen, Ari. I'm sorry. For everything. I'm sick over it. I keep thinking about you being out there with him and—" I loved her pale skin and her sharp little nose and the way she blinked in confusion. I loved the padded feel of her fingertips, the sound of her breathing, the feel of tucking her hair behind her ears. I loved when she failed to suppress bursts of laughter from ripping out of her throat, when she leaned her face gently into mine, when she tilted her head to the side in photographs, when she bit the bottom of my lips while kissing me. "You must despise me."

"What're you talking about?"

"I don't want to imagine what he said to you."

"Yes, well."

"Promise you're not angry with me."

"I promise," I said. "Not anymore."

"I wish I'd met you earlier."

She waited for me to say something but I didn't. She stood, said she'd leave me to rest, then lowered herself over my chest to deliver a cool, hesitant kiss. I thanked her for coming and turned my eyes to the floor.

—

MY PARENTS URGED ME NOT to see him. He was a drunk, they said, a degenerate, a real-life *Ben Sorer U'Morer*. I wasn't sure why I didn't listen. I was curious, I suppose, to see what shape he was in, and anyway knew I'd have to face him eventually. More than anything, I needed to actually see him before I could determine what he'd done.

I knocked at his door. The lights were off. After a few moments a weary face peered out. Bloodshot eyes examined me before the door opened fully, revealing a handsome, exhausted man in a gray Valentino suit.

"Oh." Julian's face twitched in disappointment. "Thought you might be someone else."

"Mr. Stark," I said, frowning. "My name's Aryeh Eden."

He took my left hand, closed the door behind me. "You look better than when I last saw you."

"You've seen me?"

"Briefly, when you first got here. Had to assess the damage. Your parents made me leave. Can't blame them, I guess."

We stood at the foot of Evan's bed. Evan was not a pretty sight. Wires and tubes snaked around him. His leg was in an enormous cast, suspended above him. A long cut stretched along the left side of his face, and he had burn marks on his neck, his right bicep, his chest.

"That'll scar," Julian said, gesturing at his son's cheek. I thought I made out vodka on his breath.

"How is he?"

"In a good deal of pain. He couldn't take it anymore so they, you know, morphined him."

"When do they think he's getting out?"

"Another week, earliest. I wish it were sooner. Well, of course I do. I just mean I need to get the fuck out of here."

I must have given him a funny stare. He rubbed his eyes, lowered his voice. "Not because I'm a prick, though I'm sure my son would be the first to disagree. My wife, is what I meant," he said. "My wife died here."

"I'm sorry."

"Yeah," he said, his voice ringing oddly, "certainly was an ordeal." We stood in silence. "Coffee?" He motioned toward a pot near the sink. "Tastes like aluminum, but it works."

"No, thanks."

He eyed my cast. "He did a number on you, didn't he?"

I looked at Evan, lying in bed. "He did worse to himself."

"He wasn't always this way."

"What way?"

"I used to—" He paused, rubbed his eyes. "I guess I used to think he was an unusually *happy* kid. Bit of a smartass, but full of life, loved learning. There was none of this—this fucking coldness. Not until his mother passed." His eyes were fixed on Evan's chest rising and falling. "Something in him died with her."

—

THINGS AT HOME MORE OR less reverted to the way they were before the accident. At first my father walked on eggshells, his rage muted to quiet sympathy. We ate together. He shared interesting tidbits acquired through his chavrusah. I told them about the work I was catching up on, the hurried paper I wrote for Mrs. Hartman ("The Repressed Romanticism of Matthew Arnold"), the comically abbreviated version of my paternal family history presented to Mr. Harold. (I omitted, tactically, that I was thoroughly defeated in biology, now that I missed a week of classes.) Neither of my parents broached the subject of what would happen next year, saying only that I was free to choose whatever I wanted: college, a yeshiva program in Israel, a formal Beis Medresh in Brooklyn. Only a few nights later, however, after I told them I was stepping out—I was meeting Oliver, Noah and Amir to smoke for the first time since the accident—my father stewed angrily, muttering about how I ought to look no further than my arm if I needed reminders to maintain distance from my friends. Still, I went.

"You haven't spoken to Evan yet?" Oliver asked. We were too high to drive and so sat instead at the edge of the lake, pants rolled to our knees, legs in the water, staring dizzily at the nighttime sky.

"Nope."

"Maybe you should," Noah suggested, after some hesitation.

I dipped my non-casted hand into the water, made waves. I thought about how, somewhere below, God's secret name inhabited the depths. "I have nothing to say to him."

"Come on, Drew," Noah said. "Scream at him. Tell him he's a maniac. Clear the air. Then we can all go back to normal."

Amir leaned forward, eyes grave. "You don't think he did it, you know, on purpose, do you?"

Silence.

"Jesus, Amir," Oliver said, after it'd become clear no one else was speaking. "Why would you put that in his head?"

Amir shrugged. "It *is* Evan."

"Dude. Crashing a boat?" Noah asked. "You think that's like one of his weird experiments?" We each grew quiet at this thought. "I mean, can't be, right? It's—he could've *died*."

"I'm not pretending to understand him," Amir said. "I'm just putting it out there. Would it really surprise you?"

"Yeah, actually," Noah said, trying his best to muster an air of decisiveness. "Of course it would."

"Yeah, shut up, Amir," Oliver said. "This is crazy talk."

"Right," Amir said, frowning, "because setting school grounds on fire or conjuring the dead or throwing a Picasso into a bonfire—none of that is crazy, is it? It's all perfectly normal behavior, boys being boys?"

"Okay. It was kind of fucked," Noah admitted. "But a different sort of crazy. There's harmless crazy and then there's—I don't know, murderous crazy."

"Like when he drugged me?" I said suddenly.

"Exactly," Oliver said. "Harmless crazy."

"He can be—wild," Noah said delicately. "Distasteful, for sure—"

Amir kicked his bare feet in the water. "Vile."

"Fine. Vile," Noah said. "But this is Ev. We've known him our whole lives. He was always a pretty happy kid, right? We know he wasn't this way at all, not until Caroline—not until that happened. We know what he's been through, we know the good, the not so good, and when you add all that up—the person you'd always rely on, the kid who threatened the fifth grader who used to pick on Oliver—I just don't think we can call him, well, a murderer."

Amir laid his head in the grass. "At what point do we acknowledge what's in front of us?"

"Which is?" Noah asked.

"That he's kind of nuts," Amir said. "That he really does have some sort of disturbing system or plan."

Oliver turned my way. "Let Eden decide. He was there."

I didn't answer.

—

THE CLOSE OF MARCH BROUGHT REJECTIONS. Northwestern said no. Cornell and Penn followed suit, as did Haverford and Bowdoin. (Bowdoin? I didn't even remember applying there.) I deleted the emails when they came. I didn't tell my mother.

"So. What's your plan?" Kayla would press, after an attempt to comfort me. "What're your safety schools?"

"Don't have any."

"Sensible," she said, hands in her lap, spinning one of her funky pencils through her fingers. "So then what? You're just—waiting it out?"

I shrugged, raising my hands to emphasize defeat. A searing pain shot through my casted right arm, suspended limply in a sling. "Guess so."

"But what if—"

"I know, Kayla," I snapped. "I'll deal with that when it happens."

She folded her arms. "I don't want to bother you, Ari, and I know you detest advice, but maybe you should see Ballinger. You could discuss taking a gap year and reapplying?"

"Yeah, maybe," I cut in, knowing I'd do no such thing.

—

EVAN WAS RELEASED ON A FRIDAY, some two weeks after I was discharged. It rained that day. Noah told me he was going with Amir and Oliver to visit on Saturday, but said he'd understand if I didn't feel up to joining. "These things take time, I'm sure," he said, struggling for the words. "No pressure."

I didn't go. I ate with my parents, slept a good portion of the day. When I got bored I read the *Miami Herald* by my pool. It was a long Shabbat and I was restless, but I decided that if Evan wanted to talk, he ought to come to me.

—

HE DID ON SUNDAY NIGHT. I was in bed, nearly asleep, when there was a cautious knock at my door.

"You have a—guest," my mother said tonelessly, poking her head inside.

"Who?"

"Believe it or not," she said, dropping her voice, "Evan Stark."

I straightened.

"I'm telling him to leave," she said hurriedly. "Honestly, I was so taken aback to find him that I slammed the door without actually saying anything. He's still standing there, but I absolutely do not want that boy in this house."

"Nah, it's all right." I stood. "Let him in."

He looked like hell. His right leg was in an enormous boot and he walked with a bad limp, leaning heavily on a cane. His hair was wild and he hadn't shaved in weeks, making that dark look in his eyes more pronounced. A red scar ran down his left cheek, just as his father had predicted. "Well," he finally said from the doorway to my room, after we'd stared at each other for a good while, "aren't you going to offer me a seat? I'm crippled now."

I led him to my desk chair before returning to the safety of the edge of my bed.

"You didn't come yesterday," he said, resting his cane across his legs.

"I was busy."

He looked over the books stacked on my floor. "I seem to be intruding. Or at least your mother gave me that impression." Chin up, he surveyed the contents of my room: my open closet, with my few shirts strewn around; my whiskey from Oliver; my unmade bed; the sea of loose-leaf papers and school notes engulfing my desk. "How's the claw treating you?"

"It's pretty mangled," I said, eyes on the floor.

"Want me to sign it?"

"Not particularly. Is that cane necessary?"

"The physical therapist seems to think so. I don't know, makes me look like I crawled out of a James Bond movie, don't you think?"

"No. What's with your leg?"

"I'm walking," he said. "At first they were a little worried about that. But here I am, up and moving."

A trembling, buried rage awoke somewhere in my chest. I tried blinking it off. "We're both just inordinately lucky, aren't we?"

"So they insist." He massaged his leg. "Well," he said, leaning toward me. "You're obviously hostile."

Fuck you, I wanted to say. *I don't trust you*, I wanted to say. "For good reason, don't you think?"

"Maybe," Evan said, "but how come you're not actually hostile enough to, you know, fight me or throw me out?"

"I swear," I mumbled, quickly returning my gaze to the floor, "do *not* start."

He raised his hands above his head. "You're pissed, Eden, I know, I get that. But you're too smart to really believe it was anything other than a mistake. A colossal one, no doubt, but I was only screwing around. Clearly I didn't think you'd grab the wheel—"

"Are you out of your fucking mind?" I yelled suddenly, unable to stop myself. Immediately, I glanced worriedly at my door, half-expecting my mother to rush in, brandishing a kitchen knife. "You came here to blame *me*?"

He seemed slightly taken aback that I'd raised my voice, though quickly tried recovering his usual expression of calm indifference. The effect, however, was unconvincing. Maybe it was the scar, maybe it was the sleeplessness in his eyes, but he looked, in that moment, genuinely disquieted. "Of course not," he said hesitantly. "I appreciate you even let me inside. I'm just saying it was, you know, a pretty hazy night, we got into some deep stuff, we were smoking, we polished off that bottle—"

I clenched my fists. "I don't want to hear it."

"Fine." He gritted his teeth, nodded to himself, as if consciously moving to another strategy. Paranoid, I allowed myself to wonder whether any of this was real or if it was all just performative. "Look," he said. "I came to say sorry."

"This is you apologizing?"

He played with the cane, passing it back and forth in his hands. "Yeah, as a matter of fact."

"You're sorry for what, exactly?"

"Jesus, Eden," he said, frowning, "you're not the most gracious recipient of an apology."

"We were about to fucking crash. Are you too demented nowadays to realize that?"

He shook his head patiently, as if mollifying a child. "I knew what I was doing, Eden. At least I thought I did. I was going to veer. I mean, I've done it before."

"Bullshit." And then, less sure of myself suddenly: "There was no time to veer."

"Yeah, well, maybe not. As I'm admitting, my judgment wasn't exactly unimpaired."

"You nearly killed us."

"Now that's quite the claim."

"I'm serious."

He smiled darkly, unable to help himself, and in that smile I glimpsed the Evan I knew. "I just see a few bruises."

"I keep trying to figure it out," I said, after a long beat. "What you were trying to do."

All emotion left his face again. "You know what Bloom likes to tell me sometimes? A little too often, actually?"

"What?"

"That you're the one in the group with great moral instincts. And I think he's right." Evan stretched his leg, tried not to grimace. "So just listen to what your gut is telling you."

I paused. "I don't want to say aloud what my gut is telling me."

"Cut it out, Eden." He shook his head. "If you really believed that, if you *really* thought that's what happened, then we both know I wouldn't be allowed to be sitting here with you."

His head bobbing in the bay, water spurting violently from his mouth as I struck his stomach. "I almost *did* leave you," I said, eyes on my sneakers, shocked I was actually verbalizing this. "I almost didn't pull you out."

"Yes, but you *did* pull me out, Eden. In your heart of hearts, when you had to decide? You let me live. That was your answer." He chewed his lower lip, the way Sophia did. "And now I really need a favor."

I allowed myself a forced, spiteful laugh. "You're kidding. What do you possibly want?"

"I'm facing some legal headaches."

"DUI?"

He stretched again, eyes temporarily unfocused in pain. "I'm told it may become slightly messier than that."

"How messy?"

"They can make my life unpleasant," he said. "Rehab. Prison. Both. I have a court date scheduled for the fifth."

"Better get a good lawyer."

He exhaled, rubbed his kneecap. "I—well, believe it or not, I really need your help. I need you to testify."

"Testify? It's a DUI."

"Having you there, I'm told, will make things considerably easier."

"As what? A witness?"

"As the only other person present, Eden. As the person who saw what happened, who had just as much to drink and smoke, who grabbed the wheel—"

"You want me to take the hit for you? What if I tell them I was, I don't know, forced to save us as you tried smashing us into a jetty? What if I tell them you took me out against my will?"

Evan sat there fidgeting, attempting to hold my gaze. "Or you could tell them the truth. You could tell them this was a terrible accident, an anomalous mistake. That I wasn't visibly drunk. That I've expressed to you how sorry I am, that I want to make amends with your parents and Remi's dad and anyone else who cares. You could even tell them I was reckless and going too fast and playing a stupid game of chicken and that, in your estimation, it'll never happen again. And," he added, biting his lip, making an effort to remain calm, "hopefully you could tell them that you've accepted my apology and thereby save me a rather great deal of trouble."

I considered his request. I felt a strong conviction forming in me, an instinctual sense of friendship and loyalty. I thought, for a second, that I'd forgiven him. Then I had a sudden vision of Evan gripping Sophia, their bodies collapsing on each other, their voices crying out. I willed myself into numbness and returned my attention to Evan. "I can't do that for you."

He looked me over, saying nothing, only smiling. Slowly, with effort, he rose to his feet, limped out and closed the door.

—

THE FOLLOWING DAY I LEFT math to find Sophia leaning against my locker. I paused briefly before approaching. Unwelcome clarity came over me at the realization that seeing her there still made me exuberant, despite the way she'd treated me, despite surviving the crash, despite the problem of deciding what to do about Evan. I found this thought depressing: I'd faced an objectively life-altering moment, and still what felt most monumental were ordinary manifestations of love and hope and suffering. "Hi," I said.

"Who knew you were one to stay late after a math class?"

"Had to talk to Porter about my progress, or lack thereof." The hallway was empty. The next period had already begun. "You've been waiting?"

She nodded.

"Guess that means I should be worried."

"Don't look so alarmed. It's insulting."

"Sorry, I'm just scarred. Last time I found you waiting for me wasn't much fun." Balancing my math textbook against my chest, I tried, clumsily, opening my locker with my functional hand.

She touched my shoulder, gently moved me aside. A chill descended through my vertebral column. "Your combination?"

"You want my code?"

"Don't trust me?"

"Of course I do, but I'm okay, I can do it myself—"

"You've got one working arm, your dexterity sucks."

"Thanks, but—"

"You're being kind of weird about this."

"Fine," I said, instantly red-cheeked. "Zero-seven-two-four."

She looked me over, stifled a smile. "Isn't that just the strangest coincidence?"

"You don't say."

"Believe it or not, July twenty-fourth happens to be my birthday."

"Sorry, I never got around to changing—"

She spun the lock, jiggled it open. "I mean, what're the odds? Well, I guess I'm not really asking a numbers expert, am I?"

"Low blow." I placed my books inside.

She peered into my locker. "Ari," she said, dropping her voice, "I need to ask you something confidentially."

Inexplicably, my heart soared. "Of course."

"Swear you won't be mad."

"How could I be mad?"

"Seriously. Promise."

"I promise I won't be mad."

She glanced around, making sure we were alone. "I know what Evan asked you."

I tried maintaining a stoic expression. I utilized my old strategy, focusing my attention on only one feature of her face, this time her chin, smooth and sharp and lovely. After a moment or two I failed, and when I took in the entirety of Sophia Winter's face I saw only a mask. "You do?"

"And, yeah, I don't blame you for refusing. Truly, I mean that. Actually you're probably right for saying no. It's—well, even I see that."

I studied my textbooks, the ridiculous poster of Avril Lavigne that Oliver had taped recently to the back of my locker. "Why would he possibly tell you?"

"*You* still speak to me, don't you?"

I fell silent, ungracefully gathering folders and binders into my backpack.

"You don't think I know I'm a fool? It's just—he's in so much trouble, Ari. His entire life will be ruined, everything he has left, and if it's my fault—"

"This has nothing to do with you, Soph. You weren't there, you didn't see what he was like. You haven't seen all the things he's done this year."

"I've seen enough to know I don't want to be responsible for breaking him."

I moved away, unable to make eye contact. "I don't even know what you're talking about."

"I"—she stopped, bit her lip—"I know."

"Something happened."

"Yes," she said, "something did happen. And that feeling, Ari, of undoing someone, even after the world's already had its way? Of contributing to such . . . willful self-destruction?" She played with her wrists. "I couldn't bear it, Ari."

"So therefore you want *me* to testify for him."

"For my sake. For me."

"Okay," I said, knowing then, after Yeats had shown me only in the abstract, what it was to feel pale from imagined love, "then I will."

She didn't dare move, she didn't dare touch me. Instead she looked at me with the knowledge that I was someone over whom her power was absolute. "You're much better than we are, Ari."

"I don't like when you say that."

"It's the truth. *'One man picked out of ten thousand.'*"

I dug into my pockets. The beginning of sunset cast a glassy, yellow light over us through the hallway windows. "I'm not very good at all."

—

I WAS LYING IN BED the night before we were due in court, distracting myself by flipping absentmindedly through last-minute revisions for a Hartman paper, when my mother knocked. "Something came for you," she said tersely. She handed over a thick, cream-colored envelope. "Could be a college?"

I bolted upward. "Where's it from?"

"The . . . Rousseau Institute?"

My face fell. "Junk mail."

She took my good hand. "Everything okay? You seem on edge."

"Yeah, I'm fine."

"How's your arm feeling?"

"Better."

"Seriously, Aryeh, why do you look so nervous?"

"Just this Coleridge paper," I lied. "It's due tomorrow."

"Sounds fun. And stressful, I guess. I'll leave you to it. But if you need something, you'll call?"

"I'll call."

She nodded, left me alone. I skimmed through the letter:

Dear Mr. Eden,

Thank you for participating in our annual contest. We are pleased to inform you that your submission has been awarded the Philo Sherman Bennett Prize. Please note we receive several hundred submissions each year, and that winning essays are selected by independent judges, all of whom are—

I read on. I was to receive a gold medal and monetary compensation—one thousand dollars, thanks to the generosity of the Bennett family—and my paper was to be published in an upcoming special edition journal sponsored by the Institute. What paper? I knew it was a farce, probably designed to extract Social Security numbers, though a harried Google search returned, at least at first glance, a semi-reputable website. I scanned the page: no clear mention of the cost of accepting the award, though I didn't bother with the fine print. Bewildered, anxious about what would happen in the morning, I crumpled the letter, tossed it at my desk, returned haphazardly to my paper and, soon enough, nodded off to sleep.

APRIL

Although the young may be experts in geometry and mathematics and similar branches of knowledge, we do not consider that a young man can have Prudence. The reason is that Prudence includes knowledge of particular facts, and this is derived from experience, which a young man does not possess; for experience is the fruit of years.

—Aristotle, *Nicomachean Ethics*

'd never been inside a courthouse. It was an empty, depressing room: dusty and poorly lit, with dark mahogany paneling and a tacky rendering of the American flag pinned to the wall. Before the judge's bench sat a pair of cops and a haggard-looking stenographer bent over a typewriter. The judge, the Honorable Ralph Holmes, was a middle-aged, overweight man with a booming voice and a face knitted into a permanent frown, probably from years of adjudicating deadbeats and totaled vehicles. The air conditioner seemed to be set to fifty degrees. I found it difficult not to shiver.

Evan waited outside. He wore a dark suit, the one he wore to Remi's party. He looked regal, almost, despite his scar, despite his cane. He shook my hand, thanked me for coming. I helped him inside.

"Where's your lawyer?" I figured he'd arrive with some white-shoe attorney.

"Don't have one."

"Doesn't your father know you're here?"

"He doesn't care. Actually, he'd like me off his hands for some time. Best way to do that is to lock me up." He winced as we made our way to the back of the room to await our turn. "What about your parents? Are they aware you're helping the Malach HaMavis?"

"They're very much not."

We were the third case of the morning. We rose for the judge, who glared impatiently from the bench, tapping his pencil without any particular rhythm. "No attorney?"

"No, sir," Evan said.

"Why's that?"

"I don't believe I need one."

The judge took off his glasses. "You were recently released from the hospital, as I understand it. Due to injuries sustained the night of your accident. A boating accident."

"Correct, sir."

"Did you receive that scar on your face during said incident?"

"Yes, Your Honor."

The judge grimaced, rummaged through his documents. "Police report states you had a blood alcohol level of 0.10 percent at the time of the incident. A blood alcohol level of 0.08 percent is sufficient to convict."

"I'm painfully aware, Your Honor."

"I'm finding your demeanor off-putting, Mr. Stark."

"You're not alone, I'm afraid."

"You also face charges of reckless driving," he continued, frowning. "This leaves us as follows. For the count of reckless driving, you're liable, under Florida law, to a five-hundred-dollar fine and up to ninety days in prison. For the count of driving under the influence, you're liable, under Florida law, to a fine of one thousand dollars, fifty hours of mandatory community service, as well as a one-year period of probation and up to six months in prison." He cleared his throat. "You do grasp the gravity of these consequences, young man?"

"They seem a bit draconian, Your Honor. But yes."

"Did you just use the word 'draconian' in my courtroom?"

"My apologies, Your Honor."

The judge inched forward in his seat. It was hard to imagine he'd ever faced a defendant as interesting, or as deliberately insolent, as Evan. "You seem to be a relatively bright kid."

"You flatter me, Your Honor." Evan shifted his weight on his cane, cringing some more. Then, unable to help himself: "You seem bright yourself."

"Yet apparently not bright enough to refrain from talking back to a judge. Or staying out of trouble. And if there's one thing I detest in my courtroom, Mr. Stark, it's a young man with a titanic ego and apathy for the rule of law." He smiled wickedly. "Have any ambition? Work hard in school? Do you, dare I suggest, have plans for when you graduate?"

"I cannot speak for the legitimacy of my ambition or work ethic, Your Honor. Hopefully my friend can attest to my character." He gestured toward me, allowing me to feel the full weight of the judge's stare. I swallowed hard. "The only thing I can say is that I've secured postgraduation plans."

"Oh, yes? Do share them with the court."

"I'll be attending Stanford, Your Honor."

"Stetson?"

"Stanford."

"Stanford, you said?"

"Yes, sir."

The judge frowned in disbelief. "I wasn't admitted there," he muttered.

"I'm certain the admission committee kicks itself regularly for that mistake."

I felt only fleeting anger toward Evan. I didn't understand why he cared enough about his future to request my help but couldn't refrain from sabotaging himself, though at least his irrational desire to rouse Holmes' ire had no effect on my own fate. No, bewildered as I was in that moment, I turned my anger on Sophia. She should never have put me in this position, she should've known Evan was hell-bent on self-implosion. She should never have made me expendable. She should have chosen me over him.

"How do you plead?"

"Not guilty on both counts," Evan said. "In self-defense, I offer the following motions: motion to dismiss for an unconditional delay in filing charges, for a failure of the government to preserve evidence, for insufficient evidence of a crime, for lack of probable cause, for an improper search of a vehicle and for the violation of my Fourth Amendment rights." Evan paused. "Oh, and for general governmental misconduct, Your Honor."

The court stenographer, who'd been stabbing diligently at his keyboard, released a high-pitched giggle, which he attempted to conceal as a cough. Evan remained composed, staring coolly in the direction of the bench. "Think this is some joke, Mr. Stark?"

"Hardly, sir."

The judge leaned back in his chair, scribbled further. "Stand, witness," he said, averting his eyes. "See if it does any good."

I stood meekly, cleared my throat. "Thank you, Your Honor."

Holmes raised his brows. "For what?"

I cleared my throat a second time. "For allowing me to testify, sir."

Evan looked at me, nodded, nudged me along.

"Did he give you that?" the judge asked.

"Pardon?"

"Your arm."

I looked down at my cast. "Oh. Yes."

"Your name?"

"Aryeh Eden."

"What was that?"

"Aryeh?"

"Would you spell that, please?"

"A-r-y-e-h. Or Andrew. You can call me Andrew."

"Which is it?"

"It's my Hebrew name," I said, embarrassed, "and the name I use."

"And how do you know Mr. Stark?"

"We go to school together."

"Some school. Are you going to tell me you're attending Stanford, too?"

I thought of the newest round of rejection letters I received only the day before: Brown, Dartmouth, Harvard. "No, sir."

"As I understand it, you were in the boat the night of the incident?"

I nodded.

"Communicate verbally, Mr. Eden. For the court's records."

"Yes."

"The police report excludes your blood alcohol level content. Were you drinking?"

I felt clammy. "Only a bit, sir."

Holmes peered down from on high. "It's difficult for me to imagine anyone with half a brain would get into a boat in the middle of the night with an inebriated driver—unless, of course, you weren't sober, either."

I opened my mouth. Nothing came out.

"Did you notice Mr. Stark was drunk?"

"He wasn't drinking in the boat."

"But did you discern erratic behavior?"

"I   nothing abnormal."

I felt very far off from the courtroom, my mouth dry, my voice carrying as if I were underwater.

"Well," the judge said, playing with the frames of his glasses, "what you're saying hasn't been much help, since it directly conflicts with the police report and paints you either as startlingly naïve or as a liar." He smiled pleasantly. "I will, however, give you the benefit of the doubt, Mr. Eden, and presume the former. So let's conclude. Can you tell me whether, in your own estimation, Mr. Stark is a stand-up young man, and whether this incident, despite his impertinence, is out of line with his character? That is, according to your conscience, Mr. Eden, can you recommend that I grant leniency to Mr. Stark?"

I blinked stupidly. I thought about the night, yes, the realization that we were going to crash, the look on his face, but mostly I thought of her. The night of Purim: red eyes, broken glass. I thought about how she'd stormed away at Oliver's party, even when I was vulnerable. I thought about her tears at Remi's birthday. I thought about her desperation as she stood by my locker, as she used me. She had always used me.

"Your Honor," I said, feeling Evan's knowing gaze on me. "Evan was drunk, high, reckless and put my life at risk. I have no reason to believe this was out of character."

Silence. A whirling in my skull. I could see Evan breaking into a faint smile, even with my eyes fixed firmly to the floor. "Should've chosen a better friend," the judge said brusquely. "Evan Stark, I sentence you to a fine of fifteen hundred dollars, one year of probation, fifty hours of community service and thirty days in delinquency rehabilitation." Holmes slammed his gavel, snorted. "Let Stanford do as they wish."

—

I ARRIVED AT SCHOOL BY lunch period. Soaked in nervous sweat, ignoring Sophia's text messages, I raced upstairs to the third-floor balcony.

"You're shitting me," Amir said, after I recounted a heavily redacted version of the story, one in which my condemnation of Evan was conspicuously absent. Oliver whistled a long, sad note and lit a joint.

"So what'd you tell the judge?" Noah asked. He dropped his sandwich, his appetite gone.

I perched myself where Evan usually sat. "Everything I needed to say."

"You're a good friend, Drew," Noah said, nodding.

"How's he possibly going to tell Stanford?" Amir looked genuinely devastated, despite any academic rivalry with Evan. "They won't tolerate this."

"Nah, they'll keep him around," Oliver said. "And if they don't, he'll go elsewhere. Harvard or Yale or some shit. I mean, it's Evan Stark. He's smarter than all of us put together."

"He won't be able to," Amir said quietly. "He won't go *anywhere*, actually, not with this on his record."

"Ari, you okay?" Noah asked, noticing how I cringed at this last comment. "You look like you're about to puke."

I forced deep breaths. "Still a bit tense from court," I said. Evan expelled, Evan behind bars, Evan roaming the streets. Had I just demolished his entire life?

"Hit this." Oliver shoved his joint into my mouth. "You need it."

I didn't object.

"Will the Academy even let Ev graduate?" Noah asked. "How's he supposed to miss thirty days of classes?"

"Do we even have thirty days left on the calendar?" Oliver had that lazy twinge in his voice indicating he was excessively high.

"Maybe it'll help," I said. "Clean him up."

"What?"

"Rehab," I said unsurely. "He's a mess. Something has to change. Maybe this is best for him." Another wave of nausea: green, overpowering guilt, guilt that made my insides turn. I nearly gagged.

The bell rang and we headed to Rabbi Bloom's office. I hadn't eaten all day. My stomach was queasy, my forehead burning. Rabbi Bloom gave a masterful class, discussing what he called "the Modern Orthodox paradox of opting to feel divinely obligated in a free, secular world," but I couldn't concentrate. All I could think of was the look Evan gave me when I left the courthouse.

Rabbi Bloom had me stay back after the close of the period. "Something to share, Mr. Eden?"

I felt a strange ringing in my ears. "Evan spoke to you?"

He smiled weakly. "Let's leave that for later." Did he know? It was inconceivable for Evan to have omitted my part in the story, inconceivable for him not to be bursting with shock, rage, betrayal. I tried returning Bloom's gaze, tried emitting innocence, remorse. "I was referring, actually, to your prize."

"My what?"

"I assume you received a notification?"

The letter. I'd forgotten entirely about the letter. "I don't understand."

"Those papers I assigned, after we read Sidgwick?"

"Yes?"

"I wasn't entirely up front with you, Mr. Eden."

"I don't follow."

"You wanted a plan B, as I recall, after Columbia. Here it is."

"Rabbi," I said. "I really don't—"

"One of my old PhD classmates is a professor at Princeton. Metaethics. He works on a journal that sponsors an annual contest for young thinkers. I entered your paper, Ari, I hope you don't mind. You shouldn't, really, because the good news is you won."

I rubbed my eyes—I was moderately high at the moment—and tried banishing Evan's face from my mind. "That was real?"

"It's legitimate, Mr. Eden, and quite impressive, actually. Now, nothing's for certain, but I will admit that prizewinners often enjoy successful careers at fine universities." He pushed his glasses up the bridge of his nose, offered a fixed smile. "You forgive me for entering without your permission, don't you? I didn't want to get your hopes up, the odds of winning being so low, you understand?" He offered his hand, opened the door for me. "And Ari?"

Dazed, squinty-eyed, I turned to face him. "Rabbi?"

"You did what you could for Mr. Stark." He placed his hand on my shoulder and retreated into his office.

—

RUMORS SPREAD QUICKLY THAT WEEK. Some were absurd—he was attending Stanford early, he was boycotting school, he was working for his father's fund—and some downright nasty: he'd been expelled, imprisoned, institutionalized. The truth, that he was stuck in a rehabilitation center for thirty days, his admission to Stanford on the line, circulated, too. My role in the affair, however, remained unknown.

The faculty avoided discussing Evan, refused to confirm stories. In the hallways, I received looks. My imagination descended into frenzy. I took notice of how voices dropped around me, pictured freshmen clustered at lunch, whispering about what had happened on the boat. Overrun with paranoia, I hastened from class to class, seeking refuge at my locker, lowering my gaze to the floor.

After our penultimate biology class—our lectures ending early so that we'd have sufficient time to focus on studying for the AP test— Sophia lingered in the classroom. Her normally reflective eyes were downcast. "Have a minute?"

Since my appearance in court I'd returned to avoiding her. On the day of Evan's sentencing I'd offered her the same story I'd given my friends, only to proceed to ignore her, both in the hallways and over text message. Given that she hadn't confronted me, I felt sure that Evan hadn't told her what I'd done. But I wanted to avoid deepening my entanglement of lies or, worse, watching her weep for Evan. If I stopped seeing her, I could end my heartsickness. Sophia Winter was a virus, snaking through my bloodstream, eroding my bones. To excise her from my life would be to dull a significant source of pain, to gradually distance myself from the stranger I'd become. "Actually, I'm meeting Kayla," I said hurriedly. "We're going for dinner."

Unmoved, she continued leaning nimbly against her desk, as if I'd responded in the opposite way. "Just wanted to see how you're holding up."

"I—" I frowned, uncertain how to answer. "I'm fine."

"I never thanked you. I know how difficult it must've been, and that it was terrible of me to ask you. But you did it, Ari, and you were so noble to try."

I avoided her eyes. "It was nothing. And clearly it didn't work."

"The alternative could've been worse without you."

"I don't know about that." I picked at my nails, woozy with shame.

"He starts rehab this week?"

"That's what Noah heard. But—doesn't he tell you?"

"No," she said, causing my heart to swell with joy, despite my best efforts to steel myself into indifference. "He's told me nothing." An awkward lull ensued. I calculated the distance between us: ten feet, at most, from her desk to where I stood at the doorway. "Anyway." She walked toward me, hesitating. "I won't hold you. I just wanted to thank you. And—to tell you I miss you."

She disappeared through the door and I remained in my spot, pleading with myself to wait until her footsteps grew lighter, until I knew she was gone. And yet, after only several moments, I could take no more of the sound of her feet scraping lightly against the tiled floor.

"Sophia," I called out, just before she'd reached the end of the hall-way and turned out of sight. It took her several seconds to face me, but in her movement—confident, agile, lovely—I realized that she'd known all along I'd break, that she'd never doubted the depth of my desire. "I can postpone dinner."

I sent Kayla a vague text: something about a last-minute biology quiz, an emergency study session. And then, for the first time in many long weeks, Sophia and I left the Academy together, this time through a side door.

—

WE WENT TO HER HOUSE. She snuck white wine from her kitchen, put a finger to her lips, led me up a narrow glass staircase under a solitary skylight. Her house was so big, she whispered, that no one would know I was there if we were quiet. Slightly drunk, gasping for air. Her hands combing my hair, her mouth in my ears. Heavy breathing: her fingers down my chest, my lips on the nape of her neck, all light escaping the room. Sharp, wonderful, this world of impossible desire, a world where everything was free, lonely, expanded, where all else was forgotten. I held her to my chest, my head buried in her neck, her legs entangled in mine. This was the happiest I could hope to be, I told myself. Nothing could match this moment.

We fell into dazed sleep, time suspended and spectacular. I woke eventually to the sound of tears, her body curved against mine. She held my fingers, tracing circles over her stomach. Her chest rose, fell slowly. I didn't move.

"Sophia."

Silence. Insensate darkness. It was late, nearly eight. My parents would be looking for me. Kayla must've called furiously. Sophia kept tracing circles.

"I got into Juilliard today."

I gripped her body. "That's incredible, Soph, that's—" She didn't stir. "Why didn't you tell me?"

"I couldn't."

I leaned forward, put my lips to her cheek. "You should be happy."

"I know."

"Don't you want to celebrate?"

"I haven't told anyone but you."

"Not your parents?"

"Nobody."

"You're scared what they'll say?"

The circles stopped. "Music has its penalty," she said, half of her face buried in her pillow, the other half obscured by the growing dark. "Great music happens only when things are broken, doesn't it seem that way? Is that what I want my life to be?"

Quiet shadows separated us, even as we were pressed together, skin to skin, flesh to flesh. "Soph?"

"Hamlet."

"Why'd you make me do it?"

"I've never made you do anything," she said.

"You knew if you asked I'd have no choice. You knew I'd do whatever you wanted."

She took my right hand in her own, lowered my left down her thigh. "The more we suffer, Ari, the more we inflict."

I kissed the back of her head, pulled away. I dressed in the dark and slipped out into the street.

—

MY FINAL THREE DECISIONS CAME the next day. Amherst said no. Princeton, a laughable prospect, wasn't even available to check; its server

had crashed from too many thousands of hopeful teenagers checking simultaneously. This left me with NYU, my last hope. I trembled
slightly punching in my personal code, which I'd forgotten and had
to reset. I closed my eyes before accessing the decision page. I took a
deep breath, offered a quick prayer and, slowly, opened the page:

> Dear Mr. Eden,
>
> The admissions committee at New York University has carefully
> considered your application and supporting credentials, and it is with
> regret that we must inform you we are unable to offer you admission
> this year.

I smiled weakly, moved to my desk to open Oliver's scotch. I took
a long pull, wiping my mouth with my cast. Then I took the contents
of my desk—books, loose-leaf papers, graded tests, folders, binders,
pens, all of it—and, in one fell swoop, launched everything against
the wall.

—

HAVING BEEN A STUDENT AT Kol Neshama for only one year, still uncertain whether the Academy had expanded or collapsed my universe, I
was torn throughout our final days of school between never wanting
to leave and never wanting to return. Teachers said their goodbyes,
wished us luck on finals, claimed we'd go on to accomplish great futures. (Most of us, at least; Dr. Flowers made it clear I need not bother
keeping in touch.) Rabbi Feldman urged us never to cease viewing
him as a lifelong rebbe, told us he looked forward to dancing at our
weddings. Dr. Porter, struggling to conjure pleasantries, insisted we
were a group that meant well and that sometimes that was all that
counted. Mr. Harold implored us to take down his home address
and write often. ("No email," he explained too loudly. "I won't let my
grandchildren make one for me. Give me ink or give me death. Well,
not yet, though. No death yet.") Mrs. Hartman, always the stoic, bade
farewell one final time in her singular style: "Parting is indeed such

sweet sorrow, but I'm afraid I'm not one to make a spectacle of it, lest I kill thee with much cherishing."

—

WE HAD OUR FINAL SESSION with Rabbi Bloom. He wanted to conclude with *The Natural History of Religion*. We talked mostly about the moral and emotional components of theology, or, as Oliver put it, eyes unabashedly red, "what we get out of the goddamn thing."

"Ernest Becker," Rabbi Bloom said hoarsely, under the weather, "claimed religion solved the problem of death."

"No small problem," Noah said.

"Freud, more bleakly, claimed the whole thing was nothing but a way to repress our most violent desires. Rav Soloveitchik, through his Adam I, claimed we worship because we long for vastness." He gave a worn smile. "Enter Hume, the naturalist. What did he chalk the whole thing up to?"

"Emotion," I said. I looked over to the empty chair where Evan typically sat. In his absence, a power vacuum had formed. For much of the year, I wanted to be the one sitting there, dominating, the one to whom all deferred. Now, I no longer had any desire for Evan's spotlight.

"Of what sort?" Rabbi Bloom asked.

"Fear," I said.

"Right where we started." Rabbi Bloom dabbed his nose with a handkerchief. "Fear of our future. Fear of our weaknesses. Fear of our potential. Fear of what we desire. Now, I admit Hume took this in a direction I'm not too fond of, blaming religion for all sorts of unpleasant consequences. Competition. Intolerance. Dishonesty. An utter misunderstanding of moral truth. Was he right? I can't rule it out definitively. He was, after all, a smarter man than I."

"And a nut," Amir said. "Definitely a nut."

"True," Rabbi Bloom said. "And yet, he's on to something: our monotheistic drive stems not from our desire to control but from our desire to feel."

"Feel what?" Noah asked.

"Everything." He turned to a highlighted passage in his book. "What influences us most is what Hume deems the 'ordinary affections of human life.' Our concern for our well-being. Our anxiety over what our futures hold. Our desire for romance and respect and happiness. Our fear of dying. Our hunger for food, for money, for comfort. Do you see?" He nodded to himself without waiting for an answer. "As we stumble on through the many events that make up human life, agitated and scared and laughing and trembling and crying and loving, we arrive at an epiphany: *'And in this disordered scene, with eyes still more disordered and astonished, they see the first obscure traces of divinity.'*"

"So you're saying what?" Oliver asked gruffly. "That we made the whole thing up? That all this effort is one big farce?"

"It is and it isn't," Rabbi Bloom said. "God is someone— something—we'll always need. He is the adversary against which we rage and the comfort for which we yearn. We need Him when we need something larger than ourselves to thank and something larger than ourselves to blame. We need Him to feel as if we're not alone, and we need Him to feel as if our aloneness isn't our fault. We need Him when we rejoice, when we want happiness, peace, quiet, but we also need Him when we mourn, when we experience dread, loss, insanity." He paused, looking to the empty chair. "We need Him more than He needs us. And that, I think, is what it all amounts to. So did we make Him up?" He shrugged, closing his copy of Hume, giving an exhausted smile. "Does it matter?"

—

KAYLA DROVE OVER AFTER SCHOOL. I'd been waiting for our inevitable confrontation: I never apologized for canceling on her, I'd allowed her texts and calls to remain largely unanswered, I'd blown her off in school. She wore an oversized sweater, her hair in a ponytail. When the door to my room was closed I offered scotch. She declined. I poured one for myself.

"You're drinking an awful lot," she observed.

I sat beside her on my bed. "Yeah, you're probably right."

"I don't know exactly what you're trying to prove. That you're un-happy?"

"Maybe. I don't know, either."

"Ari."

I didn't answer. I put my head against her shoulder. She didn't shake me off.

"Why didn't you ever really care if this worked?"

"That's wrong," I said, buried in her sweater. "Of course I cared."

"I don't think I believe that anymore."

"But it did work," I pointed out, "for a while, at least."

She smiled sadly. "Sure. While I deluded myself."

I straightened, leaning against my wall. "I hope you don't mean that."

"But that's what happens, isn't it? All of us, everybody, we fool ourselves into believing someone loves us the way we love them."

An awful pause, during which all I could think of was Edward, in *The Good Soldier*, failing to love Leonora. *But she had not for him a touch of magnetism. I suppose, really, he did not love her because she was never mournful . . .*

"It's just"—Kayla continued, undeterred, hands together on her lap—"you were different in the beginning. More innocent, yes, shockingly naïve, endearingly naïve, but you had—I don't know, you just had more substance." The way she was speaking reminded me of someone else. Even her pauses seemed deliberate.

"Right. And now? What am I now?"

A nod, a gritted smile.

I sipped my drink. "Damned like everyone else?"

"No. Because I don't care how badly you want to be, you'll never really be like the others."

We looked around absently. "The other night," I said, setting my drink to my floor, "when I had to cancel dinner?"

She closed her eyes. "Do I want this vocalized, Ari?"

"I was with Sophia."

"And by *with her* you mean—"

A buzzing started in my eardrums. My voice was just a sequence of nebulous noise, absent of meaning. "I'm sorry, Kayla."

She nodded, she left.

—

WE HEARD NOTHING FROM EVAN. Noah tried visiting the rehab center but was told guests weren't yet permitted. Amir called half a dozen times, only to be rebuffed. Oliver tried sending "a gift basket of sorts"; an administrator informed him that Evan was not interested in receiving gifts at this time. I made no such effort, panicked as I was at the thought of eventually being confronted, by Evan and by the others, about what I'd done.

My arm was healing well. Dr. Friedman told me I could have the cast removed after finals. Would the cast impede my academic performance? Would I require a medical note? No, thanks, I told him. It didn't much matter.

I wasted my study days, as I knew I would. With no collegiate plans on the horizon, I was growing alarmingly indifferent not merely to my grades but to my consciously self-destructive behavior. Instead of preparing during our free week I read *Faust*. I went for drives with Sophia—to the beach and back—when she needed time away from her books. I sleepwalked through basketball practices. I ambled across the street to smoke, devour Cynthia's baking, hit golf balls. I joined Oliver at Three Amigos, where his waitress friend brought us pitcher after pitcher of Rolling Rock until we staggered out, the afternoon shimmering with Florida heat, and had to call Rebecca to retrieve us. (We first tried Amir, who, boarded up studying, promptly hung up on us, his mother howling in the background.) Nighttime came, and I had an increasingly difficult time willing myself into sleep, particularly if I wasn't high before bed.

And then: examinations were upon us. Biology was a train wreck; I spent much of the test doodling and at one point caught Sophia's eyes and snorted. I raced happily through Gemara, suffered through math, impatiently endured history ("Explain the factors precipitating the 351 CE Jewish revolt against Governor Constantius Gallus"). AP English Literature, at least, was entertaining, concluding with an essay on "The Pity of the Leaves." As I handed in my exam, I realized, somewhat disconcertingly, I'd circled one line three times: *just to let him know / How dead they were.*

When I finished Hebrew, my last exam, I found Rabbi Bloom at my locker. He hadn't been texting or reading while waiting, I noticed, but motionless, entirely lost in thought. "Mr. Eden," he said kindly, glancing up as I joined him. "How'd the final test of your high school career treat you?"

The thought of offering even one more lie nauseated me. "Poorly."

He laughed. "Refreshing honesty, but worry not. It'll work out. These things do, don't they?"

I unlocked my locker, though only after a bit of a struggle. "Right, maybe."

"For what it's worth," he said, "you did quite well in my class."

"Since when do we get official grades for that?"

"Don't you think you deserve them? I daresay the reading load was as intensive as the alternatives."

"More interesting, too."

He fixed his tie, eyed the hallway. It was empty. "I was hoping for a quick word."

I shut my locker. "Your office?"

"We're fine here."

I put down my backpack. Donny emerged from a nearby classroom and walked toward us, hands plunged suspiciously into his pockets. When he spotted Rabbi Bloom, he smiled superficially, hastening the other way. "I want to begin by saying that I know there are things you're keeping to yourself, but I do hope you'll share them with me when you feel ready."

"I—yes, of course."

"Right." He smiled pleasantly, cleared his throat. "The other thing

I have to say is that Stanford called to inform me that Mr. Stark's admission is now formally under review. They requested a full report of documented disciplinary action within twenty-four hours."

"God," was all I managed, aware of a tightening in my chest.

"I assume you know why I'm telling you this?"

I failed to return his gaze. "I—no, I don't."

"It's because I trust your moral intuition. And it's because you happen to be the only other person in the entire world who knows what happened that evening."

"But I don't think I do, actually," I said, scarcely getting the words out. "It was such a blur, you know, it all happened so quickly, I don't—"

"Ari," he said, dropping his voice once more, playing with the knot of his tie, "I've spoken with Mr. Stark."

A momentary spell of dizziness, air leaking from the hallway. "But then—why hasn't he told anyone else? I mean, nobody else knows, do they?"

"From what I can discern, he has no interest in bringing to light the details of the courtroom. Maybe it's pride, or stubbornness or amor fati. But in my view? I think you did what he wanted."

I pawed nervously at my chin. "You think he *wanted* me to say that to the judge?"

"I think he wanted you to fight back." His voice softened to a whisper. "Anyway, what you did was not only blameless, given your position, but beneficial for Mr. Stark in the long run. I know I disappointed him earlier this year, but he needs help. Real help. And this, right now, is his best chance to recognize that. To be away from his father, from his friends, from me, from Ms. Winter"—at this mention of Sophia we each blushed, finding reason to avoid each other's eyes—"and to reflect on how best to heal from the suffering he's been subjected to, suffering no one should have to face, especially that young. Without you, Mr. Eden, I'm afraid he'd—well, he'd never give himself that opportunity."

"Right, well." I nodded awkwardly. "I do appreciate that."

"Now, to address the other question at hand. I can't make my decision about what to do about Stanford without knowing whether *you* can forgive him. Whether you can envision trusting him again. Because that, I believe, tells me everything I need to know."

Whatever happened on the boat had already come to pass. I was fine, Evan was fine. The world trudged onward, nobody suspected anything truly malevolent, I myself hardly did any longer. Trauma had given way to normalcy: studying, examinations, the splintering of relationships, the imminent arrival of graduation. How many more times would I even see Evan or the others again? I wondered whether refusing to forgive him signified nothing more than a desire to maintain a connection to Zion Hills, whether viewing the boat incident as anything other than an accident was merely a means of distracting myself from a bleaker alternative: that I wasn't special, that my life's biggest catastrophe was profoundly mundane. "I don't know yet."

He placed a hand on my shoulder. "You may not want to hear this now, you may not want to hear it for a long time, in fact, but you and Evan share many things, not least of which is an overpowering thirst to understand the world around you."

"Yeah, well, I'll never see it." I said so with unintended defiance. "As much as he likes trying to convince me otherwise."

"One can share certain traits without being alike, Ari. Much to your advantage, I might add. But sharing an extreme intellectual appetite, for instance, is no evil thing. And I say all this not to push you back into friendship, but to tell you that Evan relies on you, more than you realize."

I didn't bother stifling my laugh. "You think he *relies* on me?"

"Perhaps this manifests perilously at the moment," Rabbi Bloom said, "but he considers you a rival with a unique capacity to get under his skin. And in time, I'm confident, the day will come when you two might need each other."

"I'm flattered you give me such credit, Rabbi, I really am, but you're very much mistaken."

"Don't you see how he reacts when he thinks you've received preferential treatment? When he thinks you've gained on him in—

romantic pursuits?" Again, we each turned our attention down the hall, though nobody approached. "Have you ever seen him react that way with anyone else? It's because something about you, Ari, reaches him." He coughed into his hand, lowered his gaze. "I suppose, now, there's something I should admit."

I picked up my backpack. "Is it the drug test?" I said, without thinking.

He stared on blankly, pretending not to hear me. "Last year, when I received your outstanding application essay, I allowed Mr. Stark to read it."

"Yeah," I said coolly, "I know."

Neutral expressionlessness gave way to anxious smiling. "You do?"

"I mean, I've at least suspected so for a long time. He made it obvious enough."

Rabbi Bloom nodded, overtaken by a strange look of relief. "Well, imagine my delight," he said, "when I came across your writing. Here, finally, was the thinker I was searching for. An analogue. Not just someone of his caliber, but someone who could push him . . . philosophically, let's say. Someone he could push, in turn."

I put both hands to the crown of my head, over my yarmulke, stunned by the realization that monumental changes are, in the end, dictated by external forces we never discover. "You showed him my essay so he'd approve me," I said quietly. "You brought me here for him."

At first, Rabbi Bloom stood there saying nothing. While I waited for him to speak, I braced myself for feelings of betrayal or devastation. Instead, I felt nothing, not because I was numb, but because I couldn't force myself to believe I'd actually been wronged. I felt, rather, as one might upon learning some intelligent design exists, even if it turns out to be slightly crooked.

"My one regret, Mr. Eden," he said eventually, "is that I didn't get my hands on you three years earlier." He tapped my shoulder and turned down the hall, back toward his office. I stood bewildered for a few moments before reopening my locker and emptying it a final time.

—

WE HAD OUR LAST GAME of the regular season that evening. We won emphatically, securing a spot in the upcoming district playoff tournament. Noah had his jersey number retired after the game, and to celebrate we ended up at Three Amigos. After several rounds of beer and a few hits of Oliver's joint, I decided to call an Uber. It was early, not yet midnight, but I was feeling particularly antisocial and wanted to be alone. Instead of going inside when I got home, I went out back and sat by my pool, staring at the sky and the water, allowing mosquitoes to gnaw quietly at my arms. Eventually, I fell into a strange, half-sober dream: I was wandering through the golf course, looking for someone, a worm crawling between two of my fingers, a house falling in the distance, kicking up dust . . .

"Aryeh?" My mother's figure appeared at the patio door. "That you?"

I cursed, blinking in confusion. Instinctually, I opened my phone, noticing an unread email from some Joshua Robert:

Ari,

I'm glad Laurence passed along your paper. Impressive work for a high school student, and a brave leap into difficult (moral) waters. Congratulations. Do come see me on campus this fall.

Best,

JR

"You scared me half to death, you know that? I thought you might've been an intruder, honest to God." She was in her robe, scowl-faced. "Please tell me you didn't just get home? We've discussed curfew—"

"No, don't worry, Imma." I stood, groggy, and stumbled toward her. "I've been home, I just fell asleep outside for a bit."

"Outside?" She pursed her lips in distress, leaned over to sniff me. "You smell like you've been drinking."

"I can't talk now, Imma," I said, wiggling past her at the doorframe, bolting toward my room, "there's something I really need to do."

"I'm waking Abba," she said worriedly. "You're frightening me."

I grabbed my laptop from my desk, powered it on, muttering to myself as I waited for the screen to blink to life. My mother followed me into my room.

"Aryeh?"

Over a week had elapsed. Ignoring my mother, I flew about my room, searching for a forgotten red folder. After excavating my password from beneath a pile of laundry, I punched it into the server. A large, roaring tiger materialized on-screen, triumphant collegiate music blaring in the background. *YES* it said in big, orange letters. *WELCOME TO PRINCETON.*

A moment of disbelief as I stared at my computer, my mother hovering over me, the only sound in my room that grainy, low-volume fight music. "What is that? What's happening?"

I left the computer open, sank to my knees. "Thank you, God," I whispered, face buried in my hands. "Thank you, thank you, thank you."

"Aryeh!" my mother shouted, on the verge of crying.

"I got in," I said, tearing my face away from the floor and launching myself into her arms. "Imma, I think I just got into Princeton."

Full-on tears. She wrapped her arms around me and shrieked, despite the fact that I smelled of beer. I danced about my room, leaping onto my bed, my vision swimming. My father, hearing the commotion, waddled out in his pajamas. When we told him the news—my mother continuing to shriek at the top of her lungs—he blinked curiously. "Where's that again?" he asked sleepily.

"New Jersey."

"Well, then. Congratulations." He shrugged, and headed back toward his bedroom. "Maybe this'll make you happy."

MAY

The orchard now's the place for us;
We may find something like an apple there,
And we shall have the shade, at any rate.

—Robinson, "Isaac and Archibald"

At first they laughed.

"Right," Oliver said, striking a ball over the fence. "By the way, have I neglected to mention I'm headed to Harvard with Davis?"

Amir was floored, his entire worldview collapsing before his eyes. "Impossible," he insisted, even after it was clear I wasn't joking. "Sorry, Ari, I'm not saying this to belittle you, really, but you can't just, like, fucking get into Princeton. That's not how it works."

I flashed my acceptance on my phone. Noah howled and began pelting golf balls over the fence.

Amir dropped his club, traumatized. "But it—how? How did this *possibly* happen?"

"Told you motherfuckers!" Noah broke into dance, jabbing his finger at Amir. "The motherfucking kid from Borough Park!"

"Isn't there a *bracha* we're supposed to recite?" Oliver asked. "The one you make when you witness a miracle? Or at least the one for seeing a rainbow? I think there's a tropical storm coming soon, maybe we can combine everything?"

"I'm getting my dad's cigars," Noah said, sprinting toward his house. "We're celebrating."

Their incredulity didn't offend me. Something rapturous had indeed happened: what I had always viewed as the cruel logic of my existence had, remarkably, changed. The future I'd been dreading—a miserable return to my old life, this single year in Florida some gorgeous, twisted dream—was now averted. There was hope, a world beyond the world I'd never thought I'd have at all. I was self-absorbed, I was unhealthily fixated on shallow demarcations of status and success and worth, but I was not, as it turned out, inferior, nor was I trapped. I had another chance, a permanent escape into a life of aesthetics and cathedrals and poets and dining clubs. A life of prestige, a life of learning, a life of the mind.

My mother bought balloons, a cake, a yarmulke bearing the Princeton insignia. For her, the triumph of my acceptance provided validation: the boy she dragged to the library all those years ago, the boy she saved from an education-less world, regained what she relinquished. My father, with slightly different priorities, recognized my moral revitalization. I joined him at minyan the next morning and experienced my most meaningful Shemoneh Esrei in years. *Blessed Are You, Lord, Redeemer of Israel*. Dizzy with gratitude, eyes sealed in prayer, I made all sorts of vows: to stop breaking Shabbos, to stop violating kosher, to stop smoking, to again wear tzitzit. Witnessing these changes come to fruition, my parents discovered that, in the time span of *bein hashemashos*, their son had been made whole again, a new future stretched gloriously before him.

I left Noah's house light-headed from midday cigars, dropped a smug postcard for Bearman in the mail and called Sophia. She told me to come over, that she was bored and sitting by her pool. Norma let me inside, guided me out through the backdoor. Sophia was on a hammock, suspended between royal palms, wearing that shiny, black one-piece she'd worn nearly a year before at Noah's barbecue. She had on a large sunhat, sleek sunglasses; her legs were oiled, the visible parts of her stomach toned. She swung, the world swung with her: her face obliterated by light, her face returned to clarity, the tree blotting out the sun.

"A surprise visit from Ari Eden?" She closed her book, *The Beautiful and Damned*, and straightened slightly. The sun's lengthening beams seared my eyes. "What luck."

"*'My lord,*'" I said, "*'I have news to tell you.'*"

Dozens of chimes, angled from citrus trees around the backyard, sung delicately with the wind. "You and Kayla are engaged? You've bought a house and a dog?"

I wondered whether my ability to overlook such occasional bursts of casual cruelty indicated weakness on my part, a lack of self-esteem, perhaps, some depraved willingness to put myself at her mercy. I buried this thought. "Funny."

Her face dipped in and out of view as she swung, one moment returning to the shadows, the next bursting into blinding light, one moment a girl whose gloom was streaked with splendor, the next a girl whose beauty blurred with despair. A mesmerizing trance: light to dark, dark to light. I saw what I wanted, I saw what I had.

"Too soon?"

"Yes."

"My apologies. Want a drink? I'll call Norma."

"No, thanks." I moved to drag over a lounge chair beside her but she stopped me.

"There's room," she said, sliding over on the hammock. I lowered myself next to her, entangled in mesh, her left leg now draped curiously over mine. "So," she said, after a beat, "everything okay?"

I surveyed the waterfall Jacuzzi leading into a limestone infinity pool, the chaise longues floating over the shallow end, the white begonias and violet-blue periwinkles and light-pink rain lilies of the garden. Maybe this, amid all more meaningful things, turns out to be the shortest distance to joy, I thought, feeling Sophia against me: wealth, beauty, leisure. I felt myself tingling. "Great, actually."

"I don't think I've ever heard you so enthusiastic about anything." She adjusted her weight, sinking closer to me within the web, turning to face me. "Do share."

"I'm going to college."

She examined a fingernail, newly enameled in pale pink. "Some-where local?"

"Closer to you."

"The Northeast? New York proper?"

"New Jersey."

"Didn't realize this was a guessing game. Okay, then. So it's Rut-gers."

"No."

"Seton Hall?"

"What?"

"I don't know. Fairleigh Dickinson? Haven't we exhausted all the options here?"

"You're missing one."

"You've stumped me."

"Princeton."

"It's in Princeton?"

"C'mon, Soph."

Her face went slack. "You're joking."

"Apparently not."

"Princeton?"

"Princeton."

"It's just—" Her mouth went wide, she blinked unnaturally. "I guess I don't really—what'd Ballinger say?"

"So she was even more speechless. She called me to come in and take the Ivy picture. Look at it next time you're in school. Her mouth is fully agape."

"I can't believe it," she said, "Ari, I—" She lurched forward, kissed me, long and slow. I drew a sharp breath.

"It was because of you," I said quietly. "I wanted this because of you."

She was on top of me now, the hammock swaying precariously. We were both breathing heavily. "No one's home except Norma."

The world spinning on around us: the palm trees dancing in the breeze, the sun burning golden upon us. "That so?"

"Hamlet, you idiot. Come with me." She took my hand and led me inside.

—

WE DIDN'T HEAR FROM EVAN until three days before he was released—twenty-eight days since our time in court. He left word with Noah he wanted us to visit.

"He called you?" Oliver asked, looking insulted. "Suddenly that motherfucker has a phone?"

Noah shrugged. "Said it was urgent we visit."

"Urgent?" Amir said. "Why?"

"He said it's a big part of his program," Noah said. "Before he can officially graduate, or whatever they call it, heal, maybe, or evolve, he's supposed to formally make amends with those he's wronged."

"But he didn't do anything to *us*," Oliver said, glancing my way.

"He was really insistent that we all come," Noah said, reddening at the way Oliver was putting me on the spot. "And I think we should. Sign of solidarity, you know? He'll get out of there on the right foot and see there's no hard feelings."

"All right," Amir said. "Yeah, I mean, I guess I'm game to help him booome a normal human being again."

Noah turned my way.

"Nope," I said reflexively. "Count me out."

"Dude," Noah said, "c'mon, Ari—"

I imagined Evan gathering us together, only to announce the events of the courtroom. What if Rabbi Bloom was wrong? "I don't think it's a good idea," I said, visualizing the disgust with which Noah would regard me were he to find out what I did to Evan.

"Well," Noah said, "he specifically requested I make you come, even after you refuse. A personal favor, he called it."

"I really don't care what he requested."

"In fact, he told me to tell you not to be worried about whatever you heard from Socrates and to remind you that you'll have to see him eventually."

"Socrates?"

Noah shrugged. "Yeah, dunno. Figured that was some weird philo-sophical inside joke you guys had?"

Refusing to see him would only postpone our encounter—and for a grand total of three days, at that. If Evan intended to confront me, it made no difference where this happened. He had a plan in play, whether or not I acquiesced.

We drove westbound on 595, top down, everyone staring coolly into the purple sunset. The center was about forty minutes away and looked like a boutique hotel. There was a fountain in the circular driveway. The lobby was tastefully decorated: wingback armchairs, crystal chandeliers, neutral paintings of sailboats. A large TV, on mute, played local news: a reporter diagramming the path of a tropi-cal storm barreling our way over the coast.

"Actually, this isn't so bad," Amir said, taking a look around. "I expected something a bit more . . . spartan?"

"Yeah, I could probably get used to this when my time comes," Oli-ver said, putting his feet up on the side of an armchair. "Think the pool has a bar?"

Evan had a small corner room on the fourth floor. He looked more or less the same, but clean-shaven with trimmed hair. His face was slightly leaner, though not gaunt. His limp was unimproved. "Boys," he said, moving aside from the doorframe after we knocked. "Come in."

"Some place you've got, Ev," Oliver said, taking a look around. It was cramped, but not terribly. A twin bed, neatly made up, sat in the center of the room, next to two mahogany cabinets. The corner of the room had a wooden desk. His nightstand bore a small stack of books: Wittgenstein, Schopenhauer, Heidegger. There was a lone window through which faint sunlight dripped. The room had no right angles. Evan took a seat on his bed. We stood around him.

Evan met my gaze. "Eden. Thanks for actually coming."

"Yeah," I said, quickly glancing away, "good to see you."

"He put up much of a fight?" Evan asked Noah.

Noah gave a good-hearted laugh. "Hardly."

"So," Amir said, "what the hell's the emergency?"

Noah socked his arm.

"What?" Amir protested.

"What kind of opening is that?" Noah said.

"That's all right," Evan said, holding up his hand. "Apologies if I frightened you. I didn't intend to."

"Nah, buddy, we're happy to see you," Noah said cautiously. "Hear about the game last night?"

"No, sadly."

"Yeah, we smacked North Miami Country Prep," Noah said, receiving a fist bump from Oliver. "Clinched a district playoff game, baby. You'll be back for that."

"Yes," Evan said, hardly stirring, "that's right."

Oliver looked Evan up and down. "Why do I feel like you're not having normal human reactions? They have you on something?"

Evan smirked. "Don't I look clean and pure to you?"

"Nah, honestly you look like fucking, what's his name, Darth Vader with that scar. But they got to you, didn't they?" Oliver covered his face with his hands. "This place is worse than a monastery."

Evan bent over, groped under his bed, pulled out a small, black box.

"Not sure how to feel about this," Oliver said, rummaging through the contents: a half dozen pale-blue pills, a large stack of round, light yellow pills.

Amir eyed the cache. "What're these?"

"Dilaudid for the leg pain," Evan said, gesturing at the yellows. "Then amitriptyline for sleeping. I don't sleep well. My leg still kills." For effect, he attempted to lift it.

"And depression," Amir added hesitantly. "I remember that from AP Chem."

"Yeah, I guess that, too," Evan said. "What about you, Eden?"

"Eden flipped out while you've been gone." Oliver slung his arm around my shoulder. "The kid's back to his old religious ways. No more weed for him!"

"But how are you feeling?" Evan asked.

"Fine," I said.

"I see you've had your cast removed."

"I have."

"Good as new?"

I flexed. "More or less."

Oliver clapped my back. "Your star witness is a brave fighter," he said, failing to notice the way I immediately cringed.

Amir picked at his beard, ignoring my eyes. "You know, I would've liked to see Ari on the stand."

"Quite the sight," Evan said, "you have no idea. A regular Ronald Dworkin up there. He did everything he could, I'm very grateful. And it sounds as if your goodness has been rewarded?"

"Our Princeton man," Noah said. "Doesn't he look like your typical All-American frat star, now that we're done with him?"

I blew anxiously into the palm of my hand. "You heard?"

"Of course," Evan said. "It's the talk of the town."

"I'm just curious," Amir said, "the Academy is fine with this hiatus? Stanford, too?"

"Well," Evan said, leaning on his elbows, "here's how Bloom put it—"

"I thought you couldn't see anyone," Oliver said.

"My father certainly abides by that rule."

"He hasn't been here much?" Noah asked.

"Not a single time," Evan said. "But that's irrelevant. He's irrelevant. What I was saying was that my old friend Judge Holmes sent quite a letter to Stanford, advising they sever ties. So they called Bloom to learn more."

Nervously, Amir massaged his fingers. "Like what?"

"Everything. My personality. Teachers' opinions. Informal disciplinary record. What Bloom himself thought. And you know what? The old man came through."

Amir looked astounded. "Like, you're in the clear?"

"For the moment. There are caveats, though. Bloom gave me rules."

"Such as?" Amir asked.

"Let's just say he isn't terribly fond of my—extracurricular interests." I squirmed, went to sit on his desk. "I live to see another day on the condition that I cease and desist from things he finds unsavory. Basically, I'm on extreme probation. Stanford will see reports from rehab, the judge, the school. Make sure I get myself in order."

"And the Academy?" Amir pressed. "You're just off the hook with missing finals?"

"I'm taking my exams when I get out," Evan said. "But you'll be happy to know it'll be with reduced points."

Amir frowned. "Reduced points? That's it?"

"That disappoints you?"

"Not really. It's just—you bust your ass and you do everything right for eighteen years, or you just fuck up colossally and, lo and behold, it all works out nonetheless." Amir joined me at the desk. Noah patted his back mockingly.

"Speaking of fucking up colossally." Awkwardly, Evan cleared his throat. We blushed collectively at such contrived pacification. "I wanted to see you guys so that I can, you know, formally apologize. And, well, repent."

Oliver laughed. "Repent?" Noah kicked him.

"I've put each of you"—his eyes lingered on me—"in dangerous situations, and I'd like to make things right. I'd like to earn your forgiveness."

"Things are fine, aren't they, guys?" Noah said, trying to muster enthusiasm. "You really don't need to sweat it, dude."

"That may be. But I know I've been behaving—erratically all year. I've forced each of you into situations you probably found uncomfortable or bizarre or, I guess, distasteful, to put it mildly—"

"—no, no," Amir said, unable to help himself, "we just love raising the dead."

"And Ari," Evan continued, turning my way, "more than anyone else, you're the one who's suffered most from my misconduct. You're hurt because of me, and, truly, from the bottom of my heart, whether you forgive me now or not, I'm sorry. I've been through a lot this year, I've learned a lot about myself and my father and, to be brutally honest, it took me a while to figure out that the pain of losing my mother isn't something I can expect to evaporate. It's no excuse, it's just—I haven't been entirely myself, as I'm sure you're all too aware, but I'm working on it." Evan cleared his throat. "So you'll let me make it up to you?"

Noah was the first to offer a high five. "Hell yeah, bud."

Oliver shrugged. "Want us to sing a song or something?"

"Not quite. As a token of my remorse, I'd like to propose a trip."

"I'm not going back to Key West," Amir said.

"A camping trip," Evan said.

"Camping?" Oliver laughed. "Mind if we spring for a hotel?"

"Think of it as an end-of-high-school send-off. Nature, hiking, beers, fireside chats. A way for us to be together before we have to finally splinter off."

"Since when are you sentimental?" Amir asked.

"Actually," Noah said, glancing around the room for support, "I was going to suggest we take a trip this summer anyhow, before college starts. My pops keeps encouraging it. He did one with his boys back in the day and he still goes on and on about it."

"Exactly. Plus, to be honest," Evan said, "I could use a trip. I've been locked up for too long in fucking hospitals and rehabs. And I think the mountains would do us all good. Wholesome fun, right?"

"Wait, mountains?" I asked. "You do know this is Florida."

Evan smiled patiently. "Did I forget to mention that the trip is in Georgia?"

"Georgia?" Amir asked. "No. I'm not doing a fourteen-hour drive."

"Okay, so we'll find somewhere closer. That part is no biggie," Noah said delicately. "We'll go somewhere a bit more local. Who needs mountains?"

"We do," Evan said sternly. "Transportation won't be a problem, I assure you. I've taken care of tickets. All you need to do is show up at the airport."

We were quiet, too awkward to answer, until Noah approached Evan and, gingerly, wrapped him in a bear hug. Evan's face at first maintained its natural aloofness, but then, to my surprise, it adopted a thin smile, softening its features. Oliver offered some mildly offensive joke to relieve the tension, and Amir found himself laughing against his will. I remained at the desk. Evan, still being squeezed by Noah, met my eyes and nodded. I nodded back.

—

I SPENT THE NIGHT BEFORE our trip with Sophia. I packed a small meal—several rolls of her favorite sushi, assorted milk chocolates, a bottle of red wine—and snuck her through Noah's backyard into the golf course. It was a gorgeous evening: the wind hardly blowing, the sky a perfect black, sprinkled with faded stars.

"So this is it," Sophia said, a plastic cup of wine in hand, sitting with her knees at her chin, observing the sky, "the calm before the storm, they call it."

"That storm they keep talking about?" I was full now, drowsy, slightly drunk. "Noah said it wasn't real."

"He's probably right. They say it'll be Category One if it hits, but usually these things die out into tropical disturbances. But maybe you'll get your first hurricane! How exhilarating. We can't consider you a proper Floridian until you're baptized by one, you know."

"Yeah, wow, I can hardly contain my excitement." I bit open a packet of M&M's, separated several greens, offered them in the palm of my hand. She snorted, slapping away my hand. I flicked the greens toward a nearby bunker. "When would this hit?"

"Probably never, because we're still a few days away from the first of June. Worried it'll affect your little boys' trip?"

"No." I inched closer, feeling the heat of her body. "I don't want to go that badly anyway."

"Why's that?"

"I just don't."

"Who's forcing you?"

I took the wine, poured myself another cup. "It'll be one of our last times all together for who knows how long. Maybe ever."

She placed her head in the nape of my neck, breathing softly against my chest. I didn't dare move.

"Soph?" I finally asked, after holding my breath for too long.

"Yes?"

"What happens after all . . . this?" Animals chirping from the distance, some far-off hole up the course. "To you and me, I mean?"

Her head angled to the heavens. "Beautiful, isn't it?"

"It is."

"So then let's not think about that tonight."

The moon was full. "It's just that Princeton and Juilliard," I said, "really, we're only a bus ride away."

She lowered herself until her back was on the ground. She grabbed my hand, gently pulled me on top of her.

"Come to prom with me," I said.

She leaned on her elbows, weak moonlight illuminating half of her face. "I'm supposed to go with Evan, you know. He asked me at the end of freshman year, when he was still a child. He gave me a rose. We had our first kiss."

"Right," I said, my cheeks burning with heat. "Yeah, understood, then."

She leaned up toward my face. "But I want to go with you, Hamlet."

I fell forward, kissed her. We sank to the ground, arms and legs intertwined, pale lights above. Thomas Hardy, they say, spent an hour each day staring at the same painting in a local museum to commit everything—color, texture, pigmentation—to memory. This moment, I told myself, would be the painting to which I'd return, that singular burst of beauty and happiness I'd recount day in, day out, for the rest of my life, down to the slightest detail: the texture of her lips, the taste of her mouth, her vanilla scent, night rolling on around us.

—

IT WAS STILL FOGGY WHEN we left. We met outside the Delta terminal, where Evan distributed our first-class tickets. It was a short flight, just over an hour. Evan had a driver waiting when we landed, equipped with camping paraphernalia—a large tent, hydration back-packs, cooking utensils, a flare gun—and a cooler of food and beer. It wasn't a far drive to Horeb, a picturesque stretch of trails within the Blue Ridge Mountains. Our driver confirmed Horeb was an excellent choice: an elevation of nearly four thousand feet, water springs, all sorts of wildlife. "Songbirds, bobcats, coyotes, boars, deer, foxes, black bears," he lectured, "anything you want. You boys like fishing? Because there's quite an aquatic population, some delicious catches."

"Not particularly," Oliver said. "I'm more gatherer than hunter."

"Never mind that. Just get to the top. Lord, that's a view. Some tribes used to hunt there. Iroquois. The Shawnee, too, I think. There's a memorial plaque or something up there. Sacred ground."

There was a shelter, a small wooden shack, at the entrance where we mapped our trail. The kid manning the desk looked our age, perhaps younger. "If you need something," he said with a heavy Southern twang, "you'll give a holler."

Amir frowned. "You expect we'll need something?"

"I was joking," the kid said. "Nobody will hear you anyway."

"Lovely," Amir said, "and what's the deal with the storm?" I glanced out the window at a rich, cloudless sky.

The kid spat dip into an empty water bottle. "Look like a storm to you?"

"No," Amir said, "but I—"

"First time?"

"Camping?" Amir asked. "Yes, actually."

The kid waved us off. "You softies will be fine."

I was surprised by how much I enjoyed the trail, the woods still, forbidding, the air heavy and fresh and filled with the sound of running water and warbling birds. We decided to set camp at the peak. Evan wanted to see stars.

We took several breaks—to eat, to swim in a spring, to give Evan's leg a chance to rest. Evan limped the whole way through and, despite his walking stick, despite his protests, had to be assisted when the incline proved too steep.

"Maybe going to the top isn't the wisest, Ev?" Noah said, after Evan had been forced to retreat to a rock to catch his breath and wait for the pain to subside. "Let's find somewhere a bit more manageable."

Evan popped a blue pill and, wincing, picked himself up again. "Fuck that."

We were worn and sore and ravenous by the time we arrived at the summit. We picked out an isolated spot in a field and set to work pitching our tent. They smoked—I, alone, refrained, just like in the old days, and instead davened ma'ariv off to the side—and then we sat lazily, watching the sky move from blue to harsh steel to violent purple. The wind began picking up.

"Maybe it's coming after all," Oliver said, studying the sky. "That storm."

Evan disappeared into the tent and came out with our food. We roasted hot dogs and tore through snacks—protein bars, marshmallows, extravagant desserts—that Cynthia had sent up with Noah.

"So how we feeling, Ev?" Noah said, passing around frosted cupcakes while Amir set about making s'mores. "Mountain air doing the trick?"

"My stump of a leg feels like absolute shit," Evan said. "But otherwise, yes, actually. Exactly what I needed."

Amir speared a marshmallow. "Who knew you're such an outdoorsman?"

I felt peace in the sudden absence of color above, a sense of order and stillness emanating from the empty fields and ancient trees and astral skies that bled out into the world around us.

"Something about the mountains, I guess," Evan said.

Unmoved by astronomy, unperturbed by the mess on his face, Oliver crammed an entire cupcake into his mouth. "Anybody else feel weird pounding these on a camping trip? Because I feel like woodsmen aren't supposed to eat adorable frosted desserts."

I helped myself to a second. "Nope, they're delicious."

Amir raised his cupcake toward Noah. "Compliments to the chef."

"Don't look at me," Noah said.

"You've never had to cook a thing in your life," Amir said. "I was referring to your rock star mother."

"First of all, I make great pizza bagels, everybody knows that," Noah said. "But no, my momma didn't make these. She makes different cupcakes."

"True," Oliver said, "she makes those chocolate chip ones. They're amazing, better than weed, I swear."

We continued losing light. Night wasn't far off. Evan added another branch to our fire.

"So," Oliver said, "someone should tell a story."

Amir looked my way. "Give us ghost tales from the Old Country."

"All the ones I know are about demons and dybbuks in the time of the Gemara," I said.

"Like that one about pouring seeds on the ground near your bed," Amir said, "so that you can wake up to those chicken footprints that demons have? Spooky stuff. Bet Ev believes in that, huh?"

Evan was busy staring into the fire with enough intensity to infect me with secondhand anxiety. Slowly, he dragged a branch through the flames.

Amir cleared his throat. "Mr. Stark?"

"What?"

"I asked if you believed in demons."

Evan gave a slight smile without turning toward Amir. "Why would I?"

"Ari, give us a dybbuk story," Oliver said. "Frighten me out of my goddamn wits, will you?"

For emphasis I stood. I gathered the strings of my tzitzit in my hands, the way I used to when I was a child. "My first-grade rebbe told this story on an Erev Shabbat, as a treat. I didn't sleep for a week."

"Wonderful," Noah said. "Lay it on us."

"Okay. Once upon a time there was a newly married couple in Chelm."

Oliver sighed. "It's always Chelm, isn't it? The Yidden of Chelm can't stay out of trouble."

"One Motzei Shabbat," I continued, "just after midnight, the wife goes outside into a crazy storm to empty a bucket. When she comes back inside, she's choking, seizing. Her husband asks what's wrong, but when she opens her mouth nothing comes out. They call the doctor, but he's stumped. He can't figure it out, neither can any specialists in the area. So, they head to the rav."

"Love going to the rav," Oliver said, picking at his cupcake. "I do the same thing when I'm constipated."

Amir hurled a marshmallow at Oliver's face. "Shut up for once and let the man finish."

I cleared my throat. "The rav looks her over, consults a Gemara and then whispers into her ear. All of a sudden, a deep, alien voice answers, except the woman's lips aren't moving, though her stomach is swelling, getting bigger and bigger. The rav demands the dybbuk reveal its identity, and the dybbuk obliges, explaining that he was a former yeshiva student who had strayed from the derech. One evening, after hours of drinking, he'd been thrown from a horse, and because he had died suddenly, the dybbuk tells the rav, he never had a chance to repent. So, the rav promises he'll learn Torah in the dybbuk's honor, gathers a minyan, says kaddish and then the woman crumples to the floor, writhing, while the voice booms out the Shema. Her left pinky nail comes exploding off, the glass window in the room shatters and then—silence. The dybbuk is gone."

"Well," Oliver said, soothing his left pinky, "that was . . . kind of a letdown."

Amir laughed. "How did you possibly believe in that stuff?"

"I mean, I was, like, six," I said. "Plus our rebbe never lied."

Noah sandwiched graham crackers, chocolate oozing onto his wrist. "I don't even get the point of that kind of story. What's the lesson?"

Evan twirled a marshmallow through the fire. "That there's mysterious power in the universe."

I shrugged. "Or it's a little more mundane: learn Torah, don't wander and you won't wind up becoming a dybbuk."

"What about you, Ev," Noah said. "Give us something from rehab. Something . . . grittier."

"I don't have anything," Evan said. "I spent my time reading."

"Whatever you were reading was probably a horror story in and of itself," Amir said.

"Yeah," Oliver said, "your books are too damn long."

"Not what I meant," Amir said, rolling his eyes. "But really, you've got nothing? You've exhausted all your weird, little biblical folklores?"

"Sorry," Evan said. "Don't think I can help."

"Wow," Amir said, "guess rehab really kills those Kabbalistic impulses, huh?"

Evan reached for another cupcake. "Well, all but one, really."

Far-off trees respired with the wind. I looked up, readied myself to see stars. I'd Googled the basics two nights before. Find Sirius by sloping left through Orion. Free-fall slightly rightward, about the equivalent of three fists, and find Canopus. "Which would that be?" I asked.

"Levitating?" Amir said. "Or maybe stopping the sun?"

Evan leaned closer to the fire. "You've all heard of vision quests?"

I stared blankly. "As in, Native American rituals?"

"Yes."

A look of disquiet dripped through Amir's face. "What about them?"

"I shouldn't say," Evan said. "You'll call me crazy."

Noah did his best to provide a reassuring half-smile. "We already do."

"Well," Evan said, "let's just say I'm fairly confident that I've gathered enough empirical and theoretical data suggesting they might just work."

Amir snorted. "You're joking."

"It's nothing radical, really," Evan said. "Most cultures believe we benefit by losing ourselves, just for a short while. And we do it all the time, don't we? On Yom Kippur, we fast, we don't shower, we wear white. Why? To leave behind our human body, to pretend we're something else. On Purim, we drink and dress up to do the same. Plato calls it telestic frenzy, Euripides calls it a Dionysian Mystery, Islam calls it Sufism, Hindus call it *avadhuta*, Shamanism calls it a trance state. But at its root? All this stuff's the same."

"And the point," Amir asked, probing his charcoaled marshmallow, its white interior webbing his fingers, "of losing ourselves?"

"To see God, of course," Evan said.

"Come on," Amir said, "let's not start with that weird stuff again, okay? We've had a nice respite from it, haven't we?"

Blind fear woke suddenly in my chest. "Why'd you bring us here?"

"Eden," Evan said, unblinking, unapologetic, "you know I can't do it alone."

"Can't do *what* alone?" Ignored, Amir gave me a stern look. "What's he talking about, Ari?"

I stared directly into the fire. "This isn't some apology retreat," I said. "It's a trap. Another experiment."

"Okay, hold up," Noah said, seeing the way Amir was winding up. "Let's just—let's calm down, yeah? Because honestly—who cares?" He smiled, pulled at his long hair. "I mean, he flew us in first class to a mountain. If the weirdo wants to pretend this is some cultic ritual, I say why not? Indulge him. What difference does it make to us?"

I watched as Evan finished another cupcake, chewing with almost surgical intensity. "The cupcakes," I said. "Where are they from?"

Noah paused. "Wait, what?"

"Enough with the cupcakes!" Amir said. "They're not even that good."

"No, for real, I'm serious," I said. "Who brought them?"

No answer.

"He—he drugged us," I said softly, mostly to myself, feeling suddenly as if I might vomit. "He's going to try and—"

"Eden," Evan said calmly, warningly. "No need to talk ourselves into hysteria."

Amir dropped his cupcake to the ground. "Someone tell me what he's talking about."

Oliver scooped the fallen cupcake and, tearing off the dirtied side, took a greedy bite. "These puppies are laced, aren't they?"

"Ah, okay," Noah said, breaking into a relieved grin, glancing at Evan, "so you sprinkled, what, weed into the cupcakes? Dick move, I'll admit, but a stupid prank. No real harm, right?"

"It isn't weed," I said, "is it?"

Amir extracted marshmallow bits from his palms. "What'd you just say?"

Evan cleared his throat. "If we're to do this properly, the best method to shed the self is through an artificial catalyst."

Now Noah stood, drawing himself to full height, digging his sneakers into the earth. "Evan?"

Evan stared off at what little remained of daylight. "I really do advise we stay calm and do our best to think positively."

"Know what?" Amir said, rolling up his sleeves. "I've just decided I'm going to punch you in the face again."

Noah put a hand on Amir's shoulder. "No one's punching anyone. All right? But Ev, you're going to have to come clean. Let's just, you know, let's talk it out civilly."

Evan gave a regretful smile. "We were having such a lovely time."

"Ev," Noah warned. "For real. We're all your boys, but you have to cut the shit."

Evan didn't bother standing from his spot near the fire. "There are acid hits in the cupcakes."

Amir put his head in his hands. "You're such a piece of . . . please tell me you're lying? Please tell me this is a bad dream or—"

"Had I told you the truth," Evan said, matter-of-factly, as if he were merely explaining the most reasonable thing in the world, "none of you would be here."

Oliver shrugged. "I would've."

"I understand you're angry," Evan said calmly, "but I'm afraid it was necessary."

"Necessary?" Amir started at Evan, but Noah, in an effortless motion, seized him by the arm and restrained him.

"When does it hit?" My voice felt funny now. Did I always sound like this?

Evan massaged his leg. "Can't be sure. Fifteen minutes. An hour. Three hours. Who knows?"

"Okay, here's what we'll do," Amir said, running a hand through his beard, "we should vomit. Like, right now, before it's too late. We'll do it together. On three."

"It's already too late," Evan said, checking his wristwatch. "But feel free to try."

"Call me crazy, but I don't see the big deal," Oliver said. "I've been meaning to get around to LSD for some time now." For effect, he ate the last cupcake.

"This isn't a fucking joke, Oliver," Amir said. "This is—well, this is illegal!"

Oliver scoffed. "Suddenly you're concerned with what's legal?"

Amir wretched, spat, kicked at the ground. "You don't go around slipping people acid! What if something goes wrong? We're in the middle of nowhere, for God's sake."

Noah sat again, flexing his fingers in thought. "Oh, God," he said quietly. "Oh fuck."

A long pause ensued, during which I became conscious of a sort of viscous horror leaking its way through our circle. I looked at the faces of the four people around me. A year ago I didn't know they existed.

"Amir, aren't you at least curious?" Evan said. "Don't you want to see if I've been right?"

Instinctively, I touched my healed arm.

"If you were *right*?" Amir said. "Right about what? That we should've listened to Ari and realized you're off your rocker? That you never should've been allowed out of rehab?"

"Everything." He faced Amir. "Listen. I'm offering you the chance to put aside the entire world, just for a bit, and gain infinitely more. What do you have to lose? You're going to MIT. Your whole life, you've done everything to make your mother happy, your grandfather proud, your father regret leaving. You have everything coming your way, and soon you'll be working your ass off for a decade straight, with no end in sight. Just once, right now, don't you want to do something that—that has the power to frighten you?" He turned to Noah. "Noah Harris, athletic phenom of Zion Hills. Discipline, restraint, devotion for, what, fifteen long years to earn the scholarship your father decided you'd have to win before you were even born? Aren't you just exhausted of it all? And you, Eden, constantly battling yourself, still too scared to let out what you really are, even when you want it just as badly as I do? We're in these . . . these cages our whole damn lives. Don't we want to be free, even once, for a few hours at the very end of childhood? Don't you want to be absorbed in something so much fucking greater?"

Oliver licked the last of the frosting from his thumb. "Guess I'm chopped liver? Where's my pump-up speech?"

"So that's what you're running from?" Amir said, waving his marshmallow stick. "Responsibility? Facing all the shit, good and bad, we need to go through? You're just—you're weak, Ev. Weak and angry and lost. You can't handle life anymore, but know what? The rest of us are doing just fine. You think you live in this, I don't know, this exceptional moral world of secluded pain and wisdom, when the truth is you're just a sad, broken flameout."

It appeared my hand was shaking, even though the panic I felt was almost nonrepresentational, as if my body had at first failed to recognize that what was happening around me was real.

"Ev," Noah said, kindly, firmly, "everyone here is already absorbed in something greater, even if you don't realize it. And that kind of happiness or value or whatever you want to call it isn't something you get by being drugged into a stupor."

"It's not about that," Evan said. "It's about *theia mania*."

Amir threw his stick in Evan's direction. He missed. The stick landed at Evan's feet. "What'd you just say?"

"Divine madness," Evan said. "That's what I want."

"Fuck *you*," Amir said. "Because we don't."

Evan smiled sadly. "I'm afraid it's coming anyway."

—

LIGHT RAIN CAME, WENT. NOBODY spoke much. To pass time we wandered along a trail—through dogwood blossoms, through stunted oak trees, through the range's famous blue haze—until we arrived at a plunging ravine.

"Well," Amir said, eyeing the rocks below, "this seems like a dangerous place to hang out before an acid trip."

Noah shuddered at the sight of the cliff's edge. "Can we please get back to camp?"

I heard rustling in nearby shrubbery. "Is it happening now?"

"No," Evan said.

"How will we know?" I asked.

"You'll know," Evan said.

The noise grew louder, guttural, almost like braying.

"Okay, anyone hear that?" Amir asked. "Or am I hallucinating?"

"Nah," Noah said. "I heard it, too."

Evan limped toward the brushwood.

"Careful," Amir said. "What'd the driver say about bobcats?"

"Bears," Noah corrected.

"Whatever," Amir said. "Could be feral."

"Nope," Evan called from the bushes, "it's just a goat."

"A goat?"

"Someone give me a hand." Nobody stepped forward, so Evan scooped it up himself and stumbled back through the undergrowth, limping it toward the edge. It was only a baby. White, miniature horns had begun to surface on the crown of its head.

My palms tingled, my tongue felt thick against the roof of my mouth. I rolled my head, attempting to snap out of it. "What're you doing?"

"It's a sign," Evan said.

Noah began blinking manic patterns. "Of what?"

"Before Yom Kippur," Evan said, "the Kohen Gadol had a tradition."

"Jesus," Amir said. "Don't say it."

"One for God, one for Azazel," Evan said.

"So where's the second goat?" Noah asked.

Evan pointed to himself. The goat whined, struggling to break free. "Anyone have a quarter?"

Half-formed waves of pain thickened unevenly across my forehead. "What're you talking about?"

"Heads, I take the dive," Evan said. "Tails, it's our friend."

"Right," Amir said, "you'll throw yourself off?"

"One of us has to do it." Evan pointed to the sky. "He'll decide."

"Even joking about that is revolting," Amir said, unable to stop himself from wringing his hands. "Something is seriously wrong with you."

"Talk to the Kohen Gadol, not me," Evan said. "Eden, have a quarter or not?"

Obediently, realizing I was in the gradual process of wafting infinitely far away from myself, I fumbled in my pocket for a coin. "A dime," I said.

"Perfect," Evan said. "Flip it. I've got my hands full."

I was sweating feverishly. Sunset began, the fading light hurting my eyes. I took the coin, tossed it over my head. It landed a few yards behind us.

"Nice arm," Noah said.

Amir retrieved it. "Tails. Lucky you. You're saved."

Evan's lips were moving but he wasn't saying anything.

Noah touched Evan's chest. "You talking to yourself?"

Evan tightened his hold on the goat. "I—I'm not quite sure, actually."

Amir gestured behind us. "And what the hell's with *him*?" At the foot of the shrubbery, walking long, perfect circles, was Oliver, face white as a sheet. "Has he said a word in the last hour?"

Noah approached cautiously. "You okay, man?"

No answer. Oliver continued tracing the circles.

"Think it's hitting," I announced again.

"Stop saying that," Evan said.

Amir studied his hands with a look of incomprehension, as if discovering new appendages. "You really think so? I don't know."

Beams of light danced in my vision. "Yes."

"I'm not sure I like this," Noah said thinly.

"Evan," Amir said suddenly. We'd forgotten he was still holding the goat, which was now thrashing its head side to side, trying its best to gore its captor. "Let it go. Seriously."

Evan blinked in confusion. "I'm sorry."

A treacherous crack above. On cue: the rain.

"Shit!" Amir yelled, suddenly in a panic. "Motherfucking *shit!*"

"Let's get out of here." Noah's eyes moved unnaturally from left to right and back, his golden hair slicked with rain. "We need, um, to go back down the—the path to the tent. Before it hits." He put an arm around Oliver's shoulders, trying to stop him from continuing his orbit.

"Evan!" Amir pulled at Evan's shirt, rain falling harder. "We need to get out of here!"

Evan was shaking. The goat, crying out, squirmed violently, nearly broke free, causing Evan to bend and regain his hold. "It's—I have to do this. We have to pay tribute to enter."

"What the fuck are you—"

Evan hurled the goat from the ravine. An infinite fall: the goat screaming, a small cloud of gravel pitching up. Quivering, I approached the edge, trying to peer down at the remains, and then rain turned to ice, the full weight of nightfall crashing upon my back, Amir's screams morphing into something else, something far-off and inhuman. I staggered; Noah grabbed me before I stumbled off the edge, my vision dimming. And then, the mountains reappearing, throbbing in Technicolor: electric violets, sparks of vermillion, great bursts of azure. The world rearranged itself, dissolving in sliding lights, a bright rumble rupturing my eardrums, days lengthening, collapsing, life screeching on without us.

—

RABBI GLICK HAD A FAVORITE teaching: Torah unfolds thematically, not chronologically. This is useful in relaying what follows. What I saw that night didn't happen linearly, logically, within neat divisions of time. When I dream about it—frequently, always accompanied by night sweats—I do so as I experienced it, in fragments of memories: the smell of fire, endless rain, blood in my mouth, the crunch of wood. Then I wake, leaving one nightmare for the next.

When the whirling stopped I found myself in a place of pure marble. "Where am I?" I called out. Echoes rang around me. Marble floor stretched on for as far as I could make out, a diagonal pattern of gleaming black and white stones, with a row of wooden reading desks, evenly spaced, extending into the distance. No walls, no ceiling.

Evan stepped from the shadows, older, more ragged, clothing torn. He wore a crown of leaves in his hair. Faint spots of red decorated each of his hands. "We're here."

Intense light. Spangles in my field of vision. I blinked rapidly. They didn't subside. "Where's here?"

"The center of the earth," Evan said, hurrying ahead and disappearing from sight.

I turned, finding the others. Noah, in purple robes, stood tall, glowing, his hair dramatically longer and tied into a knot. Amir, bathed in white light, sat on the floor, cheeks in his palm, beard slightly thicker.

"And Oliver?" I asked.

Noah pointed behind me. Oliver, drenched in color, glasses cracked in two, his normally heavily gelled hair entirely disheveled, was staring into a silver mirror—ten feet high, dust-laden, ornately framed. At the top of the frame was a phrase carved in black lettering: PREPARE YOURSELF IN THE ANTECHAMBER, SO THAT YOU MAY ENTER THE BANQUET HALL. At the bottom of the frame, in sapphire, was an odd symbol—a backward, inverted comma hovering above the squiggle of a regular comma. Hebrew letters, I realized: two yuds, one right side up, the other upside down, or perhaps an aleph whose base had been erased, disembodying its top and bottom?

I put my hand to his shoulder. He didn't stir. "Oliver?" I peered into the mirror. There was no reflection, yet on he gazed.

"He won't answer," Amir explained. "Hasn't spoken in hours."

"Hours?" The kaleidoscopic colors were making it difficult to concentrate. I felt a deep searing in my chest. "We've been here for hours?"

"Days, more like it," Noah said. "I think I've been here for days."

The burning traveled to my throat, drying the words in my mouth. "Water," I said, fighting through a coughing fit. "Is there any water?"

Evan rematerialized before me. "Don't ask for water here," he said hurriedly. "Now follow me. We should move quickly while we can."

We were trudging through a great rain, lightning fracturing the deep-black sky, a tower in the distance, animals in my peripheral vision, moving two by two. I was Scipio, lost and small amid the spheres, looking down at Carthage from on high, the universe star-filled and splendid. We walked for ages, beating against the wind, time expanding around us. Evan, walking with a staff, and even so routinely stumbling, led us through a forest, until we arrived at a clearing in the woods. A small circle of trees flanked the mouth of a cave. Evan turned to face us. "In here."

Noah craned his neck for a glimpse inside. "We can't go in *there*. There's no light."

"Where we're going," Evan said, "we don't need light."

"And where's that?" Amir asked. "What's in there?"

No answer. Instead, Evan forged straight into the dark.

For a moment we hesitated, lingering in the storm. We had little choice. We nodded to each other and followed.

We'd entered into an orchard. Trees were lined in careful rows. Luscious fields, everything radiant and green, stretched as far as my eyes could see. Large fruits hung from branches, white flower bulbs bloomed before our eyes. Off to the side was a pond, an enormous boulder at its edge; the boulder had a clean hole at its center through which water dropped from a small spring. In the middle of the grove was a slightly withered tree, before which Evan stood. Noah wandered slowly through flowers, admiring the streak of colors. Amir, off by the brook, was on his knees, gazing into the water, a thin mist in the distance. I realized that the rain was gone, that I was dry again, that a thick layer of warmth flooded my senses and relieved my thirst. Old memories ran through me: learning to ride a bike, wrapping tefillin for the first time, my fifth birthday party, my father inscribing my first Gemara, reading my Princeton acceptance letter, sounding out *Corduroy's Busy Street* with my mother, kissing Sophia that night at the beach. I staggered about, as if tipsy, as if arriving home from a long, cruel voyage.

"Amir has the right idea." Evan broke away from the center tree, over whose bark he'd been tracing his fingers. "We'll need to get in the water."

"Evan," I said, "Oliver's gone."

Evan didn't move from the tree.

Noah hurried back through the flowers. "Oliver didn't come in here, did he?"

"We need to find him," I said. "We can't leave him out there."

Noah frowned, examining his purple robes. "Out where?"

"I don't know." I paused to think. "Near the mirror? In the storm?"

"The storm's gone," Amir chimed in, unflustered, still glued to his reflection, his nose hovering over the surface of the water.

"In here it's gone," I said desperately, pivoting in place. "Not out there."

"You see this, then?" Evan asked, walking up to us. "All of you can?"

"I'll look for him," Noah said. He spoke weakly, as if struggling to wake from a trance. "I'm going back out."

"No," Evan said, "he's perfectly fine. But he needs to be alone."

"What're you talking about?" I said. "He could be—"

Evan shook his head. "It affects us all differently. Leave him. It's important we four remain together. Really, you have to trust me."

Laughter erupted from my lips, laughter I've never heard before. "Trust *you*?"

"He's fine, I promise," Evan said. "But swear you won't leave the orchard. It's dangerous."

Noah squinted. "How's it dangerous?"

"Leaving now means never coming back."

"Okay, then," Noah said, "fine, I swear."

I walked up to the foot of the water. I could see my reflection. I thought I looked handsome, but also as if I'd aged several years. My complexion was rough with stubble, my eyes dark, tired. I had short, neat hair, a gaunt face. The longer I looked, the more I resembled an only slightly younger version of my father. "Amir, you all right?"

"Yeah," Amir said, tearing his eyes from the water. He gave me his hand. I helped him to his feet.

"Amir. Eden," Evan said. "You need to swear you won't go back out there."

"Enough already," Amir said. "I swear it."

"Eden?"

Looking at Evan, studying his scar, I knew whatever connection I still held to my old life was ending. The mostly silent boy, perched in the back row of Rav Glick's shiur in Brooklyn, New York, the one busy contemplating how best to escape beautiful things he didn't yet understand, was now gone. "I swear," I said.

"Good," Evan said. "Now we need to bathe." Carefully, he peeled off his clothing and, strolling past us, submerged himself. *Behold Nachson*, I thought. *First into the Red Sea*. We did the same, wading naked into the water.

Amir, nude, startled-eyed, stood at the edge. "I'm not going in. It's—I can't."

Evan drifted back toward the edge. "You'll have to, if you want to see it."

It was the first time I'd witnessed Amir regard Evan not with defiance, not with impatience, not with contempt, but with fear. "See what?"

Evan pushed off from the edge. "You know the answer." Amir, in turn, walked straight into the water.

"Hold your breath half a minute," Evan said. "Then meet at the tree."

The water was frigid, immediately sapping all feeling from my extremities. Underwater, I opened my eyes. Evan was staring directly at me.

When we emerged we were dry again, even before we had our clothing back on. Blood returned to my face. Feeling returned to my fingertips.

"I don't suppose anyone is hungry." Evan plucked a pomegranate from the tree—small, slightly crowned, a deep, rich crimson—and handed it to me. "One bite," he said. "Just one."

I took a mouthful, passed it to Noah. Sharp, sour, an explosion of juice. I spat the seeds, wiped my mouth with the back of my hand. The fruit made its way from Noah to Amir and back to Evan, who took the final bite, a stream of red bleeding down his chin.

Then: a stirring around us. Overhead, a whisper. The flowers swayed; the twigs beneath my feet snapped in unison. Over the water hovered a dark shape.

Amir retreated several feet. "What the hell is that?"

The dark shape fluttered gently. I had the distinct impression that the darkness was breathing, that it had been all along, waiting patiently while shards splintered and grass withered and flowers faded, while lifetimes expired and empires ended and families imploded, while man-made dreams dissolved. *If Isaiah were right*, I thought, *if God created not a wasteland but a habitation, then how to sanctify the sorrow of human life?* The darkness began moving, steadily, in our direction. I felt a hand on my shoulder. Evan, pushing me aside, stepped forward, presenting himself to the void without form.

"Evan," Noah said urgently, somewhere behind me, "get away from that thing."

I heard the sound of roaring waters, death laced with life. The darkness continued to approach, gaining speed.

"Evan!"

In the final moment before the darkness reached him, Evan snapped, turning back toward us, trying to run. Noah, Amir and I broke into a full sprint. We were only several yards ahead of Evan— Noah leading, Amir and I trailing—but Evan, with his shattered leg, was hopeless. I heard his scream; I craned my neck to watch the darkness overtake him, lost my footing, face-planted. I tried getting to my knees, the darkness approaching, nearly over me, only to discover the flare gun, which had rolled some yards ahead from where Evan's backpack landed. I grabbed the flare and, as darkness descended, launched it above my head.

The shot sailed upward for some time, a bright-orange comet impaling infinite space, a lesson in broken relativity, before losing steam and arcing downward. It fell from dewy morn to spectral eve, crumpling in an explosion of color, raining electric-neon yellows and reds.

Amir was running toward me. "What happened?" Noah raced ahead to grab Evan, who was crawling on all fours, gasping for air. "What—"

From the heavens approached a cloud of fire, within which stood a figure I couldn't make out. It looked, at first, like the *Vitruvian Man* given wings, until I realized it had four faces: a human face at the front, the face of a lion on the right, the face of an ox on the left, the face of an eagle on the back. The figure expanded, growing larger, larger, filling our atmosphere, spinning in circles. My heart stopped; its faces were now completely human: one was mine, one was Evan's, one was Noah's, one was Amir's. These faces blinked, wept, in unison. From the center of the cloud came forth lightning, and then a whirlwind.

"Blow!" Evan was on his knees now, his scar glowing. "Rage, you fucking cataracts and hurricanes . . ."

Heaps of broken images. A corpse, a lion, a donkey. Dogs eating dogs. Holding my mother's hands, walking through the ruins of Jerusalem. Sunsets, groves, oceans, summer solstices, olive trees. Bulls slaughtered on altars. Foxes running, tails aflame. Fire encircling

our town, every tree, every house, every hill. Water to blood, hail to
fire. Red doorposts, the great transgressor, the cries of mothers. A
mountain above us: we will do, we will do. Many ladders. Going up,
going down. A land of draught. Death's beautiful shadow. Cain killing Abel; Joseph pleading from the pit. Years melting: my parents
buried their parents, I buried my parents, strangers buried me. Sea-
sons, decades, centuries, eons. We four clasped hands, blurred into
one, the knowledge of everything coming together, the loft of vision,
the divine image.

I was seated in a grand, deserted hall. Everything white, clean,
gleaming. The ceiling extended as far as I could see, like some futur-
istic amphitheater. I was alone, wearing a black tuxedo, in the middle
of a row, thousands of unoccupied seats around me. At the front of
the room was a stage with white curtains. On the right wall I noticed
a framed painting: a castle, leaning drunkenly into the sea, engulfed
by a storm. Dark colors, a swirl of lighting, clouds smudged with gray,
ragged cliffs, a ship in the distance.

"Ticket, please." A small voice in my left ear. At my side a toddler
stood impatiently, hand extended. He wore a conductor's hat. His
name tag read DANIEL.

"What?"

"Your ticket, if you would." He took out a pocket watch, swore
under his breath and then returned it to his coat. "We're on a tight
schedule."

I reached into my breast pocket to find a white ticket. ROW 7 SEAT
25. A sentence in Greek was engraved on the bottom. I handed him
my ticket, which he punched and returned. "Keep this on you," he advised. "You don't want to lose it."

"What's it say?"

"Pardon?"

"The Greek," I said. "I can't read it."

"Most people don't ask."

"You can't tell me?"

He hesitated. "A deep distress hath humanized my Soul."

A more familiar voice from behind us: "Thought I'd find you here." The boy and I turned toward the entrance. Walking down the aisle was Evan, his wreath replaced with a white dinner jacket. His limp was gone, his scar was gone. I couldn't tell whether he was addressing the boy or me.

The boy looked to the ground. "You shouldn't be here." Still, Evan took the seat to my right. "You don't have a ticket."

"Of course I do," Evan said, taking one from his breast pocket. "Just not for here, it seems."

"You're not staying, then?" I asked Evan.

He shook his head. "No, sadly. I have another viewing to attend."

"Really," the boy insisted, "you mustn't linger. It's imperative we begin promptly."

"I'll be only a moment," Evan said.

"How do you know him?" I asked. "Daniel?"

"I don't. Not really." The painting on the wall caught Evan's eye. He pointed, chuckling softly. "You could've had anything and you chose that?"

"I didn't choose anything," I said. "I don't even know what it is."

"*Peele Castle in a Storm*," the boy chimed in. "Beaumont."

"I suppose it suits you," Evan said.

The lights dimmed.

"Think that's my cue." Evan stood again. "Best of luck, Eden." He took the boy by the hand and led him toward the entrance. The curtains rose. A long, flimsy screen descended onstage.

"Not what we did shall be the test when act and will are done," boomed a voice from within the orchestra pit. The screen began to glow. A pale orb. Two eyes, blinking in unison. A nose. Lips. My face. "But what our Lord infers we would had we diviner been." Darkness. My film began. Nothing but a thin, still sound.

—

I WAS FACE-FIRST IN THE GROUND. For some time I blinked at darkness. My lips were cracked; I crawled, I breathed dirt, my palms bled. Eventually, after what seemed like hours, I managed to stand. The storm had passed. I stumbled, dizzied, phantom pain pulsing in my right arm. I cringed in the too-bright sunlight, waiting for my eyes to adjust. I was in the fields near our tent, the ground uprooted. Large, splintered oak trees littered the floor, along with scattered debris: wood, garbage, a dead red fox. I tried screaming, nothing came out. I waited for the first wave of panic to subside, wondering how long I'd been out, whether the others had left without me. *I sure should see / Other men here: but I am here alone.*

I began walking, searching for clues. "Noah!" I called madly. "Evan! Amir! Oliver!" Echoes.

I walked for half an hour until I found Oliver. He was sitting on a boulder, head in hands. His glasses were beside him, snapped evenly in two. For the first time, I realized how rail-thin and diminutive he was. He looked, in this moment, nearly emaciated.

"Oliver." I hobbled toward him. He didn't look up. "Oliver," I said, sitting beside him, "you all right?"

He raised his head. "Ari."

"Yes?"

"I can't see."

"Figured," I said, looking again at his glasses. "Your glasses are—"

He shook his head. "My eyes."

"What do you mean?"

"They're not working."

"I don't know what you're—"

"Ari, there's no light, there's, I . . . I'm blind!"

"What?"

"I'm fucking blind, I can't see shit, I—"

"No, okay, hold on a second," I said, breathing strangely, leaning toward his eyes as if I knew to examine for something, "I can help. There's got to be an explanation, right? Maybe you have dirt or, like, I don't know, a splinter? Let me—"

"A splinter? You think I have a fucking splinter? Eden, I'm telling you I literally cannot see anything."

Think rationally, I told myself. Ward off the onset of panic. Recognize that foreign chemicals still coursed violently through your bloodstream. Determine whether this was imaginary, still part of the hallucination. Pray this was part of the hallucination. "Oliver," I said, despairing at the sound of my own choking voice, "where were you? Why didn't you go in with us?"

He faltered over a rock. I steadied him. "Go in where?"

"The cave," I said impatiently, "leading into the—"

"All I remember is seeing bronze gates," he said unhappily, "and then not being able to see anymore." He put his hands to his knees. His face was streaked with earth. "Someone was there with me."

"Which one of us?"

"A stranger. Wearing tefillin."

"Tefillin?" I paused. "Then of course it was one of us. Who the hell else would have tefillin out here?"

"I didn't bring. Neither did Noah or Evan or Amir."

"I did."

"Were you wearing them last night?"

"No, but—"

He tried walking again. I stopped him. "I don't understand what you're saying," I said. "How could—what do you even think any of this means?"

"I don't know what anything means. All I'm saying is what I saw."

"Okay," I said frantically, allowing our limping to continue onward, "okay, so let's just think for a second, let's piece this together. We can fix this, right? We can—right, so you saw a guy wearing tefillin and then . . . so what happened then?"

"I told you, the lights went out."

"You mean the acid kicked in."

"I'm hallucinating blindness right now, too, then?"

I was silent.

"It was real," he said. "Something I wasn't supposed to see."

—

WE WANDERED. WE FOUND TREES snatched cleanly from the earth, roots intact, teeth marks in bark, carvings in the ground. We considered giving up on finding the others and devised an alternative plan: I'd leave Oliver somewhere relatively secure and go directly for help, making my way back to the entrance, a trek I knew would take most of the day. Then we heard wailing.

Oliver, ears perched, desperate for direction, shot his arm northward. "Over there."

We climbed through a thicket into a field, expecting to find another goat. Instead we found Amir, hunched over, drenched in mud, inconsolable. Beside him sat Evan, chin at his knees, clothing torn, hair clotted with blood.

"What in the—" I sat Oliver on a boulder. Amir and Evan weren't speaking. I wasn't certain they even realized I was there. "What . . . what happened?"

Evan didn't answer. Eyes unfocused, he gazed several yards past me, toward the lone tree in sight. Amir, still sobbing, attempted to speak, but managed only paroxysms of unintelligible half-words.

"Amir," I said. Vertigo deepened in my skull. I felt, all at once, unsteady on my feet, confused as to where the ground ended and mental phenomena began, the physical reality of my body glaringly incompatible with the physics of the world around me. "You have to talk to me."

Amir grabbed my collar, pulled my face toward his own. He was convulsing. Unformed grief took hold in his eyes. "We need help, Ari, I don't think we can save him—"

"What? Save who? I—" I tried shaking Amir off. "Amir, save who?"

Without looking my way, Evan raised his arm and pointed toward the tree. "He's there."

"What's happening?" Oliver thrashed about, almost as if his body were seizing. "Ari, what the fuck's happ—?"

Slowly, I approached the tree, a sugar maple. Greenish-yellow flowers bled softly from the branches, falling gently on a body resting at its roots. Noah was lying on his back. His eyes were open, staring up at the sun. His mouth was closed, his enormous arms crossed over his chest, his legs straightened. His long, blond hair was ragged, but with no evidence of blood. He looked, really, as if he were only sleeping, if not for his eyes, frozen in beatific terror.

I took a single step back. My vision swam, my breathing came with labor. Despair, a violent, all-encompassing despair, the sort I imagine precedes the end of normalcy, the end of clarity, the end of happiness, introduced itself to every cell in my body. I couldn't tell whether I was cold or hot, sitting or standing, speaking or silent, sentient or dreaming, dead or alive.

A comforting deafness pressed itself temporarily against the world. I wanted this numbness to persist, I would've given anything to remain in that anesthetized half-life. Then I heard the sound of Amir moaning, of Oliver crying out as he lost his footing and fell to the ground, and with that I knew the world had returned to me. We had no cellphone reception, I thought with strange lucidity, we had no other flare guns, we were hours from the entrance to the trail, we had no fellow campers in sight. I kneeled, finally, over Noah's body and felt for the pulse I knew wasn't there.

"No use." Evan appeared behind me. "He's gone."

I tried, desperately, pumping Noah's chest without knowing what I was doing.

"Ari," Evan said hoarsely, "leave him."

I keeled over, sick. After some heaving, sweat pouring from my face, I looked back at Evan. "You did this."

His gaze was off in the distance, somewhere in the miles and miles of green forest, in the blue mountaintops that floated, tenderly, into a mist of pale clouds.

"You killed him," I said.

He turned to me. His eyes were dark and eerie, sliding in and out of focus. "Don't." His voice hardly constituted a whisper. "Please."

I launched myself. We fell, rolled. I threw punches, most of which he deflected, though several landed effectively enough, allowing me the satisfaction of feeling the pressure of his skull against my bleeding knuckles. Evan wouldn't strike me. Instead, when I wouldn't stop, he grabbed my fists and, in one fluid motion, threw me on my back. I craved the pain, I let it build—in my arm, in my back, in my head—before I forced myself upright. Evan was already standing, though his leg appeared to be threatening to buckle. Oliver, lying helplessly on the ground where I'd left him, had been reduced to incoherent screaming as he pounded his fists into dirt. Amir, regaining himself, had rushed over at the sight of our wrestling. He stood between us, arms extended weakly, breaking us up, and so I nodded and pretended to limp back toward the tree. When Amir's hands fell to his knees, when I noticed Evan doubled over, I charged again to take him by surprise. This time, Evan swung, in self-defense, and connected with my face. There was a loud, beautiful crack. I went horizontal. All of the ugliness in the world went with me.

JUNE

The Sages taught: When the Temple was destroyed for the first time, many groups of young priests gathered together with the Temple keys in their hands. And they ascended to the roof of the Sanctuary and said: "Master of the Universe, since we did not merit to be faithful treasurers, let the keys be handed to You." And they threw them upward, and a kind of palm of a hand emerged and received from them. And the young priests jumped and fell into the fire.

—Ta'anit 29a

The helicopter found us, rushed us to a small, local hospital. The medics told us it was Thursday: we'd arrived at Horeb on Tuesday, and somehow Wednesday was gone. I remember rousing momentarily, just as we took off. The pilot muttered about how the area looked like Sodom and Gomorrah, overturned.

Curious prodding ensued at the hospital. I received stitches. Evan's leg was in rough shape. Oliver's vision still hadn't returned. Amir was untouched, save for minor bruises. We were each treated for dehydration and trauma.

They were baffled by Noah's death. They were running tests, they claimed, they should know more soon. Theories formed, interrogations followed. What kind of LSD? Had he fallen ill? Where did we find shelter during the storm? Their last question, presented with lowered voices, made me nauseous: did I suspect foul play?

One by one, our parents flew up. What happened to their boys? Why didn't the doctors know anything? Another IV in my veins, I heard from down the hall what I'd been dreading most: the sonic cry of Noah's mother and father.

In my own room, my mother retreated from me, her body crumpled against the door. "How could you do this to us?" She asked this several times, eliciting nothing but silence. My father, beside her, wept into his hands.

—

NOAH WAS ALL ANYONE IN Zion Hills spoke about. People wept openly in the streets, in the butcher, in shul. I was reminded, all the while, of the way I thought of Noah when I'd first moved to town: hero, marvel, everyone's favorite son.

Nasty rumors circulated, too. By the time we returned home, we were no longer victims in the public eye. They found LSD in our systems, weed in our belongings; our stories conflicted radically, even the parts we weren't frightened to share. The truth—that we didn't know what happened, that we had no explanation for Oliver's onset of blindness or Noah's death—was beside the point. TRAGIC TEENAGE CULT, one headline read. ACID TRIP KILLS BASKETBALL STAR. Allegations became increasingly outrageous: group sex, animal sacrifice, colonizing the forest, conspiring to murder Noah.

The difficulty with that last theory, of course, was the continued failure to diagnose Noah's death. There'd be no autopsy, Cynthia decided, despite the protests of the police and the hospital, as it'd be a desecration of the human body under Jewish law. There were no clear signs of trauma. It didn't seem as if he'd overdosed. There were no traces of poison, no signs of violence. It was shocking, it was heartbreaking, it was grotesque and it remained unanswerable: the death of Noah Harris was a medical mystery.

Late Thursday night, Eddie Harris knocked on my front door. My heart endured a glacial plunge. I thought, at first, he'd come to confront me, to shake me until at last I provided real answers. But Eddie was gentle, disoriented, half-shaven, scarcely capable of concentrating on full sentences. He looked as if he'd been tranquilized, and I realized he likely was.

"Ari," he said, refusing to cross the threshold of my doorway, pawing at his eyes, "Ari, what am I going to do? What are any of us going to do?"

"I know," I said. "I know."

"This was my little boy, Ari. This was the . . . the absolute pride of my existence."

"Eddie," I said, the words forming too slowly in my mind, my surroundings sterile now and out of focus, "you should know he was the single greatest person I've ever met."

He cried, which in turn made me cry. We cried together, standing at my doorway.

"I came here to ask—" My head was on his shoulder. I was prepared in that moment to submit myself: for questioning, for capital punishment, for anything that might possibly diminish Eddie's grief. "You don't know how much my boy valued your friendship," he said, wiping at his face, "and Cyn and I adore you, adore your parents. And, well, we want you to know we don't blame you for what happened, for whatever happened out there and . . . Noah was always going on about what a freaking genius you were, a, uh, a real wordsmith. He always insisted that, did you know?" Eddie lowered his voice, released me from his grip. "Would you speak at the funeral? Would you do that for us?"

I told him it'd be an honor. We shook hands. I felt sick.

—

THAT NIGHT I DREAMT OF NOAH. I was sitting in a lecture hall when suddenly he came ambling down my row, muttering apologies as he climbed over legs, targeting the seat to my right. He wore his usual smile, despite the fact that his blond hair was streaked with twigs and luminescent dust.

"Sorry to drop in unannounced," he said, sinking beside me. His voice was unchanged. His left eye, I noticed, had turned a slightly lighter shade of green than his right.

We shook hands. "I didn't expect to see you for quite some time," I said.

"How long has it been?"

"Only a few weeks."

"That's right." He slung an arm around the back of my chair. "Still getting the hang of the whole time zone conversion thing." Someone in the row ahead turned, delivering a glare. We nodded our apologies.

"How long can you stay?"

He checked his wristwatch. "Till dawn breaks. Can't really miss my shift."

"I—I don't understand," I said, lowering my voice. "How'd you get here?"

"Alone. They make you go alone."

"They do?" And then, furrowing my brow: "That's not what I meant."

"I got here the same way I got there in the first place."

"Fine, never mind that. What's it like there?"

"Well, it's pretty damn busy," he said. "Not much time for yourself, not much privacy. Good intramural leagues, though. You'll never believe who's on my team."

"Who?"

"Afraid I can't reveal that." And then, leaning forward, dropping his voice: "But let's just say our power forward once gave a pretty rousing spiel in Gettysburg." He winked and put a finger to his lips.

"Can you—" I paused, leaned closer. "Can you tell me about God?"

"What about Him?"

"What's He like?"

Noah sighed. "Always with the questions, Ari. Don't you enjoy some mystery?" When I shook my head he pointed to the front of the hall, at the lecturer onstage. A familiar figure—small, scrawny, no older than eight—was on his tiptoes, scratching equations on the blackboard. I raised my brows in surprise. Noah laughed, doubling over, gasping for air, and then I woke.

—

THE FUNERAL WAS LATE AFTERNOON, right before Shabbat. They picked a plot in the center of Grove Street Cemetery, next to where Cynthia's father, Noah's namesake, was buried. There was a service first in the chapel—cramped, heavily carpeted, dimly lit—in which everyone fought for seats. It was unimaginably crowded, standing room only. I sat, with my parents, toward the front, near the Samsons and Bellows. The Starks hadn't come.

It was a long service. Noah's older sister, a senior at UCLA, had a difficult time relaying much between sobs. Rabbi Bloom, when he went, stressed that "Noah Harris was the embodiment of *lev tov*, a good heart to which all clung." Extemporaneously, Rocky stood to speak, only to insist that Noah was the most impressive athlete handed to the Jewish people since Sandy Koufax.

When it was my turn, I walked slowly to the lectern, glancing at the coffin beside me before turning to the crowd. I could see people waiting outside the chapel, unable to gain entry. My gaze moved from Oliver, in his dark shades, to Amir, mournful and, shockingly, shorn of his beard, to Sophia, her delicate crescent of a face formerly but no longer the answer to every question I'd ever posed. I cleared my throat, too loudly, into the microphone, fumbled for the mostly incoherent notes I'd scribbled when I couldn't sleep. Sophia, her arm around Rebecca, eyed me sadly.

"'*Who mourns for Adonais?*'" A rush of disassociation: I gripped the lectern, lifted my head to the crowd. Undifferentiated faces blinked at me, faces of a world reduced abruptly to anonymity and flickering movements and indistinguishable forms of private sorrow. "Today, in this nightmare, we mourn Noah, our Adonais. Eulogizing his dear friend John Keats, the poet Percy Shelley wonders why it is we dread waking from this dream of life. Beyond this world, Shelley claims, awaits peace. Here, however, 'tis we who are '*lost in stormy visions*,' we who '*decay / Like corpses in a charnel*.' If this is the case, then what is it that . . . that shatters us in these moments?"

The other time I'd been to this cemetery, I realized, was with Noah. Several hundred yards away, Caroline Stark rested in the earth. "The day I met Noah Harris," I said, voice choking slightly, "happened to be the day I met the first true friend I've ever made. It would be impossible, really, for me to overstate the extent to which his kindness had a profound impact on me." Oliver's unseeing eyes were on the floor. Amir glared in my direction. Why had I ignored his calls, why had I pretended to be asleep when he arrived at my house the previous day? He needed a friend, I needed him, but whatever instinct it is that makes us crave human connection had gone quiet within me, despite my desperation to switch it back on.

"The meraglim, sent forth by Moses to scope out the land of Israel, encounter the Nephilim, the titanic sons of Anak. *Va'nihee vi'anaynu ka'chagavim vi'chane hayinu b'aynayhem*, the spies report. *We were grasshoppers in our sight, and so we were in their eyes, too.* Noah, we all well know, was a giant. To look up at Noah was to be reminded of your own size—in physical stature, doubtless, but also in empathy, in kindness, in all that combines to make an unfailingly good human being. And yet, for all his greatness, never did Noah even once allow himself to look down upon others. Noah, instead, was a person who respected and protected his friends at all times. More than anyone else I know, he was capable of fitting into all situations, he was a person who never once had a cruel word to say about anyone else, he was a person who insisted, even when others wouldn't, even when— well, even when I wouldn't, on maximizing only the good in someone, despite . . ." I dropped a page of my notes, paused to retrieve it from the floor, noticed the words no longer made sense, entire sentences unraveled. "Despite evidence to the contrary. And so . . . I'll always remain grateful"—I coughed into the microphone, trying to make sense of what happened to my life—"even if I'll always be puzzled, that someone like Noah Harris decided to take me under his wing. I don't think anyone can understand fully what it was for an outsider to walk into a room, any room, with Noah as a friend and feel a sense of comfort and security that the person who lights up everyone around them suddenly—"

Surges of color, strange geometrical disturbances. I blinked, I steeled myself against these intrusions of hallucinatory light. From my peripheral vision, I noticed Evan snaking through bodies, tears bleeding to his scar. In those eyes, I'd seen many things before: I'd seen vengeance, I'd seen bereavement, I'd seen a strange sort of deadness, I'd seen pride, I'd seen rage. Now, however, I saw only an inhuman blaze. Even from the podium, even before the crowd, I knew he was allowing me to see this so that I'd know nothing remained in him. I stared for a moment, and then he retreated, hobbling through the exit.

"What I want to say, I suppose," I said, snapping back to myself. I knew what the crowd was thinking, I knew they were right: my friend's death was our fault, my fault. I didn't deserve to be up here. Perhaps I didn't even deserve to be alive. I folded whatever was left of my speech into my pocket. "More than anything right now, I want to feel what Shelley ultimately describes—some great upsurge of all-encompassing beauty, a *fire for which we all thirst*' that connects us, that sustains us with love. I want to believe that hovering above us is something unshakably true, or at the very least something that's . . . I don't know, cathartic. Something that makes sense of what's happened, even if it resists human comprehension. But it's just—" My voice broke, it appeared. I waited for tears; tears didn't come. "Kierkegaard deems Hashem's inability to communicate with mankind 'infinitely deeper than sorrow.' But that sorrow reciprocates. We strive, each day, to live connected to God, and yet in this moment, when our need for Him is greatest, He feels most distant. And that's why we fear death, isn't it? Because Shelley's only partially right: there is a fire after which we forever chase, it never really leaves us, but no longer does it fortify. It's at death that we understand, finally, that the fire is meaningless, that God is incommunicable. Sometimes, devastation is—I don't know, shapeless, maybe. Sometimes we admit we have no real answers. Today, in truth, I have nothing left."

—

MOVING FROM UNTRUTH TO TRUTH, Leo Strauss taught, was not a transition of joy but of "unrelieved darkness." Such was the period following Noah's death. Prom was canceled. Our senior trip to D.C. was canceled. Our hard-earned district playoff game was forfeited, Rocky unwilling to stomach the slaughter we'd receive without Noah. Entire days were spent confined to my bedroom, diseased with a spiritual self-revulsion I felt wholly and unremittingly. I skipped the mandatory practice session leading up to graduation. Amir continued leaving frantic messages, though mostly I ignored him. Sophia called, I called back, we never spoke. I heard from nobody else. I scarcely ate, I endured cold sweats and spiked temperatures and fever visions: piano notes, inaudible whispers, amphitheaters. My surroundings turned black-and-white. I sat on the floor of my room, back to the wall, facing the door, knowing in my heart I could no longer hope to recognize what might prove beautiful or lasting.

—

ENTIRE NIGHTS PASSED CHANGELESSLY, my conscience deformed, lost somewhere in the dark ceiling. *I've seen divinity face-to-face*, Jacob mused, after wrestling the angel, *and yet my life has been preserved.* Did he, did Abraham, did Isaac, did anyone ever really carry on with normal life after communing with God, or did they, too, find reality derailed? When I did drowse, I dreamt of gardens and whirlwinds and letting Evan drown. These dreams always ended the same way: with Oliver, Amir and me forming a circle around a body. After too many nights of such torture I could endure no more. Ambien, Sonata, Restoril—anything I could get my hands on. They worked well enough when mixed with vodka, hurling me into dreamless states of unconsciousness. And this was all I wanted: the bliss of oblivion.

—

AGAINST MY WILL, I ATTENDED graduation. "You're too close to entering some—" I was in bed, my mother before me, hand over her mouth. "I don't want to say it, Aryeh, I don't, but you're heading for a kind of . . . unsalvageable depression, God forbid." I was forced upright, I was dressed, I was in the car, I was onstage. It was joyless, the ceremony. Oliver didn't attend, neither did Evan. When Rabbi Bloom called my name, he scarcely made eye contact as he handed me my diploma. A memorial video was shown in Noah's honor. A new award, presented to the graduating senior best embodying the athletic, interpersonal and moral achievements of Noah G. Harris, was given to Amir.

"Congratulations," I said, after the ceremony concluded. I stood with Amir in the corner of the ballroom, near a table bearing salads, challah rolls, cold cuts.

Amir had the award tucked under his right arm. "Where *the fuck* have you been, Ari?"

"Nowhere," I said. "I've been nowhere."

"You just don't answer calls?"

"I answer some, don't I?"

"Barely."

"I know, I'm sorry, it's just . . . the truth is, I almost feel like we shouldn't be speaking," I said. "And I know this is fucked, I do, really, but it's—maybe we're not supposed to fall back into anything resembling normalcy? Maybe we're not entitled to anything that even somewhat looks like . . . regular life? I don't know. Does that—do you know what I mean at all?"

"No, I don't know what you—" Amir paused as Donny walked by to fix his plate. He nodded, warily, in our direction. We nodded back. We were used to this. Everyone avoided us. "You and I, we're the last ones standing. Speaking is *necessary*, you understand me? It doesn't mean we're forgetting . . . what happened. It just means—it means we need each other, because who the hell else is there?"

I touched my eyes. "Where's Oliver?"

"Not in great shape," Amir said. "I talked to his mom for a while yesterday. She said he's still with all these specialists who can't figure out why he's so unresponsive to different therapies. I think they're really starting to worry that it's, you know, that it's permanent."

I saw my parents lingering near the exit, anxious to leave. Rabbi Bloom had already disappeared, eager as he was to avoid Amir and me. Sophia, on the other side of the room, stood with her back my way, accepting congratulations from a crowd of parents. "And—Evan?"

"I mean, I've tried," Amir said. "Haven't seen him or heard from him at all."

"Not since the funeral, you mean?"

"What? No, he had the audacity to skip the funeral, remember? And you'd know how I feel about that if you maybe ever answered the fucking phone."

"Wait, but," I said, "I—I saw him there, just for a second. When I was speaking."

Amir frowned. "What are you talking about?"

"Yeah, I—he darted out as soon as we made eye contact."

"No," Amir said, "I *really* don't think he was there. He's been totally incommunicado—"

"Amir." Suddenly I was hot around the neck. "I'm telling you I saw him."

"Right." Amir clenched his clean-shaven jaw, looked at me strangely. He was rather dignified beardless, I thought. A new person. "Right, okay, then. It's just—well, Ev's been hiding, you know, since Bloom axed him."

"What?"

"I thought you knew. Again, I only left you, what, three voicemails about it?"

"I didn't—"

"Evan's expelled, Ari."

I didn't care why Evan was out while we were permitted to graduate. Maybe Evan had told Rabbi Bloom the truth. It didn't matter. "He's the one who deserves the worst," I found myself saying, my voice rising. "He's the . . . Evan's the cause of all our—"

Amir nodded behind me. I turned: Sophia was waiting, still wearing her cap and gown. A scarlet tassel, signifying her status as valedictorian, hung below her eye, just where Evan's face featured a scar.

"Hi," she said, after Amir left. She wore no makeup. She raised a plastic cup to her lips. I noticed it was empty.

"Sophia."

"You're a hard person to get on the phone."

"You're the same way," I said.

"I think we've been evading each other," she said.

"Yeah," I said, "maybe that's true."

"Well, I want to tell you that you spoke beautifully. At the—at his funeral, I mean."

What had it been like wearing a face nobody remembered? What had it been like not thinking about the moral fissure dividing who we were from who we envisioned we'd grow up to be? "Oh."

"I think he'd —" Sophia pursed her lips, remembered how to smile. "I *know* he'd be immensely proud, Hamlet."

Outside, floodlights punctured the darkness of the soccer fields. Human beings, I decided, need crowns of mourning, not veils of ignorance. Why pretend we don't know our station? Why pretend we don't know living demands grief, and grief requires submission, and it is only submission that ensures humanness? I kept staring out through the window. Whatever drifted outside, in those fields, had found its way inside.

She said: "We should probably, finally, talk."

"Okay," I said, "let's talk."

"Sophia?" Mr. Winter approached; I received a cautious glance. "We should head out if we're . . . going to make that dinner reservation."

She nodded, he stalked off. "I get the sense he's heard about me," I said, once we were alone again.

"Yes, well, everyone has, Hamlet."

What I wanted to say was: I wish I were erased. What I said instead was: "Yes, I know."

—

REBECCA CAME TO SEE ME that night. "I want to give you one more chance to come clean," she said. She refused to come inside, so we went for a walk down the very street she traversed every Friday night with Noah, the very street on which they shared their first kiss, the very street she figured her children would roam in a not unimaginably distant future. "Everyone tells me to sever ties, you know. But it doesn't feel right. I don't think that's what—I don't think Noah would've appreciated that. And for my own sake, Ari? For my own sake, I need the truth. Please, I just—it's time to finally hear truth."

I told her as much as I could explain logically. This proved fruitless. Despite my swearing, she didn't believe that we didn't willingly take acid, that we had no credible memory of the night, that we woke to find him dead. "What are you hiding?" Her hands were in her face, she was yelling. "I don't understand what you could all *possibly* be hiding from me?" How was I to explain what I'd seen? How could I make her understand what I didn't?

She stopped abruptly in her tracks, turned toward me. "I don't care what Sophia or Bloom or Eddie or Cynthia thinks." She stopped crying. She was close to my face. "I don't care what *anyone* thinks."

I stepped backward, away from her. "I don't—what does that mean, Rebs?"

"It means I don't trust you anymore. It means I—somehow, I misjudged you. We all did, I think. Because you weren't who you were supposed to be, Ari. You turned out to be—" She pulled at the ends of her hair. "Everything changed once you came into our lives."

Rebecca left me, disappearing down Milton Drive. I missed Noah terribly. I stood under a streetlight, resigning myself to new and everlasting loneliness.

—

SOPHIA CALLED A FEW DAYS later, as I knew she would. She asked, at first, how I was holding up. Not well. Was Kayla around? No, and she knew it. Breathless silence. In time: did I have anyone? My parents? Amir? Yes, I lied. Yes, of course. But how was *she*? "Trying to keep life from disintegrating, I guess you can say."

"Probably we're a bit late for that," I said. "All of us."

"People are worried about you, Ari. Amir calls a lot. Asks if I've heard from you, asks me to check in."

I took my cellphone off speaker, held it to my ear. "Know something, Soph? All I wanted, ever since it happened, all I wanted is to just—I don't know, to mourn. To fucking—" Rage was impermanent, time was impermanent, injustice was impermanent, my body, above all, was impermanent. "And I only wanted to mourn with you. But why? Why do I feel like you're the only person in the world who understands?"

"Ari."

"Why am I always—why am I so fucking desperate to wrest just one last second of happiness with you?" I paused, bit my lip. "Why didn't you come when I needed you?"

"I'm not sure how—" I listened to her breathing, phone blazing against my cheek. "Why'd *you* do this, Ari? Why did you romanticize me like this? So—so *unsustainably*. You've insisted, from the very beginning, on building me into some kind of . . . I don't know, some idealized entity just because you decided you wanted me. Just because the person you choose *has* to be special, doesn't she? Has to be world-changing, has to be—"

Months earlier, in a session with Rabbi Bloom, we discussed Avicenna's Floating Man. Imprisoned in an Iranian castle, Avicenna pictures a human ushered accidentally into existence. This poor creation, forever suspended in air, never experiences material reality, and yet he is capable, through no power outside his own reflection, of knowing himself. Hearing Sophia's voice only faintly, random assortments of disembodied sound, I fell and I fell and I fell like this Floating Man, a bundle of impulse and perception fluttering irrelevantly over the abyss of matter, removed always from the human world.

I realized, eventually, that the line was quiet again. "Sophia?"

Somewhere on the other end she cleared her throat. "I said I'm leaving for New York next week."

I frowned. "Already you're leaving?"

"Well, I need to go up and get settled and—"

"Right."

"And I need to get away from here." *Isn't everyone supposed to love home?* "I don't want to come back anymore."

"I don't blame you," I said. "So you're really calling to say goodbye, aren't you?"

"Yes," she said. "I am."

"I just—" No longer could I tell whether we were whispering or screaming.

A hesitant lull. "Yes, Ari?"

"I just need you to know—" Her ice-gray voice. Those opalescent eyes I made out before dawn, amid the unfamiliar shapes of my room. Her infinite loneliness, dignified and seductive, a loneliness worse than mine, never to be breached. "Please, I—I'm telling the truth, Soph. About what happened with Noah, I mean."

"I do believe you," she said, without hesitating. "At least, I think I do. And every day, since you've come back, I've been trying to convince myself of one thing."

"Which is?"

"That you're different than he is."

My eyes were attempting to cry, but it appeared my body had forgotten exactly how to do so, which I found strange, considering it hadn't been long since I last cried, so far as I could remember. "I—I'm nothing like Evan."

After the longest time: "I love you, Ari."

"I love you, too."

"Goodbye, Hamlet," she said and hung up.

—

MY PARENTS MADE ARRANGEMENTS. They found a buyer for the house, an apartment in Brooklyn. They were ready to go back, even my mother. I asked how soon. Within the next few weeks, they said, after I'd left for college. I told them an apartment would be too small for all three of us. They said they'd be alone going forward.

—

LATER THAT WEEK I RECEIVED a call from Amir. "Ari," he said urgently, after I ignored the first several rounds of ringing, "where are you?"

Early evening. I was home, drifting into one of my pill-induced fogs. Augustine's *Confessions* was open on my lap, though I didn't remember removing it from my shelf. "Why?"

"I need your help."

The desperation in his voice threw me. "You okay?"

"Yes, I—it's Evan."

"Evan?"

"They withdrew their offer."

"Stanford?"

"Yeah."

Grief eats away its heart. I closed Augustine. "Good," I said. "He can go to hell."

"Ari, listen to me. He's in a rage, he's—it's frightening." That dark space again: inhale, exhale, focus on the panicky voice on the other end of the line. "We need to do something."

"Not *our* problem." I despised how I sounded, despised the way my room was, at that moment, performing a delicate pirouette into the fading light. "Not anymore."

"Ari!" Was Amir shouting? "He's—I really think he's going to hurt himself."

It wants to be like you, from whom nothing can be taken away. I shut my eyes, resting the phone against my face, stretching my arms into the air. "How do you know?"

"He totaled his car. Do I need to remind you what he's capable of in this kind of state?"

"Well, I—why are you calling *me*?"

"Who the hell else is there besides us?"

I thought this over. "Bloom?"

"Bloom's the one who called Stanford, Ari. There's Sophia—"

"—I didn't say Sophia—"

"—but she hasn't answered."

I was silent again.

"Are you home or not?"

But my sin was this: that I looked for pleasure, beauty, and truth not in him but in myself and his other creatures. I pitched *Confessions* against my wall. "Yes," I said, fighting against the spinning in my head, willing the world to come back to me.

"I'm coming for you," Amir said. "We need to find him."

The search led me instead to pain, confusion, and error.

I sprang from bed, threw on clothing. I waited in my driveway, streetlight trickling over me. The weather had been oppressive since Noah died: sweltering days and nights, starless skies, heavy winds, unusually rainless stretches that left our lawns brown and desiccated. The heavens were in mourning, protesting what had befallen South Florida. Amir was there within minutes, soaked in sweat, hands unsteady on the wheel. I had the urge to run across the street and grab Noah.

"He called about a half hour ago," Amir explained, driving frantically, swerving to avoid a mailbox, craning his neck for any sign of Evan. "To tell me about Stanford."

"Where did he say he's going?"

"Well, he didn't, obviously. He was going on about Bloom and what happened in the mountains and about—" An involuntary pause as he swallowed at the thought of what he was saying. "He said he thinks he might know what we need to do to atone."

"Atone?"

"Yeah, I mean, he was literally raving. I tried calming him down and convincing him to let me come see him, but he said he was heading out and wouldn't tell me where."

He wasn't home. He wasn't walking the streets. He wasn't in the library. He wasn't at the lake. He wasn't in Three Amigos. We called Oliver (his mother answered, only to immediately hang up), Donny, Rebecca, Remi, Gabriel, everyone. Amir called Sophia again. It went straight to voicemail.

"I think we should give up," I said, still replaying the sound of Sophia's voicemail message in my mind.

Amir braked fast at a red light. "Can you stop fucking saying that? We can't, okay? We can't just forget about it."

I didn't face him. "He's not our responsibility anymore. He's not my friend anymore."

The light turned green. Amir, fists shaking, floored the gas. "I'm trying the Academy."

"Do whatever you want," I said, "but take me home first."

A pause. "You're not actually going to make me do this alone?"

"I'm sorry," I said, "but we—I don't think you should be doing this at all, Amir."

"You think we have some kind of choice here, Ari? You think you can use what happened to Noah as an excuse to abandon everybody? To give up on living, like you're the only one who's affected? You think that's what Noah would've wanted from *you*, of all people?" He stopped, voice threatening to break. "You think, after all else, he'd want to see you become this . . . this fucking shattered and selfish, in the end?"

Debilitating guilt infested every inch of my body. "Fine," I said, breaking my gaze from the rearview mirror. "The Academy."

We drove in silence. It was fully dark now, and the Academy at nighttime had an eerie feel. The guard gate, surprisingly, was open. Flickering, silver lights bathed the sides of the building. A few cars were parked in the lot, as well as a small bulldozer and a dumpster. Garbage and desks were piled high outside the entrance. Classroom lights were on. A solitary figure limped through the model temple.

"Evan!" Amir called out through his open window. We parked diagonally, claiming two spots, and, cautiously, approached, hovering at the border of the miniature city. Wind sobbed in my eardrums. I grabbed my yarmulke to stop it from soaring into the night. "We've been searching everywhere."

Evan looked up, his eyes narrowed into blue slits. "Why are *you* here?"

I knew, of course, he was addressing me. "I don't know," I said.

He was shivering visibly in the wind. "He—Amir put you up to this."

Amir took a step toward Evan, entering the Outer Courtyard. "Enough of this, Ev," he said gently. "We're here to help."

A fragile laugh. "With what?"

Several more steps forward. Amir crossed now into the Inner Courtyard. "Help you."

Evan released a strange burst of laughter. "I'm afraid I'm nearly beyond help," Evan said. "Actually, we all are."

"No, actually, we're not," Amir said, pleading. "Because I know this is—well, this *is* fucked up. But even if it doesn't seem like it right now, we can heal, Ev, all of us will figure out a way to heal. You're going to need some time, but this won't define us, you understand me? We're each going to rebuild. You can reapply, if you wanted, you can do something to prove that you've—"

"You really think I—" Evan blinked feverishly, placed his hands over his head. "Amir, you actually think I give a fuck about where I go to school?"

Amir glanced my way for help, but I remained motionless. "Yeah, Evan. I do. Because you always have, rightfully so. I don't like to say this, you probably won't ever hear me vocalize this again, but you're brilliant and you deserve it, and I know you have a certain . . . emotional connection with the school and—"

"It was all I had left of her," Evan said, receding into himself. "It was all I had left."

"Evan." I rocked on my feet, hands in my pockets, uninterested in his mental wanderings. I had little awe left for Evan Stark. "Why did you come here?"

He retrieved the lighter from his pocket and, as I'd seen him do many times before, flicked it on, off, on, off. "You think this is beautiful?" he asked, gesturing toward the temple itself. He used the lighter to illuminate the intricacies, tracing the stone stairs, the hechal, with its chains of gold, its cedar-lined walls, its carvings of flowers and palm trees and cherubim. He paused over the Kodesh HaKodashim: the oversized menorah, the showbread's gilt table, the incense altar. "Here," he said, gently fingering the veil—a mixture of blue, scarlet and deep purple—that covered the wooden Ark. "I really think, maybe—I think *this* is where we went."

Amir gave me a look of apprehension, which I ignored. This time, however, I inched closer. "Where's that, Ev?" Amir asked. "What did—where did we go?"

"The innermost chambers," Evan said quietly. "The Holy of Holies."

Amir went on biting his nails, staring intensely, running mental calculations.

"Think about it," Evan said in the face of our silence. "Think about what happens to those who enter the Inner Sanctuary?"

"They die," Amir said.

"The problem is that it worked," Evan said, "it actually worked." The fire from the lighter trembled in Evan's hand, casting him in fragmented light, accentuating his scar. "This whole time, when you mocked me for my experiments, I was—I was actually right, wasn't I? You know it as well as I do."

"Right about what?" Amir said. "You think we did something *right*? You think Noah's death *worked*?"

"No, I mean that—you know what the Zohar claims? That we each contain just a tiny splinter of the inner sanctum," Evan said, still resting over the veil. "And so human sacrifice—death, the thrill of a holy death—tears apart the veil, unleashing into the world whatever lies behind the curtain."

Amir put his hands to his knees in defeat. I stepped past him. "You know what?" I was shouting, unable to see straight. "You *are* fucking crazy! That night on the boat, you really were trying to kill me, and I never should've listened to—"

"Eden, I'm not trying to—what if this is our only chance? You don't understand that Noah's death tore down the veil!" Evan yelled over the wind. From his pocket he removed a flask. Instead of swigging, he doused yellowish liquid over the model temple. A benzene stench spread toward us.

"What the—?" I took a step back. "What are you doing?"

"I really think—I *know*, actually, that we performed what few other humans ever have." Evan returned the emptied flask to his pocket. "We saw God and we fucking survived! We *were* worthy, Eden, we—in the end, we really were, weren't we? But when we tore down the veil, when we peeked at divinity, we left our world exposed to the . . . to the inner sanctum, I think. And now—I just"—he put his hand to his scar—"we have to reseal, I think we have to before anything else happens to us, before anything else is consumed, but I just don't—"

"Listen to me," Amir said, desperate, "you're—you sound unhinged. We need to all—" He trailed off, studied Evan's face. "Evan, what happened to you?"

Evan stared past Amir, focusing on me. "Before you dropped into our lives," he said slowly, "she wasn't in Kenya."

"I don't know what that—"

"Actually, she'd never even been to Africa. All that was a lie."

Suddenly it was crucial I didn't blink. "What? So where was she?"

"Hiding," Evan said.

Amir frowned. "What're you talking about?"

"She was with her parents, boarded up in Connecticut. She was *supposed* to go on that program. That part was real. But things changed, and she needed to—to disappear for a while. So, Kenya was the cover-up."

"I don't understand." I stepped toward Evan. "What was she hiding from?"

Facial features dissolving under the weight of a boundless, vaguely ecstatic grief, Evan nodded. "She was pregnant."

His words hung senseless over the model temple. A dull ache came on in my forehead. The first time I kissed her, her high heels in my hands, her tears on my neck. Wrapped around her in her bedroom, frightened to stir, cracking open an eye to convince myself it was real. My need to be adequate, my stomach inverting itself, gorgeous delirium, the hope I was complete now, healed now, happy now. She wasn't mine and, in truth, I never quite had her—nights here and there, shifting dreams, moments that never lasted. Sophia Winter never once belonged to me. "No, but, I don't—" I touched the crown of my head. Not even twelve months before, I was obsessed with tragic grandeur. In the time since, I'd seen life extinguished, I'd seen grief's hold over all people. Since I first learned to read, I'd wanted, more than anything, never to submit to the smallness of my existence. Now, I despised myself for ever having that desire. Now, I would've given everything for a final taste of that smallness. "Then all this time—but the baby?"

"She has dreams, Eden, doesn't she? Juilliard, medical school, Carnegie Hall. Having him would've meant giving up everything. But after everything that's happened to me? I—well, I wanted him. Desperately. And I—it ruined us, I know that now. It ruined us, and in a way, I guess, it ruined everyone."

Before Amir or I could object, Evan put the lighter to the veil, which shriveled in seconds. He moved to the altar, the flame glowing an incandescent orange as it spread. Amir dove at Evan, attempting to seize the lighter, but Evan, in a surprisingly violent motion, threw him off, sending Amir crashing through the Inner Courtyard, which flattened beneath him. By the time I helped Amir to his feet the Kodesh HaKodashim was gone. Evan sent his foot through the hechal, launching fiery pieces of the chambers into the surrounding shrubbery.

We watched the temple burn. Wind carried fire from the bushes to the palm trees, the garbage piles, the desks. I imagined Jerusalem under siege, Titus slitting the curtains, the steps of the sanctuary running with bubbling blood. Anything beautiful, Evan once recited in class, must first wear a monstrous mask. ("Friedrich Stark, everyone," Amir had said at the time, extracting a laugh even from Rabbi Bloom, "our new philosopher to be born!") These, of all things, came to mind.

Amir threw fistfuls of dirt at the burning desks. Amplified by gasoline, however, the fire had already leaped to the top of the mound and toward the school. I dragged my foot through shrubbery, stomping at sparks, singeing the bottom of my jeans. Under my sneakers, an index card, half-blackened, torn from the temple walls: *Such seems your beauty still. Three winters cold / Have from.* Evan stood in what remained of the Outer Courtyard, flames at his elbows, Jerusalem embers beneath his feet.

I found myself yelling at neither Evan nor Amir in particular, pointing at the lights in the building, the few cars in the lot, realizing there were people inside. Cinders swam gently through the air. I dialed 911. Fire snaked from the very top of the palm trees to the second-floor window, climbed to the third floor, descended into the building's underbelly, bathed us in an incoherence of bright light.

Sirens in the distance. "We can't wait," Evan said. He stumbled, dazed, coughing through smoke. "I didn't mean for—we have to get whoever's inside." We charged toward the front door, pausing before the flames. My vision blurred; I breathed fumes; the air stung my face, burned the top of my hair. Macabre screams from above. Unbearable heat, night collapsing over us, the door gone now, given over to fire. Amir tried forcing us back; Evan refused to retreat. Above, a brilliant red neared the top of the building, crowning us in a golden aureole. *Raze it, raze it, to its very foundation.* Ashes rained upon us, ashes covered our faces.

Firefighters arrived, throwing Evan aside, rushing into the inferno. Evan remained frozen to his spot. His leg gave, so he stayed there on the ground, gazing into the flames. Helmeted men, unfurling fire hoses: water surging in the dark, vaporizing in a fit of hisses. Cars pulled up, neighbors and students and parents pooled into the street, crowded the gate, watched Kol Neshama burn. Medics, policemen, fire volunteers, construction workers. Gio, Niman's uncle, Lily's parents, Gabriel's family, Donny and his younger siblings, Kayla and her parents, Rabbi Feldman sobbing into his handkerchief. In the very back, Rabbi Bloom, glassy-eyed, dressed in a dark suit, his thin silhouette cutting a strange shadow against the curb of the street.

It was summer: who would be inside? A woman—Gemma's mother?—claimed there was a yearbook meeting. The first firefighter out had retrieved a girl, someone coughing violently, a junior who'd apparently been tapped by Davis to take over as literary editor of the yearbook. Davis and Lily emerged next, unconscious, escorted into an ambulance. Orders to evacuate fell unheeded. The fire had been contained but refused to shrink. More commotion: the junior, recovering on a stretcher, began rattling off names. Gabriel Houri. Jennifer Benstock. Elana Levy. Solomon Katz. Harry Lasser. Sophia Winter.

I doubled over, blood pounding in my ears. *From the depths I have called You.* Chaos. Stretchers. One thousand lights. *O God, if You record iniquities, O Lord, who will stand?* A faraway voice: do you ever feel outside the world? A pale figure—aristocratic cheekbones, sharp lips, ash-stained—on someone's shoulders. Evan, marked with dust, beat his fists against the ground. Someone grabbed at my shoulders, it was my mother, I couldn't get up. *And He will redeem Israel from all their iniquities.*

The silence burst. All sound rushed back, the sound of wailing, the sound of burning, the sound of wind. Evan stood and looked hard at the fire. Rabbi Bloom broke into a run. A stretcher hurried past us: the ambulance was gone. For a moment Evan waited, giving Rabbi Bloom a chance to catch him, and then he hurled himself headfirst into the flames.

EPILOGUE

Who alone suffers, suffers most i' th' mind,
Leaving free things and happy shows behind.

—Shakespeare, *King Lear*

I didn't tell anyone I was coming. I had a conference in Manhattan; on a whim, I boarded a subway during a free afternoon and found myself ascending on Fiftieth Street. It rained on and off as I walked the streets of Brooklyn, trying to find the new apartment, receiving confused stares from black-hatted yeshiva students. I wandered past the old places, past my house and local restaurants, past Torah Temimah and the park where we'd played ball. I kept thinking that, even in the rain, it wasn't all nearly as gray as I remembered, but beautiful, in fact, full of life, joy, purity. I thought about the feeling I had before I moved, standing in my emptied room. It is, more or less, the way I've felt since I saw Noah lowered into the ground.

Outside the apartment building I bumped into a man with a large black coat and payot at his shoulders. He held hands with a toddler and was sweaty and disheveled and looked as if he were running late. He gave a brief glare, muttered rapidly in Yiddish. It was, I realized, my old friend Shimon Levy.

"Shimon!"

He stopped in his tracks, surveyed me up and down. I was clean-shaven, my hair cropped. I wore a brown bomber jacket. His eyes went to the thing missing from the top of my head. "Aryeh?" A low, awed voice. *Blessed are You, Lord, who revives the dead.*

"I can't believe it," I said. We shook hands. "Is this your son?"

Shimon played uncomfortably with his payot. "My youngest."

"You have more?"

"Baruch Hashem," he said. "Three beautiful children."

"Wow, I—that's incredible, Shimon. Really. Who'd you marry?"

"Remember Esther Leah Epstein? Reuven's cousin?"

I bent over to face his son, who eyed me suspiciously, lollipop in mouth. "Shalom aleichem. What's your name?"

The boy shut his eyes, cleaving to Shimon's legs.

"Yossi." Shimon put his hands on Yossi's neck. "I'm surprised. Usually he takes to strangers."

I straightened. "I'm so happy for you," I said. "Sounds like you have a wonderful family."

"The Rebonu Shel Olam has treated me with abundant chesed." He paused, checked his wristwatch.

"So," I said, glancing around, "you live nearby?"

"Over on Cedar. Near the yeshiva."

"Do you work there?"

"No, I'm in kollel. For *parnasah*, though, I'm an electrician." Yossi, from below, yanked impatiently at Shimon's tzitzit. "But where are *you* now?" He lowered his voice, shielding Yossi from my answer. "Your father I see in shul."

"I'm still in school, after all these years," I said. "But somewhere far away."

"Still go to libraries, then, yes?"

I smiled. "I do."

"The libraries—those books—they worked out for you?"

My scarf fluttered in the wind. Above us, a roiling sky. "No," I said. "Quite the opposite."

He glanced down again at his son. "When did you—stop?"

"I'm afraid that's not a simple question."

"But what happened to you?"

"Something I'm trying to forget," I said in a quieter voice.

"Do you think"—Yossi tugging violently at his legs now—"do you think you'll ever return?"

I studied the face of my oldest friend's child. After a long pause: "Yes, actually," I said. It was true, I realized then. It had always been true. "I will."

We hugged, said goodbye. I watched him go, watched him gather Yossi into his arms and kiss his cheek. The last time we parted, I'd escaped, like I'd always wanted, and he'd remained behind. Shimon Levy, in the years since, had uncovered the inexhaustible dream: family and community, faith and culture, stability and kindness, order and depth, the courage to live as we all might, were we conscious of infinitude's daily touch, were we liberated from longing, were we content to beat interminably at some ideal. I, in turn, roamed through wet streets, looking on at the world around me, discovering what a monstrous thing it is to be alone. Hillel cautioned against separating from the community, and yet Hillel hadn't lived my life. The rain resumed. I decided to walk back to the train.

—

WE HAVEN'T SPOKEN ONCE IN the last seven years, Evan and I. Occasionally, I've considered sending emails—composed when the sleeping pills don't work like they used to—though I always delete them in the morning. I don't do this because I miss him or feel sorry for him or have something to tell him. I do it because Evan, I know now, is like I am, or rather I am like Evan. Amir and Oliver found happiness; Evan is the only one, I suspect, who suffers like I do. This is why I was secretly and perversely delighted when, last week, I received the following letter:

> Eden:
>
> *I hear you'll be in the northeast. I wonder if you'd entertain meeting me. There is, I imagine, much to say.*
>
> —E.S.

Attached was a picture of the five of us. I'm not certain when it was taken, though I had a feeling it was from Remi's birthday party, considering we were all wearing dark suits. It was a relic. There was Noah, front and center, taller than we were, handsome and beaming, his blond hair the brightest part of the photograph. He had one arm around Amir, who wore a sly half smile, and the other around Oliver, short, well manicured and, chin up, defiant. On the far right was Evan, unsmiling, hair gelled, eyes dark and knowing. Then on the left, almost an afterthought, I stood, smiling uneasily, noticeably out of place. Scribbled on the back of the picture was a tag from Euripides: "Terrible is it to desire it . . . but also terrible not to desire it."

—

I MET HIM AT SOME quiet bar near Union Square. Hardly anyone was there. He arrived before I did and picked a table in the far back. I almost didn't recognize him. His hair was at his shoulders now. He had a thick beard, the sort people grew in mourning, which worked to cover the entirety of his scar, save for a small patch just under his eye. His skin was ruined, he looked a great deal older. He had a cane leaning against the table and, apparently, something of a nervous tic that caused his fingers to quiver slightly. He didn't notice me until I sat across from him.

For a long while we stared, said nothing. He didn't offer his hand; I was glad, because I wasn't certain I'd accept. Finally, he smiled—a worn, sad smile—and cleared his throat. "Still drink whiskey?"

I nodded.

He limped over to the bar, returning with two tumblers. "On me," he said, handing me the drink.

"What do you want?"

Several times he blinked. I got the sense he couldn't control it. "Never one for small talk, Eden."

"Neither are you."

He put down his whiskey. "I'm not actually supposed to drink.

Stomach's fucked. Never been the same since." He was referring, I assumed, to the time he entered the fire.

"Thought maybe it was because you're back in rehab."

Another self-hating smile. "No more rehab."

"Tell me," I said, "how was prison?"

"Prison was—difficult. Prison was remarkably unenjoyable."

"And afterward? Where were you then?"

"You didn't follow along in the papers, with the rest of Zion Hills?"

"Can't say I did."

"There was some time in a ward," he said. "And that was also rather unpleasant."

I spun my tumbler in careful circles. I found these rotations oddly comforting, probably because they reminded me that I was, in fact, grounded to my own world, one that existed quite apart from his, and that seeing Evan again need not diminish my sense of self-sovereignty. "Are you—crazy?"

He leaned back in his chair, winced slightly, readjusted his positioning. "Some people in my life seem to think so."

"And what do you think?"

"I say we all went a bit mad."

"What are you doing in New York?" I asked.

"Just passing by," he said. "I'm not really here."

We drank more in silence. It occurred to me that the last time he and I had shared a drink was on a motorboat.

"So," he said eventually, "do you speak to anyone anymore? Oliver?"

I laughed slightly. Shortly after high school, Oliver visited Israel on some half-year traveling program. Within weeks, he dropped out of the program and entered a Beit Medresh in Har Nof. He married his rabbi's niece and never came back. Apparently he now has several young children, teaches *cheder*. His eyesight never returned. He wears thick, tinted glasses and goes by Eliyahu Elisha, his Hebrew name. He and I, as I consider during late-night musings, traded lives. He, like Shimon, got the better deal. "Only Amir, really," I said. "Though less and less these days."

"He's in medical school, isn't he?"

"He just finished," I said. "Helped that he graduated college in three years."

"Of course he did." Evan put fingernails to his teeth, only to pull away his hand. "I hear he's getting married."

"He is."

"Good for him. He's always been the one who coped best, hasn't he?"

"Turns out he's the greatest of the five of us," I said. "After Noah, at least."

The name drew silence. I strained to make out the music in the background. I watched waiters roam the room. I found it simultaneously beautiful and devastating to consider that the other human beings around us had no knowledge whatsoever of our two lives.

"With what happened, though—you have to question that sometimes," Evan said, "don't you?"

I blinked into my tumbler. "Question what?"

"Well, I mean, Amir survived . . . untainted, it sounds like," Evan said. "He wasn't wounded. He's had all the normalcy, all the success."

"If you're actually suggesting that Noah was impure or defective or whatever the fuck you believe because he—"

Evan put up a hand, the way he used to. "There's a world of difference between being not pure and being *impure*, Eden."

I shook my head. "I'm not talking about this."

Evan allowed his gaze to move about the room before returning to me. "All right, then what about you, Eden? Still seeing someone special?"

I chewed on the insides of my cheeks. "No, I—that didn't work out."

"For now, at least. How long was it?"

"About a year and a half."

He touched his cane, as if for support. "What happened?"

I didn't answer, so he lit a cigarette. He did so, I noticed, with his old Cartier lighter. "And Bloom? Ever hear from Socrates?"

"Here and there," I said. Rabbi Bloom resigned after the fire, taking up an ad hoc lecturer position at Rutgers. From time to time we exchange letters. He visited once, when I was a college freshman. We walked the campus, went for coffee. I tried thanking him, right before he left, for helping me get there but failed to find the words. Sometimes I send updates—about my dissertation, not life. He responds, without fail, quickly and with detailed, handwritten notes, pointing out arguments I perhaps hadn't considered, books I might find useful. I don't listen to his recommendations. Mostly it's an excuse to talk to the man. "What about you?"

He put a finger to his scar, though I wasn't certain if he realized he was doing this. "It wasn't his fault, what happened to us."

"Well, of course not."

"He thinks so." He chewed his lip. It was a familiar act. I put the tumbler back into motion. "And for a while, I did, too. Now I don't. Now I realize the man was more of a father to me than Julian ever was."

"Yeah? What about all that Nietzschean gibberish about self-creation? About being your own father?"

He shook his head with distaste, allowing the cigarette to dangle from his lips. "That's not for me anymore." Smoke twined between us. The smell nauseated me. "So I looked you up online. I even read the description about your research."

"I'm flattered, truly."

"Hegel, tragedy, guilt, sentiment." He smiled. "Have I taught you absolutely nothing?"

A friend once warned Tennyson that humans cannot live in art. After college, however, I set out to do just that. I'm writing on what Coleridge calls "implicit wisdom deeper even than our consciousness." My aim is to prove that, in Hegelian tragedy, moral intuition mandates a belief in the inevitable triumph of our ethical institutions, even at the expense of a hero's self-destruction. What I mean by this is that sometimes the world demands one person's devastation so as to secure salvation for everyone else and prevent the unraveling of what has, until now, been holding us together. I like this idea. The department claims to like it, too, if I ever finish the project. "I should hope not," I said.

"An inveterate idealist, you are. Maybe that's a good thing. Actually, probably, it's a wonderful thing." A waiter, frowning, requested Evan stop smoking. Evan apologized and put out the rest of his cigarette. "Know what I believe in?"

"I can only imagine."

"How about this? I believe certain people are damned to be unhappy."

"So?"

"Don't you agree?"

I wanted to be embarrassed by the question. I wanted my cheeks to redden the way they used to when I'd first arrived in Zion Hills. As it was, I didn't flinch. I caught a glint of my reflection through a window behind Evan's head. Studying my features, I missed my childhood in Brooklyn more intensely than I ever had before. "Sure I do."

"What do you do about the solitude?" He stirred his drink. "I mean, maybe you should marry *her*, after all."

I looked away from his face. "Pardon?"

"It's just that, for me, the worst horror of all, even after all these years?" He looked at me with defeated eyes. "It's that feeling of moral aloneness. It's always been the feeling I've never gotten rid of."

I finished my whiskey, crossed my legs. I prepared to submit the question I'd been wondering, with varying degrees of intensity, for some seven years. I'd been able to bury it for temporary stretches, even as I knew this question—properly or not, meaningfully or not— measured my existence. Faced with the prospect of vocalizing it now, I found it resisted simple articulation. "If *it* never happened," I said, slowly, struggling for words, "I want to know how you imagine things would've ended, if left to—to a natural course."

"Natural course?" Evan smiled pitifully, sipped. "You, of all people, don't really believe in life divorced from divine intervention?"

"No," I said, "but I believe in a life divorced from what you've done."

I started thinking about things I'd lost years before. I thought about that winding staircase and about what a casket looks like lowered into earth and about a pomegranate bleeding in my hand. I thought about how I felt more Jewish now that I was alone and capable of relinquishing my birthright than I ever did in Brooklyn or Zion Hills. I thought about how surviving requires finding something that possesses the mind so thoroughly that nothing else matters. I thought about how sorrow, in the final analysis, probably does elevate, so long as you convince yourself that being untouched by yearning means you were never really worthy of experience. I thought about how we never really do manage to recover fully from whatever first wounds us. I thought about how human memory probably has a habit of rendering things more profound than they ever really were. I thought about how some find God while trying to lose Him and how others lose God while trying to find Him.

"Ari," Evan said, his voice thin, "do you ever miss it?" He fumbled for a second cigarette, though didn't light it. I felt, for the first time in many years, an urge to become excessively drunk, but I didn't touch what remained in my tumbler. Something in me had been gone for quite some time now, but in this moment I felt its absence most profoundly.

"I don't want to talk about it," I said.

"But that clarity, that recognition of looking upon the most beautiful thing either of us or any other human will ever see, that sense of—of divine intoxication?" He removed his unlit cigarette from his mouth, stored it in his pocket. "That's what it was, Eden. Divine intoxication."

"You know what Oliver told me, after I first found him?" I asked this in a voice that wasn't mine. "He said we weren't supposed to see any of it. And he was right, I think. That's why everything happened."

It was hot, suddenly, even with the light fading around us. After the long pause: "Ever think about returning?"

"Yes," I said. "Nearly every day."

"I'm going back." He finished his drink and stood. "Forever."

ACKNOWLEDGMENTS

Yeats wanted to ground literature on the three things that Kant believed rendered life livable: "Freedom, God, Immortality." To that list, I submit family, friends and teachers, without each of whom this book could not exist.

Susan Choi's support of the embryonic version of this manuscript helped propel me into motion. I am grateful for her mentorship and inspiration.

John Crowley shared his wisdom with me, embracing the story's mysticism and humor. I appreciate his graciousness and his confidence in my potential.

Emily Forland, my agent, believed in me from the moment she suspected that my manuscript sounded like her "cup of tea." She helped actualize my lifelong dream, providing brilliant guidance, vision, calm and cheer each step of the way. Thank you, also, to everyone at Brandt & Hochman.

Sara Birmingham, editor extraordinaire, improved this book immeasurably. I am lucky to have worked with and befriended someone with her depth of insight and expertise. I am indebted to Martin Wilson, my publicist, whose kindness and tireless effort opened life-changing doors. My thanks, additionally, to Ashlyn Edwards, whose invaluable contributions ensured that new audiences discovered the novel, and to Meghan Deans, Miriam Parker, Helen Atsma, Sonya Cheuse, Elizabeth Yaffe, TJ Calhoun and the entire team at Ecco and HarperCollins.

I remain thankful for my teachers and professors, from my high school and yeshiva days to college, graduate school and, now, law school. I have been privileged to study with giants—masterful, caring thinkers whose teachings endure and enrich each aspect of my life.

I am blessed with exceptional friends, for whom I am continually grateful. Thank you for the encouragement, endless laughter and infinitely entertaining material. (I jest. This book, I promise, is not about you.)

My paternal grandparents, Joseph and Selma Hopen, nurtured my literary interests from an early age. I miss them deeply. My maternal grandparents, Kalman and Irene Talansky, champion my pursuits on a daily basis. I have loved poring over this book with my grandpa, whose incomparable devotion resembles that of a parent toward his own child.

My siblings, Jessica and Josh, support me in every capacity. We are inseparable and lean on each other at all times. The fierce bond I have with my sister and brother—and now my brother-in-law, Charles—is one of the great joys of my life.

I reserve my deepest gratitude, now and forever, for my parents, Gary Hopen and Beth Talansky-Hopen. They are my original—and constant—editors, they are my role models and they are the finest, most selfless people I will ever know. My parents have given me everything. Any virtue of this book functions as but a reflection of their love.

ABOUT THE AUTHOR

DAVID HOPEN is a student at Yale Law School. Raised in Hollywood, Florida, he earned his master's degree from the University of Oxford and graduated from Yale College. *The Orchard* is his debut novel.

THE ORCHARD

David Hopen

A Roading Group Guide

A CONVERSATION WITH DAVID HOPEN

Originally published in Alma, a Jewish culture publication, in December 2020. (Reprinted with permission.)

One of my favorite aspects of this book is just how deep you dive into a very particular world that doesn't often get the mainstream treatment. I personally have never read a novel set in a Modern Orthodox community, and I'm wondering, does the world of Zion Hills at all resemble the MO community you grew up in?

Zion Hills bears no resemblance to the community in which I grew up. It's very much a fictionalized city—aesthetically, financially, geographically. In forming this world, however, I wanted to draw from elements critical to my own childhood and to the warm, wonderful community where I was raised.

Having attended yeshiva day schools, I was interested in replicating the feel of a dual-curriculum education, in which long days are split between Judaic and rigorous secular studies. Flitting seamlessly from morning prayers to AP classes involves a beautiful synergy. I wanted to encapsulate that complex, fascinating balance, the way a structure centered on meaningful ritual need not preclude participation in society. I also aimed to provide a sense of the profound, lifelong friendships formed at this age and in such communities. And finally, I viewed South Florida as a perfect backdrop for this story, both atmospherically and in terms of envisioning a modern Eden—at least for someone fleeing an old life and seeking dazzling sunlight, beauty, freedom.

Let's talk about names. Your main character, Ari Eden, gets called at least six different names in the book: Aryeh, Ari, Drew, Andrew, Eden, and Hamlet. How did you decide when to use each name and what was the significance of switching between them?

Oftentimes, the decision was natural. I lived with these characters for long enough to extract an accurate sense of their personalities and interactions. Certain contexts called for affectionate nicknames, other times for distance. More broadly, though, names function as devices by which to track progression. Ari explores the moral weight of bearing a Hebrew name, and the way religious identity interacts with a fundamentally contemporary environment. This is a novel involving internal evolution as well as the art of projection, and so what characters might be called in given moments coheres with the ways we actively reform ourselves, with the way we reckon constantly with the link tethering who we hope to become and where we currently stand. One midrashic commentary on Genesis features God asking Adam to select his own name. That sense of liberty—and power—animates Ari's ability to peer both inward and outward so as to fashion for himself a name.

The title of the book, the central theme, and ultimately a huge part of the plot are based on the Talmudic story of Pardes, or the orchard. It's a simple story I've read before, though I never really felt like I could *quite* understand it. When did you first learn the story of Pardes, and what drew you to center your novel around it?

I've always been drawn to this myth, which I first encountered in yeshiva. In my view, the story gives insight into how we view the human capacity for holiness while also raising questions useful for forming religious, and civic, identities. Whatever occurs within the orchard—

both in the Talmud and in my novel—demands that we consider the relationship between what is good and what is moral. And it also asks that we ascertain what it means to lead worthy lives, and what ultimately becomes of our natural longing for transcendence. These are questions I was eager to explore through fiction, and I think these are questions faced by anyone interested in finding meaning in an increasingly changing world, particularly given how COVID has reshaped the structure of daily American life.

There's a lot of conversation around an author's responsibility, especially one coming from a minority community, to translate—or not translate—certain words, phrases, and terminology that readers might not be familiar with in their writing. This book is rife with Hebrew and Jewish terminology—did you ever question whether you'd need to define anything? And why did you ultimately decide to leave them as is?

The question was short-lived. Hebrew expressions are present on occasion, but very much contextual. The goal was to build an authentic, immersive environment, and sometimes glossaries prove distracting. One of the great joys in reading about different cultures, in my own experience, is discovering the beautiful details of new worlds, and so I wanted to be careful about shattering the fourth wall or lessening the experience of plunging into a story. And if philosophical discussions about the works of Sidgwick, for example, don't receive such treatment in the novel, why should assorted cultural phrases be treated with heightened caution? My hope is that this makes for a reading that is perhaps slightly deeper and more absorbing.

The book is filled with references and quotes from Jewish thinking, philosophers, classic literature, etc. Were there any guiding texts you turned to again and again while writing the book?

Writing this novel as an undergraduate—and revising while earning my master's—led to a natural synthesis between my fiction and academic work. My research centered on studies in literature and in moral and legal theory, and so thinkers whose work I consumed featured in this story, both conspicuously and indirectly. Poets like Shelley and Wordsworth and Yeats played important roles while developing the manuscript, as did works ranging from Shakespeare to Fitzgerald to Ronald Dworkin to the Talmud. Ari's hunger—for learning, for experience—initially finds fulfillment through independent reading, and I wanted that literary feeling of grandeur and exploration to permeate *The Orchard* and define its characters.

One theme throughout the book is this idea of whether one must suffer to ultimately experience joy. I'm wondering how much of working on this book over the years felt like suffering, and how much like joy?

Writing necessitates labor. Whether producing a novel in this fashion—embarking on the story as a high school senior, completing a draft during free moments as a college student—makes for an easier or more difficult reading experience remains uncertain. But I do know that this book was a joy to write. I loved living with this book over the course of many—and pivotal—years, I loved watching as it evolved from a passion project to a serious prospect to a fully developed work alive in the world. The ideas and characters have served as my constant companions since I was eighteen, traveling with me to new schools and new countries, a coming-of-age tale that came of age with me.

Have you noticed any stark contrasts between the feedback you get on the book from Jewish readers vs. non-Jewish readers?

In truth: no, I haven't. Perhaps because the novel contains so much, each reader undergoes an individualized experience entering *The Orchard*. I think, in some circles, there is an expectation that Jewish readers, familiar with particular practices of Modern Orthodox life, more easily extract certain nuances from the story. And yet, overwhelmingly, I'm told this is absolutely not the case, and so I admit that I've really enjoyed feedback that pushes back on such assumptions. The story might unfold in a religiously insular backdrop, but its themes are universal.

So you're now in your first year of law school. Do you see any crossover between your passion for writing and your interest in law?

Considerable overlap exists. Law impacts how I approach fiction, magnifying the moral impact of language, the way words find life beyond the page. At the same time, my writing career allows me to approach law in a humanistic fashion, to envision the real-world effect that theory has on human lives. Each side enriches the other, and pursuing these two spheres in unison has been a wonderful privilege.

QUESTIONS FOR DISCUSSION

1. Despite expressing skepticism, Ari and his friends consistently participate in Evan's experiments. To what extent is each member of the group accountable for the events that unfold? Does their participation reflect any genuine belief in Evan's theories?

2. Rabbi Bloom involves himself in the lives of his students, revealing a particular interest in pairing Evan and Ari. Was Rabbi Bloom correct in likening Evan and Ari? And how do you view Rabbi Bloom's motives—is he sincere and well meaning, or does he overstep critical boundaries?

3. In the essay with which Ari applies to the Academy, he writes: "Happiness shall elude you, and yet you shall pursue it. We never reach permanent happiness, but we move steadily after its shadow, both physically and spiritually. We creep closer and closer toward God, each time halving the distance, but what we stand before is only an approximation. We move to new places, we visualize new achievements, but the yearning remains, because a life devoid of longing is not, in the eyes of the Talmud, a life fit for a human." Does this essay successfully encapsulate

Ari's philosophy in life, or does Ari ultimately grow distant from these ideas? More broadly, does the content of the essay find confirmation or rejection throughout *The Orchard*? How do you relate to this notion of "yearning" in your own life?

4. Ari's relationship with his parents evolves over the course of the story. How does the emotional structure of the Eden family change? In what sense is Ari similar to and different from his parents? Do these similarities and differences impact your understanding of the way Ari values family?

5. Sophia plays piano in different contexts throughout the novel, both formally and informally, such as at Oliver's house party, the school recital, and in her own bedroom. Do these performances register differently? In what ways does each performance offer insight into Sophia's character? If her music, as Ari suggests, functions as a means of escape, then how—and why—do other characters find ways to escape? Do they have a right to flee?

6. Ari's evolution is continually analyzed—by his parents, by Sophia, by Kayla, by Evan and the others. Such scrutiny occasions moments of self-introspection during which Ari wonders whether he has surrendered fundamental aspects of himself or simply developed into the person he always hoped to become. Does Ari lose himself, or do his religious, social, and intellectual decisions fulfill what he envisioned for himself while in Brooklyn? Are there specific inflection points that landmark Ari's spiritual journey? Do you think, in the end, that Ari will return to religion in some capacity?

7. Within "the orchard," Ari and his friends experience life-changing visions. What might these visions represent? Does each character's response to the aftermath of the orchard alter how you conceptualize their personalities?

8. The group spends considerable time studying foundational works of the Western canon, but does so under the guidance of a rabbi and within the context of a Jewish school. What is the interaction between religious and secular studies throughout the book? Do you think these two worlds enrich each other or prove incompatible?

9. When Ari moves to Zion Hills, he is exposed to a previously unknown world of wealth. How does this dynamic come to bear on the story? In what ways are Noah, Amir, Evan, Oliver, and Sophia shaped by their respective financial realities?

10. The Talmudic myth of the rabbis entering Pardes looms over the novel. How do the different fates of those four rabbis find analogues—or revisions—in the five members of Rabbi Bloom's study group? Why is it that Oliver fails to join the others in entering the orchard? Is there a correlation between each character's role in the orchard and level of happiness? And how do you think such happiness measures against the happiness experienced by Shimon in the epilogue?